COCO MAN

A Novel

Laken Hyson Schmalz

Copyright © [2024] by [Laken Schmalz]

All rights reserved.

No portion of this book may be reproduced in any form without written permission from the publisher or author, except as permitted by U.S. copyright law.

For my real-life Abuelas.
Dolores, for telling me scary stories disguised as life lessons.
And to RaeAnn, for instilling a love of reading in me so deeply that I wrote a book.

Contents

1. The Red Light (2010) — 1
2. Present Day (2022) — 15
3. The Spit Wad (2007) — 22
4. Present Day (2022) — 31
5. The Cardinal (2010) — 36
6. Present Day (2022) — 45
7. The Brown Spot (2009) — 48
8. Present Day (2022) — 56
9. The Cliff (2010) — 62
10. Present Day (2022) — 67
11. The Egg (2008) — 75
12. Present Day (2022) — 82
13. The Spoiler (2008) — 85
14. Present Day (2022) — 92
15. The Arm (2010) — 97
16. Present Day (2022) — 107
17. The Wailing Woman (2011) — 110

18.	Present Day (2022)	119
19.	The Footprints (2011)	122
20.	Present Day (2022)	131
21.	The Lost Sister (2012)	135
22.	Present Day (2022)	141
23.	The Ouija Board (2012)	145
24.	Chapter 24: Present Day (2022)	155
25.	The Confession (2012)	159
26.	Present Day (2022)	168
27.	The Necklace (2006)	172
28.	Present Day (2022)	177
29.	The Static (2013)	181
30.	Present Day (2022)	193
31.	The Last Talk (2013)	196
32.	Present Day (2022)	206
33.	The Casket (2013)	211
34.	Present Day (2022)	223
35.	The Teeth (2015)	230
36.	Present Day (2022)	240
37.	The Morgue Pizza (2015)	244
38.	Present Day (2022)	254
39.	The Cemetery (2015)	261
40.	Present Day (2022)	273
41.	The Reunion (2016)	280

42.	Present Day (2022)	290
43.	The Map (2018)	297
44.	Present Day (2022)	304
45.	The Best Day (2019)	307
46.	Present Day (2022)	313
47.	The Feeling (2021)	321
48.	Present Day (2022)	325
49.	The Link (2022)	329
50.	Present Day (2022)	336
51.	The Last Memory (2022)	341
52.	Present Day (2022)	350
53.	Present Day (2022)	354
54.	Present Day (2022)	357
55.	Present Day (2022)	363
56.	Present Day (2022)	367
57.	Present Day (2022)	372
58.	Epilogue	378
	Acknowledgements	382
	About The Author	383

Chapter One

The Red Light (2010)

Palmer Lane sat in front of her bedroom vanity attempting to apply eyeliner for the third time that night. She had picked out a new eyeliner at the drugstore earlier that day and she was determined to apply it evenly to both eyes. Palmer stared into the mirror with her mouth open, chin down and her dark green eyes unblinking. She was almost done creating the perfect line of black above her left eye when she was startled by two large hands grabbing her from behind, just under the armpits. Palmer gasped and she dropped the eyeliner as her whole body jerked. A roar of laughter erupted from behind her and she saw a mischievously delighted face in the reflection of the mirror just as she turned with her fists curled.

"CALUM WHAT THE FUCK!" Palmer hit the boy in the chest with the outside of her fist.

He put his hand over the area she struck and continued to laugh so hard that he doubled over trying to gain control of himself.

"Seriously Cal you almost gave me a heart attack!" she said breathlessly.

"I'm so sorry! You were so focused!" Calum laughed as he slipped his long lean arms around her neck and hugged her from behind. "Seriously, you've been reading too many ghost stories, it's got you all jumpy," he chuckled.

Palmer and Calum looked at each other through their reflection in the mirror, Calum with a big stupid grin on his face and Palmer with an annoyed but loving smile. Palmer and Calum had been high school sweethearts and were now in their first year of college. He was right though, she had been reading too many ghost stories. She had been up late the night before reading The Shining.

Palmer took a second to study Cal. He had grown up some this year. Where he was once lanky he now possessed some muscle tone. His dark hair was almost black and always seemed to be disheveled no matter what he did. While his hair always seemed to look like he just woke up it somehow worked for him. He had eyes that he always claimed were blueish green but that Palmer swore were gray. Much to his dismay, he had not gained any facial hair so his sharp angular face was perfectly smooth. Calum had a smile that always looked like he was up to something. He had random moles that littered his sun-kissed body. Palmer was obsessed with these large singular freckles since she on the other hand had pale skin and not a single freckle anywhere. Calum was tall, which was great for Palmer since she was considered fairly tall for a girl. Calum gave her a squeeze and flung himself onto her unmade bed.

"You about ready to go?" he said with arched eyebrows.

She turned back to the mirror rolling her eyes. Her heart stuttered. For a moment she thought she saw something in the corner of her room, reflecting back to her in the mirror. Something shadowy and

Chapter One

The Red Light (2010)

Palmer Lane sat in front of her bedroom vanity attempting to apply eyeliner for the third time that night. She had picked out a new eyeliner at the drugstore earlier that day and she was determined to apply it evenly to both eyes. Palmer stared into the mirror with her mouth open, chin down and her dark green eyes unblinking. She was almost done creating the perfect line of black above her left eye when she was startled by two large hands grabbing her from behind, just under the armpits. Palmer gasped and she dropped the eyeliner as her whole body jerked. A roar of laughter erupted from behind her and she saw a mischievously delighted face in the reflection of the mirror just as she turned with her fists curled.

"CALUM WHAT THE FUCK!" Palmer hit the boy in the chest with the outside of her fist.

He put his hand over the area she struck and continued to laugh so hard that he doubled over trying to gain control of himself.

"Seriously Cal you almost gave me a heart attack!" she said breathlessly.

"I'm so sorry! You were so focused!" Calum laughed as he slipped his long lean arms around her neck and hugged her from behind. "Seriously, you've been reading too many ghost stories, it's got you all jumpy," he chuckled.

Palmer and Calum looked at each other through their reflection in the mirror, Calum with a big stupid grin on his face and Palmer with an annoyed but loving smile. Palmer and Calum had been high school sweethearts and were now in their first year of college. He was right though, she had been reading too many ghost stories. She had been up late the night before reading The Shining.

Palmer took a second to study Cal. He had grown up some this year. Where he was once lanky he now possessed some muscle tone. His dark hair was almost black and always seemed to be disheveled no matter what he did. While his hair always seemed to look like he just woke up it somehow worked for him. He had eyes that he always claimed were blueish green but that Palmer swore were gray. Much to his dismay, he had not gained any facial hair so his sharp angular face was perfectly smooth. Calum had a smile that always looked like he was up to something. He had random moles that littered his sun-kissed body. Palmer was obsessed with these large singular freckles since she on the other hand had pale skin and not a single freckle anywhere. Calum was tall, which was great for Palmer since she was considered fairly tall for a girl. Calum gave her a squeeze and flung himself onto her unmade bed.

"You about ready to go?" he said with arched eyebrows.

She turned back to the mirror rolling her eyes. Her heart stuttered. For a moment she thought she saw something in the corner of her room, reflecting back to her in the mirror. Something shadowy and tall, like a person. But when she whipped her head around there was nothing. Just her tattered horror movie posters pinned up with thumbtacks. That had been happening a lot lately, shadows in the corners of her vision that disappeared when she looked harder. Maybe she really was reading too many horror novels. Best to lay off the Stephen King for a while, she thought.

"Seriously Palmer, you good?" Calum asked, concern lining his face.

"Yeah— I'm fine. Just thought I saw something. It was probably a smudge on my mirror," she gave him a weak reassuring smile. He looked back at her unconvinced.

She turned back to her mirror to finish getting ready. But just then she noticed that her eyeliner shot up from the corner of her left eye all the way up to her eyebrow. She must have jerked her arm when he had scared her and she was still applying her eyeliner.

Her mouth fell open in shock and frustration before she made eye contact with Cal again in the mirror and they both howled with laughter. Calum gripped his stomach and rolled on her bed laughing loudly, the previous offputting moment forgotten. Eventually, their laughter boiled down to giggles when they both heard a knock on the drywall by Palmer's bedroom door. In the door frame was Palmer's mother, beautiful with long dark brown hair and a smile on her lips.

"What is so funny in here?" She said with an amused shake of her head.

Calum had left the door open when he snuck up on Palmer. He was well-versed in the rules of the house. Leaving the door open when Palmer and Calum were alone in her room was a firm rule no matter how old they were. Palmer and Calum Murphy were nineteen years old and in their first year of college but they both still lived at home.

They hadn't necessarily decided on attending the local college for each other, but that had been an added bonus. They had decided to attend the small Colorado college for different reasons. Palmer had told her parents she was staying because she was still unsure about what she wanted to do with her life. She didn't feel comfortable going away to college when she didn't even have a major picked out. It wasn't completely untrue. But in reality, Palmer stayed for her grandmother whom she was extremely close with. Palmer's grandmother was starting to have more and more health problems with every passing season. Palmer wanted to be close, just in case.

Calum on the other hand had stayed because he had a tendency to get into trouble and his parents had wanted to keep a closer eye on him. Additionally, his grades were not the best and it was easier for him to get into their hometown liberal arts college.

"Nothing," Palmer responded to her mother's previous question with a smile on her face as she wiped at her ruined eyeliner.

"What are you guys up to tonight?" asked Palmer's mother, arms crossed but still smiling. She looked between them with loving eyes.

Palmer's mother liked Calum, which was a miracle considering that most parents would have thought of Calum as a bad influence. Palmer was uniquely able to see past Calum's faults to his big heart, and she had always felt that her mother was able to do the same.

"We've got a party to go to!" Hooted Calum with that wicked glint in his eyes.

Palmer's mom rolled her eyes and looked at her daughter fixing her makeup at the vanity.

"Text me the address please," Palmer's mother said seriously. "And be home by two o'clock," she said, narrowing her eyes. "Nothing good—," "*ever happens after 2 am.*" Palmer finished in unison with her mother.

It was a common saying her mother had repeated to her time and time again.

"I know Mom," Palmer said with reassuring eyes.

Palmer's parents didn't enforce rules as strictly as other parents did but they definitely worried.

"Who's going to be the designated driver?" She said looking at Palmer.

Her mother knew Calum couldn't be trusted to be DD. He was notorious for enjoying himself a bit too much. On more than one occasion Palmer had called her mother for a ride when Calum had said he would drive but had ended up having too much fun.

Palmer wasn't stupid enough to drink and drive and her parents had always said they would rather her call them for a ride if she needed to. Well, her mother had at least. Her father was a little more old school and was the one to 'bring down the hammer' so to speak when Palmer bent the rules.

"Me. I've got class early tomorrow" Palmer responded, standing up.

She had finally finished her makeup. She turned to give herself a once over in the mirror, making sure not to look too closely in case her eyes betrayed her again. Palmer had creamy white skin and dark brown, wavy hair that went past her shoulders. She had large moss-colored eyes, dark lashes, and full lips. She examined her ample curves in the mirror and adjusted her white t-shirt and faded blue jeans. She wore ruby red earrings in each ear and a gold necklace with a Virgin Mother pendant on it. Her grandmother had given her the necklace years ago.

Palmer slipped into her brown UGG boots as her mother continued to caution them about their night plans.

"Give your dad a kiss on the way out. Oh! And your grandmother is in the kitchen. Stop and give her a kiss too!"

"Got it."

"Hey," her mother said, making a point to make direct eye contact with her daughter. "I'm serious. Text me the address. I've watched way too much Dateline and I.D. TV to let you just waltz out without me knowing where you're going".

"Got it!" Palmer said, exacerbated.

Calum still lounged on Palmer's bed scrolling through his phone.

"Cal. Up. Let's go," said Palmer.

Calum popped off the bed with a dramatic jump and hugged Palmer's mom on his way through the door.

"Later Mrs. Lane!" he said.

"Seriously Cal. If you don't stop calling me Mrs. Lane YOU'RE going to end up on I.D. TV. It's Emilia." She threatened with a smile.

They had been going back and forth about this for years. Emilia Lane had been only 21 and married a year when she had Palmer and did not appreciate being called Mrs. Lane or Ma'am. Calum was well aware but continued to tease her, just as Emilia continued to threaten him.

Palmer's mother was beautiful. She was petite and olive-skinned. She had dark brown eyes and long, thick brown hair. Palmer was always jealous of her mother's complexion. Thanks to her father's genetics, she had been cursed with paper-white skin. The type of skin that doesn't even tan. It just burns.

"Bye Mama, Dad's in the garage?" Palmer asked, kissing her mother's cheek.

"Yes. Working on his truck," she responded.

Palmer walked through the house with Calum trailing behind her, scrolling through his phone. When they got to the living room she turned to him.

"Sit," she said.

"Roger that," He said and smacked her solidly on the ass.

Palmer swatted at him. Calum dodged her, plopped himself on the comfortable sofa, and started to scroll through his phone again.

Palmer continued to make her way through the house to the garage. She left Calum in the living room on purpose. It wasn't that her dad 'disliked' Calum so much that he was just somewhat indifferent to him. Palmer was under the distinct impression that her father tolerated Calum's presence because she obviously loved the boy so much. But Chuck Lane was the definition of unmovable.

Palmer's father was a towering bear of a man. He was burly and tall. He sported a constant gray shadow on his large sharp jaw. He was a man of few words 75% of the time, but the other 25% of the time he was telling raunchy jokes that had everyone around him laughing till they couldn't breathe.

Palmer understood why he looked at Calum with concern, she was his baby girl. And Calum rarely took anything seriously. Plus, she was sure Chuck was aware of the trouble Cal had gotten into in the past even if she had never told him. She was certain her mother had shared that information with him. Her parents were a rarity among her friends since they were still together and very much in love. They often displayed their affection for each other publicly and their children often joked about it making them sick.

Palmer opened the garage door and Chuck turned to look at her from under the hood of his old truck. He looked her up and down and responded with a grunt, turning back to his work. In Chuck's language, that was his way of saying she looked nice.

"You going out?" he said, turning back to fiddle with some old wires and cables.

"Yep. Love you," Palmer said, kissing his cheek.

Chuck grunted again in acknowledgment.

"Be careful," he responded, taking a pull of the beer set on the stool next to him.

Palmer smiled a sweet smile at him, turning and leaving him to his Thursday night activities. Palmer walked back down the hall toward the living room, stopping in front of her younger brother's door. Her brother Shawn leaned back in his gaming chair with a controller in his hands. His thumbs feverishly worked the controller as he spat profanities in his headset to whatever soul had the misfortune of playing Call of Duty with him on the other end. He sensed Palmer's presence and glanced her way. She smiled, one eyebrow up, and flipped him the bird. He smiled, rolling his eyes, and did the same. Shawn turned back to his game and let loose another string of offensive curses.

Palmer made her way to the kitchen. She could smell corn masa and savory meat. She walked through the doors and found her grandmother rolling tamales. Palmer walked up and kissed her grandmother on the cheek.

"Goodnight Abuelita. I'll stop by your house in the morning to help you sort out that one closet," Palmer said.

Palmer's grandmother kissed the air toward Palmer's cheek. Her focus was on the task in front of her. Palmer's Abuela was a typical Hispanic-American grandmother. She had short, curly, gray hair and soft brown skin. She always wore an apron and was ready to force-feed anyone who walked through her door. Her face was warm and had deep wrinkles from a life well lived.

"Good. I need all the help I can get. I want to do a garage sale next weekend,". Palmer's grandmother loved to shop at thrift shops, resale stores, antique stores, and estate sales. Some would say she loved them too much, so much so that her house was constantly filled to the brim with her finds. Most people called the things in her grandmother's house junk. Palmer called them 'treasures'. Once or twice a year Palmer would help her grandmother clean out her entire house so the 'treasure' didn't pile up too high.

"Where are you going?" Abuela paused and looked at her nice outfit. "You look pretty," she said.

"Just going out," Palmer replied. Palmer started walking toward the door to leave the kitchen.

"Ok. Don't stay out too late. That's when The Coco Man comes out," Abuela said with a wink.

Palmer chuckled. The Coco Man was a scary story she had been told since she was little. Her grandmother and mother had told her the story to keep her well-behaved. She waved to her grandmother without looking back and made her way down the hall back to Calum.

Palmer had left the room already. She never saw her grandmother continuing to stare at the empty door frame where Palmer had been for a long while. Her hands were still covered in masa. The smile slipped slowly from Abuela's face, replaced with worry and fear. Fear for her granddaughter.

A few hours later Palmer was sitting in the kitchen of a house she had never been in before. Calum had heard of the large get-together from a friend of a friend. He always seemed to know when and where the parties were. She sat at a round kitchen table with several other girls, mostly locals or friends from her college classes. The party was crowded and loud. The music was turned up all the way and she almost had to yell to speak with the people around her.

Palmer spotted Calum through the wide kitchen entrance. He was in the living room surrounded by a large group of people. They were all laughing, likely at something Calum had said. Calum was nothing if not the life of almost every party. His eyes found Palmer's and she felt her heart skip a beat. His eyes were full of mystery and mischief. He threw her a wink and turned his attention back to his friends. Palmer glanced down and noticed he had a soda in his hand instead of a beer. Strange. That was out of character for him.

She tried to focus her attention back on the conversation in front of her but she paused. In the crowd, between several people, she could have sworn she saw that eerie tall shadow again. Palmer leaned forward trying to get a better look. People were leaning and moving slightly, caught up in conversation. She had to swivel her head from side to side to try and get a better view. Just when two people moved slightly apart she saw a face. It was pale and screaming in agony, its mouth gaping open. Eyes crazed with fear.

Palmer lurched backward in her seat, the legs of the chair making a loud honking sound on the linoleum. She stood in that same instant and the chair toppled backwards. The party had stopped, and all eyes turned toward her. No one was speaking but Sexy and I Know It by LMFAO was still blaring on the shitty speakers. When she glanced back to where the face had been there was nothing there, only empty space.

A flush crept up her chest and cheeks as she realized that she probably looked like a crazy person. Palmer couldn't figure out what was going on with her lately. The freakouts were becoming more frequent. Palmer felt like her sanity was slipping away from her like butter on a hot skillet. She felt a familiar panic starting to settle deep in her chest.

A warm hand snaked from her shoulder to her neck and caressed gently. She turned and tilted her head to peer up into Calum's smoky eyes. They were clear and bright. He smiled and kissed her lightly. She closed her eyes and tried to steady her heartbeat. He smelled like cigarette smoke, rain, and his favorite body wash. She loved his smell. Palmer heard the party sounds go back to normal and she took a deep reassuring breath.

"Let's go baby," he said gently and she opened her eyes. Sturdier now.

Calum took her hand, leading her out of the house and to the car. No one looked their way, mostly out of respect for Calum she imagined.

"Keys?" He requested.

She eyed him sternly.

"No alcohol tonight?"

"Not a drop," he smirked.

Hmm. She thought, throwing him the keys. She watched him quizzically as he stalked to the driver's side of the car. He climbed in and she followed suit, sliding into the passenger side. The cool night air and Calum's easygoing demeanor calmed her earlier unease.

On their way back to Palmer's house they talked just like they always did. He was careful not to ask about her freak-out at the party. She was happy to let it go and not talk about it. Cal had his window rolled down. It was late September and still warm outside. Fresh mountain air breezed into Palmer's old jeep and it whipped through both of their hair. Calum had plugged in his iPod and they listened to some of the music he had Limewired earlier that day. Calum talked about the music he downloaded, parts he needed for his car, and some other parties that were happening that weekend. Palmer talked about the classes she liked and didn't like, her grandmother's garage sale plans, and how much she missed her best friend Jessica who had gone away to college.

Jessica had moved almost four hours away to attend a University in a bigger city. Jessica had moved into a dorm with five other girls and had crazy stories to tell Palmer about University life every time she called. Her Facebook was full of pictures of the large campus and Jessica's new friends.

Was Palmer jealous? Yes. Absolutely. But not of Jessica, of Jessica's new friends. Because they got to be with her and Palmer didn't. They had been friends since the first grade and had been nearly inseparable ever since. In fact, she planned on attending University with Jessica the following year once she got over the guilt of leaving her grandmother behind and she felt more comfortable deciding on a major. That was always the plan.

Palmer often wondered what Calum's plan was. He wasn't big on planning ahead, he was more of a 'live in the now' kind of guy. Always had been. But he loved Palmer. That was a fact. She had always assumed in the back of her head that he would follow her wherever she wanted to go.

Calum stopped at a red light and glanced over at Palmer. Calum was wearing his signature sly grin. Palmer loved that grin. It was like he had some devilish secret that only she knew about. It always caused her to smile back, even when she wasn't in the mood to smile. His smile was contagious.

She had one of those moments where you just want to pause and take a mental picture of how perfect everything is. To capture this feeling of pure happiness and bliss, just to bottle it up forever.

"Hey, who is The Coco Man?" Calum asked.

Palmer had to pause and smile at his sudden random question. He must have heard Abuela's joke from the kitchen earlier.

"It's nothing," she said smiling. "He's like..." she took a moment to think. "He's like the Hispanic BoogeyMan," she said with a small laugh.

Calum smiled at her description and looked ahead, lost in thought. The atmosphere of the car changed. Cal's smile faded and he became serious. He looked into her eyes. Really looked into them, studying her. Searching for something he'd never really looked for. The moment felt like it lasted an eternity.

Finally, he reached across the car and put his soft hand on the side of her face. His fingers were in her hair and his thumb caressed her ear. Still, he stared into her. The stare was strangely intimate for him.

Palmer had been with Calum since Freshman year. She had been the Bonnie to his Clyde for the last five years, which felt like a lifetime at their young age. They had endured everything life had thrown at them so far, hand in hand. And here they were, she thought, with their whole lives ahead of them.

Palmer's eyes started to water and a single tear slid down her cheek. Calum leaned closer and kissed the tear away with his lips. He leaned back and looked at her with that deep penetrating stare again. Searching from one eye to the next. What was he looking for? She could no longer hear the loud music bumping through the car. The music was drowned out by the ringing in her ears.

"I love you." he whispered.

"I love you too." she echoed back.

Calum leaned in and kissed Palmer. Gently at first, and then with a sense of urgency and passion. Palmer had the odd feeling that he was kissing her goodbye. But that was ridiculous. He was her everything. She had only ever loved him and she had every intention of only ever loving him. The desperate kiss continued. His fingers fisted in her hair and his other hand grabbed the back of her head. Palmer let out a small whimper as he bit her lower lip and kissed her deeper. The kiss eventually simmered and Calum pulled away, resting his forehead against hers. They both closed their eyes.

When Palmer opened her eyes he was already looking at her. He said something that they had said to each other a million times over the past five years. They had said it so often that it was almost like a mantra to them.

"Forever?" he asked seriously.

He had never said it as if it were a question before. Normally when he said it he stated it as if it were a fact. But not tonight. Why was he so serious right now? Calum was never serious. He was all smiles and jokes usually. Calum had the unique gift of turning everything into 'no big deal'. It was one of Palmer's favorite things about him, he could make light of anything. But this newfound seriousness had her heart aching. Maybe her weirdness was finally taking its toll on him.

"Always," she said, looking back at him sincerely. She meant every word.

Then the light turned green.

Calum smiled at her description and looked ahead, lost in thought. The atmosphere of the car changed. Cal's smile faded and he became serious. He looked into her eyes. Really looked into them, studying her. Searching for something he'd never really looked for. The moment felt like it lasted an eternity.

Finally, he reached across the car and put his soft hand on the side of her face. His fingers were in her hair and his thumb caressed her ear. Still, he stared into her. The stare was strangely intimate for him.

Palmer had been with Calum since Freshman year. She had been the Bonnie to his Clyde for the last five years, which felt like a lifetime at their young age. They had endured everything life had thrown at them so far, hand in hand. And here they were, she thought, with their whole lives ahead of them.

Palmer's eyes started to water and a single tear slid down her cheek. Calum leaned closer and kissed the tear away with his lips. He leaned back and looked at her with that deep penetrating stare again. Searching from one eye to the next. What was he looking for? She could no longer hear the loud music bumping through the car. The music was drowned out by the ringing in her ears.

"I love you." he whispered.

"I love you too." she echoed back.

Calum leaned in and kissed Palmer. Gently at first, and then with a sense of urgency and passion. Palmer had the odd feeling that he was kissing her goodbye. But that was ridiculous. He was her everything. She had only ever loved him and she had every intention of only ever loving him. The desperate kiss continued. His fingers fisted in her hair and his other hand grabbed the back of her head. Palmer let out a small whimper as he bit her lower lip and kissed her deeper. The kiss eventually simmered and Calum pulled away, resting his forehead against hers. They both closed their eyes.

When Palmer opened her eyes he was already looking at her. He said something that they had said to each other a million times over the past five years. They had said it so often that it was almost like a mantra to them.

"Forever?" he asked seriously.

He had never said it as if it were a question before. Normally when he said it he stated it as if it were a fact. But not tonight. Why was he so serious right now? Calum was never serious. He was all smiles and jokes usually. Calum had the unique gift of turning everything into 'no big deal'. It was one of Palmer's favorite things about him, he could make light of anything. But this newfound seriousness had her heart aching. Maybe her weirdness was finally taking its toll on him.

"Always," she said, looking back at him sincerely. She meant every word.

Then the light turned green.

Chapter Two

Present Day (2022)

P almer opened her eyes. It was difficult. It felt as though her eyelids were glued shut. She tried to blink the fogginess on her corneas away. She was vaguely aware of a sharp pain in her arm and a dull throbbing pain in her head. She blinked harder, squeezing her eyes shut. Palmer tried to rub her eyes but when she lifted her arm she realized she was attached to something. She opened her eyes again. Everything was so white, too crisp and clean. The large fluorescent light above her glared and made her crusty eyes water. She could make out robotic, rhythmic beeping in the background. She wondered where she even was.

She finally cleared her head enough to realize she was in a hospital. She finally looked around her. She was in a small room with lots of monitors. She had an IV in one arm and a blood pressure cuff on the other. Fuck her head hurt. On the tray next to her sat a small vase filled with the whitest roses she had ever seen. There was a duffle bag on the ground to her right and next to it, in a large chair was a man. He looked exhausted, but even so, she could tell how handsome he was. His golden hair was almost strawberry blond. It was cut short but she could tell that if he let it grow out it would be a little curly. He had a short gingery beard and full lips that had parted in his sleep.

He was definitely older, probably in his 30's she thought. She could see the beginning of wrinkles on his face like in the corners of his eyes and mouth. He was dressed in gray sweatpants and an athletic shirt that showed off his muscles. Woah. Correction, huge muscles. She thought he might be a cop. He looked like a cop if she ever saw one. No, a cop would be in uniform. He was sleeping sitting up, with his neck in what looked like a very uncomfortable position. He had large dark bags under his eyes, and under those bags she noticed a brush of light freckles on his large, somehow commanding nose.

She tried to sit up and was forced back down by a jolt of pain. She couldn't pinpoint where the pain had come from. It felt like everything hurt. She must have made a sound because the man jolted upright. He looked at her and became visibly relieved.

"Oh my God, Palmer! You're awake. You scared everyone to death. You've been out for hours. How are you feeling? What do you need?" said the man in a deep voice.

He had stood up and leaned over her, brushing her dark hair back and out of her face. Palmer tried to move away from his unwelcome touch. She had no idea who the hell this guy even was. She looked up at him confused and he kissed her forehead. Palmer flinched but the man didn't seem to notice, he was a little frantic. It was then that she realized her head was bandaged. Thick gauze wrapped around the entirety of her head.

"Hold on!" he said urgently. "Let me get the doctor!"

He squeezed her hand and rushed out of the large door at the front of the room. The door closed behind him and she was alone. Palmer looked around. Yep. Definitely a hospital. Fuck. Chuck was going to kill her. She wiggled her fingers and then her toes. Everything checked out as far as she could tell. She thought for a moment that maybe she had been in a car accident.

A woman wearing light blue scrubs and a stethoscope came into the room with a kind but concerned look on her face, the strange man right behind her. The doctor looked up at the beeping monitor and then back down at Palmer.

"Hey hun. My name is Dr. Walters. How are you feeling?" she crooned to Palmer in a sweet, calming voice.

The doctor was tall, lean, and beautiful. She had, perhaps, the kindest eyes Palmer had ever seen. The doctor started adjusting things as soon as she finished speaking but then looked at Palmer expectantly.

"I'm ok— I think. My head hurts. Can I have some water?" Palmer said with a croak.

Palmer had become acutely aware of her dry lips and parched tongue.

"Of course." Dr. Walters answered.

But before the doctor could get her some, the strange man reached for a cup that had been sitting on a tray next to him, offering her a sip. He bent the straw so she barely had to move. She peered at him with a quizzical look and then cautiously took a long drink. This guy had absolutely zero sense of personal space. Dr. Walters seemed to take note of her apprehension.

"Do you remember what happened?" asked the doctor.

Palmer shook her head with wide eyes.

"You were found unconscious in an abandoned house." The doctor paused to let Palmer absorb this information.

She looked at the strange man and the anguished look on his face. Palmer turned her attention back to the doctor.

"Have— have you called my mom and dad?" she said in a rough voice.

Damn her throat was so scratchy. The man replied instantly.

"I did, they're on their way. They should be here in about four hours. Oh! I need to text your mom that you woke up!" he said.

The man reached into his sweats and pulled out a phone. He started texting fiercely. Dr. Walters was still studying Palmer with assessing eyes.

"Don't worry, Susan is covering the shop. I'll text her next to let her know that you're okay," the man said to her, distracted by his texting.

He took a second to look up from his phone and at her with steady reassuring eyes. Palmer looked back with apprehension. The man and Dr. Walters looked at her expectantly, waiting for her to speak.

"Who?" she asked, trying to put an emphasis on how confused she was.

"SUSAN." The man said to her slowly.

He glanced at the doctor and then back to her.

"She works for you at the shop? You hired her last year to help out—," He looked at her hopefully.

"Ok— and— what shop?" She looked at both of them for the answer but they only gawked.

Dr. Walters's eyes widened and the man... the man's face crumpled. He looked like he might vomit. The doctor put her hand on his shoulder reassuringly. Palmer realized the man was holding back tears. It was painful to watch especially since Palmer had absolutely no idea what was going on. She felt bad for him, whatever he was going through. But she also felt awkward. She had no clue who he was or why he was even there. Palmer considered briefly that he might be one of her dad's friends.

After a few moments, Dr. Walters turned to Palmer with her hand still on the man's shoulder. She placed her other hand on top of Palmer's and said in a low voice, "Palmer, I'm going to be right back ok? Just give me a minute and I will come back and explain what I can."

Palmer nodded her head in agreement. She was even more confused. She hoped her parents were hurrying. She wasn't sure what was taking them so long to get there.

Several minutes passed and Dr. Walters returned to the small hospital room. She pulled up a short rolling stool next to where Palmer lay in the bed. The Dr. sighed and said,

"Alright. Palmer. I know that this may be hard, but I need you to try and tell me the last thing you remember."

Palmer focused and tried to think back.

"I don't know—," she whispered. "Everything is foggy."

She was thinking hard and it was starting to make her head pound even harder. Trying to think of what happened last was like trying to sort through puzzle pieces from different puzzles that had been mixed together.

"Ok," Dr. Walters said calmly. "How about we start with the basics? Can you tell me what year it is?"

Palmer took her time answering. She had a flash to a term paper she had written for British Literature, under the title she had put the date.

"2010," she said with confidence. Dr. Walters closed her eyes gently and lowered her head slightly. She took a long breath before she said,

"OK. Palmer. I think that you are experiencing some Retrograde Amnesia. Are you familiar?" she asked.

"Um, yeah I think so. I'm not remembering some things?" Palmer said slowly.

"Yes, exactly. But let's not panic. I am going to order some tests and I am going to do my best to get to the bottom of this so you can return to your family," she said with that gentle smile she was gifted with.

Palmer sucked in a breath, relieved. Her family. She needed her mom and dad. She would even be glad to see her douche of a brother Shawn.

"Ok," she said.

After Dr. Walters had left the room Palmer was alone for the first time since she had woken up. She felt like a woodpecker was trying to make a home in her head, it was pounding so hard. She lifted her hands to cover her eyes while she got a grip and noticed they were shaking violently. This was it, she thought. She had finally lost all her marbles. It had always just been a matter of time but it had finally happened.

Over the next few hours, Palmer was poked, prodded, and put through several large noisy machines. She hadn't seen the strange man again so she hadn't been able to ask who he was. She had to admit she was curious.

Finally, she was back in the small hospital room. They had dimmed the lights when she asked. Her head was still throbbing and the harsh lights didn't help. She must have dozed off amid worrying about which looney bin they would admit her to. She was hoping for a Patch Adams type of mental hospital and not a Shutter Island kind of situation.

She was awoken by trembling hands holding hers. When she opened her eyes she saw her mother. She felt her entire body relax in relief from her presence. Her mother's eyes were brimming with tears and she smiled a loving smile. Palmer looked to her left where another pair of hands were gripping her other hand. These hands were enormous and rough. Her gaze traveled from the hands to the arms, and then up to the face. It was her dad. His eyebrows were knit together in concern.

"You ok baby?" her mother said next to her.

Palmer turned. "Yeah I'm good, glad you're here now." She said with a smile.

Her parents looked at each other and then Palmer heard someone by the door clear their throat. It was Dr. Walters.

"Ehem." She cleared her throat one more time.

Dr. Walters introduced herself to Palmer's parents, shaking their hands. Then she turned to Palmer with a steady look.

"Palmer. I have asked your parents to be here while I talk to you about what's going on. Is that okay with you?" she asked.

"Yeah, of course." Palmer turned back to her mother. "What's going on? Where is Shawn?" she asked.

Her heart dropped. Palmer realized she didn't know where Cal was. Maybe he was hurt too. There was no way in hell she would be in a hospital and Calum wouldn't be right next to her making light of the situation.

"Where is Calum?" Palmer asked wide-eyed.

Her mother's face caved in on itself and became very grave. Almost heartbroken. Her father's hands tensed on hers.

"FUCK." he said in his gruff voice.

Chapter Three

The Spit Wad (2007)

Palmer sat at her desk taking notes. She was hunched over, her dark hair acting as a curtain blocking her face. She played with her necklace and jiggled her right leg as she focused. Periodically she looked up at the whiteboard to make sure she was keeping up. She was listening intently to her Biology teacher as he rambled on about Mitosis.

"The order of Mitosis is as follows; Interphase, Prophase, Metaphase, Anaphase, Telophase, and Cytokinesis. Mitosis is also known as somatic cell division..." the teacher said as he wrote on the whiteboard.

School had been in session for almost a month. It was Palmer's freshman year. There was only one high school in her small hometown. Most of the kids in her grade she had known since Kindergarten. However, there were a few that she didn't know, and they stuck out amongst the rest like a sore thumb. Friend groups had already been established for years and new kids had a difficult time finding their place.

There was one kid though, whom she didn't recognize, that had made fast friends with multiple different clicks. He was very friendly and easygoing from what she could tell. She hadn't met him yet but she had caught him staring at her from time to time.

She had asked her best friend Jessica about him casually at lunch one day. Jessica was a wealth of current gossip and information. Jessica had said his name was Calum Murphy. She also said he was homeschooled up until now, which surprised Palmer.

Homeschool kids were usually pretty easy to recognize, they had a certain way about them. They dressed differently, packed weird food for lunch, raised their hand too much, blurted out weird facts, etc. Palmer could go on and on. But the boy had an air of coolness, he was almost aloof. He definitely didn't dress like a homeschool kid. He dressed in band t-shirts and faded jeans most days. Today he was wearing checkered vans and a black zip-up hoodie. He was tall and lanky, with perfectly messy black hair. His eyes were what caught her attention though. They weren't blue or green but almost gray. And they were piercing. Her heart skipped a beat every time she caught him looking at her, which was often.

She felt him looking at her frequently. Palmer was well acquainted with the feeling of being watched. That prickly feeling on the back of your neck. The light burning sensation into your back and face. The sinking of your stomach. The gnawing feeling that if you just turned around, you would see eyes looking back at you. She was also well-versed in ignoring that feeling.

The boy known as Calum Murphy was so accustomed to staring a hole into her that Jessica called him Palmer's stalker. He hadn't spoken to her though. He never even got close to her. Which was odd, especially since he seemed to be so friendly with literally everyone else but her.

She felt his gaze on her and she looked up and to the left. Sure enough, the boy was turned back and looking right at her with an unreadable expression. They made eye contact. Palmer's cheeks reddened and she quickly turned her focus back to her work.

A minute or so passed and she was hit in the chest with a tiny wadded-up piece of notebook paper. It was a spit wad. Gross. She looked at the wet ball of paper now sitting on her desk and glanced up. Calum was looking at her with a hollowed-out pen in his mouth. He set it down and a wide grin spread across his face. His chest was shaking and she realized he was silently laughing.

Her mouth opened in amused shock. Her face must have been hilarious because Calum's laughter was no longer silent. A bubble of laughter escaped his chest and the whole class looked at him.

The teacher turned, dry-erase marker still in hand.

"Mr. Murphy, do you have a question?" he said in a stern voice.

Calum straightened and attempted to smother his smile.

"No sir," he managed.

"Then I suggest you keep your focus on the board Mr. Murphy. Now, as I was saying—," the teacher continued on, turning back to the board.

Palmer continued note taking but Calum turned his head to the side and caught her eye again. He gave her a mischievous smile and turned back. Palmer blushed and tried to focus on cell division.

Class ended and Palmer gathered up her things, shoving her books into her bright red backpack. When she was finished she slung the pack over one shoulder, headed out the door, and towards her locker. She would need to change out her books for her next few classes. She turned a hallway and there, leaning casually against her locker, was the new kid. She walked up slowly with a smile on her face and stopped in front of him.

"Hey," he said. As if this were their normal routine.

He slid sideways to lean on the next locker so she could open her own.

"Hi—," she responded.

She unloaded her books and selected the next ones she would need, shoving them into her backpack.

"That's a cool necklace," he said from above her.

"Oh, thanks," she said. "My grandma gave it to me".

"Looks old," he said.

"It is," she responded.

"You like movies?" he asked.

She stood up, slinging her heavy backpack over her shoulder again. She wondered vaguely why he never seemed to have a backpack. His hands were in his pockets. She repeated what he had just said again in her head, pausing.

"Do I like movies?" she asked, looking at him puzzled.

"Yeah, movies. You know. Motion pictures, flicks," he said with a smile and started walking her to her next class.

"Everyone likes movies," she said.

"Wanna go see Jennifer's Body this weekend?"

"With you?" she asked.

"Yeah," he looked her up and down with a smirk.

"You don't even know me," she said apprehensively.

"Of course I do, you're Palmer. Calum," he said pointing at his chest.

"I know," she said matter of fact.

"Perfect. So, it's a date?"

Palmer bit her lip. He was so forward and didn't look even a little embarrassed. She realized he was looking at her expectantly. He must have taken her silent, quizzical look as consent.

"Sweet, save me a seat at lunch," he said.

A while later, Palmer fidgeted in the lunch line next to Jessica.

"Stop being weird," Jessica chastised Palmer. "I still don't understand. So the stalker asked you on a date and said he would meet you for lunch? Just like that. Out of nowhere?"

"Basically. We're going to the movies at some point, no details on that. And he said save him a seat at lunch," Palmer said, chewing her nails.

"You agreed to the movie date?"

"Yeah, I mean I think so. I want to," she decided.

"Ok. So, we like him?" asked Jessica.

Palmer gave Jessica a meaningful look, taking a deep breath.

"Oh shit. You LIKE like him!"

Palmer shushed Jessica loudly just as someone tall reached between them for a tray.

"Excellent, I was hoping just for one like but TWO likes is even better for me," Calum said, putting an apple on Palmer's tray.

Palmer was stunned. He had heard everything. She could die from embarrassment. Jessica looked equally shocked.

Calum looked at Jessica with a puzzled look, then turned to Palmer.

"Who's this?" he asked Palmer, indicating Jessica with a nod.

Jessica's expression went from shocked to livid. Palmer was still frozen, Calum slid her tray down the line for her.

"I'm her best friend 'stalker'," Jessica explained in her sassiest voice.

Calum clutched his chest like he had been physically wounded.

"Stalker? How dare you. I am NOT a stalker. Just— her biggest fan," he said, turning and winking at Palmer.

Both girls laughed out loud and Calum grinned, pleased with himself. When their trays were full he carried his own tray as well as Palmer's tray to a nearby table.

"I like him," Jessica whispered to Palmer.

Palmer smiled at her best friend, biting her lip. When they reached the table Jessica declared that she had forgotten she had made plans to sit with the cheer squad. Palmer felt panic boiling in her stomach as her best friend turned and left her alone with the boy. But one look at Calum's welcoming face had her relaxing.

Palmer took the seat across from him. He smiled at her broadly, she smiled back. He picked up his fork, reached over, and took a bite of her macaroni and cheese. Palmer laughed at his forwardness.

"What even is this?" she said apprehensively.

"Our first date," Calum answered matter of factly.

"This is a date?"

"Of course," he said with another mouthful of her mac-n-cheese. "Unless you have a boyfriend?"

"No. I do not have a boyfriend," she laughed.

"Perfect. But I already knew that. I asked around."

Palmer raised her brows at him in question and surprise.

"I'm your biggest fan remember?" he said amused.

She laughed at that.

"Great. Now that that's out of the way, tell me about yourself," he said.

"What do you want to know?"

"Everything," he replied.

She could tell he meant it. She wasn't sure what to tell him. Palmer must have taken too long to answer because he started to ask her questions in rapid-fire succession.

"What's your favorite color?"

"Green," she responded.

"Not red?" he asked and jerked his chin to her backpack.

Palmer shook her head. "No. Green." She said confidently.

"Lucky number?"

"Nine."

"Do you have any secret talents?"

"Um— I can juggle?"

"Hot."

"Juggling is not hot," Palmer said in a giggle.

"I bet it is when you do it," he said, winking at her.

Palmer rolled her eyes and smiled.

"You are the strangest person I think I have ever met," she said, shaking her head.

"I bet you like it though, right?" Calum asked seriously.

Palmer couldn't believe how forward this kid was. He was fearless. She wondered if he ever got embarrassed.

"Maybe," she replied. "Can I ask you just one question real quick?" Palmer asked.

"Sure."

"Why are you doing this?" she asked, gesturing between them.

He chewed his food and pondered her question. Finally, he answered.

"Let me ask you a few more questions and then when I'm done I'll answer that," he replied.

Palmer was confused and intrigued. She had never met anyone like this. He was so quick.

"Alright, continue," she said.

"Favorite animal?"

"Cats."

"Siblings?"

"One. A brother."

"Oof," he remarked. "Younger or older?"

"Younger."

"Phew," he exclaimed, pretending to wipe sweat from his brow.

Palmer giggled.

"What's your favorite food?" he asked.

"Chicken Alfredo."

"Shit that's a good answer," he said. "Favorite movie?"

"Halloween."

Calum looked at her comically. "Halloween is your favorite movie?" he asked.

"Yeah. Laurie Strode is my hero," Palmer admitted. "WWLSD is sort of my motto," she admitted timidly.

He cocked his head in question, "What?" he asked.

"WWLSD. What Would Laurie Strode Do?" she said slowly. She was feeling a little embarrassed now that she had said it out loud.

"Ahhh—" he said before moving on. " Favorite book?"

"The Shining."

"Ok, so you're a classic horror girl. Interesting, I would have pegged you as the romcom type. No offense," he added the last part as he noticed her bunched eyebrows. He pointed to the table in the corner of the gym. It was filled with emo kids. Their hair was dyed black, side bangs hanging in their face, heavy black eyeliner. All of them were hunched over, listening to music and talking amongst themselves. "Are you sure you shouldn't be sitting over there?" he said with a smirk.

Palmer tilted her head back and laughed.

"That. Right there," he said seriously.

"What?" she asked.

"That's why I'm doing this. Your laugh. I've never heard a better one," he said.

"My laugh," she said, disbelieving. "You decided to hit me with a spitball today and sit with me at lunch because you like my laugh?" she asked.

"Yeah but... I mean you're also VERY easy on the eyes," he said comically.

She laughed again and he stared at her with a small smile.

"The laugh is what hooked me, but it's that undercurrent of darkness you've got going on in these," he said, pointing at her eyes with two fingers. "That's what's pulling me in".

Palmer froze, her smile fading into a frown. She felt a little exposed and uncomfortable. Like dropping your diary and it opens to a very personal page in front of someone.

"Alright let's talk about this date, I'm thinking Friday night..." Calum said, pushing right past the awkwardness. And just like that Calum wedged himself firmly into Palmer's life and heart.

Chapter Four

Present Day (2022)

Dr. Walters looked back and forth between Palmer's parents. What she saw must have given her some silent answer because she continued as if she had never been interrupted.

"Palmer, remember how I told you that you were found in an abandoned house?"

Palmer nodded slowly.

"Well, it would seem that at some point you hit your head. Pretty hard I might add," she said. Again she looked between her two parents.

"I mentioned you had something called 'retrograde amnesia'. Now I'm very hopeful that this will not be permanent. You should start to gain back your memories over time. Especially the more you continue with your normal daily routines," explained Dr. Walters.

"Ok—," Palmer said, closing her eyes. "So— I'm missing some memories. Some time? Like—, how much time?" Palmer was relieved, a little amnesia was no big deal. She'd seen Resident Evil.

The three people in the room looked at each other with worried glances. The silence felt like an eternity. Finally, Chuck spoke in his bluntest voice.

"Twelve. You're missing twelve years."

More silence. Palmer's world slipped out from under her and she felt almost numb. Words wouldn't come. She realized her mouth was hanging open. She focused on breathing. The rise and fall of her chest. Minutes passed and she finally spoke.

"Twelve years," she said. It wasn't formed as a question. She could see from their faces that they were serious.

"Twelve years," her father repeated back and Dr. Walters nodded.

Her mother, Emilia, still hadn't moved an inch. Nor had she taken her eyes off her daughter. More silent minutes passed. Finally, Palmer was able to speak again.

"So it's—," she started to say, counting on her fingers.

"2022," replied her father.

"How old am I?" she whispered.

"Thirty-one years old," replied Emilia with a weak smile.

Palmer took a minute to absorb that information. She didn't *feel* thirty-one. She looked at her hands. They looked the same. Except... her nails weren't chewed down to the quick. That was odd. She had a nasty nail-biting habit. She had tried everything. Lemon juice, hot sauce, the rubber band method, meditating. No luck. She always reverted back to that nasty habit. But there they were. Perfectly manicured almond-shaped nails.

She then looked up to her parents. Holy shit. She stared at them. Now that she really looked, they were different. Her father's salt and pepper hair was more salt than pepper. And the stubble on his chin was almost completely white. He had more wrinkles and his skin looked more leathery than she remembered. She noticed his giant hands were rougher as he clasped hers. And her mother, still beautiful, had aged very gracefully but had still aged. Her tan skin was still glowing but there were wrinkles near her eyes and her lips looked different. Additionally, there were small streaks of gray in her dark hair, especially around her elegant face.

Palmer's anxiety was skyrocketing. She could hear her own heartbeat. Even with both of her parents holding her hands she felt like she was about to fall off a cliff. Her ears started ringing.

"You never answered my question," she said in a small voice.

She was afraid of the answer they were avoiding. Her chest hurt and her stomach felt hollow. She began to tremble.

"What question?" Chuck said not meeting her eye. He didn't want to answer. More seconds ticked by.

"Where's Calum," she said, willing Chuck to look up.

Her father took a deep breath and managed to make eye contact.

"Not here baby. He ain't been around for a long time." He said the words as kindly as possible but he looked like he was glad they were true. Palmer didn't believe him

"You're lying," she said confidently.

She had never accused Chuck of lying. Hell, no one ever had. Chuck Lane was the most honest man most people knew. He wasn't offended by these words. Instead of Chuck responding, Emilia finally spoke.

"Palmer, he's been out of your life for a long time. You have a good life now. A GREAT life even. You're happy. I promise," said her mother.

Tears were streaming down Palmer's face now and her breathing was ragged. She was about to start crying. This wasn't real. She was dreaming. She gathered herself enough to take a deep breath and say steadily,

"Cal would never leave me".

The words hung in the air. Both of her parents were looking at her with pity in their eyes and Dr. Walters backed up into a corner to try and give them some privacy. Time passed and still no one responded. So she repeated herself but louder.

"CAL WOULD NEVER LEAVE ME!"

She started to try and sit up. This wasn't right. None of this was right. She couldn't breathe. There was no air. Eventually, Chuck spoke again.

"He didn't leave you, baby," he said with certainty. "You left him. A long time ago".

Finally, like sprinklers being turned on in the Spring, Palmer began to cry.

Dr. Walters left the Lane's to comfort their daughter. She wasn't needed for this part. They would console her until Palmer calmed down enough to listen to the medical jargon Dr. Walters had to tell her. Nothing she said now would register with her patient, but she had a feeling she was needed elsewhere. She was right.

Dr. Hartman Roth sat in a chair just outside the door. He was still in the same clothes as yesterday. His wrinkled t-shirt stretched over large muscles and he was slumped over, head in his hands.

Dr. Walters could hear Palmer's muffled cries of anguish and her parent's soothing words from the other side of the door. Hartman had likely heard everything. She walked up and squatted in front of him. She placed a hand on his shoulders and he looked up. God he looked terrible, she thought.

Dr. Walters and Dr. Roth were colleagues. Friends even. She has known him and worked with him for years. She respected him. But right now she had to remind herself that he was off duty. He wasn't Dr. Roth right now.

Hartman's eyes were red and puffy. He had large bags that had slowly been forming since the night before. He was ghostly pale and wore an expression of pure heartbreak. He looked like he had the weight of the world on his shoulders.

"Dr. Roth," she said in her soft reassuring way.

She wasn't quite sure what to tell him. He already knew the odds were good. Theoretically, Palmer SHOULD gain back her memory... eventually.

"It's going to take time," she decided to say.

He took a long time to respond.

"She doesn't remember me. She doesn't remember us," he said in a deep hollow voice.

It wasn't a question. He was well aware that Palmer's current memories did not include the life she shared with him. Dr. Walters shook her head solemnly.

"I'm very confident that she will regain her full memory in time. She's been through a traumatic event," said the doctor.

Hartman closed his eyes and ground his teeth.

"I didn't protect her. I should have—," his words drifted off.

"We both know that's not true. We still don't know exactly what happened," she said, squeezing the shoulder she held.

Hartman's eyes opened and he was looking at the door with a clenched jaw. It was as if he was trying to look through the solid wood, straight through to his wife that lay on the other side.

Chapter Five

The Cardinal (2010)

Palmer fidgeted on a stool. Her mother, Emilia, had pulled the stool from the living room into the master bathroom. Palmer was facing the large mirror above the double sink. Emilia stood behind her with a curling iron in Palmer's hair.

"Hold still. You don't want a burn mark on your neck for prom," Emilia commanded.

"I'm trying," she replied.

Palmer wished she could bite her nails but she had gotten acrylic nails the day before with her best friend Jessica. She didn't know why she was so nervous. It was just prom. How many adolescent TV Shows had she seen that depicted prom as just another silly high school ritual? A million. That's how many.

She had been excited for months. Emilia had taken her to several dress shops but Palmer couldn't find anything she wanted. Weeks later Palmer and her grandmother were at a garage sale when Palmer spotted the dress. It had cost only three dollars and Emilia had taken it out a little to fit Palmer's curvy frame.

The dress was red and bright. The red dress was held up by thin straps and stopped mid-thigh, showing off her toned legs. She had borrowed red strappy heels from her mom to complete the look but she had a large purse that had a pair of white Converse sneakers inside for later. She was sure she couldn't stand in heels for too long.

Palmer's little brother Shawn popped his head into the room.

"Hey Mom, can I open up the other bag of Hot Cheetos? Dad is hogging them in the living room but I want to play Grand Theft Auto in my room," Shawn said.

"Why don't you just get a bowl, fill it up, and take it to your room?" Emilia replied.

"Ugh..." Shawn groaned. He looked at Palmer, then down to her dress.

"You look like a giant menstrual cycle," he said with disgust.

"SHAWN!" Emilia yelled.

"You don't even know what a menstrual cycle is, skid mark," Palmer replied to Shawn.

"Pfft whatever," he said, walking back down the hall.

"Have fun running over prostitutes!" Palmer yelled in Shawn's direction.

"What?" Palmer's mother asked. Her face was confused.

"That's all he does in that game, Mom," Palmer said with a smirk.

"It is not..." Emilia's face had drained of color.

"Yeah, okay ma," Palmer laughed under breath. "Uh... mom?" Palmer looked pointedly at the lock of hair that was burning under her mother's curling iron. Steam coming off of it at an alarming rate.

"OH! Jeez!" Her mother jerked and hurriedly released the curl.

Emilia continued to curl Palmer's hair for a few more minutes. She was lost in thought about whether Palmer was telling the truth. She shook her head, deciding that was an issue for later.

"Have you heard from Jessica?" asked Emilia.

"Yeah she should be here any minute," replied Palmer.

Palmer and Jessica had made plans to meet at Palmer's house to finish getting ready before their dates came over. Jessica was going with her long-term boyfriend Chad. They had been 'On again, off again' since middle school. And they were currently going through the 'on again' phase much to Palmer's dismay. Chad was an "ass hat", as Chuck liked to say. Palmer thought he was alright but Jessica deserved better. He had a tendency to break up with Jessica when it was convenient for him. But for now, he made her happy, and anything that made Jessica happy made Palmer happy.

Palmer's mom continued to curl her daughter's long dark hair as she berated Palmer with questions about their evening plans. A few moments later they heard a loud bang and both women jumped. Jessica had let herself into the house and not bothered to stop the screen door from banging. Palmer heard her dad curse loudly from the living room.

"DAMN IT Jessica!" he bellowed.

"Sorry Chuck!" Jessica hollered as she scooted around the man lounging in a lazy boy.

Jessica came running into the already cramped bedroom. Jessica was short and petite. She had long blonde hair and hazel eyes. Jessica had chosen a long strapless purple dress that accentuated her boobs. In her hands was a matching purple purse and a pair of glittery heels that were much higher than Palmer's. Jessica could get away with higher heels since she was so small. On top of that, she was much more agile than Palmer since Jessica was a cheerleader. Jessica's already beautiful blonde hair was made even brighter with highlights and sun-kissed skin she had obtained via tanning beds over the last few weeks.

"IT'S OUR JUNIOR PROM!" She yelled as she screeched to a halt next to Palmer.

Emilia had just enough time to get the curling iron out of the way before Jessica nearly tackled Palmer off the stool in a bear hug. The two girls giggled uncontrollably.

An hour later both girls were fully primped and ready for the night when a knock sounded at the door. The girls were upstairs in Palmer's room putting on some finishing touches to their makeup when they heard the sound. They looked at each other and suppressed another round of giggles. They ran to the window and peered below to the front porch steps.

Down below Palmer and Jessica could see the top of Chad's head just before Emilia had let him in. Chad was wearing a black suit and purple tie to match Jessica's dress. No doubt she had coordinated with him so they would match. Chad looked crisp and clean, Palmer imagined he smelled like too much Axe body spray. She was sure Chad was sitting downstairs on the couch next to Chuck's lazy boy making conversation. Chad played for the local high school football team just as Chuck had so conversation always seemed to be easy between the two.

Palmer looked at her alarm clock and winced. Calum was late. Palmer wasn't surprised, he rarely ran on time for anything.

"Jessica! Chad's here!" Hollered Emilia up the stairs.

Jessica gave Palmer a big smile and two thumbs up before she raced out of the room and down the stairs. Palmer could hear her high-pitched scream when she saw Chad and imagined her rushing to jump on him.

Palmer turned her head to look out the window again. Just as she did so an old Toyota Corolla pulled up. The driver-side door opened with a creak and out stepped Calum. He wasn't wearing a suit. Instead, he had opted for dress pants and a white button-up. He had a gray tie on and she had to assume he borrowed it from his dad. He adjusted it unsuccessfully as he walked up the sidewalk. The tie was loose and Calum had his hands plunged into his pockets as he approached.

Just before Calum reached the door he looked up, straight at Palmer's window. Their eyes met and his lips spread into a smile. She beamed back at him. He often had a toothpick in his mouth and he had one in it now, making his smile even more devilish. He pushed the door open, not bothering to knock.

Palmer turned toward the door to make her way downstairs to Calum when she heard another loud bang. She assumed it was the screen door again slamming closed. But the sound had come from behind her. She stopped in her tracks, turning slowly back to the window. There was a smudge now on the previously sparkling clean window. Palmer walked closer. The smudge was nearly the size of her fist.

She looked under the window to where the roof jutted out. There was a small red mass of feathers lying there. Palmer unlocked the window, wrenching it up and opening it with both hands. It was a bird, she realized. She stared at it and an odd feeling washed over her. She had the strongest urge to pick it up.

She leaned out and reached her hand toward it. She paused. She wasn't the type of person to touch random things, especially animals. But she watched as her hand reached out and picked up the bird in her perfectly manicured hands. It was a cardinal. Palmer had never heard of a cardinal coming to this part of Colorado. Southwestern

Colorado never had cardinals for some reason. Every once in a while, they would be spotted in the easternmost part of the state, but not here. Palmer watched as its heartbeat slowed near its little throat until it finally stopped. Then she stared into its black lifeless eyes for what felt like forever.

"Palmer! Cals' here!" her mother yelled.

Palmer jolted, her mother's voice pulling her out of the trance. She started to shake. Not knowing what to do she placed the bird back on the roof where she had picked it up. She closed the window and locked it.

After taking a steadying breath, Palmer brushed at her dress before she walked to the stairs. She decided to put the unpleasantness of the dead bird behind her. Determined not to mention it and spoil the night.

But as she approached the stair she couldn't help thinking about how the red of the cardinal perfectly matched the red of her dress. Bright red. Like fresh blood.

"That's enough of that," she muttered to herself. She forced a smile to her lips. It was prom night after all.

She began to walk down the stairs carefully, rolling her ankle was a very real possibility in these shoes. She held onto the railing as she descended and caught Cal's eyes to her right. He was leaning against the wall, as far away from Chuck as possible. His eyes looked her up and down slowly as she took the steps one at a time. His gaze made her skin feel like it was on fire. His usual smirk was gone, instead, his toothpick hung from his mouth and almost fell to the floor. All thoughts of the cardinal were forgotten.

Palmer cringed as she realized she was having a real-life corny movie moment. She was making a dramatic stair entrance like in She's All That with Freddy Prince Jr.

The moment was broken by a camera flash. Emilia had started taking pictures.

"Alright guys, let's head outside so I can get some pictures while the lighting is still good," explained Emilia.

Outside Palmer's mom took what felt like an endless number of photos. She had the four of them move all over the yard and arranged them just so. From time to time Emilia would look at Calum and he would give her a flirtatious smile.

Calum and Chad weren't exactly friends but they got along just fine for the sake of the girls. They were from different social circles. Chad was popular and hung out mostly with the jocks. Chad was in shape and clean-cut. He stood up straight and always had an uninterested look on his face. Calum on the other hand was known as the friendly neighborhood stoner and class clown. Calum was long and lean. He slouched and often looked disheveled. And while he looked like he had a carefree attitude, his eyes were always assessing.

When Emilia had finally gotten her fill of pictures they were ready to say goodbye and leave for the prom. Chad headed back inside and came out with a small box. He handed it to Jessica and she hurriedly unfastened the ribbon that held it together. She jumped up and down in excitement, letting out a squeal.

"Oh Chad I love it!!!" she said.

Inside the box was a corsage. At its center, there was a purple orchid surrounded by baby's breaths. It was beautiful. Jessica pulled it out and handed it to Chad to tie on her delicate wrist. Once it was placed just right Jessica ogled it, turning her wrist back and forth.

Calum nudged Palmer with his shoulder.

"Don't worry, yours is in the car," he said with a smile.

"Seriously?" Palmer responded.

She hadn't expected him to get her one. It didn't really feel like his style.

"Super serious," he said with a mocking face.

She genuinely couldn't tell if he was joking. The teens said goodbye to the Lanes. Jessica hugged Emilia and Chuck, they were like second parents to her. Palmer moved to her mother and Emilia kissed her on the cheek and gave her a tight hug. Palmer turned to Chuck who gave her a side hug, never taking his eyes off Calum. Calum was pretending not to notice.

"Have fun," Chuck grumbled.

The couples had planned on driving separately. Jessica and Chad made their way hand in hand to Chad's mom's SUV he had borrowed. Jessica was walking so fast she almost pulled Chad off his feet.

Palmer and Calum walked to his Corolla together, separating so Calum could walk around to the driver's side. Palmer pulled open her door and looked down. On her seat was a clear box with a corsage inside.

"Shit," Calum said as he looked at the box.

The flower's inside had wilted in the hot car. Palmer looked up at his face. He was making an apologetic smile and shrugging. They both laughed. She picked up the box and hopped in the car. Once she was sitting she opened the box. The flowers were the exact same green as her eyes. She looked to Calum again. And he smiled sheepishly.

"It's a green rose. I looked up how they make them like that. It's a mutation. A little flower mutant. Like a Ninja Turtle. It's nothing." he said as he started the car.

Palmer was touched that he even went to the effort. She imagined Calum going to a florist and picking something out for her and it warmed her heart. He had put actual effort into doing this. For her.

Before he could put the car on drive she leaned over and made him meet her eyes. She held them there.

"Hey," she said, "It is NOT nothing."

He gave her a half smile as he rolled his eyes and gunned the engine. As they pulled out Palmer looked back at her parent's waving them off. Just above their heads on the roof, she could see a little speck of red.

Chapter Six

Present Day (2022)

Emilia Lane sat next to her sleeping daughter. She watched as Palmer's chest gently rose up and down. Palmer's eyes were red-rimmed and her nose was pink from crying. Their earlier conversation with her had not gone well. They thought she would eventually calm down but she never did. When Dr. Walters returned she had offered Palmer a light sedative and Palmer accepted willingly. The sobbing had turned to steady tears and gasping breaths. Eventually, her tears were silent. Finally, she drifted off to sleep. Palmer had been too distressed to ask more questions of them.

Emilia thought that Palmer had taken the news of her amnesia well enough at first, but the idea of Calum no longer being in her life had been too much to handle. Emilia reminded herself that Palmer's heart was only nineteen years old, not thirty-one. Emilia took a steadying breath as Chuck came through the door.

"She asleep?" he asked.

"Yeah," she whispered back.

"Hart's outside, he's a wreck. What the fuck happened?" said Chuck.

Emilia shook her head in response.

"No one knows how she ended up at that shack of a house. She didn't text or call anyone to let them know where she was going. Not even Hart". He paused. Looking at his daughter. "The police are searching the house and surrounding woods as we speak, we should get an update if and when they know anything," he said checking his phone.

"How's Hart?" Emilia replied.

"Not great, but he's holding up. I told him to go home and try to sleep a couple of hours and I would call him with any updates. I can't believe this".

A few minutes passed. The Lanes watched their daughter slumber. The bandage around her head had been removed and replaced with some gauze. She had needed twenty stitches to close the giant gash on her forehead. Additionally, her arms had started to bruise.

"Do we tell her when she wakes up?"

"What part?" asked Emilia.

There was a long pause.

"Jesus," Chuck muttered. He took a moment to collect his thoughts. "I think we start with telling her about Hart. The doctor lady said the sooner she gets back into her routine the sooner she can start piecing her memories back together. We got lucky, this could have been much worse".

Emilia shuttered at the thought.

"Ok, she said. "When she wakes up we tell her. How do you want to do it?"

"Fast. Like a bandaid," Chuck decided. "We give her a few minutes to absorb it and then we bring Hart in. I say we hold off on Shawn or Abuela for now."

They looked at each other in the way people who have been together for decades do. Letting a silent conversation flow between them.

"I hate this", Emilia said.

"Me too," agreed Chuck.

Just then Palmer's eyes fluttered open. She looked at both her parents. Finally, she settled on her mother.

"What about Jessica?" she asked. She was almost scared to get her answer about her very best friend. But the smile on her dad's face gave her hope.

"Jessica's got herself a handful of kids now, and another one on the way. We called her when we knew you were ok and we've been updating her. She's been dying to talk to you but we weren't sure what you were ready for," said Chuck.

Palmer gawked. Jessica. Her best friend. Had a 'handful' of kids. And was pregnant. She absorbed this new information. Nodding her head. She was certain her face didn't show how shocked she was. She gulped.

"I want to talk to her," Palmer said.

Her parents looked at each other in silent agreement. Her mother answered.

"I think that's a great idea! Wonderful. Oh... it will have to be through Facetime though. She lives across the country," answered Emilia enthusiastically.

"Ok," Palmer started to say. She considered and said seriously, "What the fuck is Facetime?"

Chapter Seven

The Brown Spot (2009)

Palmer sipped her coffee on her grandmother's porch swing, enjoying the crisp autumn air. She had a thick quilt on her lap and her feet were covered with chunky white socks. One foot pushed off the ground rhythmically to keep the swing gently moving. Palmer closed her eyes and inhaled the scent of fall. One hand was warmed by her cup of coffee and the other was tucked into the quilt. She loved this quilt. It was Abuela's and it smelled like her. Church perfume and tortilla dough. It had tiny strips of fabric all woven together to create a colorful masterpiece held together with a crimson trim. She liked to feel the red stitches with her fingers. The quilt usually sat folded on Abuela's old worn-out couch but today she had brought it out here to enjoy her coffee.

Fall in Colorado was beautiful but unpredictable. Colorado weather could be 'bipolar', often having a mind of its own. Some years summer would hold on tightly, not allowing Fall to come until nearly Thanksgiving. Then winter would swiftly wipe all traces of Fall away with heavy snow. Sometimes as soon as the leaves started to change in September they would be washed away by rain. Leaving the tree's barren until spring. However, this year fall had arrived gently in late August and lingered well past its time.

She heard the shuffling of her grandmother's slippers approaching.

"Hola mi hita, what are you doing out here? It's freezing. Are you crazy you'll catch your death," Palmer's grandma said. Everything Palmer's grandma said was usually accusatory but in an endearing way.

"I'm fine Abuelita. It feels nice. Besides, I have the quilt and some coffee to keep me warm," Palmer said, raising her steaming cup as evidence. Abuela made a disapproving clicking sound with her tongue.

"Those aren't the only things trying to keep you warm," she said, glaring at the street. Calum was pulling onto the street in his dusty old Toyota Corolla. Abuela's lips were pierced together in a thin line. Like Palmer's father, her grandmother was also not a big fan of Calum.

When Cal's car finally reached the section in front of her grandmother's house he honked loudly.

"Hey weirdo what are you doing?" He hollered out his open window at her.

She should be angry with him. He had promised to text her last night but of course, he never did. He had most likely gotten caught up socializing at a party.

She smiled despite herself and set her coffee down. She laid the blanket in a heap on the swing and turned to kiss Abuela goodbye. Her grandmother put her hand on Palmer's cheek, pulling Palmer's attention back to her. The sternness that was in her grandmother's face was gone. Replaced by something sad and far away. Like someone looking at an old photograph of a loved one.

"Hita, be careful ok? With this...," she said, pointing to Palmer's chest. Where her heart was. "Comprende? That boy is slick. I have known slick men in my life. You think you're bueno until all the sudden you are no bueno. Tu sabe?"

Palmer's first instinct was to defend Calum. Yes, he was aloof and irresponsible sometimes but he was hers. Abuela was being overly protective. However, before Palmer could get too defensive she marked the genuine look of love and concern on her grandmother's face. Palmer's righteous indignation deflated and she smiled kindly at her abuela.

"Thank you abuelita. I hear you. I will be careful. I love you. Don't forget your pills," Palmer said as she stepped off the porch. She walked down the steps to Calum.

He was gorgeous, like always. His black hair tousled, full lips spread in a cheeky smile. His skin was flawless and lightly tan. Mysterious gray eyes gleamed at her under thick black lashes. She went around the car to the rolled-down window of the driver's side, leaning in to kiss Calum.

Calum put his hand behind her head and pulled her to him through the window. She put both hands on his face. He kissed her like they hadn't seen each other in years. When in fact they had just seen each other yesterday. He always kissed her like that. He released her and stepped out of the car. His long lean body was toned and agile. He swept his dark hair out of his eyes and put his hands in the back pockets of her sweats. She put her hands in his back pockets as well. He had a good butt, warming her hands in his pockets was just an added bonus.

"Seriously, what are you doing?" he asked.

"Just drinking my coffee," she purred.

Damn him for making her forget all about his absence in communication last night she thought. Calum was talented at charming her into forgetting his mishaps.

He turned toward the house and yelled toward her grandmother, "Morning Grandma Rivera!" Palmer's grandmother pursed her lips together, threw her rag over her shoulder, and turned to go back inside. She insisted everyone call her Abuela, everyone that is except Cal.

Miraculously Abuela's dismissiveness had zero effect on Calum. He turned to Palmer.

"Wanna go for a ride?" he asked.

"Right now?"

"Yeah, I got something I wanna show ya."

"What happened to texting me last night?" she jested at him with a smile.

Calum smacked himself on the head comically. "I'm an idiot baby, you know that. At this point, it's probably something clinical. Come on, go put some shoes on. I'll make it worth your while."

Palmer smiled. She knew not to ask for details. He wouldn't give them to her. Calum loved surprises. And he was very spontaneous. She was certain he had thought of this little surprise right before he drove over. Planning ahead was not his strong suit.

"It's probably a tumor," she said jokingly about his forgetfulness. She turned toward the house just when he responded.

"IT'S NOT A TUMA!" in his best Arnold Schwarzenegger impression. Quoting Kindergarten Cop. Palmer giggled.

She jogged inside. Grabbing her boots from the mud room and slipping them on quickly. She stopped by a mirror to drag her fingers through her hair, adjusting her red headband. She examined herself for a quick second and shrugged before heading to the kitchen.

Her appearance didn't really matter, Calum never really seemed to care one way or the other. When they were together he always treated her like she was the apple of his eye. His attitude toward her remained the same whether she was wearing a short skirt and heavy makeup or if she was wearing pajamas and hadn't showered. Today was the latter.

She stopped in the kitchen and poured her half-drunk coffee into a to-go mug while her grandmother stirred something in a pot. She paused, deciding to grab a granola bar before racing outside. Calum's surprises were always fun but he never really thought ahead. This little surprise excursion could take all day and he might not have thought to pack food. She grabbed a second granola bar for him as well as a couple of bottles of water just in case.

"I'll see you later mi amore!" Abuela yelled as Palmer disappeared.

Before she headed out the door she grabbed her jacket. Better safe than sorry. She truly had no idea where Calum was taking her. Palmer jumped as she heard Calum's car horn beep at her to hurry up.

"Jeez, ok! I'm coming, I'm coming..." she muttered to herself.

She jogged to the car, opened the door, and slid inside. Calum beamed at her, pulling her into another kiss. He kissed her again, long and hard. When he finally released her they were off.

Twenty minutes later they were leaving town. Calum was blasting music through his crappy speakers. Palmer's feet were on the dash. She enjoyed her coffee and Calum's awful singing. She patiently waited for the surprise. 20 more minutes passed.

They started to climb up a mountain. The colors of the trees around them were becoming more and more breathtaking. At first, most of the trees around them were green, but as they drove they slowly began to turn yellow then orange. The orange quickly turned to shades of red. Palmer sat up. Calum looked over and grinned at her. They continued their ascent up the mountain. It was one of the most beautiful things Palmer had ever seen. The road wound up and up, the air getting thinner as they went.

Eventually, they reached their destination and Calum pulled to the side of the road. He got out of the car and beckoned for her to do the same. Palmer got out, breathing in the mountain air. It was drastically colder up here. She shut the car door and made her way to Calum. He was standing on the other side of the road. She came up next to him, heart pounding.

There was only a foot or two of concrete before the road gave way to dirt that disappeared over the edge. They were looking out over a cliff. The road they had taken spiraled up this mountain so high that she was able to see for miles. There was a vast valley of trees below them.

There were thick green trees; Douglas firs, spruce, ponderosa pines, and white firs. But there were also trees that bled into other warm colors; rocky mountain maples, aspens, cottonwood, oaks, and even chokecherry bushes. The colors were spectacular. Gold faded to corral and saffron, then to maroon and crimson.

Palmer's eyes widened, her breath catching in her chest. She reached for Calum's hand. They stood like that for a long time, not speaking. Her eyes scanned every inch of the view. It was spectacular. No matter how long she looked, her eyes could never drink in enough detail. No photograph or painting could do it justice. This was one of nature's miracles.

"You know," said Cal "there's a small house down there, just along the river. There's got to be a road somewhere that leads to it but I can't find it."

"I don't see anything?" said Palmer.

"You've got to squint," he replied and pointed out into the distance.

Palmer followed the direction of his finger and stopped breathing. There it was. At first, it was just a small brown spot. She felt a chill creep up her spine and her mouth filled with saliva. She looked harder and realized it was a house. It was surrounded by deep woods on three sides and the river on the other. She had a strong urge to get as far away from it as she could.

Had she been here before? Why was she reacting this way? She was being ridiculous. Suddenly she remembered the copy of Amityville Horror on her nightstand and shook off her dread. She really should read more self-help books instead. It was just a house, and she was being silly. She turned her attention to the boy beside her.

Finally, she swallowed and spoke,

"Thank you for bringing me here," she said.

"Of course," Calum responded nonchalantly.

Palmer turned to him then.

"I love you," she said.

"What?"

"I love you," Palmer repeated.

Calum blinked. Obviously stunned. He considered for a moment.

"Are... you sure?" he finally said.

Palmer pretended to think about it for a second. Teasing him.

"Yes. I'm sure," she said finally.

Calum bit his lip.

"Why?" he asked after some time.

This puzzled Palmer. She didn't understand the question. Finally, she smiled.

"I just do," she responded.

"Thank you," he said genuinely, still surprised at how genuinely she said this.

They turned back to the view, gazing again at the colors. Calum bumped Palmer with his hip lightly.

"I love you too, by the way," he said, not looking at her.

Palmer smiled to herself and grabbed his hand. For a while they just stood like that in silence, happiness flowing between them. Palmer knew Calum would ruin it by saying something stupid here soon, but he continued to stand with her silently.

Palmer reached toward her neck, grasping the necklace she always wore in her hand. A gold Blessed Mother pendant that always gave her comfort. It was usually warm from contact with Palmer's skin. But right now, at this moment, it was ice cold.

Chapter Eight

Present Day (2022)

Palmer was sitting up in her hospital bed. Emilia was typing on a laptop getting ready to video call with Jessica. The nurse was clearing a side table, another potted plant had appeared on it after her nap. When everyone was set up Emilia made the call to Jessica, placing the laptop in front of Palmer with a gentle smile. Palmer watched the screen intently. She was anxious to speak with her friend. The computer made a doorbell noise and Jessica's face popped onto the screen.

Jessica was still beautiful. She smiled with all her teeth at Palmer. Although her face was a little rounder it was glowing. Her shoulder-length blonde hair was cut shorter than Palmer had ever seen it.

"Hey honey," she said sweetly.

"Hey," Palmer replied shakily.

Palmer had started crying silently.

"You hangin' in there?" asked Jessica.

"Yeah, I think so," she replied. "They told me you're a mom!" Palmer said this with a small laugh and tears still streaming down her face.

Jessica was crying now too.

"I am. And your Godmother to every single one of them!"

Palmer's breath was ragged now. A minute passed and the two best friends cried together in silence.

"I'm sorry I can't be there," Jessica finally said.

"Oh my god, don't be stupid. I understand. I'm just so relieved to talk to you. I want to know everything. Did you marry Chad?"

"GOD NO!" Jessica barked, laughing.

Jessica started to tell Palmer all about her life. She rambled on about her husband, her kids, her nursing job, and about how she is a stay-at-home mom now. Palmer loved when Jessica got on a roll like this. She was an excellent storyteller, making everything just a touch comical. Eventually, there was a lull in the conversation and Palmer realized this was her chance. Palmer looked up and away from the screen. She caught her mother's eye.

"Hey Mom, I was hoping to talk to Jessica alone for a bit."

Emilia looked to the nurse who must have nodded in silent confirmation because they both slowly made their way out. When the door closed Palmer looked back to Jessica on the screen. Palmer took a deep breath. Jessica had a reserved, knowing look on her face.

"What do you want to know?" asked Jessica.

Palmer had thought long and hard about what questions she would ask her closest friend. She couldn't remember the last twelve years of her life. What were her twenties like? She felt like a time traveler like in the movie The Butterfly Effect with Ashton Kutcher. Palmer chewed her lip.

Finally, she said, "Am I happy?"

Jessica took a relieved breath.

"Palmer. You are so incredibly happy. I promise you," she said with pleading eyes.

Palmer clenched her jaw.

"Tell me."

Jessica knew what Palmer meant. Jessica took her time. Palmer didn't know but Emilia had called her an hour ago and gave her a 'pep talk'. She knew that Palmer was fragile right now. She knew that Palmer had a nervous breakdown yesterday. Emilia had given her the green light to tell her the basics. She had also told Jessica that she and the nurse would be on the other side of the door should Palmer need them. Still, Jessica did not relish the idea of putting Palmer in any more distress than necessary.

Finally, she started to tell Palmer about her life.

"Well, you came to University with me! We had... honestly probably too much fun," she laughed. Palmer smiled.

"You graduated with a degree in business. You own a second-hand shop. It's amazing. YOU'RE amazing," she emphasized.

Palmer believed her. She loved thrifting. She had always preferred antiques over new things.

"You love it. You go to thrift shops, garage sales, and estate sales all over and you buy things. You resell them at your shop. You find the coolest things. Oh! You found my engagement ring for me!" Jessica exclaimed. Her left hand shot up into the frame and a large glittering ring flashed.

"It's beautiful," Palmer marveled at the giant ring on her friend's finger.

Palmer knew Jessica was holding back some really big information. The mention of Jessica's ring only served as a reminder of the biggest question Palmer had. When she had woken up from her nap earlier she had stared at her hands, trying to find some evidence of aging twelve years. She had found nothing. She had, however, noticed a thick line on her ring finger. The skin there was lighter. As if she had worn a ring there on a sunny day. It was very faint but under the harsh fluorescent lighting of the hospital, there was no mistaking the tan line.

Palmer stared at her friend.

"I'm... married?" she finally asked. Apprehension was evident all over her face.

Jessica gave her a genuine smile and her eyes willed Palmer to understand.

"Yes."

Palmer nodded her head, and Jessica continued.

"His name is Hartman. And he is...he is everything I could have ever hoped for you".

Silence.

"He loves you. So much. And you love him Palmer. You love him so much."

Palmer sat in silence. Her ears were ringing again but she was coaching herself into taking steady breaths. More silence.

"Palmer?" Jessica had never wished for the ability to teleport until today. She would do anything to be there right now, holding her friend.

Palmer breathed but it turned into a sob.

"I'm sorry," she said, trying to get a hold of herself. "It's just a lot".

"I know. Take your time," Jessica replied. Palmer took a few more minutes to steady herself.

"Calum?" she finally asked.

Jessica's face became serious. And her voice changed. Jessica was usually bubbly and lighthearted. But not now.

"He's gone babe," she said crisply "long gone".

Palmer blinked. She was being curt with her.

"Do you know why?" asked Palmer.

Jessica made a disgusted noise.

"It's a long story."

Palmer looked at her expectantly but Jessica's facial expression made it clear that was all she was willing to say about the matter.

"Jessica, I need you to do me a favor."

"No."

"Jessica," Palmer said with force. "You owe me. How many times did I cover for you in high school? How many times did you copy my homework? How many times did I hold your hair back…"

Palmer was prepared to go on for hours if she needed to but Jessica interrupted her.

"Ok, ok! Jesus Palmer," Jessica swallowed. "Fine. I'll do it".

Palmer looked at her meaningfully. Jessica understood that Palmer wanted her to say it.

"I'll call him," Jessica rolled her eyes in agitation.

She knew this was a bad idea. Jessica put her head in her tired hands.

"Thank you, Jess," Palmer said. She could finally breathe. Palmer wasn't stupid. She knew this was a bad idea too. Dr. Walters had told her multiple times that she needed to start getting back to her current life if she wanted to get her memories back. But Palmer knew what she had to do.

"I need to hear it from him. In person. I need him to tell me. I just do Jess," she was shaking her head and wiping tears from her eyes.

Jessica breathed in and out.

"Ok," Jessica replied. "But then we talk about what you're avoiding".

Palmer knew exactly what she was talking about. Hartman. Palmer refused to think about it long. She needed to know about Calum. She needed to see him. Her life had not turned out the way she thought it would.

"Ok," she agreed. "But I want to talk to him in person. I want to hear it directly from his mouth".

"Your parent's are going to fucking kill me," Jessica cursed.

Chapter Nine

The Cliff (2010)

Palmer sat in the musty backseat of Calum's car eating sour straws and listening to Jessica discuss her new favorite television show. Jessica's boyfriend Chad was slumped against the backseat window next to Palmer. He was dead asleep. Calum drove with one hand on the wheel, the other hand held a Monster energy drink. Jessica blabbered on in the front passenger seat, using her hands excessively to describe the plot of the show. Jessica had a tendency to get car sick if she didn't drive or sit in the front.

The four of them had decided at the last minute to drive to the beach. It was the summer before college and they were trying to soak up every minute. Palmer had never seen the ocean. When Calum had discovered this he had immediately begun to hastily plot this road trip with Jessica. Jessica had dragged Chad along reluctantly.

Chad had been to the beach many times, he had grandparents that lived in Florida whom he visited often. Jessica had been to the beach a handful of times on different vacations with family. As for Calum, Palmer knew for a fact that he had been to the beach on numerous occasions because of the family photos displayed in his house.

He had never mentioned it but Palmer had deduced that Mr. Murphy had a sailboat somewhere. There were many pictures of Cal's dad with a sailboat in their home. In fact, one of the many bathrooms in the expansive house was nautical themed to Palmer's amusement. She wouldn't put it past Calum's family to have a beachside condo somewhere. But Calum had never brought it up.

Jessica continued to ramble on while Calum listened absently. Chad snored loudly next to Palmer. He had been asleep for at least half the trip.

"That's why it's called Pretty Little Liars. Because literally all of them are liars. You can't trust anybody in the show. The plot twists with every single episode. It's impossible to figure out who 'A' is. It's driving me nuts," exclaimed Jessica.

"It's not impossible. You just need to have Palmer watch the first few episodes and she'll tell you exactly who this 'A' is," Calum responded.

Palmer rolled her eyes in the back seat. She had one hand on her necklace, twirling the pendant between her thumb and forefinger. She caught Calum's eye in the rearview window and he winked at her.

"No way. I'm not watching it with her until I absolutely have to. I really like this show and I don't want her to ruin it for me," Jessica said.

"Ok. Can we stop talking about me like I'm not here?" Palmer responded.

"No offense honey," Jessica responded, smiling back at Palmer. "If I get desperate I promise to have you watch it with me so you can do that creepy crystal ball thing you do."

"I've told you a million times, I'm not psychic. They just make shit really predictable these days."

"Sure hun. But you've got to admit, it's kinda creepy," Jessica said gently.

"It's not creepy," Calum said, eyes on the road. He tilted his head considering. "A little spooky maybe," he resolved.

Palmer had actually forced herself to watch a couple of episodes of Pretty Little Liars since Jessica was so into it. Palmer had concluded pretty quickly that it wasn't her thing. However, she was pretty sure she knew who 'A' was after the first episode. Now that the show had been running for over a month she was certain she knew. It was Mona Vanderwaal, obviously. Allison was alive somewhere. And Palmer was pretty certain that the dead body they found was going to be her twin sister.

"Whatever," Palmer replied finally. "How much longer until we're there?"

They had been driving for nearly twelve hours.

"It should only be about another hour," Calum responded.

They left home at five in the morning. Each of them took shifts driving for three and a half hours each. Overall it hadn't been too bad of a drive even though Calum's car smelled like cigarettes and mildew. The hours had flown by, Palmer couldn't believe they had been driving the entire day.

The last hour of the trip flew by with the sounds of Cal and Jessica arguing over various topics. Every once in a while they would rope Palmer into the argument hoping she would support their opposite viewpoints. Palmer mostly rolled her eyes and tried to appease both of them. She was usually neutral, Switzerland.

Eventually, the car took a wide turn and there it was. An endless expanse of glittering blue water. Palmer sat up, placing her hand on the window.

"Chad! Wake up, we're here!" Jessica yelled toward the back. She was attempting to wake up the drooling mass of jock sleeping next to Palmer. He didn't move.

Jessica grabbed an empty Gatorade bottle off of the floor between her feet and chucked it at Chad. It bounced off his massive forehead with a loud thud. Palmer, Cal, and Jessica all sucked in a breath. Instead of waking up, he yawned, readjusted himself, and started mumbling in his sleep.

"Clear eyes... full hearts... can't lose," he muttered between yawns and immediately fell back asleep. The other three passengers stared at him.

"Did he just quote Friday Night Lights in his sleep?" asked Cal with a smirk toward Jessica. Jessica just glared back at him.

"You have the BEST taste in men," he said in Bobby Boucher's voice from Water Boy. Jessica flipped him the bird and Palmer chuckled.

Palmer turned her attention back to the window and watched as the Pacific Ocean crept closer and closer. They were still on a curvy road on a cliff's edge overlooking the ocean. Being from Colorado they were all used to driving on roads near ledges. This was different though. Instead of a mountain ledge that dove down into massive trees that grew up the incline, this was a bare, rocky drop. It was beautiful. Palmer could see cliffs out in the distance in front of them as well. She looked back to see if there were even more behind her.

Her eyes stopped on the last curve they had taken. Out on the ledge, there was a figure, just past the railing. A woman maybe? The sun was glaring in a way that made Palmer put her right hand up to her eyebrows to shade her eyes. When her eyes found the figure again her blood froze. It was the shape of a woman with a long white nightgown on. It was filthy. The woman had long dark hair, flowing behind her in the California breeze. Palmer was holding her breath. The woman turned toward the car, somehow looking right into the rear passenger side window. Looking right at Palmer. The car was too far for Palmer to make out the woman's face but she watched as the woman raised her arm and pointed. Her finger extended right toward Palmer.

Palmer blinked and the woman was gone. Just an empty cliff's edge.

"Palmer?" Calum said. "What's wrong? You look kinda sick?"

"She's probably car sick, you insensitive ass. You've been taking these curves way too fast. Here honey," Jessica said, handing Palmer a plastic bag supposedly for vomit.

"Ew Palmer, don't hurl in here! I'll pull over. Seriously think of the smell," Cal said shuddering.

"As if this car could smell any worse," Jessica said pointedly.

"You guys I'm fine," Palmer said weakly. She took a deep breath.

"Okay," Jessica said unconvinced. "At least drink some water ok?"

Palmer uncapped a Fiji water and took a long chug. It was a little warm but she didn't care. She looked behind her one more time, making sure the woman was gone. When she was satisfied she turned her eyes on the ever encroaching ocean before her. She did her best not to think too hard about what she saw. Or what it meant. Or how often she was starting to see things.

Chapter Ten

Present Day (2022)

P almer had finally gotten to take a shower. It was marvelous, even with the nurse who had to help her in. She was wobbly on her feet and still sore in random places. She had avoided looking at herself in the mirror before the shower but now that the nurse had left she decided to take a good look. Palmer let her hospital gown fall to the floor. Her naked body was littered with bruises and scratches, especially her arms. Her upper arms were the worst, and one of her knees was completely bruised.

She looked like herself. She didn't look old. She was fuller though. Her breasts were larger, and there was a small pooch on her lower stomach. She had the beginning of love handles. Her body had softened and she didn't hate it. Her hair was longer, it hung halfway down her back. Her eyes were the same olive green. Her skin was still pale like a vampire's she thought to herself. She was still Palmer. Just a little older. She had dreaded the moment she would have to look in the mirror, thinking it would cause her to panic again. But her reflection had made her feel better.

Palmer caught the shadow of something in the corner of the mirror. But when she flicked her eyes over to see what it was it was gone. She turned to look behind her. There had been something in the corner next to the toilet. But it was gone now she thought. Maybe she was still concussed.

Palmer turned back to the mirror only for her heart to jump into her throat. A blood-curdling scream escaped her mouth. Her hands reached for her face to cover her eyes and she stumbled backwards. In the mirror was a naked woman. Like herself. Only this woman's face was made of nightmares. Bulging, bloodshot eyes stared back at her. A too-large mouth hanging open to reveal too many teeth and a black hole. Her body was dirty and covered in dried blood and bruises. The limbs were too thin and posed awkwardly.

Palmer had fallen to the floor when a nurse burst in.

"WHAT IS IT, WHAT'S WRONG, I NEED HELP IN HERE!" the nurse cried out.

Palmer had peeled her gaze away from the frightful image in the mirror when the nurse burst in. Now she looked back. Only there was nothing there. Palmer stared at the mirror. Shocked.

"I... I am so sorry. I think... I think I might be going crazy," said Palmer.

The nurse held a hand to her full chest breathing heavily. She must have sprinted to get her.

"Don't be sorry dear. Whew. You gave me quite a fright. Haha!" said the nurse, laughing off the stress. "And you're not crazy. You've been through a lot".

The nurse helped her up, dried her off, and got her into a clean hospital gown. She was guided back to the hospital bed. Her hair was cold and wet but it was clean. She sighed with relief. Before the incident, she had even gotten to brush her teeth as they had started to feel 'fuzzy'. She was no longer hooked to the IV or any of the monitors. She was glad for it. They were making her feel claustrophobic.

She knew Jessica would do as she asked. When would he come? Where did he live? What was he like now? Her mind had started to wander, thinking of all the possibilities. A knock sounded on the door and Emilia popped her head in.

"Hey baby! Feel better?" she asked.

"Much," Palmer lied. Obviously the nurse hadn't informed her mother about the bathroom freak out.

Emilia walked to Palmer's hospital bed and started fussing with the sheets. When Emilia was satisfied she bushed Palmer's hair back out of her face

"Hun. It's time," Emilia smiled at her daughter.

Palmer was nervous. She knew what her mother meant.

"Your daddy's gonna bring him in. We'll stay for a minute and then give you some privacy."

Emilia wasn't giving Palmer an option. It had been twenty-four hours since the incident, and everyone was pushing her to start embracing this life she couldn't yet remember. Getting back to her regular routine was critical to her recovery. Dr. Walters had said this to Palmer repeatedly.

Palmer breathed deeply. What was her husband like? What was their story? She had too many questions. Where should she even start?

"Ok," said Palmer. "Let's do it".

Palmer nodded and smiled. Pleased with her daughter's reaction. Emilia walked to the door and popped her head into the hallway. She must have given some silent signal because Palmer heard a chair scoot and steps come to the door.

The strange man walked in. The man that had been sleeping next to Palmer when she woke up. His eyes were bright blue, his hair golden. A shadow of a beard covered his face and full lips spread into a weak smile directed at her. Chuck was behind the man with a hand on his shoulder. They were nearly the same height. Impressive, considering her dad's height.

"Hartman?" Palmer said slowly.

She understood now. The man had been sleeping in the chair next to her because he was her husband.

The man nodded his head.

"Palmer," he replied.

His voice was deep and rumbly. Palmer glanced at the open chair next to the bed, the one he had slept in. Silently indicating that he should sit. He crossed the room and sat leaning forward. Chuck and Emilia exited quietly, shutting the door behind them. Silence hung in the air.

"Well this is... shitty," she said with a laugh. The tenseness in the room lighted. Hartman smiled wide and genuinely as he rubbed at his tired eyes.

"Yeah," he agreed. "Really *shitty*". He emphasized the 'shitty'.

Palmer smiled just as big as he did, she couldn't help it.

"So, it would seem we are married," Palmer said, still smiling. This moment with him could have been awkward. After all, she didn't know him. He was a stranger to her. But there was something about his presence that made her comfortable, even brave.

"Yes. We are husband and wife," he said with humor.

She giggled.

"So... how are we supposed to do this?" Palmer asked him.

"Hmm... well," he thought about it. "Have you ever done speed dating?"

Palmer rubbed her lips together.

"I can honestly say I don't know if I ever have," she replied with a smile.

"Oh God, I'm so sorry. Shit! What is wrong with me? That was, that was so stupid," he said, angry with himself.

Palmer laughed. It was a full belly laugh.

"You think this is funny?" he said, gesturing between them.

"A little," she said, still laughing. "We're married, but I have no idea who you are. It's a little funny. I've got this whole Jason Bourne thing going on, minus the skills."

Hartman shook his head smiling.

"I was going to say that when people do speed dating they ask each other a bunch of basic questions to get to know each other. We could try something like that?" he said.

"Yeah, but you already know me," she said, then paused. "Right?"

Hartman's face softened. His eyes were gentle, and the bluest blue Palmer had ever seen. He had a light smile on his lips and he tilted his head.

"Yes Palmer. I know you."

Palmer blinked and warmth spread through her. She clenched her fists and gulped. This man KNEW her. He was her husband. He must know her in every way possible. His words were extremely intimate for someone she couldn't even remember meeting. She tried to make her breathing look normal.

"Ok,' she said, swallowing again.

He was leaning forward in the chair, legs spread. His elbows rested on his knees, hands clasped. Palmer realized how close he was. His masculine smell filled her nose. It was musky and woody. She eyed him curiously.

"How long have we been married?" she asked.

"Six years."

"What's your last name? Whoa. Our last name? Did I take your name?"

"Roth, and yes you did."

Palmer paused.

"Palmer Marie Roth," she said the name out loud like it was a spell that could bring her memories back. It didn't.

"You have no idea how happy it makes me to hear that name," he said sincerely.

His face was visibly relieved. The worry lines around his mouth and eyes smoothed out. Maybe the words were a spell? They certainly had a drastic effect on Hartman. She looked at him for a moment more and continued her questions.

"What do you do for a living?"

"I'm a doctor," he replied.

"Oh!" She was shocked. She figured he was a cop, maybe a lumberjack or something. She knew that was ridiculous. But he was massive. His muscles bulged through his shirt and his shoulders were extremely wide.

"You're surprised?" he asked.

"No," she started. But then she started to tell the truth. "Well, kinda. I just never really saw myself as the 'marrying a doctor' type."

"I know. You've said that before."

"Ahh," she pondered that. "What kind of doctor?"

"I'm an Oral Surgeon."

He said it like it was no big deal.

"That sounds... prestigious," she responded.

He smiled.

"Thank you, but I'm basically just a fancy dentist".

"I married a *dentist*?" Palmer said with feigned disgust.

Hartman laughed, it rumbled through his big chest and it felt like it shook the little room. Palmer found that she liked making him laugh. She continued with her questions.

"We have a house?"

"Yes."

"Is it big?"

"Yes," he said with another laugh.

"Well I should hope so, I'm married to a doctor for God's sake."

He roared with laughter at that, and she found herself laughing too.

He reached forward to touch her hand. She flinched. The laughing stopped.

"I'm sorry," he said. "I think, I think I forgot for a sec."

"No, I'm sorry. I didn't mean to," she said back to him. She really was sorry. The hurt on his face was painful to look at.

"I just miss you so much," he said. His voice quivered.

Moments passed. She was surprised by how peaceful she found his presence. Finally, she asked the question she had been saving.

"Hartman?"

He looked up at her then, love in his eyes. Hearing her say his name had his heart aching.

"Yes?" he responded. He would do anything to keep her talking to him.

"Do you know why I was in an abandoned house?" she asked.

Hartman looked back at her with his jaw clenched. Like he was holding back secrets on his tongue. His eyes drifted to her arms. Palmer followed his gaze. He was staring at the bruises on her arm. Just then she realized that they were patterned. She hadn't noticed that before. They were small circles, formed into a kind of arch. There were five of them on each arm. They were fingerprints. Like a hand had grabbed her by both arms.

She swallowed, looking up at Hartman. He slowly turned his gaze from her bruises to her face. They're eyes locked. Palmer's eyes were scared, worried. Hartman's were darkened, angry. Palmer had a frightening thought and all of a sudden she really wished she wasn't all alone with this man she hardly knew.

Chapter Eleven

The Egg (2008)

Palmer walked to class trying to ignore the bickering of her two best friends.

"Vampires are hot Cal, get over it", said Jessica.

"I'm not arguing that vampires aren't hot! I'm saying vampires have been hot for a long time. It's not new. Dracula, The Lost Boys, Interview With a Vampire, Buffy for fucks sake. I'm saying you're obsessed with the stupidest vampire movie I've ever heard of. Vampires don't sparkle, Jess. Your chick brain has you all messed up," he replied.

Jessica looked like she was going to explode. Her lips were pressed together tightly, her eyes lethal.

"First of all, fuck you. Second, how do you know the vampires sparkle if you've never seen the movie ass-wipe?"

Calum was speechless, then smiled.

"Touche Jessica. Touche," he replied.

Jessica looked triumphantly at Palmer. Palmer knew for a fact that he had seen the movie because last month he drove her to a theater two towns over to watch it so they wouldn't run into anyone they knew.

"You told her?" he cried.

"No. I told her we went and saw 'Quarantine'. You told her just now, because you're an idiot," Palmer said.

He looked at both girls, shaking his head.

"Fine. I saw it for research purposes. Purely academic. I concluded that it was stupid," he said confidently.

Jessica rolled her eyes as they walked into class. They had third period together this semester. The classroom was large, and instead of desks, it had big tables that sat four students. The trio sat closest to the back. They kicked their bags under the tables and waited for the rest of the class to file in as well.

Their high school was fairly small so their Home Economics class was taught by their gym teacher and the football coach, Coach Davis. He was a large man who had a tendency to wear polo shirts two sizes too small. Thus making his pot belly more evident.

"Alright, settle down now. Last week we went over food and nutrition. This week we will be covering family planning and wellbeing, and next week we will be going over household finances. I'm going to need everyone to partner up," he hollered with his hands on his hips.

Calum turned to Palmer quickly, grabbing her by the shoulders.

"Dibs!" he said directly to Jessica.

He looked down at Palmer and winked, scooting her chair closer to him.

"You're a child," Jessica said to him under her breath.

Jessica turned to the person sitting on her right and shuttered. Marcus Nelson had sat next to her. Palmer and Jessica had watched him pick his nose and eat it in the sixth grade. They would never be able to forget. On top of that, Marcus had a pet ferret. Not only did Marcus smell like said ferret, but he also had a tendency to talk about said ferret constantly.

Palmer felt Calum holding in a laugh next to her. She elbowed him hard.

Coach Davis cleared his throat, bringing everyone's attention back to the front.

"Alright, now that we're all paired up I would like everyone to turn to chapter six in your textbooks and read this week's assignment with your partner while I pass out the eggs".

Palmer and Calum skimmed the chapter quickly while Jessica read the chapter out loud to her partner. Marcus wasn't slow but Jessica enunciated every word as if he was a toddler.

The assignment was simple. They would be given an egg and expected to take care of it as if it were a baby for an entire week. They would need to keep a log of everything they did to care for the egg during that week. At the end, they would be required to write a paper on what they learned from this experience.

Calum and Palmer finished skimming the assignment at the same time and looked at each other a little horrified. Just then Coach Davis made his way to their table with his carton of eggs, holding one out for Calum to take.

Calum put his hand out hesitantly, accepting the egg. He turned to Palmer and smiled wolfishly. Just then the egg slipped from his hand and cracked open on the tiled floor. Calum's face froze in shock as he looked down at their class project. Palmer smothered a gasp with her hand, and Jessica howled with laughter next to them.

"Mr. Murphy. Are you kidding me?" said Coach Davis, annoyed. "You fumbled it in the first ten seconds."

"Coach. I'm so sorry I don't know what happened," Calum looked up at the man desperately.

The entire class was looking at them amused.

"Alright," Coach Davis said. "I'll give you one more, but don't think any of you can just replace these with eggs from the grocery store. My initials are on the bottom of each egg with MY handwriting. If any of your eggs break you will have to come to me for another one. Each time they break I will be taking off points from your final project. Understood?" he turned, asking the class.

Everyone nodded in reply. Then he turned to Calum and Palmer, pulling another egg out of the cartoon. Calum put both hands out this time to accept the egg. Couch Davis shook his head at him.

"Not you butterfingers," he said to Calum. Coach nodded to Palmer, indicating she should take the egg.

She accepted it with an amused smile. Coach Davis eyed Calum with apprehension before turning back to his desk. Palmer was stifling a laugh. Calum put a finger up to stop her imminent jesting.

"Not a word Palmer," he said. "Not a word."

Palmer smirked, holding the egg gently in her hands. She rolled it lightly in her fingers, feeling the soft texture of the shell. She felt the weight of it in her palms, it was so small. Palmer found her thoughts wandering to ideas of the future that she had never really considered. She was daydreaming of her future and what it could look like.

"Hey," Calum said next to her, causing her to look up. "Where'd you go?"

Palmer shook herself and smiled.

"Nowhere," she lied.

Half an hour later the bell rang. Students shuffled toward the door. Palmer leaned down to pick up her backpack with her free hand. The other hand was gently clutching her and Cal's textbooks. Palmer and Cal walked to her locker together. Cal chatting with and fist-bumping a number of people on the way. Cal never stopped at his own locker,

Palmer wasn't even sure if it had anything in it. She had never seen him carry around a backpack or any textbook.

Finally, they stopped in front of her locker and she started to open it. Calum finally turned toward her, concern etched on his face.

"Hey Palmer, you good? You look a little tired," he said.

"Geez thanks," Palmer responded, blowing a lock of hair out of her face.

"Don't get me wrong, you're still the most stunning creature I've ever had the fortune of gazing upon," he said. He grabbed her arm and began kissing it comically like he was Pepe Le Pew from The Looney Tunes.

"You are my reason for living my love. Muah, muah, muah," he said in a French accent. She was previously mistaken. He wasn't impersonating Pepe Le Pew. He was Gomez Adams and she was Morticia. She laughed and tugged her arm away.

"Gross, you're slobbering all over my arm," she huffed through her smiling teeth. "I'm fine, I've just been having trouble sleeping. Bad dreams," Palmer said, lowering her voice.

"Still?" said Calum. His expression changed from groovy to concerned.

"Yeah," she responded. She started to fill her red JanSport with the books she would need for the next several classes. "It's always the same one..." she muttered quietly.

Cal swallowed. Palmer thought he might ask about the dream. Instead, he high-fived some kid dressed like a Juggalo walking past. The guy's headphones were blasting Insane Clown Posse so loud anyone near him could hear it. Palmer hoisted her backpack up onto her back and began walking to her next class. Calum followed close behind. Palmer felt the coolness of the egg in her hand as she walked. She didn't bring up her sleeping issues again.

Later that night Palmer was at her grandmother's house helping cook enchiladas. Her grandmother was wearing one of her usual aprons and was frying tortillas over the stove. Palmer sat at the counter and helped cut tomatoes and lettuce. Palmer was staying the night with her grandma.

Palmer and her brother Shawn often stayed the night here on weeknights. It was comfortable and the food was good. Abuela was less like a grandma and more like a second mom. They loved her and genuinely enjoyed spending time with her.

"I don't think I understand the point of the egg. It's like an experiment?" Palmer's grandmother said. She was flipping tortillas with her bare hands.

Palmer and Cal's egg sat on the island counter where Palmer worked.

"It's for Home Ec. I think it's supposed to teach us about the responsibilities of parenthood," Palmer said, chopping.

"That is ridiculous. An egg is nothing like a baby mi hita. I can tell you that much," Abuela said. "Watch the stove for me real quick. I need to grab something from the pantry".

Palmer's grandmother left the room and Palmer could hear her rummaging around. Palmer accidentally sliced her finger mid-chop.

"Ouch!" she said, dropping the knife with a clang. Palmer put her finger to her mouth. She tasted the copper taste of blood. She looked up and noticed that the egg was starting to roll off the counter. "No!" Palmer cried out, reaching out to try and stop it. It was too late. The knife clatter had somehow shaken the surface of the counter and the egg's stability.

The egg fell to the floor in a loud crack. Palmer was ready to curse but something stopped her. She had expected the egg to crack open and expose its yellow runny insides. Instead what she saw was red and wrong. The insides of the egg looked like veins, blood, and boogers. It made Palmer want to retch.

Palmer's grandmother walked back into the room quickly.

"What?!" Abuela exclaimed. She looked down and saw the bloody egg. Palmer felt like the world had stopped. Her ears were ringing. Palmer's grandmother made the sign of the cross. Using her fingers to touch her forehead, her chest, her left shoulder, and finally her right shoulder. They stood frozen like that in the kitchen for a long moment. Palmer's bloody finger dripped a little on the tile.

The fire alarm went off and they both jumped. Her grandmother turned quickly to the stove and saw the burnt tortilla.

"Ay Dios mio..." she said under her breath. She pulled the tortilla off of the stove.

Palmer couldn't stop staring at the egg.

Chapter Twelve

Present Day (2022)

Palmer was still staring at Hartman. He was staring intensely back at her. Palmer glanced at the door and silently wished for her parents to come back. She didn't want to be alone with this man, even if he was her husband. She still didn't know what happened to her. Palmer looked back down to the hand-shaped bruises. She lifted her right hand and gently placed each finger into its corresponding bruise. Her elbow was raised at an odd angle in the air trying to match the handprint. As she did so she made sure she could see Hartman in the corner of her eye.

Palmer willed herself to remember what had happened to her but nothing came. The idea that she truly couldn't remember twelve years of her life, let alone the trauma she had recently gone through, weighed heavy on her heart. How could this be happening? How could this be real?

Palmer was starting to feel panicky. She was feeling too hot and it felt like something was on her chest. This was too much. Palmer's eyes blurred and her ears started to ring. The room felt like it was spinning. Hartman must have noticed her increased distress because he stopped looking around, focusing only on her. His gaze gave Palmer goosebumps.

"Are you ok? What do you need?" he asked.

He was desperate to do something for her. She felt like she was starting to hyperventilate.

"Um, could you maybe get me some water?" her words were shaky.

This couldn't be real. This wasn't happening. Hartman reached for her cup of water. Realizing it was empty he said, "Hold on, there's a fountain down the hall," he said, leaving the room.

Palmer was alone, listening to her heart pound in her chest. Her mind was reeling. She felt like she might faint.

Hartman came back and gave her sips of water, leaning the straw toward her with his fingers. Palmer flinched away from him at first but then after assessing him decided to comply. Palmer's chest was hurting, she felt dizzy. She must have looked how she felt because Hartman's handsome face was etched with concern.

"I'm going to find your nurse ok? Sit tight," he said, squeezing her clammy hand. She had an awful urge to yank it away. She didn't know him and she didn't know how she ended up like this. The awful thought that she had earlier came back up. What if he had something to do with it?

Hartman left the room again to get a nurse. Minutes passed, he must have had a hard time finding the nurse Palmer thought. Good. She needed to get her shit together, she told herself.

Palmer focused on taking deep, steady breaths. She remembered taking a yoga class in high school where the instructor had them attempt to meditate. She tried to remember how he had guided them through a 'grounding exercise'. She closed her eyes and attempted to calm herself.

Just then she heard a knock on the door. Eyes still closed she called for whoever it was to come in. She finally felt like she was gaining back some control over herself as she opened her eyes and exhaled. She was expecting the nurse or Hartman. But it was neither of them.

A tall man had come into the room. He was wearing dark denim jeans and a black t-shirt. His arms were covered in colorful tattoos and he had a short dark beard. Palmer looked at him confused. But then the man smiled. It was a wicked side smile.

Palmer's heart lurched in her chest. She knew that smile intimately, she would recognize that smirk from a mile away. All of the control that she had thought she gained back slipped from her grasp again as all of her thoughts emptied from her skull. Panic flooded back to her tenfold.

It was Calum.

Chapter Thirteen

The Spoiler (2008)

Palmer and Calum were on his parent's couch watching The DaVinci Code. Palmer was lying flat on her back, legs on Calum's lap. He had pulled the down comforter off of his bed and dragged it into the living room for their movie night. The white comforter covered both of them. Palmer had a giant bowl of popcorn resting on her belly and was slowly bringing fistfuls to her mouth. They both watched intently.

Palmer liked her popcorn extra salty and buttery. Calum did not.

"Dude, how can you stand to eat that?" Calum said.

"Stand what?" Palmer responded without taking her eyes off the TV.

"The popcorn, it's way too salty. Again," he said, shaking his head.

"No it's not, you're just a pussy," she responded.

Calum put a hand to his chest in mock offense.

"Madam! Language!" he said in a bad British accent.

Palmer rolled her eyes and continued to watch. It was nearly nine o'clock. Palmer wondered to herself where Calum's parents were. She realized she hadn't seen them puttering around the house and checking up on them.

Calum's house was enormous. She was never really sure what his dad did for a living but assumed it had something to do with finances. He dressed like a lawyer and when he was around he always had his phone pressed to his ear. Mr. Murphy was usually yelling at someone on the other end as he hurried to some appointment. Palmer could count on one hand the number of times he had bothered to speak to her. Sometimes he would lower the phone long enough to say something to Calum but it was always brief and never personal.

Calum's mom, on the other hand, was a hoverer. She considered herself a 'stay-at-home mom' even though her only child was a teenager. She spent most of her days cleaning the expansive house, reading Good Housekeeping, crocheting, and making dinners her husband rarely had time to eat. Mr. Murphy often worked late.

Mrs. Murphy loved Palmer. Palmer always made a point to be respectful and clean her plate when she was over for dinner. Mrs. Murphy considered Palmer to be an excellent influence on her usually ill-mannered son. Even so, Calum's mother didn't like to leave them alone for more than ten minutes at a time. She always found a reason to come into the room. She would start vacuuming the pristine carpet. Other times she would bring them snacks they hadn't asked for. Sometimes she would come into the room randomly and start working on her current crochet project in the corner.

"Hey, where are your parents?" Palmer asked.

Calum's lips formed a tight line and he spoke without taking his eyes off the TV.

"Oh, they're actually out of town," he said with almost believable indifference.

Palmer's breath caught. Out of town? Why hadn't he mentioned anything? She let a couple of moments pass.

"And... they left you home alone?" she said, disbelieving.

The deceit was clear on Calum's face now. He was a good liar but Palmer could spot his deception from a mile away. He sucked on his front teeth with his tongue and tried to hide a small smile.

"Well, no not exactly. I'm supposed to be staying at Harry's for the weekend," he responded.

The air seemed to change, heavy with tension. They had never been truly alone together. They had been sneaking chased kisses between classes for almost a year now.

Palmer had kissed boys before. In the 5th grade, a boy in her class asked if he could kiss her while they were waiting for the bus. The kiss was quick and silly, both of them giggling after. And in the 8th grade, Palmer had played spin the bottle at her first 'boy/girl' party. She had leaned over an empty vodka bottle and kissed a friend's older brother in front of a circle of partygoers. That kiss had lasted maybe a second longer than her previous kiss, and the group around them had hooted in excitement. Palmer had blushed for the next two hours.

But kissing Calum was completely different. Calum's lips were warm and wet and his breath hot. When he kissed her his hands held her waist, causing her brain to go blank. But their kissing had always been short, interrupted by the school bell or Calum's mom.

They hadn't ever discussed sex together. However, Palmer's best friend Jessica had recently lost her virginity to her boyfriend Chad. Jessica had shared every salacious detail with Palmer, leaving Palmer intrigued but terrified. Calum had turned sixteen last month and Jessica knew sex was a frequent topic amongst his friends. It seemed like these days sex was all anyone wanted to talk about. Yet, that particular topic hadn't come up when they were together.

Jessica had overheard Calum's buddies asking him if he and Palmer had "done it yet'. Jessica had of course immediately gone to Palmer with the details of the conversation. Jessica had said Calum responded to the questioning by shrugging and telling the group of boys it was none of their business. Jessica was impressed by his discreteness but Palmer wasn't surprised.

Calum didn't like to talk about his personal life, and that included Palmer. He didn't hide his feelings for Palmer. Quite the opposite actually. If anything, he had a tendency to embarrass Palmer with his public displays of affection. He made it abundantly clear to everyone around that he and Palmer were very much together. He kissed her without hesitation whenever and wherever he wanted. There was zero question that Palmer was Calum's from the first time he spoke to her. He just never liked to share details about himself with others. Palmer respected that about him.

Calum and Palmer were both tense at the idea of being completely alone. Palmer had stopped eating the popcorn, her mouth had gone dry. Calum swallowed hard. They were both breathing a little harder. Minutes passed. Palmer rubbed her lips together and they continued to watch The Davinci Code in silence. They usually watched horror movies on movie night since it was Palmer's go-to genre but Calum had insisted they watch something 'normal'.

Palmer finally said, "I bet this Sophie chick is going to be related to Jesus somehow".

The tense moment was over.

"What?", he asked.

"The girl with Tom Hanks, I bet she's one of the descendants they're talking about," she responded.

Calum looked at her astonished.

"Fuck! Palmer, are you kidding me? Did you just ruin another movie for me?" Calum said jokingly with a hint of seriousness.

She had ruined the plot of several movies for him in the past year.

"You swear to God you've never seen this?" he asked.

"NO!" she explained.

"If that ends up being what happens I'm going to be so pissed Palmer. You seriously have to stop doing that," he said, shaking his head.

"Sorry..." she said weakly.

He was playing with her but she could feel his annoyance. Calum had been waiting to see this movie for a while now and Palmer was fairly certain she had spoiled the plot. She was incredibly gifted and guessing how movies, books, and shows ended.

Palmer sat up with a grunt and handed the popcorn bowl to Calum.

"I'm gonna get water," she said standing up.

She made her way to the kitchen. She reached for a cabinet full of cups on her tippy toes, selected her favorite cup, and turned to the sink. As she did she saw a dark figure in the doorway. She jolted, dropping the cup. Not again, she thought. Please not again.

But when she turned it was just Calum. Her heart relaxed back to a normal rhythm. He was leaning against the door frame, hands in his pockets. There was a look in his eyes that Palmer had never seen before. He was nervous. His jaw was clenched as he watched her intently.

She picked the cup back up, filled it with water, and took a long drink. She could feel his eyes on her the entire time. When she had drunk her fill she set the glass on the counter and moved to the door he was semi-blocking. She met his eyes as she went to move around him. She brushed against him as she passed. She only made it a few steps when he grabbed her hand and spun her toward him.

Calum crushed Palmer's lips with his own. The kiss was hard. He smelled like fresh laundry and she noticed he tasted like mouthwash as his tongue explored her mouth. Her hand remained in his and his other hand reached for her free one. They remained in the doorway like this for several minutes, kissing and holding each other's hands.

Calum started to lead her backward toward the couch. His mouth remained on hers. Palmer kept her eyes closed, relishing his attention. Her legs eventually hit the back of the couch and she fell back into it. Calum clumsily collapsed on top of her. Their lips separated and they stared at each other for a moment catching their breaths. Palmer bit her lip. Calum looked deeply into both of her eyes before he kissed her jaw and then her neck. His hands roamed up her waist to her breast. He squeezed lightly and she moaned quietly.

His mouth returned to hers and kissed her again with his warm tongue. Butterflies erupted in her stomach. His hand continued to knead her breast. His hand traveled to the bottom of her maroon shirt and crept underneath. She felt his fingers travel to her bra and he squeezed again. His kisses had quickened.

Palmer became acutely aware of his pelvis pressing against her own. Warmth spread through her belly. His hand slipped under her bra and she gasped. A low growl rumbled from his mouth into hers. She felt his soft palms rub against her nipples. Her entire body felt electric. He continued to kiss her like this, massaging her breast. Eventually, he switched to the other breast. It felt amazing.

He started to kiss her neck again as he removed his hand from her chest. His hand traveled to the top of her low-rise jeans. He started to fumble with the buttons. Her stomach flipped.

"Calum," she said hoarsely.

He looked at her then with pleading eyes. She could feel his hardness pressed against her.

"I don't— I'm not—," she started to say.

"Ok," he said shakily.

Calum swallowed hard and kissed her once more on the mouth.

He helped her sit up and they settled back into the couch. The movie was still playing but the air was hot. Calum got up.

"I'll be right back," he said, walking out of the room.

Palmer sat there trying to catch her breath. She tried to focus on the movie, hoping it would calm her thumping heart. The movie was coming to an end.

Tom Hanks had discovered that his co-star was a descendant of Jesus Christ and Mary Magdalen. Palmer heard Calum's voice from behind her and she jumped.

"Son of a bitch," he mumbled.

His eyes were on the screen.

"Remind me not to watch movies with you anymore," he shook his head with a smile.

Calum sat down next to her, putting an arm around her shoulder.

Chapter Fourteen

Present Day (2022)

"Calum?" Palmer said in a whisper.

"Hey," he said apprehensively.

Palmer was speechless. This was Calum. Her Calum. He was twelve years older. He was a man now. She couldn't believe her eyes. Here he was, mere feet away from her. She studied his face. It was the same face, except for the beard she thought.

Yet there was something different. She couldn't place her finger on it. He was even taller than she remembered. He was dressed casually like he usually did. But his outfit was more put together, more grownup.

Then she realized what was so different about him. It was his eyes. They were wrong. They had lost that playfulness that they had always held, his twinkle. Instead, his eyes were vacant, hollow. He was haunted by memories Palmer had lost.

She wanted to go to him. She wanted to fix that look and smooth away the worry in his brow. But she was frozen in shock. Calum stayed just within the door, not daring to move toward her.

"Jessica called me," he said.

"I asked her to," Palmer's voice was still a whisper.

"Mmm," he said, acknowledging her statement.

This wasn't right. This wasn't them. He looked scared to come anywhere near her. He looked uncomfortable that he was even there. But his eyes. They were full of longing for her.

"Calum?" Palmer whispered again.

Calum swallowed. "You really don't remember. Do you?"

Palmer shook her head slowly.

Calum scratched his head and ran his hands through his hair.

"Are you ok?" he asked.

Calum looked at her painfully.

Palmer had barely heard what he said over the pounding in her ears. Her panic and confusion had skyrocketed.

Just then the door opened and Hartman walked in with a nurse. The nurse walked straight to Palmer, checking her over. At first, Hartman didn't notice Calum, he had been too worried. When he finally noticed someone else was in the room he turned to Calum, a confused look on his face. And then the room became so tense Palmer could barely breathe.

Hartman's jaw had clenched so tight she could see the muscles in his cheeks. His back straightened and his eyes hardened. His lips were a tight line. He had squared his shoulders to the other man. Somehow he had made himself look even bigger, she saw him take a deep breath as his built chest rose and fell.

Calum sneered at her husband through a mocking smile. His tattoos shifted as he clenched his fists. Though he was leaner than

Hartman he was a little taller. His face had shifted into a look of malice. These men hated each other she realized.

It felt like the men faced each other for an eternity. The nurse continued to check Palmer, asking her questions that went unanswered. Palmer couldn't hear anything. The nurse was completely oblivious to whatever was going on behind her.

The door opened again and Chuck stood in the doorway. He saw the look on Hartman's face and immediately went on alert, scanning the room. Chuck spotted Calum and he looked almost as angry as Hartman. Chuck composed himself quickly and stepped between the two. Calum and Hartman didn't take their eyes off each other.

"Alright guys," Chuck said. "Let's take this out in the hallway huh?" he said companionably.

The men didn't move.

It was Hartman who finally spoke. He looked dangerous but his words were calm.

"What are you doing here?"

"I was invited," Calum said with contempt.

Calum glanced at Palmer. Hartman's eyes followed. Hartman moved a few steps then, blocking Calum's path to Palmer.

"Hartman," Palmer said.

Her voice had been louder than she intended. Hartman turned his neck and turned to her. He was asking her a question with his eyes.

"I want to talk to him. I NEED to talk to him..." she pleaded.

Hartman looked unsure but nodded his head. He moved to the door, still eyeing Calum. Chuck gave a warning look to Calum, putting his hand on Hartman's shoulder as he got close.

"We'll be right outside," Chuck said to Palmer but directed the words to Calum.

Hartman looked at Palmer before completely leaving, making sure this was what she wanted. When she nodded, so did he, accepting her decision. He didn't look happy about it.

Palmer's father and husband walked through the door.

The nurse had caught onto the fact that something odd was going on. She was looking at Palmer with concern. Palmer felt like everyone was acting ridiculous. It was just Calum.

"You're looking a little better, your color is coming back. Keep sipping on that water for me ok? Do you need anything else?" said the nurse.

"No I'm good, thank you so much," Palmer said absently.

The nurse walked to the door then, eyeing Calum up and down before she walked out. The door shut behind her. Calum and Palmer were alone again.

"Well that was awkward," Calum said sarcastically.

Palmer just stared. What the fuck was that? Why was there so much tension?

"Can you sit please?" she asked.

Calum looked appalled that she had asked him to sit next to her. He started to protest.

"Palmer..."

"Please," she commanded and gestured to the empty chair.

Calum reluctantly moved to the chair, staying as far away from her as possible. He settled in the chair but looked uncomfortable.

"You look good," he finally said. "Considering..."

He looked around the room and continued to talk almost absently as if this wasn't incredibly weird.

"Jessica was a real delight on the phone," he said sarcastically. "She said you had been in some kind of accident. That you couldn't remember anything from the last decade or so. Must have bumped your noggin pretty hard huh?" he rambled on.

He was putting on a show. He was trying to act like he didn't care, like he felt fine. He was playing it cool. But Palmer knew him. She knew what he was doing.

"Cut the shit Cal," she said.

He looked at her then, shocked. He rubbed his beard.

"Fucking talk to me," Palmer said. Her voice was full of panic.

His cool demeanor shifted into one of pain and concern.

"You REALLY don't remember," Calum said softly. It wasn't a question.

Palmer reached her hand to him, tears had started streaming down her face. She hadn't realized just how scared she was until now. With the comfort of Calum's presence, she let her new reality consume her. True fear spread through her body. The last twelve years of her life were gone and she had no idea what happened during them. The person she was, the life she had was gone. She was lost. She had no idea who she was supposed to be now. On top of all that she was genuinely worried she was losing her mind. Her mind flashed back to the horrifying naked woman in the mirror just minutes ago. Palmer outstretched her hand to Calum, her eyes begging him to take it.

Calum looked at her hand dumbfounded, his mouth hanging open. His bulging eyes went to hers. His face crumpled.

"Palmer..." he started.

"Please," she begged, her voice pained.

She was desperate. Calum's resolve broke. He scooted his chair closer, taking her trembling hand in his and bringing it to his cheek.

Chapter Fifteen

The Arm (2010)

Palmer hated camping. She had seen the Friday The Thirteenth franchise in its entirety multiple times. She had said this to Calum and Jessica but they had insisted on going up to the lake for the night. A lake. With teens. Great. They were practically begging for a Jason Voorhees type encounter. She voiced this opinion but was promptly ignored.

The entire graduating class was going. They were going to have a bonfire. At least they hadn't depended on her to pack or plan anything she thought.

It was the last summer before everyone went off to college. Jessica was going to a big university, and Palmer and Calum were going to stay behind for a year, attending the local college. Palmer was content with this plan but was apprehensive about being separated from Jessica. Part of what kept her sane was knowing Calum would be here too. She supposed that was the main reason she agreed to go camping. Calum could make even the most grueling experiences fun. Plus she wanted to spend as much time with Jessica as humanly possible before she left.

Palmer's strange experiences were starting to happen more frequently. Shadows in the corners of her eyes. Feeling like she was being watched. She was barely sleeping at night. She tossed and turned in her bed, getting her legs twisted in the sheets. Sweating through terrible nightmares. She did everything she could to forget the nightmares when she awoke in the morning. Nightmares, more like NIGHTMARE, Palmer thought to herself. It was always the same one. She shook herself and focused on the current nightmare in front of her, camping.

Palmer sat in a lawn chair next to Jessica. They sipped wine coolers while they watched Calum try miserably to set up their tent. Unfortunately for Palmer, Calum was insistent that she experience 'real camping'. Apparently, this included a tent. Chad had borrowed his parent's camper for him and Jessica to sleep in. Palmer would be lying if she had said she wasn't jealous.

"You good buddy?" Jessica said for the fifth time.

"Yes. Jessica. I am just peachy," Calum grumbled sarcastically.

He had waited too long to start putting up the tent. It was already starting to get dark. But he was Mr. Social. When they had arrived he insisted on talking to every single person he knew. Before they knew it the mosquitos were coming out.

Calum had chosen a place further from the bonfire than everyone else. Palmer had insisted on this. She wasn't a fan of smelling like smoke. Calum's tent was a little wonky, likely due to the four beers he had already drunk. Calum stood back, hands on his hips, looking at his finished task.

"You're going to sleep in that?" Jessica said.

"Hey Jessica, do me a favor and shut up," Calum responded.

Jessica smiled. They loved to raz each other. Jessica gave Calum the bird, he shot one right back.

Chad walked up, he was definitely more than four beers deep. He stumbled to Jessica and kissed her enthusiastically.

"Hey, baby!" he slurred.

Jessica rolled her eyes. Chad looked at the tent then.

"Whoa, what happened to your tent?" he said.

"Nothing, it's perfect," Calum said, annoyed.

"Here let me help," Chad said, moving to the tent.

Within a few minutes, Chad had straightened the tent and staked it securely. When he was done he dusted off his hands and turned to Jessica. He scooped her up in his arms, carrying her off to the noisy party. Jessica giggled and pretended to protest. Palmer watched them make their way to the bonfire, worried that Chad would fall with her best friend in his arms.

"Damn. Even drunk, that prick does everything better than me," Calum mused.

Palmer smiled. Calum took her hand, pulling her up. He kissed her. Her head tilted up and his hand slid down her arm to her palm. Hand in hand, they headed to the party.

Palmer had an absolute blast. Palmer laughed with high school friends, reminiscing about the past. She had cooked her own hot dog on the fire as well as her own marshmallows for 'smores. Calum showed her how to make the perfect 'smore. It had taken forever, he made her slowly rotate the marshmallow next to the fire. Not too close, not too far. She had eaten it but it was just ok. When his back was turned she purposefully burnt the next marshmallow till it was black. It was delicious.

The night crept on. People were gathered around the bonfire in hoodies to keep warm. There was loud music bumping through the open night air and Calum was in his element. Palmer sat on a log, she was starting to get tired. She stood up and stretched her back, arms clasped and in the air.

Palmer caught the flicker of something strange in the fire. She brought her arms back down and stared harder into the flames. There it was again. Palmer leaned forward. Her eyes searched among the logs trying to see something, anything. Just when she was about to give up she saw it. It was long and pale, contrasting with the rest of the wood. It was an arm. She could see the slender fingers on the end of it. They were burning. The skin peeling away like old paint, revealing muscle and tendons underneath. Palmer's eyes swept up the arm to the shoulder, then to the neck.

Palmer froze. There was a body in this bonfire. Under the logs, they were burning a body. She wanted to scream but she was frozen. The head and the rest of the body were covered by heavy sticks and logs. Palmer could only see the arms, shoulder, and neck. Like a freestyle swimmer moving their arm up out of water.

Palmer saw something shiny glint on the neck of the body. Her hand instinctively went to the religious pendant around her neck. Palmer looked down at her favorite accessory and looked back up again. But the arm was gone. The body was gone. It was just a lighter-colored log. Maybe a piece of aspen tree. Her eyes searched the entire bonfire for any evidence of what she saw. There was nothing there. Just her mind playing tricks on her again. The lack of sleep she told herself. She took a deep breath to steady herself. She pushed the dread and fear down deep, plastering a smile on her face and joining the conversation next to her. Then she joined another conversation and another. The night rolled on and she began to feel normal again.

Normal. Palmer thought. She needed to feel normal. She needed to feel alive. She needed to push this darkness out of her and fill it with life and light.

Palmer caught Calum's eye from across the fire. His gray eyes were fixed on her, causing a shiver to run down her spine. He started to make his way to her.

Palmer and Calum hadn't gone all the way yet. She was sure his friends had asked him casually about it. Anytime the subject was brought up in front of her Calum would skillfully evade answering. It wasn't any of their business anyway. They had fooled around and gotten close on many occasions, but Palmer always pulled back just a little. Hesitated. And Calum never pressured her. But things had started to shift between them lately. Palmer had started to catch Calum staring at her with need in his eyes. And she had started to look at him the same way.

When he reached her he kissed her softly and made to pull away and walk her to the tent in the dark, but she held him there. Palmer deepened the kiss. She gripped the front of his shirt in her hands. His mouth was so warm. He ran his hands down the sides of her waist and around to her ass. She moved her lips to his ear.

"Let's go back to the tent," she whispered, nipping at his ear.

A flash of shock ran over Calum's face before he replaced it with his playful grin. Palmer grabbed his hand and handed him the flashlight, indicating he should lead the way. Calum slowly guided them through the darkness, zigzagging through trees, until finally, they came to their spot.

Calum unzipped the front of the tent, allowing Palmer to go in first. They slipped off their shoes and crawled inside. Calum had set up their mats, sleeping bags, and pillows. He handed the flashlight to Palmer while he zipped the tent shut. He turned, facing her on his knees. She was also on her knees, flashlight facing him.

Calum took the flashlight from Palmer and set it in the corner, facing away from them. The light in the tent dimmed. They were both breathing heavier than normal.

"Are you su..." Calum started to ask her a question.

"Yes," Palmer said breathlessly.

Calum's eyes widened and his mouth opened before he snapped it shut, taking a breath. He moved closer to her so their knees were inches apart. Her breasts were pressed against him. She was still looking at him as she pulled her shirt up and over her head. Cal was frozen, hands at his sides. He looked down at her and to the tops of her breasts spilling from her black bra. She was breathing heavily, nerves fluttering in her stomach.

Palmer kissed his lips gently, moving her hands under his shirt. Her fingers traced up his toned abdomen to his chest. She could feel his heart pounding. He hadn't started to kiss her back yet, he was still immobile. She glided her fingers back to the bottom of his shirt and pulled it over his head, throwing it to the side.

Palmer started to unbutton her jeans with shaky hands when he finally moved. His hand held hers still and she looked up into his eyes. She saw only love and understanding. She trusted him. Calum cupped the back of her neck and lowered her down to the brick-colored sleeping bag, kissing her gently.

Calum's kisses were slow and deep. He held the back of her neck with one hand while the other explored her bare skin. His hand cupped her breast and squeezed gently. Palmer gasped lightly and he groaned in her mouth. He sat up and slowly helped her remove her jeans. Once they were off she reached behind her and unlatched her bra, letting it fall off. Calum gazed down at her, his eyes absorbing every detail.

"I love you," he said. "I'm going to love you forever."

It was the most intimate thing he had ever said to her. There was zero humor in his voice.

"Forever?" she asked in a husky voice.

"Always," he promised, and then he lunged at her.

Calum's lips crushed against Palmer's. His hand roamed up her sides again and this time to her bare breasts. His palm caressed her peaked nipple and she lost her breath. His soft tongue roamed her mouth and urged her on. His hand roamed to her other breast and he used his thumb to caress that nipple. Her body was starting to shake with adrenaline.

Palmer's hips came up and found his pelvis. His hardness was pressed against her and it was all she could think about. She tugged his jeans off urgently and he tossed them to the side. She used her hands to slowly feel her way from his chest to his abs, then to his hip bones. He shuttered harder and harder the lower her hand crept. She used her fingers to play with the band of his boxers.

"Palmer..." he said breathlessly into her hair.

Finally, she plunged her hand into his shorts, finding him.

"Fuck," he begged.

Palmer stroked him, drunk on the power she had over him at this moment. He was so soft. Calum began to trail kisses down her neck to her breasts. He took a nipple in his mouth, sucking gently. She ran her free hand through his thick head of hair. His kisses moved lower, to her abdomen. As he did so he moved his cock away from her curious hand.

She huffed in frustration but was quickly quelled by his fingers gently playing with the thin piece of lace that covered her sex. Palmer shuttered. His kisses trailed back up to her mouth.

Calum pulled back and looked into her eyes, asking silently for permission to continue. Her answer was a trusting smile, her heart was in her chest. She loved him so much, she wanted to give him everything. Palmer trusted Calum more than anyone else in the world and she wanted him to know it. To feel it.

Calum's fingers gently pushed her panties to the side and found her sex. She was soaking wet.

"Oh my God, Palmer... Fuck. What are you doing to me?" He whispered in her ear.

Calum's fingers gently explored her sex while her mind slowly unraveled itself. She was lost in him.

"Calum please," she begged.

Calum reluctantly paused his kissing and exploration to pull his wallet out of his discarded jeans. He quickly pulled out a condom and pulled off his boxers, exposing himself fully to her. Just before he was about to roll the condom he made eye contact with Palmer and saw her fear.

"Palmer, it's ok. Babe if you're not ready we don't h..." he started to say.

"I'm ready," she interrupted.

She gave Calum a solid look and urged him to continue. He nodded his head in answer, rolling the condom on. He laid on top of her slowly, never taking his eyes off of her. Palmer leaned up and kissed him softly as she wrapped her legs around him. They were both shaking slightly in anticipation.

Calum lined himself up with Palmer's entrance and slowly pushed himself into her inch by inch. Palmer gasped as he bumped against resistance. Calum paused and stared into her eyes, silently asking her if he should continue. She answered by cupping his face with her hands and kissing him.

Calum pushed past her barrier and she cried out into his mouth in pain. He buried his face in her hair, continuing to slowly rock his hips.

She could smell his body wash and smoke from the campfire on his skin.

Palmer's pain simmered to a dull ache and eventually, she started to find her pleasure. She started to move her hips against his, tightening the hold her legs had on him. Calum started to speed up, his heavy breaths turned to grunts. Palmer's hands slid down his back and then up again.

"Calum," she said breathlessly.

Hearing her say his name had been too much, he erupted. Calum cried out in her hair, shuddering through his release. Finally, he collapsed on top of her, utterly spent.

Palmer couldn't help the trembling that had taken over her body. She had a million different emotions fighting for her attention. She had the horrifying feeling that she was going to cry. She inhaled but it came out a sob. Calum raised himself quickly and searched her eyes. They were brimming with tears.

"No, what... why..." Calum stumbled for words.

Concern and fear took over his face.

"I'm ok, it's ok!" Palmer explained tearfully. She smiled and gave a weak laugh, "I'm happy, they're happy tears!" she said, trying to wipe the wetness from her face.

"Ok..." he said. "Well, maybe stop. You're freaking me out."

They both laughed loudly at that.

Calum helped Palmer clean herself and put on her pajamas. Her limbs were still shaking violently. Eventually, they were both comfortable in their sweatpants and tucked under open sleeping bags. Calum turned the flashlight off and pulled Palmer to him tightly.

Calum fell asleep within minutes, but Palmer lay there listening to the sounds of the forest. She told herself it was just the wind whistling through the trees, but she could have sworn she heard the sound of a woman screaming.

Chapter Sixteen

Present Day (2022)

Calum gripped Palmer's hand in his tightly. His head was dipped low.

"Please talk to me Cal, I'm so scared," she said tearfully.

Calum took a shuddering breath. He was holding back tears.

"I'm here," he said. "I'm here."

They sat like that for some time. It was Palmer who spoke first.

"You have a beard."

Calum laughed. "I'm thirty-two years old Palmer," he said comically. "It happens".

Palmer nodded.

"It's kind of gross," she smiled.

He smiled again.

"You look exactly the same," he said, looking at her thoughtfully.

"Lies. I saw myself in the mirror earlier," she joked. She tried not to think about what else she had seen in that mirror.

"You always look beautiful to me," he whispered.

"What the fuck happened Cal?"

Calum flinched. Pain streaked his face.

"You left," he said finally.

"That's what they said, but I wouldn't have left unless there was a reason. Something happened. Something big".

Palmer had never seen his face look like this before. He looked like he was breaking in front of her. He looked desperate and haunted.

"It wasn't just one thing Palmer. I fucked up. A lot. It was a lot of fuck ups," he choked. He was going to start crying.

Palmer squeezed his hand. She didn't want to push him too hard too fast. He was being heartfelt. He was so sad and fragile-looking. She decided to change the subject a bit.

"You have tattoos," she gestured to his arms.

She started to look at them closer. There was a two-headed snake that wrapped around one forearm. The other had a naked pinup lady on it as well as some other small intricate tattoos that blended together. The tops of his hands had bones drawn on them to make them look like skeleton hands. She wasn't quite sure what the tattoos turned into as they disappeared beneath his short sleeves. She noticed his neck then, he must have had some tattoo that started on his chest but came up to his collar. She couldn't quite make out what it was. When she mentioned the tattoos he looked down and tried to hide the naked lady she had already seen. Her brow furrowed.

The tattoo had been of a busty woman with dark hair. She was fair-skinned and had a dark green background behind her. Palmer turned Calum's hand in hers, forcing his arm to rotate. Exposing the pinup tattoo. Calum allowed her to study it. Palmer thought she looked a little familiar. The woman's head was tilted back in a laugh, her bright green eyes glittering. Written sideways alongside her body were some fancy letters that were a little hard to read. After a moment she realized it said 'FOREVER & ALWAYS' in all cursive caps. It was then that she realized why the woman looked so familiar.

Palmer's jaw dropped. Her other hand came up and she hit Calum in the chest, hard.

"Ow! Fuck Palmer," he exclaimed.

"IS THAT ME!?" she said angrily.

Palmer was trying not to yell so Hartman and Chuck wouldn't come in. Calum grinned.

"That's exactly how you reacted when I first got it," he was holding back laughter. "I thought you would be flattered back then. You were not impressed."

"Yeah, no shit dumb ass! I'm naked on your arm!" She was shocked. 'What were you thinking!"

"I was 20, and high. I wasn't thinking. I didn't do a lot of thinking back then Palmer," he said.

His voice had gotten serious again, his face haunted. She hated it. But she knew that there was no going back. Only forward. She needed to know what happened. She needed the gaps in her memories filled. She needed to know how she had gotten here.

"Tell me about you. Your life," she said. She was still seething from the realization that she was permanently branded on Calum's arm, naked. But she needed answers.

Calum groaned. "It's not a very nice story Palmer."

"Tell me anyway," she said.

Chapter Seventeen

The Wailing Woman (2011)

"Palmer, can you run back to the car and grab another blanket?" said Palmer's mother Emilia.

"Yeah sure thing!" Palmer said. She raced through the grass and across the parking lot to her mother's SUV and grabbed a picnic blanket from the back. She jogged back quickly.

"Where do you want it?" Palmer asked her mother.

"Mmm... maybe over there under those trees?" Emilia replied.

Palmer walked over to the spot and began to spread the blanket out. It was the annual Rivera family picnic and her mother's entire family would be coming to the park to eat, drink, and play horseshoes. The children would play on the playground while the adults relaxed and caught up with each other's lives.

Palmer's family was huge. She had more aunts, uncles, and cousins than she could count. Family reunions were always a big event. The majority of her immediate family lived in the same small Colorado town and got together for dinner often. But her enormous extended she realized it said 'FOREVER & ALWAYS' in all cursive caps. It was then that she realized why the woman looked so familiar.

Palmer's jaw dropped. Her other hand came up and she hit Calum in the chest, hard.

"Ow! Fuck Palmer," he exclaimed.

"IS THAT ME!?" she said angrily.

Palmer was trying not to yell so Hartman and Chuck wouldn't come in. Calum grinned.

"That's exactly how you reacted when I first got it," he was holding back laughter. "I thought you would be flattered back then. You were not impressed."

"Yeah, no shit dumb ass! I'm naked on your arm!" She was shocked. 'What were you thinking!"

"I was 20, and high. I wasn't thinking. I didn't do a lot of thinking back then Palmer," he said.

His voice had gotten serious again, his face haunted. She hated it. But she knew that there was no going back. Only forward. She needed to know what happened. She needed the gaps in her memories filled. She needed to know how she had gotten here.

"Tell me about you. Your life," she said. She was still seething from the realization that she was permanently branded on Calum's arm, naked. But she needed answers.

Calum groaned. "It's not a very nice story Palmer."

"Tell me anyway," she said.

Chapter Seventeen

The Wailing Woman (2011)

"Palmer, can you run back to the car and grab another blanket?" said Palmer's mother Emilia.

"Yeah sure thing!" Palmer said. She raced through the grass and across the parking lot to her mother's SUV and grabbed a picnic blanket from the back. She jogged back quickly.

"Where do you want it?" Palmer asked her mother.

"Mmm... maybe over there under those trees?" Emilia replied.

Palmer walked over to the spot and began to spread the blanket out. It was the annual Rivera family picnic and her mother's entire family would be coming to the park to eat, drink, and play horseshoes. The children would play on the playground while the adults relaxed and caught up with each other's lives.

Palmer's family was huge. She had more aunts, uncles, and cousins than she could count. Family reunions were always a big event. The majority of her immediate family lived in the same small Colorado town and got together for dinner often. But her enormous extended family lived further away. They came from all over; New Mexico, California, and Arizona to start. This was their chance to all get-together. Palmer had so many relatives on her mother's side that she didn't even know everyone. She was introduced to new family members at almost every gathering

Palmer loved these family reunions. She loved having a big family. This year she was particularly excited because she was bringing Calum. She wanted him to meet her family, she wanted them to love him. And for him to love them. Calum was important. He was her family too.

The party had started an hour ago and people were still finding her and greeting her. Tios and Tias would hug her and kiss her cheek. They would ask her how college was going, and what she was studying. They would ask about her parents and her brother Shawn.

Her mother was mingling and still setting out food. Chuck, her father, was telling filthy jokes to a group of Palmer's cousins, second cousins, and Tios. Chuck was not a Rivera but had married into the family when he had married Palmer's mother. He must have reached the punch line because they all tipped back their heads laughing. One of her cousins shot beer out of one of his nostrils and the laughing started again. Chuck gave the young man a giant slap on the back to help his choking, nearly knocking him forward. Shawn was on the grass lawn playing frisbee with a couple of cousins his age.

Where the hell was Calum? Palmer had told him when to be here. She knew he tended to be late for everything but this was crazy. He was over an hour late now. Someone somewhere started blaring Suavemente by Elvis Crespo on crappy speakers. Probably out of their car. A ruckus cheer rang out.

Just then Palmer's grandmother walked up to her.

"Hita, what is wrong? Why are you so sad in the face?" Abuela asked.

"It's nothing, I'm just looking for Cal. He was supposed to be here by now," Palmer replied. Her eyes were searching the parking lot for any sign of his car. Maybe it broke down? It was pretty old and shitty.

"Come. Sit down here with me and your Tias huh? Forget about the boy. When he comes he comes," Abuela said. Palmer's grandmother pulled Palmer by the hand over to a small circle of women sitting in a semicircle of lawn chairs.

Palmer made her way around the circle to kiss each woman on the cheek in greeting. They were all related to her in some way or another. Palmer took a seat in the remaining empty lawn chair. The women sat and gossiped for hours. They had already served their husbands and were now picking off their own plates.

The ladies talked about everything and nothing. Palmer mostly drowned out the chatter. Instead, she listened to the rushing sound of the nearby river and the cheering sounds coming from the game of horseshoes. Periodically she checked her phone for any message from Cal.

She had texted him at least ten times asking where he was and if he was ok. She was starting to worry. The sun was beginning to make its descent, and the mosquitos were coming out. He could still make it, she thought to herself. The family reunion could go on still for hours. It usually went well into the night. They would need their phone flashlights to find their cars.

Palmer heard the conversation around her change. The group of women had somehow gotten off the topic of how to get grease stains out of denim and were now telling spooky stories. She heard her Tia finish whatever story she had been telling.

"It was a chupacabra! I swear!" Tia said. All the women tipped back their heads laughing. Palmer knew who the chupacabra was. It was her family's version of the sasquatch or bigfoot. According to the stories he was like a little vampire creature with red eyes and he drank the blood of animals left outdoors. Mostly livestock. In the stories, it was usually a goat.

Palmer knew this was a story meant to scare little kids into staying in their bed at night. But she also knew for a fact that not a single person in her family would ever allow one of their pets to sleep outside. Dogs and cats were always brought inside when it got dark, just in case.

Palmer loved it when her family told scary stories like this. Maybe it's what had sparked her love of horror movies. Palmer could remember being a little girl and listening to her grandmother tell her spooky tales before she went to bed. Sure they were scary but they also made Palmer feel almost giddy, excited.

The laughter and conversation of the women died down. The sounds of the rushing river behind them became louder.

A couple of the women smiled at each other knowingly. Anticipating what came next. One of the women started speaking,

"Shhh.." she said with her eyes wide and a finger to her lips. "Do you hear that?"

Palmer strained her ears to listen.

"That there," the tia said. "You can almost hear her crying..."

Palmer smiled and sat back in her chair. She knew this story. She had been told it a hundred times.

"Hush," Palmer's grandmother said with a stern face. "Don't joke about her like that. You ask for trouble. She is no joke,". Abuela spoke sincerely.

"It's just a story Maria..." one of the other women tried to say.

Abuela gave the Tia a hard look.

"What story?" said a young girl who had joined the group. Palmer didn't recognize her. She must have been one of her Tia's children's children. Or something complicated like that she thought to herself.

"La Llorona," replied Palmer's grandmother in a sad voice. The women became deadly quiet, as they always did when Abuela spoke. The air seemed to get heavier, the sounds of the night louder.

"The Wailing Woman?" replied the young girl.

One of the Tias spoke next.

"A long time ago a woman went out for a picnic with her husband and baby. They chose a place much like this area, near a river. They laid out a blanket and spread out their lunch. They ate and laughed. They realized they could no longer hear the baby babbling. When they turned to look, the baby was gone. It had crawled to the river and was swept away. The woman, in her panic, followed in after the baby and was also swept away. They say you can still hear her walking up and down the river, crying for her lost baby," the Tia finished quietly.

The sound of the nearby river became even louder. The insect noises became more hushed.

"Was it this river?" the young girl asked worriedly. She looked in the direction of the river.

"Probably not hita. It's an old story, like El Cucuy. Every time someone tells the story it's a little different. It changes. Like a game of telephone. They say it's this river or that river. At this point, it's every river," a Tia said.

"El Cucuy?" asked a girl nervously.

"El Coco. You guys call him The Coco Man now", someone answered her and the girl shivered. In fact they all shivered a little, happy to move on.

"I was told the story of the wailing woman differently. I was told she killed herself days or weeks later. Too much grief," said another.

"I heard that she drags kids into the river and drowns them, thinking they are her lost child," another chimed in.

"I heard the woman became distracted listening to her husband. She was too in love with him. Infatuated. He was smooth, tu sabe? A slick talker. She was charmed by him. She forgot about her baby, lost in his words. Only for a moment. That's why she was distracted," said the woman closest to her grandmother.

The women fell silent. Lost in thoughts about the story. Thinking about what they would do if it were them, or their babies. Contemplating the weight of The Wailing Woman's sadness.

"Who was she?" asked another younger girl in a small voice.

Multiple women opened their mouths to speak but Abuela spoke first.

"She is all of us," Abuela said absently. She was looking off into the distance.

Palmer looked up at Abuela in confusion, eyebrows knitted together. All the women were looking at Abuela. Moments passed.

"What do you mean Abuela?" Palmer finally asked.

Abuela took a deep breath and looked from face to face. She was the matriarch of their family. The oldest living female relative for every woman in this circle. She began to speak and they all listened.

"Why do we tell each other these stories over and over again? The details never the same. Always changing. Evolving si? It's a lesson. A warning. La Llorona could be any of us if we aren't careful. She could be our daughter or our daughter's daughter," she said the last part looking right at Palmer. Abuela held Palmer's stare.

Suddenly Palmer was grabbed from behind. Her heart flew up into her throat and she gasped loudly. All the women in the circle jumped, and several of them made strangled noises. Even Abuela was startled and her hand flew to her chest.

Calum had snuck up behind her and attempted to scare her as a joke. Palmer heard his laughter before she saw his face.

"Jeez! Calum! You scared me," she said breathlessly.

Calum bent down to kiss her, his lips lingering on hers longer than she was comfortable with in front of family. Palmer had to break the kiss. She could taste alcohol and smell weed on him. She fought back her annoyance to introduce him.

"Ladies, this is my boyfriend Calum!" She said with forced cheer. The women smiled at him apprehensively. They were still recovering from the earlier shock. Abuela's face was irritated and stern. It usually was when Cal was around.

Calum went around the entire circle shaking every woman's hand. A bit more enthusiastically than appropriate. His smile was off. When he made his way back to Palmer she stood up.

"Cal, can I talk to you for a second?" she paused. "Over here," she added, looking in a secluded direction.

"Yep!" he said with that weird sleepy smile.

She grabbed his hand and led him over to a shadowy area away from everyone else. When they stopped Cal immediately tried to kiss her but she moved her head to the side. He stumbled forward, bumping into her.

"Are you drunk?" she asked.

"I've had a few," he answered with a smirk.

Palmer threw her hands up in exacerbation.

"What is wrong with you? Seriously Cal? This was important. You knew that. This is my family," she said accusingly.

"So what? I'm a little buzzed. It's a party, Palmer. I'm good. Introduce me. Let's do this!" He was swaying to the right.

Palmer paused. Her eyes were burning. She realized she was about to cry and sniffed. She started to turn around, embarrassed and not wanting him to see her like this.

"Palmer?" He put his hand on her shoulder and forced her to look at him. His smile was gone, replaced with concern.

"Oh my god, Palmer. I'm so sorry. I...", he started. He looked down at himself. "I'm sorry".

Palmer sniffed again and wiped at her now wet eyes.

"I wanted them to love you," she said. "Like I love you," she added.

Calum took a deep breath and started rubbing his eyebrows between his thumb and forefinger.

"Palmer. I'm sorry, ok? I lost track of time and I wasn't thinking," he said, not looking at her. Calum was rarely serious. "Forgive me?" he said looking up at her.

Palmer was still angry but his sincerity was moving. He looked genuinely sorry. It was hard to stay mad. He must have seen her resolve soften because he gave her a weak smile and pulled her in for a hug.

They stayed like that for a good long while. Just hugging. Finally, Calum spoke, speaking into her hair.

"What do we do boss?"

Palmer made a quick assessment. Making a decision.

"Let's just go home," she concluded.

"What about them meeting me and falling in love with my devilish charm and handsome face?" he said. "I really feel like this could be the night I finally win over your grandma..." he added with a hint of humor.

Palmer laughed despite herself.

"I don't think so bucko. Besides, the party is pretty much over. There's always next year".

They ended their hug and started to walk to the car hand in hand.

"Next year," said Calum definitively.

They walked through dewy grass in silence. The stars were starting to reveal themselves. The sound of insects was deafening and the party music was starting to fade. One sound though seemed to drown out everything else. The sound of water moving quickly over rocks and pebbles. Water lapping up onto the gravel shore. The river.

Chapter Eighteen

Present Day (2022)

Palmer sat in the hospital room with Cal. Twelve years of lost time weighed heavy between them. Palmer's hand tightly clasped his. She was so tired. The events of the last couple of days pressed down on her. Her head was hurting worse and worse with every passing second. She felt like that security guard that Michael Myers killed with a hammer to the head in Halloween II.

She was waiting for Calum to open up and talk about his life. The life she knew nothing about. The silence was killing her, so she decided to start asking questions.

"What do you do?" Palmer finally asked.

"What do you mean?" he responded.

"Like for a living," she answered.

Calum shrugged.

"All sorts of stuff I guess. Odd jobs mostly. Right now I work for a logging company. But, I've done all sorts of things,"

"Do you still live at home?" she asked. She was referring to their hometown.

"Nah. I bounce around a lot. I've lived all over the place," he said looking at his shoes.

Palmer looked down at their joined hands. She was afraid to ask her next question.

"Are you... are you married?" she asked slowly. Acid filled her stomach.

Calum looked up at her then. Looking her in the eye. He shook his head.

"No Palmer. I've never been married," he said, dropping his voice.

He held her gaze for some time before she broke his stare. She swallowed and tried to look anywhere else. The pounding in her head seemed to worsen. She released him, bringing her now free hand up to her forehead. She pressed the heel of her hand in hard and groaned.

Calum started to speak.

"Palmer?" he began to say.

Just then the door burst open and Hartman rushed in. Almost like he had been standing near the door anticipating her distress. Her sound of pain triggered him to interrupt. He moved quickly to her side. Calum slid out of his way and toward the back of the room.

"What's wrong?" Hartman asked Palmer. "WHAT DID YOU DO?" he said menacingly toward Calum. Hartman had puffed himself up again. Doing that magic trick again where he makes himself even bigger than he already is.

"Easy RoboCop," Calum responded. He had a cold sneer on his face. "I didn't do anything," he put his hands up in a mock imitation of defensiveness.

"My... head..." Palmer ground out the words between her teeth. Her vision was getting blurry. The lights glaring. Just then a stabbing pain sliced through her temples and she gasped. She could barely make out Hartman hollering down the hall to a nurse for help.

Darkness was creeping in from the outer corners of her vision. She felt like she was going to faint. She blinked, trying to clear her vision. She saw Hartman's massive body sticking out of the door, still calling for aid. She blinked again and saw Calum in the farthest corner of the room staring at her with an odd look on his face. Usually, Calum wore every emotion on his face. Humor, playfulness, happiness, mischievousness, joy, impishness, etc. The emotions she was used to seeing on his face were gone. Something horrifying was in his expression. Something Palmer had never thought she would ever see there. Something that scared her to her core.

Nothing.

There was absolutely nothing on his face. No emotion. Like a sinister manikin. And his gray eyes were staring right into hers. His eyes seemed to darken as she stared. Her mouth fell open. There was something behind him. Someone. But that was impossible. They had been the only three people in the room. She tried to focus her dark, blurry vision.

And then she saw it. It was the woman. The woman who had been haunting her life for years. It stood behind Calum. Bloodshot eyes bulging out of its head. Mouth open in a mid-soundless scream. Its jaw opened impossibly wide to reveal a black hole.

Everything went black and quiet. Something miraculous started to happen.

Palmer started to remember.

Chapter Nineteen

The Footprints (2011)

Palmer was singing along to Someone Like You by Adele as loud as humanly possible in her car. Her rabbit's foot keychain was swinging from the ignition with her keys, a rosary hung from the rearview mirror. Every once in a while the cross of it made a little clinking sound on her stereo.

"NEVER MIND I'LL FIND SOMEONE LIKE YOOOOOU-UUUUU. I WISH NOTHING BUT THE BEST FOR YOOOOOOOUUUU..." she belted.

Palmer had texted Calum after her late-night midterm study succession for Statistics 101. He had texted back that he was at a house party, begging her to come. She was still a little wired from her iced coffee earlier so she figured she might as well. He had sent her the address.

"SOMETIMES IT LASTS IN LOVE BUT SOMETIMES IT HURTS INSTEEEEAAAAD, SOMETIMES IT LASTS IN LOVE BUT SOMETIMES IT HURTS INSTEAD..."

Palmer had just turned onto the house's street so she turned the music all the way down to focus. She was reading the house numbers.

"Damn," she muttered to herself. It was one of the nicer neighborhoods in their town. The houses were massive. It was so late that most of the lights were off. The further she drove down the street the further apart the houses became, making the darkness even worse. She made a mental note to keep her eyes out for deer. Out here they had a tendency to jump out in front of your car.

Giant ponderosa pines and Douglas firs crowded together between the properties. They loomed on the edges of the street like guardians of some dark secret. Palmer was worried she had missed the house because the last one was quite a ways back, but the road continued on. Just when she thought she should make a U-turn she saw a long line of cars parked on the side of the street. She pulled behind the last one and unbuckled. She grabbed her phone and her keys. She checked her makeup in her visor mirror. Satisfied she got out of her car, slamming the car door behind her.

Palmer slipped her vermilion jacket on. It was autumn and the night air was frigid. She started to walk toward the still-invisible house. She remembered to press the lock button on her car clicker. The answering honk sounded ominous in the dark. She continues walking past car after car. She was starting to get annoyed with how far away she parked when she remembered what kind of creatures lived in Colorado forests.

She thought of big black bears that love to come close to town just for the buffet in people's trash. She thought of mountain lions. How they stalk their prey. She started to walk faster. Her brain started to play tricks on her, making the outdoor sounds more sinister than they were.

Then Palmer remembered how close they were to The Southern Ute Reservation and Navajo Nation here in their little corner of Southwest Colorado. She had gone to school with many indigenous kids. She recalled a story they had told her once. A story about a creature called a Skin Walker. A malevolent human that had the ability to turn into animals. She had been told she would know when she saw one because the animal "wouldn't look quite right". She wasn't anxious to figure out what that meant.

Palmer's pace quickened. She was about to pull out her phone to call Cal and use its flashlight when the house came into view. It was an enormous log house with giant bay windows. She could hear the bass of shitty dubstep music and she breathed a sigh of relief.

When Palmer finally reached the front steps she could see a handful of people on the front porch. They were chatting, smoking cigarettes and marijuana. She pushed past and opened the front door. The music blasted into her face. She started to search for Cal.

Her eyes scanned faces as she walked through the house. She saw a few people she knew from school and waved quickly, continuing on with her search. She walked past people playing cards and lounging on sofas with red solo cups in their hands. The door to the garage was open and she squeezed in. People were milling about along the wall watching four people play a round of beer pong. No sign of Calum.

Palmer turned around, heading back into the main part of the house. Brushing past tipsy partygoers, she found a hallway that was somewhat secluded. Where on earth is Cal? She pulled out her phone and texted him. As soon she heard the little woosh of the text being sent off she heard the muffled ping of Calum's phone. Palmer thought it had come from behind a door just to her left so she walked toward it.

Palmer could hear several voices coming from behind the door. She turned the knob and opened the door. Just in time to see Cal bent over someone's office desk snorting white powder up into his left nostril. Palmer froze, from shock or confusion she wasn't sure. Calum had a lazy grin on his face as he straightened himself. There were a handful of other people in the room. His gaze swept over them, landing on Palmer. The grin slid from his face, replaced by a blank expression.

Palmer was still halfway through the door but in less than a second she was turned around and back out in the hallway. She left the door open behind her and she walked down the hall in a daze. She couldn't hear anything anymore. Not the sound of the bumping music, not the buzz of crowded chatter, not even the sound of Calum calling her name from far away. She needed air. Fresh air. Maybe a moment to herself. She was walking swiftly, nimbly dodging crowds of people. She was desperate to find an exit.

There. She could see a sliding glass door in the back of the living room. Palmer continued to move fluidly through people. Her body felt numb. All she knew was that she needed some space. The house was making her feel claustrophobic. The air was too thick in here with all these bodies. Her brain was too full of thoughts.

Palmer finally made it to the door. She fumbled with the handle but was able to slide the large door open a foot or two. She slid through and out onto a back porch. The icy night hit her in the face. She commanded herself to take deep breaths of the fresh frigid air.

The backyard was as massive as one would expect. The giant lawn was appropriately yellowed for fall and it stretched out to pavement and then to a swimming pool. The owner of the house hadn't put the winter cover on the pool yet and Palmer could see vapor escaping up from it. Home swimming pools aren't very common in Colorado since there are really only about three months out of the year when swimming pools are actually usable due to the weather. However, they weren't unheard of. Especially for the wealthy, which obviously whoever owned this house was.

The back porch lights were on so Palmer could see further out past the pool to even more yellowed lawn that crept up to the forest. The trees hugged the line that separated them from the grass. Like there was some invisible force field keeping them at bay.

Palmer walked down the back porch steps and across the lawn. Still needing to get as far away from the house as possible. She continued to take steadying breaths. She reached the pool's edge and hugged herself, tucking her cold hands into her armpits for warmth.

Palmer heard the slide of the door she had just come through. She whipped her head around to see Calum running toward her.

"PALMER!" he yelled from the porch. He was still jogging toward her. "Jesus, Palmer, I've been looking for you everywhere. You disappeared," he said as he finally reached her side.

Palmer looked at him in silence. Calum was acting cagey. His eyes bounced around all over the place, never really looking at her. He pushed his hand through his hair.

"Look," he started. "I know what that looked like back there," he was gesturing with his hands. "Well, actually, it kind of was what it looked like back there, but it's not what you think. I've never done anything like that before Palmer I swear. That was the first time. It was..." he paused. "Peer pressure," he finally said. "I know that sounds lame and cliche. Look. It's really not that big of a deal, I swear. I swear," he said

Palmer just continued to stare at him. Calum rolled his eyes.

"Seriously Palmer. You're going to turn this into a big thing?" Calum said with annoyance. She couldn't believe it. HE was annoyed. With HER. She took a moment to collect her thoughts.

"Cal," Palmer started. "I honestly don't even know what to say to you right now. I don't know what's going on with you," she said, shaking her head.

"I said it's nothing. Just let it go, Palmer," he said.

"I don't think I can Cal. I'm worried about you. This isn't you."

"Palmer for fucks sake. Stop being so melodramatic. Look, honestly, I can't deal with this right now. Why don't you just go home? I'll call you in the morning when you've had a chance to cool down," he said. He started to turn away from her. Effectively ending the conversation.

Part of Palmer was trying to figure out what the fuck just happened, the other part was wondering if he was actually about to walk away from this conversation. From her. She watched his back as he walked back across the grass, up the porch stops, across the porch, and through the sliding glass door. Just like that.

Palmer stood there in shock. This night had not gone as she had imagined. She had known he would probably be a few drinks in when she got here. When was he not? She thought she would find him playing a fun round of King's Cup where he would be charming everyone around him. Then he would see her. His face would light up like it usually did when he spotted her. He would pull her onto his lap and beg her to join in. Palmer would decline over and over because she would obviously need to drive him home.

Palmer imagined that she would have to all but drag him away from the party but he would relent when she kissed him on the neck like he liked. They would drive home laughing about this and that. She would tell him about the study session. Maybe when Palmer pulled up to his house he would tell her that his parents were still out of town and she should spend the night, with a wink. Calum would lead her by the hand to his bedroom, where they would spend the rest of the night tangled in each other's naked, sweaty limbs.

But that is not what happened. Not at all.

Instead, Palmer was devastated, alone, and scared. Scared for what was happening to Calum. Scared that she didn't know how to help him. Part of her thought maybe he was right. Maybe it really was nothing and she was overreacting.

Palmer's thoughts were reeling. Distracted, she took a step back. Forgetting that she was standing on the edge of the pool. Where she thought her foot would make contact with concrete, it instead slid into the frigid chlorinated water. Her body quickly followed suit. Before Palmer's forehead bounced off of the edge of the pool, she thought she had seen a dark figure just outside the tree line. Then everything went hazy.

Palmer could feel the freezing water soak her jacket and her jeans. She felt it in her socks, in her ears. It was inside her she thought. It was filling her lungs. Everything was slow and blurry. She couldn't seem to tell her body to move. Palmer felt the bottom of the pool on her tailbone when she had sunk all the way down. She could feel herself losing consciousness but she tried to blink it away, to no avail. Her vision became dark just as she felt someone grab her by the hand.

Palmer woke up colder than she had ever been in her whole life. Her throat was on fire, her head felt like she had been hit with a baseball bat. Her vision was blurred but was starting to clear. Calum was above her, along with twenty to thirty other people who must have come out to see what was going on.

"PALMER? PALMER?" Calum was yelling at her. He was shaking her by the shoulders. "Someone get a fucking blanket!" he shouted at the crowd of people. Several of them took off toward the house.

"Palmer, holy fuck, are you ok?" he was crying. Tears were falling down his cheeks. Palmer had never seen Calum cry before. She reached up and touched one with her index finger. Her hand looked like a corpse's, thin and whitish blue. Cal leaned into her hand and started to cry harder.

"I'm.." Palmer started to speak but had to clear her throat. "I'm ok, I'm ok," she croaked out.

"Thank God," Calum said through choked tears. "Jesus fuck, Palmer," I've never been so scared in my life." He bent over her, putting his forehead to her own. "I'm sorry," he whispered.

Palmer started to sit up, Cal's hand holding her neck gingerly and guiding her up. Someone from the crowd loudly protested that she shouldn't do that but she ignored them. Obviously no one had called 911 due to all the illegal substances. Right when she had gotten into a sitting position someone came up and placed a warm blanket around her.

"Come on, let's get you inside by the fire. We'll get you warmed up and into something dry. I'll call us an Uber to take us back to my house," Cal said. He helped her up onto her feet. "You're gonna have a nasty bruise," he said, touching her forehead gently. Palmer winced.

"Did you save me?" she asked him.

"No?" he responded. "I saw you fall in and hit your head from an upstairs window. I ran down here as fast as I could. You were already up on the pavement. You must have pulled yourself out and passed out. I was the first one here. Everyone else just followed me," he finished. He started to guide her toward the house with his hand on her lower back.

Calum was still talking to her when she absent-mindedly looked back beyond the pool and toward the woods. There was nothing there. No shadow. Then she looked at the edge of the pool where she had fallen in and apparently pulled herself out. She saw a massive wet spot where she had laid their unconscious. But a few feet from that she saw a few smaller spots leading toward the forest. They were already starting to dry.

Palmer could have sworn those wet spots were bare human footprints.

Chapter Twenty

Present Day (2022)

Palmer woke up to someone forcing one of her eyes open and shining a bright light into it. When they had released her eyelids and moved the light she realized it was Dr. Walters. Palmer couldn't focus enough to figure out what she was saying at first. But finally, Dr. Walters's voice registered with Palmer's brain loud and clear.

"Palmer, can you hear me?" Dr. Walters said gently. Palmer blinked rapidly trying to also clear her vision. She was seeing little spots float around the room. Palmer nodded then.

"Yeah," she swallowed.

"I think you had a panic attack. Totally normal considering everything you've been through. Most likely you hyperventilated, causing you to faint. Again. Normal," said Dr. Walters, smiling.

Palmer looked to her other side and saw Hartman towering over her. Worry etching his eyebrows, his eyes assessing every inch of her for injury or harm. She realized her hand was firmly grasped in his giant fist. His hand was so big it swallowed up hers. It made her think of King Kong when he grabbed that tiny blonde lady and climbed all the way up the Empire State Building. The urge to tug her hand away was still there, but getting better.

"I'm ok," Palmer finally said. "Just a massive headache still".

Palmer cast her gaze around the room and saw her parents off to the side trying to stay out of the way. They were holding each other and smiling at her. Dr. Walters started to speak again.

"Well, I've already given you the max dose of the medication you are on but there might be another we can add to your medication list. It could help. Let me see," Dr. Walters was talking and typing on a large computer that pulled out from the wall. Presumably ordering the medication she mentioned.

Palmer looked at the corner where Cal had been before she fainted. It was empty. She looked around the room, he was nowhere to be seen. Hartman must have caught onto what she was thinking.

"He's not here," Hartman said between clenched teeth. "He weaseled out as soon as we realized you were fine and had just fainted,".

Palmer made a disappointed and concerned face. She could hear her father grumble from the side of the room.

"I'm sure he'll slither back at some point, he always does," muttered Chuck under his breath.

Palmer looked down at herself. The blanket that had been covering her had been moved around, probably when the nurses and Dr. Walters had been assessing her. The blanket was askew and she could see her feet sticking out the bottom. She looked at them for a long moment before she spoke.

"I think... I think I remembered something," Palmer said to no one in particular.

Dr. Walters stopped typing and looked over at her. It seemed like everyone leaned more closely to her.

"What did you remember?" Hartman asked first.

"It was nothing really, just a party that I went to in college. I fell in the pool. But I had no memory of it before," she said, shaking her head.

"I remember that!" said Emilia. "You came home the next morning with a huge egg-shaped lump on your head and a nasty bruise. Your dad and I thought you had been drinking but you swore up and down that you hadn't been and it was just an accident."

"That's right," Palmer started to say. She scrunched her face. The memories were starting to come back to her but they were foggy. "You and Dad accused me of lying. You thought Cal had somehow been responsible and I was making it up to protect him. We got into a huge fight. I remember!" Palmer said enthusiastically.

Her parents smiled mildly and Hartman squeezed her hand in encouragement. The room was tense but she didn't care. Palmer was finally feeling like things were going to be ok. She could see the light at the end of the tunnel.

"The memories you're missing should start flooding back now. It could take hours, days, weeks, months. We never really know. The human brain is fascinating," Dr. Walters said. She was smiling and shaking her head in wonderment. "Let's just take it slow and monitor how things go".

Palmer was feeling light-hearted and hopeful. She reached up to grab a hold of her necklace to reassure herself. But it wasn't there. She looked down at her chest and checked all over her neck with her fingers.

"What is it?" Hartman said. He had gone on high alert again.

"My necklace. My Virgin Mary one that Abuela gave me? I'm not wearing it. Do I not wear it anymore?" she asked, looking at Hartman and then her parents.

"No, you still wear it all the time. You never take it off," Hartman answered her first. He looked to Dr. Walters. "Did the EMTs or the hospital take it off when she got here?" he asked.

"Not that I know of," responded Dr. Walters. "But I'll check."

"Don't worry, we'll find it. I'll call the detectives working on your case. Maybe it fell off at that house. They're still searching it for evidence," Hartman said.

They had told Palmer that she had been found in some abandoned house. They weren't sure why she had been there in the first place. She had hit her head hard enough that twelve years of memories had flown right out of her.

"Ok," she said weakly. She felt naked without the necklace.

Chapter Twenty-One

The Lost Sister (2012)

Palmer woke up from one of those weird afternoon naps. The kind where you open your eyes and you're all sweaty and stiff. The kind of nap where you wake up with no idea where you are or what time it is.

Palmer realized fairly quickly that she was at her grandmother's house. The display cabinets full of clutter were a dead giveaway. She kicked off the blanket from her now too-warm body. It must have been late afternoon, she guessed. The sun was glaring through the west-facing window. Palmer could hear her grandmother clattering in the kitchen. Abuela must be getting ready to make dinner, she thought.

Palmer sat up. She stretched her neck from side to side trying to work out the kinks in it from falling asleep on the couch. Hey necklace was sticking to her damp skin in an odd way and she adjusted it. She stood up to go check on her grandmother. One of her knees popped loudly and she flinched. Only twenty years old and already starting to fall apart, she thought to herself and smiled.

Palmer had finished her first year of college. It was the end of summer and soon she would be moving several hours away to go to the same university as Jessica. As a matter of fact they would be moving into a sophomore dorm together here in just a few weeks. Palmer was so excited. They had already picked out decorations.

Palmer had finally decided to major in business. She wasn't sure exactly what she would do with that degree but she knew she could do a lot of different things with it. Palmer missed Jessica so much this last year and she was so excited to get a real college experience with a dorm and everything. But on the other hand, Palmer would miss her family, especially Abuela. Palmer had told herself that she would try and spend as much time as possible with her grandmother this summer to make up for the time she would miss with her over the school year.

By some small miracle or his father's money, Calum had also been accepted to the university. He had already rented a house just off campus with four other guys. Palmer was glad he would be coming too, one less person for her to miss. Plus maybe getting some distance from this town and his parents would be good for him, she thought.

Palmer could hear loud snoring coming from the other couch. Shawn was asleep with his mouth hanging wide open. There was a large drool spot under his chin. He had offered to drive Palmer over here when she said she was going to Abuela's for the afternoon. He had recently gotten his license so he jumped at the chance to drive literally anywhere. Plus there was always the promise of food.

Abuela had been watching her shows when Palmer and Shawn arrived. They must have fallen asleep. It was easy to fall asleep in their grandmother's home. Maybe it was the deep sofas and excessive blankets. Or maybe it was just Abuela's calm, welcoming presence.

Palmer started walking in the direction of the kitchen. She decided to let Shawn sleep. She looked around the living room. It was crammed tight with comfortable couches and chairs that faced a large oak entertainment center with a box television set inside. The entertainment center had glass front display cases on either side of the television. Behind the glass, there were at least twenty different nativity scenes all made with varying materials and colors. The walls were covered in different pieces of art that Abuela must have taken a fancy to at one point or another. Their mismatched frames somehow made the space cozy.

There was a large well-loved Persian rug beneath her feet as she strode out of the living room. Palmer passed through a hallway that had her grandmother's collection of catholic crosses tightly hung next to each other on both sides of the wall. There were more and more of the crosses every time Palmer came over. Finally, she turned right and padded into the kitchen where her grandmother was molding raw meat into little balls with her hands.

"Good morning sleepy head," her grandmother said with a smile.

"What time is it?" asked Palmer. There was an infinite number of clocks in her grandmother's house but none of them held the actual time. There were too many for her grandmother to make sure they all had working batteries, let alone set them.

"Almost five o'clock," Abuela said. She wiped at her forehead with her forearm. Careful not to get the raw meat on her.

Palmer walked to the cabinet over the sink, selecting a cup and filling it with water. She chugged it greedily. When she had drunk her fill she filled the cup one more time, setting it over to the side for later. Then Palmer washed her hands so she could help her grandmother with dinner. She dried her hands on an embroidered hand towel that hung from the oven handle and pulled out a stool to take a seat. Abuela moved the bowl of raw meat toward Palmer, inviting her to start making little meatballs with her.

They worked in amiable silence for a time. Finally, Palmer spoke.

"Do you have any plans for the weekend Abuela?" she asked.

"Mmm. I think your Tias are coming to pick me up on Saturday real early to go garage sale shopping if you want to join?" she responded. Abuela was referring specifically to her sisters. She had four of them.

"Maybe. I'll let you know," Palmer said smiling. "I love how close you are with your sisters. I wish I had a sister. Somehow I don't think Shawn would go garage sale shopping with me when we're older," Palmer finished with a laugh. Abuela laughed as well.

"Having sisters is one of my greatest blessings," she said, scooping up more meat into her palms. Abuela looked up at Palmer, her face saddening. "Did you know I actually had another sister?"

Palmer looked up at her, shocked. She had no idea. No one had ever mentioned her.

"What?" Palmer responded.

"Yes. Gabriela," Abuela whispered the name of her fifth sister. Abuela began to roll meatballs again to distract herself. "She was my favorite sister. Don't tell your Tias," she said pointing a meat-covered finger at Palmer. Abuela was silent for a moment. "She was lost to us. A long time ago. Before your mother was born."

"What happened?" asked Palmer. She was almost afraid to ask any questions right now, but she wasn't sure why.

"No one knows for sure. She disappeared one day. Gabriela was a young woman when she... when we lost her. A few years older than you. My parents called the police. They came and asked us questions but never did much. The police told us she had probably run away with a boy. But we all knew she would never have done that. She was... la mejor de nosotras. Understand? She was... the best of us. Gabriela was sweet and kind. She never had a bad word to say about anyone. Ever. Your great-grandmother and great-grandfather were heartbroken when she disappeared. Never the same. We were angry with the police when they insisted that she had run away," Abuela looked up at Palmer then. "Only something terrible would have taken Gabriela away from her family. From us. We all knew. My father and the other men from church would go look for her in the woods all over town. My siblings and I called every hospital around. We stapled her picture to every post we could. We paid to put her picture in the paper for a year even though it was expensive and we didn't have the money."

Palmer was shocked. No one had ever told her this story. Gabriela was never mentioned in any stories or brought up in conversation. She was just now even learning about her. Abuela continued the story.

"After a few years, my siblings and I bought a tombstone for her and had it placed in the cemetery. Just so that my parents had a place to go and remember her. For all of us to put her to rest. We knew she was dead," Abuela finished, clearing her throat.

"Why doesn't anyone talk about her?" asked Palmer.

"Mmm," Abuela mused. She was thinking hard. "I think it upset your great-grandparents too much when we talked about her so eventually we all stopped. Even after they died we kept it up without even thinking about it. Maybe too much pain even for us still."

"You — you really have no idea what happened to her?" Palmer asked.

Abuela considered Palmer's question before answering. "I found a notebook in her room, a few days after she left. She had hidden it somewhere my parents wouldn't find. I had hoped it was a diary that would tell us where she went but it was nothing. Just notes and scribbles, but on the sides she wrote a name over and over again. Nick, Nick, Nick Nick. She wrote it in big fancy writing you know? We did not know any Nick." Abuela sighed. "I showed my parents and they told the police but they did nothing. My father though — he hunted down every Nick in town after I showed him. Asked them questions. Grilled them. But it was how you say —" Abuela paused, trying to find the English phrase. "A dead end," she finally finished.

"Abuela, I'm so sorry," Palmer said. They were both crying now.

Both women reached meat-covered fingers toward each other and held hands across the countertop. Letting the moment hang in the air. After a minute Abuela released Palmer's hand and clapped her's together. Shaking off her sadness.

"Alright, I'll wash my hands and start making the broth. You finish up making the albondigas, ok?" Abuela said, turning toward the sink.

Palmer let her grandmother change the topic to more light-hearted subjects like who hadn't been to mass lately and how much more expensive the grocery store on this side of town was. Her grandmother rambled on about what was happening on Days of Our Lives and Palmer's uncle's diabetes. Palmer understood her grandmother's need to wash out the sad conversation with mundane conversation, so she let her talk and talk while she cooked.

But Palmer's mind kept going back to their previous conversation. To the lost sister.

Chapter Twenty-Two

Present Day (2022)

P almer was being wheeled down a long hospital hallway. She watched as tile lines passed under her feet. Her mother pushed her slowly past closed doors with beeping monitors behind them. Palmer's mother had insisted that Palmer needed fresh air. Dr. Walters had given her blessing but only if Palmer promised to stay in the wheelchair. Palmer felt like that was a little bit ridiculous since her legs seemed to work perfectly fine. But she agreed anyway.

Palmer's mother, Emilia, had bundled Palmer up beneath a thick coat and layers of blankets. Thick socks had been rolled onto Palmer's feet and the blankets tucked underneath. Palmer thought vaguely that she hadn't been this coddled since she was a toddler. Hartman had watched the entire ordeal from the side of the hospital room. He stood rigid with his fists clenched at his sides. Like he was trying not to bundle her himself. Palmer was thankful, she was still a little uncomfortable around him. Silly as that sounds.

Palmer had put two and two together and assumed it must be wintertime. It was a little shocking to realize that she didn't remember what time of year it was. *Duh*, she thought to herself. Of course, she didn't know what season it was. She couldn't even remember what year it was.

Emilia Lane expertly maneuvered Palmer down several hallways and into an elevator. They were both silent up until now. Neither one of them was quite sure what to say to the other. Hartman had stayed behind someone reluctantly to give them some time alone. The two women had left him talking to Dr. Walters. Palmer was the first to speak.

"So—, how was the last Harry Potter movie?" Palmer asked.

"What?" her mother responded with confusion.

"The last Harry Potter movie? The Deathly Hallows Part 2? It was coming out soon I'm pretty sure but—," Palmer knocked on her head with her knuckles. "I don't remember how it was," Palmer finished.

Palmer and Emilia both paused. Then they both started laughing hysterically. Palmer's mother laughed so hard she had to cross her legs and bend over. Palmer gripped her abdomen and howled. The elevator doors opened and their laughing died off into giggles. They wiped at their now-damp eyes and continued on their way. The awkwardness of earlier was gone.

Palmer's mother told her all about the differences between the last Harry Potter movie and the book while they made their way outside. The hospital had a little paved garden area where presumably patients or visitors could come and walk around. It was getting late in the afternoon and the sun already starting to disappear behind the far-off mountains. Emilia chose a spot to park Palmer and took a seat on a bench next to her.

"Hey Mom, where were you and Dad when the hospital called you? The huh... big guy, mentioned that you were still a few hours away when I woke up," Palmer said. She wasn't quite sure what to call Hartman and she felt weird saying his name. Too intimate.

"Oh, well your father and I actually moved to Arizona several years ago. We were sick of the cold. We're only nine hours away," said Emilia.

"Do I still live here?" Palmer was referring to her hometown. Palmer had already figured out that they were at her local hospital.

"Yes. You and Hartman settled here. Your choice I'm sure but he's never seemed to mind. Quite frankly I think that man would follow you anywhere," her mother said. She was smiling at Palmer but Palmer wasn't in the mood to talk about Hartman right at this moment.

"Where is Shawn?" Palmer asked, changing the subject.

"Arizona," Emilia said quickly. She wasn't making eye contact with Palmer. Palmer had the distinct impression that her mother was avoiding talking about Palmer's brother, Shawn. Emilia changed the topic quickly.

"It wasn't the hospital that called us," her mother said.

"What?" It was Palmer's turn to be confused.

"Earlier you said that it was the hospital that called us. But it wasn't. It wasn't the police either. It was Hartman. He called us first. So we got on the road as fast as we could".

"Oh," Palmer said.

"He was the one who found you," Emilila said.

Palmer looked at her mother shocked. No one had mentioned that to her. In fact, everyone had been tiptoeing around giving her any kind of details as to what happened or how she was found. Probably worried about her fragile state of mind. Palmer couldn't blame them. To be honest she was feeling pretty unstable. Half the time she felt like she was going crazy, and half of the time she felt like she was drowning. She was just trying to absorb everything slowly.

Soon she would need to start asking the harder questions. The ones that would upset the axis on which her current world balanced. But not yet. For now, she was content to breathe in the fresh air next to her mother and watch the sunset. It smelled like a snowstorm might be rolling in.

In a window, several stories above the two women stood a hulking man looking down at the scene. And several parking lots away sat another man with gray eyes peering through his rearview mirror, monitoring the scene as well.

Chapter Twenty-Three

The Ouija Board (2012)

Palmer was walking backward towards Calum's room. She and Calum were kissing each other feverishly, Calum leading her by the waist. When they reached his bedroom door she could hear him fumble with the door knob and push it open with a small thud. He was gripping her hips with his fingers, the tips of them digging into her love handles. When they had made it a few feet into the room she heard him kick the door shut behind them with a loud bang. His lips never left hers.

Calum continued to back her into the room. After a few more steps Palmer's ass bumped against his desk and he lifted her onto it, settling himself between her legs. Palmer had threaded her fingers through his soft black hair. Calum started to kiss her jaw, traveling down to her neck and pulling off her cherry scarf. Palmer took her shirt off revealing her bra underneath. Then she reached toward Cal, pulling his old Blink 182 t-shirt off.

Calum unclasped Palmer's black bra and threw it across the room. He immediately took one of Palmer's nipples into his mouth and suckled it roughly before pulling on it with his teeth. Palmer's back arched and she panted as he switched to the other nipple.

Calum blindly fumbled with the buttons of Palmer's jeans and she reached down to help him. As soon as her zipper was down he found her with his fingers and began to stroke her most sensitive spot with his index and middle finger. Not only did he know every inch of her but he knew every button to push to tip her over the edge. Calum kissed the tops of her breasts and made his way up her throat and to her jaw. He plunged his soaked two fingers inside of her.

"Say my name baby," he rasped into her ear.

Palmer's inner muscles clenched in pleasure. "Cal," she said breathlessly. She was so close.

"Say it again," he growled.

Palmer came then. "CAL," she yelled and tilted her head back, exposing her neck. Calum took his free hand and placed his palm on her throat, squeezing ever so slightly. Possessively.

Then they quickly and clumsily took their clothes off as fast as possible. When they were both totally naked Calum reached into the drawer of the desk and pulled out a condom. He put it on in a flash and began kissing Palmer again but even harder now. Their tongues slid together with urgency.

When Calum finally plunged into her she gasped. Calum stroked her long dark hair and gathered it into his fist. Her legs were locked around him and he gripped her hips for more control. They were panting. The desk under them bumped into the wall loudly but they were both too wrapped up in each other to care about his roommates.

Calum locked eyes with Palmer as he found his rhythm.

"Forever?" he grunted between his labored breaths. Palmer placed her hand on his cheek.

"Always," she cried out. Another orgasm racked her body.

Calum looked down to where they were joined and came with a groan, pulling her as close as possible to him. The sweat from their bodies mingled and Palmer felt him shudder inside her. Palmer kissed him on the cheek over and over again. Blissfully happy.

Five minutes later Palmer and Calum were lying in his bed, totally spent. Palmer had changed into a pair of Cal's sweatpants and thrown on one of his plain white t-shirts. Calum had also changed into sweatpants but hadn't put on a shirt. Calum was lying in the bed flat on his back. Palmer was curled into him, her head resting on his arm. She was trailing small circles onto his chest and abs.

"I had my Marketing final today," Palmer said. "I think it went well,"

Calum grunted in response.

"How did your biology final go? That was today, right?" she asked him.

"Look, can we not talk about school right now? Let's talk about something else. Anything else. The guys and I are having a party tonight if you want to stay. Someone told Todd about this game called Edward Forty Hands where you duct tape forty-ounce bottles of beer to your hands at the beginning of the night and no one will help you take them off until both bottles are empty. Get it? Edward Forty Hands, Edward Scissorhands?" Cal laughed.

Calum had been avoiding talking to Palmer about school for weeks now. Palmer almost never saw him on campus anymore. His avoidance was starting to bother her.

"While that does sound entertaining to watch, I still have a couple more finals this week and I really need to study," she responded.

Cal grunted a nonverbal response at her again. Palmer thought he was acting weird. She decided enough was enough.

"Talk to me, Cal. What's going on?"

Calum took a deep breath and sighed. "Look, I just don't think college is for me".

"What?" Palmer responded. She had known he was a bit of a slacker and lacked motivation but he had never said anything about not wanting to go to college anymore.

"It's just not my thing, ok?" he responded defensively.

"Is it your grades? I can help you get them back up next semester. I'll tutor you," she said, desperately wanting to help him.

"I SAID IT'S JUST NOT FOR ME," Cal said with his voice raised. Palmer froze. Calum took a steadying breath. "I haven't been to class since midterms Palmer. My grades were shit but it's more than that. I just don't want to do it anymore. The college thing."

"Ok," Palmer said. "People don't go to college all the time. I know it's not a big deal, I was just trying to help. You've never said anything about dropping out so I was confused."

"Ok," he said. He still sounded annoyed. "Can we just drop it please?"

"Sure," she said. She was also starting to get annoyed.

Palmer sat up. She wanted to go home. She hated it when he was in a pissy mood like this. She started to crawl over him and out of the bed. She couldn't get out on her side since the bed was pushed up against the wall.

"Palmer, don't be like that," Cal said.

Palmer was trying to find her jeans from earlier but she accidentally grabbed his. When she did, a little plastic baggy fell out of the front pocket. It landed on the hardwood floor in front of her. Palmer and Calum both looked at it. Cal began to speak.

"Palmer —" he said in a panicky voice. But it was too late. She had already seen what was inside. Palmer whirled toward him.

She wasn't going to let him gaslight her this time.

"THAT'S IT CAL," she exploded. She was moving toward him, pointing her finger at his chest. "I've had it. What the fuck is going on with you? This is so fucking stupid. YOU'RE being fucking stupid. Drugs? Oh my God, Cal. You idiot," Cal was trying to stand but Palmer poked him so hard in the chest that he fell back down.

"It's more than that though, isn't it? You've changed. You're not YOU anymore. You keep pushing me away so I don't look too closely at what's going on with you, but I'm done with that. No more excuses, no more bullshit. Talk to me. Now, Cal," Palmer was shaking with anger.

Calum sat up, swallowing. He looked like he was about to speak but instead of words, a sob came out. To Palmer's astonishment, he was crying. He leaned forward and rested his head in his hands.

"Palmer, I —" Cal started to say. "I'm sorry. I'm so sorry," Palmer could see his back rising and falling erratically in his sobbing. "I don't know what's going on with me either. You say I don't seem like myself. I don't *feel* like myself either,"

Palmer moved to him. He must have sensed her resolve because he sat up and hugged her around the middle. Cal buried his wet, tear-stained face in Palmer's chest. He held her tightly while she stroked his hair. Palmer buried her face in his head of hair. Relishing the familiar smell of his shampoo.

"Do you still love me," he asked her. His voice was muffled, his face still buried in her breasts.

"Yes," she said solemnly.

"Forever?" he asked.

"Always," she answered automatically. It was their little mantra they said to each other all the time. They stayed like that for several minutes. Holding onto each other.

"It's going to be ok," she murmured. "We're going to figure it out."

"No more drugs," Palmer finally said.

"No more drugs," Cal responded. He was still clinging to her.

"No more alcohol," she said.

"I'll moderate how much I drink," he resolved.

Palmer pulled away from him then. She couldn't believe he was bartering with her right now.

"What?" she said, shocked.

"Come on Palmer. You can't expect me to stop drinking altogether. That's not realistic, we're in college," he said.

"No. I'M in college. Remember. YOU'RE dropping out," she said with annoyance. "I can't believe you Cal," her previous anger was bubbling back up to the surface.

Cal was starting to speak, but she was over his excuses for tonight. She had already turned, grabbed her keys, and left the room. She walked out of the house and to her car. Calum didn't follow. Palmer drove back to the dorms. All the way there she thought about the little baggy and the little yellow oval pills inside.

It was nearly dark when Palmer got back to the dorms. She used her key card to get into her and Jessica's room. However, when she opened the door she was stunned. She had expected to open the door to find Jessica lying in bed studying with the lights on and music blaring. Instead, Palmer found that the room was dark, lights off. But with lit candles scattered on every surface and even on the floor. Their amber lights cast an eerie glow over the space. There were five girls sitting on the floor in a circle. The room was silent.

All at once five heads whipped up to look at her and every single one of them screamed. Palmer jumped, a small yelp escaping her. Several of the girls had scrambled away from the circle. A few of them clutched their chest and necks.

"It's just Palmer!" Palmer heard Jessica yell. "It's just Palmer," she repeated.

"Holy shit!" one of the girls exclaimed.

"What the fuck!" Palmer yelled.

Now, with the help of the hallway light sneaking in through the open door, Palmer could see who the five girls were. It was Jessica and four girls from down the hall. Palmer could also see that they were all in their pajamas and that they were circled around an Ouija board.

"You almost gave us a heart attack!" Jessica exclaimed. "I thought you were staying at Cal's?"

Palmer's stomach ached as she remembered what had happened earlier. Something was going on with Cal. Something more serious than she was equipped to handle. It was all going to come to a head soon and she needed to figure out what to do. How to reach him.

"I changed my mind," Palmer responded. She hadn't talked to Jessica yet about the changes she was noticing in Cal. So many people already had a low opinion of him, she didn't want Jessica to be one of those people. She felt a responsibility to protect and defend him. Palmer knew if she told Jessica what was going on Jessica would be the opposite of helpful.

Jessica would tell Palmer to leave him. Jessica had broken up with Chad freshman year of college and had been happily single ever since. She had often hinted at how much she wished Palmer was single too so they could 'have the full college experience together'. 'The full college experience' to Jessica meant hooking up with whatever boy she felt like that week.

No. This was Palmer's problem to figure out. She alone would find a way to help him.

Several of the girls in the room said hello to Palmer or waved at her nervously. It was clear Jessica had bullied most of them into playing.

"How did you do on the Marketing final?" Asked one of the girls from Palmer's class.

"Pretty good I think. I'm more nervous for tomorrow's finance one though," Palmer admitted.

"Oof, me too," the girl responded with a worried look. Clearly she was thinking that she should be studying instead of playing spooky games with her friends.

"Want to join us?" asked Jessica.

"Playing Ouiji? Pass," said Palmer. She was still standing in the doorway. "I'm just gonna grab my backpack and I'll study in the commons."

"C'mon! It will be fun. Well," Jessica said looking at the room and the other four girls. "Maybe not that much fun. We've been at it for thirty minutes and nothing has happened yet. Other than you scaring the shit out of us".

"Like I said, pass," Palmer said. She had enough weird shit happening in her life, she didn't need to go asking for any more. "Haven't any of you guys seen The Exorcist? Or Paranormal Activity?" Palmer asked the group. All of them either shrugged or shook their heads.

"Whatever, your loss," replied Jessica, irritated with Palmer's dismissiveness. She turned her gaze back to the circle. "Alright, girls let's try a couple more times before we call it a night huh? Everyone, hands in."

All the girls put their fingers on the planchette, the little triangle with the glass circle in the middle. Palmer moved around the girls and towards her desk on the other side of the room where her backpack, books, and laptop were.

"Are there any spirits here that wish to talk to us? Are there any spirits here with a message from beyond?" Jessica said to the room. Just then the planchette moved and the girls screamed in unison. Palmer jumped again and looked at the board full of letters. The glass on the planchette was perfectly placed over the word 'yes'.

All of the girls had removed their hands from the board. Frightened looks on their faces. Palmer smiled to herself. She knew how this worked. One of the girls had moved the eye, but there were so many fingers on it that no one would ever be able to tell who.

"Whew!" Jessica exclaimed in excitement. "How exciting! Ok let's keep going. C'mon hands in, hands in," she encouraged them. Palmer had stopped piling books into her backpack to watch in amusement.

"Jessica, maybe we sh..." started one of the girls

"Don't be such a baby, come on," Jessica pushed. The girls obeyed.

"Spirit. How long have you been dead?" Jessica asked the room. No answer.

"Ok. Spirit. How did you die?" Jessica persisted. Still no answer. Jessica started to get frustrated.

"Your name! Tell us your name Spirit! Who are we talking to?"

The planchette finally moved again in a sharp jerky movement. The girls all gasped but this time they kept their fingers on the game. The planchette paused on each letter and the group of girls said the letter out loud.

"G," they said in unison. A few seconds passed and then they all said, "A". More seconds passed and the room felt a bit heavier. "B," they said and the planchette moved back up to the top. It came back down again and the girls all said "B". The candles flickered. Another few seconds and the planchette made its final movement. "Y," they said finally.

Palmer wasn't breathing. She had bitten down on her tongue. The tang of blood filled her mouth. Goosebumps covered her skin. She could feel someone behind her. Their breath on her neck.

"Gabby?" Jessica said. And then the candles all winked out.

Chapter Twenty-Four

Chapter 24: Present Day (2022)

Palmer's mother wheeled her back to her room. Hartman was waiting for them when the elevator doors opened to the floor her room was on. He escorted them back to Palmer's room. Obviously giving up on trying not to hover.

"So — how was the fresh air," Hartman said awkwardly. He was trying to make conversation.

"It was good!" Emilia said enthusiastically. Obviously trying to encourage him. Palmer said nothing. She was too tired to make idle conversation right now. Hopefully, he wouldn't start talking about the weather, she thought.

"Looks like it might storm later on," he said. Palmer snickered and he looked at her puzzled.

When they finally got back to the room she noticed there was a tray of food on the side table. Her stomach rumbled. She had no idea when she had last eaten. Hartman and Emilia helped Palmer back into the bed. Hartman expertly removed her IV from the little hook on her wheelchair and moved it to the one on her hospital bed. Palmer had to remind herself that he was a doctor. *Dr. Roth*, she said to herself.

Emilia excused herself to find Palmer's father, Chuck. Palmer's mother turned and gave Palmer a meaningful look before she left the room. *Be nice,* the look had said. Palmer tried not to roll her eyes.

Hartman was adjusting the side table so that the food sat right in front of her. There was a small vase with perfect white roses placed neatly inside. It was taking up too much room so he grabbed it and moved it over to the counter by the sink. Palmer remembered that she had seen that specific bouquet when she first woke. The leaves looked so clean and soft, like little clouds. She could tell even from here that their thorns had been carefully removed.

"Who are those from?" she asked.

He looked embarrassed. "Oh um, me." He continued to adjust things in the room nervously. There were several vases of tall colorful flowers. "You always talk about the roses your grandmother kept in her garden when you were a kid".

Palmer wasn't ready to talk, let alone think about Abuela yet. She tried not to linger on the word he had used. Kept. Past tense. No, she wouldn't linger on that. Instead, she thought about how soft her grandmother's roses had felt, their sweet smell. Hartman had brought white roses but Abuela's had been a deep red. Palmer didn't dwell on that either.

"Huh," she said under her breath. Obviously her *husband* would know something like that. She didn't think she had ever mentioned how much she loved her grandmother's rose garden to anyone before. But somehow Hartman knew.

Hartman took a seat next to her in the chair where she had first seen him. He looked at her and then at her plate. Palmer was pretty sure he would start feeding her himself soon if she didn't start to eat. So she picked up her spoon and started to take small bites of her mashed potatoes. The hospital had made chicken fried steak, mashed potatoes, gravy, and green beans for dinner. There was also a little container of green jello on her tray. To the side of her tray, there was a lidded cup filled with ice water. It was full of the kind of ice that was perfect for crunching on.

"So — husband," Palmer said jokingly, trying to break the tension. She gave him a weak smile. Hartman laughed and let out a sigh. "You seem to know me pretty well."

Hartman shrugged. "Well I should hope so, we've been married for four years."

"Four years!" Palmer nearly choked on her food. "We've been married for four years?"

He looked at her lovingly. "Four years, two months, and 3 days."

Palmer stared at him for a moment, then stabbed into her chicken fried steak. "Wow, so you like — *know me* know me." Her cheeks flushed, realizing that she had probably slept with this man.

Hartman smiled at her. "Yeah Palmer, I *know you* know you."

Palmer had a thought. This was her husband, her partner. Maybe he knew about everything. Even the things she avoided talking about. Her biggest secret.

"Hartman, can I ask you a question?"

"Palmer, you can ask me anything," he responded. He looked so hopeful.

Palmer played with her food a little. Moving the fork through the gravy and mashed potatoes, making a little river. "Do you know about — the stuff that I see sometimes?" She didn't meet his eyes.

"You mean like the woman?" he asked.

Palmer almost gave herself whiplash looking up at him too fast. "You know?" she whispered.

Hartman spread his hands out, palms up. "Of course I know Palmer."

Palmer was shocked. She didn't know this man but the Palmer from her past, the Palmer she had forgotten, knew this man well enough to share this.

"Do you — believe me?" she had never felt so vulnerable before.

Hartman spoke with absolute certainty "Of course I believe you."

Relief filled Palmer. Someone believed her. Maybe she wasn't crazy.

Hartman continued. "Palmer, I will always believe you. And I might not know everything about you. That's the best part about being married. I learn new things about you all the time. But I like to think I know most things. Or at least the big things. And the small everyday things that make you, YOU." He was smiling now. "I know that you hate spring. Your favorite snack is chips and salsa but your favorite food is chicken alfredo. I know that you keep the soundtracks for Rocky Horror Picture Show and The Phantom of the Opera in your car at all times. I know that you don't have a single freckle anywhere on your entire body and it drives you nuts. I know that you tell people the scariest book you ever read was The Exorcist but it's really The Haunting of Hill House, because Nell loses her mind. I know what mug you prefer to drink your coffee out of in the morning. I know that I love you and that you love me. Even if you don't remember right now."

Chapter Twenty-Five

The Confession (2012)

The university cafeteria was buzzing with noise. Droves of people were coming in for the dinner rush. Many of the students were just finishing up their afternoon classes, hoping to get a bite to eat and relax with friends before returning to the dorms. The cafeteria was massive. Harsh iridescent lights glared from the ceiling to expose old rubber tile flooring. The smell of soup permeated the air along with Fabuloso floor cleaner, a noxious blend.

Palmer sat at a small two-person table in the back staring at nothing. The white noise of student chatter did nothing to drown out the thoughts screaming in her mind. Palmer's undereyes were stained a deep blue from a lack of sleep. Her usual glossy, thick brown hair was greasy and thrown up into a bun. Her lips were pale and chapped. Palmer had been getting less and less sleep lately. It had been several months since the incident with the Ouija board and things had gotten so much worse.

She should be happy, she thought. Things with Cal were going great. The day after their fight about his drug use and drinking she had woken up to him knocking on the door to her dorm. When she had opened it he had immediately wrapped her into a hug and said how sorry he was. He had told her how things would be better, how he would be better for her. Palmer was so freaked out from the Ouija board the night before that she was just glad to be in his presence. But he had been true to his word. Things had gotten better.

Calum had been like his old self. Happy and fun, warm and loving. He had still dropped out of college, for now. When Palmer had asked him what his parents had said he mostly brushed it off, saying he told them he was taking a break. He had told Palmer that they thought he would eventually start classes back up. Palmer thought he probably would too.

A few weeks after their fight Calum had gotten a new tattoo. He already had a handful of tattoos that littered his body but he had seemed particularly excited about this one when he left for his appointment. He had refused to tell Palmer what it was he was getting or where it was going. Palmer only had one rule and that was 'NO FACE TATTOOS'. She didn't want to date Mike Tyson. She had reiterated this rule to Calum and he had only smiled mischievously and agreed.

Hours later he had come back to her dorm and she had nearly punched him when she saw the naked picture of herself on his forearm. Palmer had kicked him out of her dorm and refused to speak to him for two days. But she was weak and eventually, she forgave him, even though she still hated it. She was beyond embarrassed that it was on display all the time. She prayed no one could tell it was her. Jessica had laughed when she first saw it but later when they were alone she confessed to Palmer that it was the most romantic thing she had ever seen. Palmer tried her best to think of it that way. He would just have to wear long sleeves around her family, she told herself. After a while, Palmer started to warm up to the tattoo. She would never, ever tell Cal though.

Cal had been true to his word about the drinking and the drugs as far as she could tell. He would nurse one or two beers at parties but other than that she didn't see any evidence that he was using drugs. He seemed ok, more than ok if Palmer was being honest.

But while things with Calum had improved, the strange occurrences that had plagued Palmer for years were happening more and more frequently. Shadows in the corner of her vision, a woman's face in the mirror that was not her own for just a split second. Palmer would be alone in a room but have the uneasy feeling that she really wasn't alone. At night she would lay awake wondering if she was losing her mind.

Palmer had taken a psychology course last year. She remembered that she was the right age for schizophrenia to present itself. This fact was what worried her most often. But then she would remember that Jessica and four other girls had been in the dorm that night with the Ouija board. That was not in her head.

Gabby. The Ouija board had spelled out the nickname for someone named Gabriella. What were the odds that the only real-life tragedy in her family was her missing great-aunt? Palmer could still remember the night that her grandmother had told her the story. She could still feel her grandmother's soft hand in hers as Palmer comforted her. Ever since that night Palmer's mental and physical health had started to decline. She was losing weight and her skin was even paler than normal.

Palmer continued to stare into space, her mind replaying all the unexplainable things she had seen or felt. Her eyes weren't fixed on anyone in particular but then one person came into focus between the crowds of people. Calum was walking toward her with a lazy grin. His gray eyes were fixed on her, his black hair disheveled and perfect. Palmer smiled despite her exhaustion. Calum knew Palmer's schedule by heart. She assumed he must have been on campus with friends and decided to meet up with Palmer knowing she would most likely be in the dining hall about now.

"Hey good lookin'," Calum said as he got closer.

"Hey you," Palmer responded. Calum pulled out the chair across from her and moved it to her side, plopping himself down into it. His excessively long legs were sprawled out in front of him.

"You look like shit."

"Gee thanks," Palmer laughed. Calum started to eat the now cold food in front of her. One of his hands wrapped around her shoulder and played with the piece of hair that had escaped her bun while the other crammed cold french fries into his mouth. Palmer closed her eyes and tried to relax.

"You got any studying to do tonight?" he asked.

"Nah, I'm pretty much caught up with everything."

"Wanna go see a movie? I'll let you spoil The Woman in Black for me?" Cal said with a wink.

"It wouldn't be fair, I read the book," Palmer said and yawned loudly. "I'm exhausted," she said. "Can we just go chill in my room? Jess is still seeing that guy with the turntable. She won't be home until late, I think he has a show or something."

Cal shivered. "She's still seeing the DJ guy with the snake? Ugh. He's even worse than that one with the moccasins."

Palmer laughed. Jessica's dating choices were usually pretty interesting. "I don't know. I still like this guy more than that one with the little braid?"

"Babe, that was a rat tail, and yeah ok I'll give you that. At least DJ Python isn't sporting a rat tail."

Palmer shook her head with a grin while Calum shoved the last few french fries into his mouth, grabbed her tray, and stood. Palmer stood up too and followed him. He tossed the old food into the garbage bin and stacked the tray for her. Then they made their way through the crowd, out the doors, and into the bitter winter air.

There were at least two feet of snow on the ground, still frozen from the last snowstorm a week ago. But the pavement was clear, having been shoveled by the college maintenance crew. Palmer shoved her hands into the pockets of her brick-colored puffer jacket. Calum only had on a flannel over his shirt, he rarely wore appropriate weather attire.

They talked about everything and nothing. Calum talked about his roommates and their drama with girls, Palmer talked about her classes. Before they knew it they were at Palmer's dorm. Palmer opened it with her key card and let Calum inside. Calum fell onto Palmer's twin-size bed and kicked his shoes off onto the little rug. He was so tall that his feet and ankles hung off the end of the bed.

Palmer took off her jacket and hung it up in her wardrobe. She turned back to Cal. He was lying face up with his hands tucked behind his head. His eyes were closed. Seeing this Palmer decided to put on some comfy pajamas. She stripped down to just her panties and pulled out a flannel sleeping set. Palmer dressed in front of the wardrobe mirror. She had pulled the bottoms on and went to put on the top when her eyes flicked to Calum in the mirror. His eyes were open and taking in every inch of her. Heat flooded her core and her bare breasts felt heavy as his gaze lingered on them.

Calum's eyes finally made their way up to Palmer's. His eyes locked onto hers and she shivered. Palmer slipped the nightshirt over her head, the fabric grazing her now hard nipples. Her head popped out of the hole and she tried to find Calum's dark gaze again in the mirror's reflection.

She could still see him lying in her bed looking at her but standing next to him by the bed was a woman. The woman. Long dark hair, filthy white nightgown, muddy bare feet, and the most horrific face imaginable. Her bloodshot eyes were open as wide as possible. Her mouth hung open inhumanely wide. And her shaking arm was raised and reached toward Palmer.

Palmer screamed and covered her eyes. She tried to get away from where she knew the woman had been but in her blindness she ran face-first into the wardrobe, almost knocking it over. Calum was already up and next to her. He straightened the wardrobe before it fell. Then he grabbed Palmer by the arms and shook.

"Palmer! Jesus! Fuck, what is it? What's going on?"

Palmer was still covering her eyes and sobbing. Calum shook her harder.

"No no no no no no—," were the only words she could say.

"PALMER!" Calum yelled in her face and she felt him shake her so hard her feet almost came off the ground. Her brain rattled in her skull.

Finally, she opened her eyes. She immediately looked to where the woman had been. There was nothing there. She looked all over the room. Nothing. Palmer looked to Cal then. He was looking at her like someone looking at a bomb.

"What the fuck was that?" He said between gritted teeth. Palmer thought that he was still shaking her for a moment before she realized her body was shaking now all on its own.

"I... I...," she started to speak but coherent words wouldn't come out.

"Holy shit," Calum said, dragging his hand through his hair. He led her to the bed and forced her to sit on the edge. Then he walked to the dorm door, opened it, and peered into the hallway. Clearly he was trying to see if anyone was around to hear her fit. Satisfied that almost everyone was still at the cafeteria for dinner, he shut the door. Calum turned to Palmer with an angry look and strode toward her.

"Palmer. Get your shit together. You're freaking me out. You need to calm down and tell me what just happened." He pulled out the chair at her desk, placed it in front of Palmer, and took a seat. Calum gave her a hard stare and Palmer swallowed. She took a deep breath and tried to steady herself. It was time, she decided.

"Sometimes — sometimes I see stuff," she said.

"Like what kind of stuff?" Calum responded.

"Shadows mostly I guess? Sometimes I just feel like someone is watching me. And then — there's this woman."

"A woman?"

"Yeah. Sometimes I see a woman. But only for like a split second. It's so fast. Like a blink. She's there and then she's not."

"Is that what you saw just now?"

"I think so. She was right next to you and then she wasn't," Palmer was starting to feel better just talking about it. A weight was starting to lift from her chest.

"When you say 'sometimes' you see things. What do you mean?" Calum asked.

"It's been happening a lot more than it used to —," Palmer started to say.

"Used to? How long has this been going on?"

"I'm not sure? I don't remember when it first started. Around when I started high school I think?"

"Jesus Christ," Calum held his head in his hands.

"Cal I'm scared, I can't eat, I can't sleep. I just keep seeing her face over and over. I feel like she's always just here," Palmer waved her hand in some empty space to her right. Cal reached up and grabbed her arm, putting it back down at her side.

"Palmer. Listen to me," Palmer looked at him with a hopeful expression. This was Calum. He knew her better than anyone. And now he officially knew everything about her. There were no longer any secrets between them. He would help her, she thought. He would fix this. He would know what to do.

"You need to stop," Calum said.

"Stop what?" Palmer was confused.

"Stop acting like a crazy person."

Palmer felt like he had punched her in the stomach.

"You're stressed. You took on too many classes this semester and you always take your grades too seriously. You're pushing yourself too hard. All these years of watching horror movies and reading scary books have given your imagination too much fuel. Plus you're homesick. That's all." Cal was holding both of her wrists now. His voice was stern. "You say you're seeing stuff. No, you're not. Ok? It's just stress and you're hyper fixating on it. It's going to be fine."

Palmer was shocked. This was not the response she had expected from him.

"But Cal I —," she started to speak but he interrupted her.

"STOP. Palmer, don't talk about it anymore. Seriously. What happens if you keep entertaining this idea? What happens? You're going to end up being committed somewhere. They're going to put you on medication that turns you into a zombie. Do you want that? Because I don't. So you're going to stop talking about it. You're going to straighten up and get it together. Got it?"

Palmer had started to cry. He had never spoken to her like this before. On top of that, he had voiced all of her fears. She really was going crazy. A sob escaped her lip and she tried to raise her arm to wipe her snot on her sleeve but Cal was still holding her wrists down.

"Palmer, answer me. Do you understand?" he said firmly and a bit louder. Palmer nodded her head. He was right. She needed to get her shit together before she was too far gone to come back.

"Come here." He grabbed the back of her head and pulled her toward his chest, holding her. Her tears were rolling down her cheeks and into his shirt. "Everything is fine. I love you. Forever."

Palmer sniffled and wrapped her arms around him. "Always," she said.

Chapter Twenty-Six

Present Day (2022)

Palmer was sleeping restlessly in her hospital bed. She had dreamt of snow falling gently and silently in a mountain forest. Fat white snowflakes clinging to the earth. It was beautiful and should have been a lovely dream, instead it was a nightmare. The snow was falling so thickly that she couldn't see more than ten feet in front of her. The cold was penetrating her very soul, paranoia ran rampant through the dream. Someone was out there with her.

Palmer's eyes flashed open. She was sleeping in her hospital bed, curled up on her side. A thin white blanket covered her. She could hear the annoying beeping of the machine in the room with her. She could see the red glow of the pulse oximeter on her index finger. There must have been a smaller light somewhere behind her acting as a night light because while the room was very dim she could still see.

Palmer turned over to her other side, minding the cords that seemed to be attached to her. As she did she noticed someone was standing by the closed door. It was Cal.

Palmer paused. "Hey you," she said. She offered him a small smile. He returned the gesture.

"Hey."

"I'm surprised you're back," she said. Calum's brows furrowed and he looked at his hands.

"Are you?"

Palmer considered and answered, "No. I guess I'm not."

Calum looked around the room and scratched his beard. "I heard the nurses say that you're starting to remember things." Palmer thought that he seemed to be looking anywhere but at her.

"Yeah, I'm still missing a lot but bits and pieces are starting to come back," Palmer replied.

"Mmm..." he said as he continued his assessment of the room.

"I haven't remembered why you left yet though," she said in a low voice. Calum's eyes flashed to hers.

"I didn't leave Palmer. You did," he said matter of factly.

Palmer shook her head, "No. I loved you Calum. I remember that perfectly well. I would not have left you for anything. You were everything to me." Palmer's eyes were watering, her vision blurring with tears.

Calum's jaw tightened, he looked up at the ceiling and closed his eyes. "Fuck Palmer."

"Will you come sit?" Palmer gestured to the chair by her bed. Calum looked at it and her apprehensively. Finally, he walked slowly over to the chair and sat. "Where did you go earlier?" Palmer asked him.

"I had some stuff to do. Plus it was getting a little intense in here," he shrugged.

"Why'd you come back?"

Calum took a long breath. "Well, I saw the walking mountain you call your husband leave a few minutes ago and I saw my opportunity. He's not a big fan of mine."

Palmer had some questions about that but decided to stay on track. "But why did you come back?" He was looking at his hands again.

"I think the masochist in me wanted to see if you remembered…"

"Remember what Cal? What are you waiting for me to remember?" For some reason, Palmer's heart rate picked up. The beeping from the monitor picked up pace as well. Calum looked up at it. When his gaze came back down to hers his face was expressionless. Palmer swallowed.

"I uh — got you something." Calum broke the silence and reached into his pocket. He pulled out a small green velvet jewelry box and tried to hand it to her. Palmer hadn't raised her hand to take it so his arm remained outstretched awkwardly.

"You got me something?" Palmer wrapped her arms around herself. "You got me jewelry?" She was confused. "You've never gotten me jewelry before. Or at least not that I remember?" She could feel the beginning of her headache returning.

Calum's face dropped and he frowned down at the jewelry box. "No Palmer. I never gave you jewelry. Trust me, there are a lot of things I wish I had done differently." Calum ran his hands through his hair. "Please Palmer, just take it. It's a gift."

Palmer hesitantly took the small box from him. She stroked the forest-colored velvet with her thumb before popping the lid open. Inside the box was a silver necklace with a silver and blue pendant with the Virgin Mary displayed. It was shiny and brand new. There was still a little tag attached to the chain.

"What is this?" Palmer whispered.

"It's another necklace with Mary on it. I noticed that you weren't wearing that old one you always wear when I saw you earlier and figured you maybe needed a new one. This is a Catholic hospital so they had a ton in the gift shop."

Palmer stared down at the necklace. She cleared her throat and closed the jewelry box, setting it beside her on the bed.

"Thank you," Palmer said with a weak smile.

Calum smiled back with a genuine smile. "You're welcome. Look, I'm sure He-Man will be back any minute to hover over you for the rest of the night so I better get going," he said as he stood up.

Palmer felt herself start to panic. What if he left and never came back?

"Will you come back?" she blurted out.

Calum looked down at her apprehensively. "Maybe. Try and get some sleep." Calum leaned down and kissed her on the unbandaged part of her forehead. "Tell Popeye to lay off the spinach for me?" He was referring to Hartman. "Night," he said as he walked out.

Palmer sat alone in her hospital room, staring at the door where Calum had just left. She felt uneasy. Like there was still someone else in the room with her. But there was no one. Still, the heaviness of someone else's presence lingered.

Palmer looked to her side where the box with the new necklace lay. She reached for it and rolled the box in her hand before leaning way over and setting it on the side table well away from her. There was a pit in her stomach. Something was coming.

Chapter Twenty-Seven

The Necklace (2006)

Tomorrow was Palmer's fourteenth birthday. She was sitting on the back porch of her grandmother's house reading Salem's Lot while Shawn ran through the sprinklers. Abuela was tending to her garden well away from the trajectory of the hose. Abuela had the most beautiful rose bushes Palmer had ever seen. They lined the entirety of the back fence. The bushes bloomed large red roses all summer long, their petals fat and soft as butter. And they smelled amazing.

Palmer looked up and watched Shawn narrowly escape the arc of the water that was automatically moving down and then back up in a sweeping motion. He let out a yell of victory. Abuela was deadheading her flowers but paused to look at Shawn's fun. She yelled out her encouragement.

This was Palmer's chance, she thought. Palmer stood up and set her book down where she was sitting.

"Abuelita! I'm going to go inside and use the bathroom! I'll be right back!" Palmer yelled across the yard. Abuela just waved back at her in acknowledgment. So Palmer headed inside. She walked through the sliding glass door and into Abuela's kitchen.

The kitchen was clean and tidy but packed with shelves that displayed different vintage dish sets. Abuela had a thing for collecting dishes. Palmer made her way down the hall with all the crosses. She passed the bathroom and turned to go up the creaky stairs to the second level of the house. The stairway wall was covered in framed photos of their family. All of Palmer's Tias, Tios, Cousins, her Mother and Father, her brother, and herself. They all smiled back at her as she snuck up the stairs.

Once Palmer had made it up the stairs she stopped and looked through the window that showed the backyard to make sure Abuela and Shawn were both still occupied. Satisfied, she continued on her mission. She passed several doors until she found the one she wanted. Palmer put her hand on the knob and took a deep breath before opening it.

Abuela's room wasn't necessarily off-limits. There wasn't a sign that said 'KEEP OUT'. Abuela had never forbidden her from going in. But it was filled with Abuela's most treasured items as well as her most fragile knick-knacks. So Palmer's younger cousins were discouraged from going in there lest they break something. Palmer remembered being younger and how afraid she was to come into Abuela's room because she was certain she would break something important. Right now, standing in the middle of the room, she was feeling that feeling again.

Abuela's bedroom was the master bedroom of the house so naturally, it was the largest. In the middle of the room was a queen-sized bed with a canopy bed frame. The bed was covered in a floral down comforter and big fluffy decorative pillows. On the foot of the bed was Palmer's favorite of all Abuela's quilts. On the farthest wall was a door that Palmer knew would lead to the master bathroom.

Abuela's room was carpeted with old eighty's style teal carpet. Open display cabinets could be found on multiple walls, filled to the brim with porcelain or glass items. The window in here opened to the front yard so Palmer would need to work quickly. She scanned the room for what she was looking for.

"Ah ha!" Palmer whispered to herself. She started to walk to the back corner of the room next to Abuela's vanity where there was a small armoire just for jewelry. It was about a foot and a half wide and four feet tall. It was made of cherry wood with six small drawers and a top lid that opened up to reveal a mirror and storage for rings. Additionally, the sides of the armoire opened up as well for necklace storage.

Palmer wasn't sure what she was looking for. She just wanted to borrow something to wear to her birthday party tomorrow. Something sophisticated and adult-looking. She would ask Abuela later tonight if she could maybe borrow a piece of her jewelry but Palmer wanted to know what her options were first. That way when Abuela took her up here she would already have an idea of what she wanted to ask for.

Palmer started opening up drawers and peering into them one by one. She saw glittering costume jewelry, gold rings that held little rubies and emeralds, her great grandmother's pearl necklace, necklaces her mother had made for Abuela during her mother's beading phase, silver, and gold hoop earrings, dangly earrings with different colored stones... so much jewelry Palmer was starting to feel a little overwhelmed. She was thinking the gold hoop earrings would be a good choice so she tried to pull them out. But they were all tangled up in a gold chain.

Palmer did her best to untangle the hoops from the chain when she realized the chain was actually a necklace. Finally, she got the hoops free and decided to take a closer look at the necklace. The gold chain held a small oval pendant just smaller than a dime. On the oval was the image of the Virgin Mary with her arms down, and palms up. Around the image were the words 'O Mary Conceived Without Sin Pray For Us Who Have Recourse To Thee'. She had brought the necklace closer to her face to read the words and realized that the pendant wasn't an oval at all but a tiny little octagon. There were eight tiny defined edges that were shinier than the rest of the pendant. It was beautiful.

Just then Palmer heard a creak from the doorway to Abuela's room and she looked up. Abuela was standing there watching Palmer.

Palmer jumped. "Abuela! I — I'm sorry. I was, I just —," she couldn't find the right words.

"It's ok hita," Abuela said, a light smile playing on her face. Abuela began walking toward Palmer.

"I was going to ask you later if I could borrow something to wear to my birthday party tomorrow. I was just curious," Palmer explained. Abuela made it to Palmer's side and looked down to the necklace that Palmer carried. Abuela's expression was blank.

"Is this what you want to borrow?" Abuela's eyes didn't leave the necklace as she spoke.

"Um — yeah, I think so? Is this ok? It's beautiful," Palmer said.

Abuela swallowed. She took Palmer's hand that held the necklace and closed it with both of her small wrinkled hands. "You should keep it, hita."

"What? Seriously!" Palmer exclaimed. "Really?"

"Yes," Abuela said with a weak smile.

"Oh my gosh. Thank you, Abuelita!" Palmer kissed her grandmother on the cheek and turned to the mirror to put the necklace on. Abuela helped her with the clasp while Palmer held up her long dark hair.

Palmer looked at the necklace and smiled broadly in the mirror. Abuela was behind her, an unreadable expression on her face.

Chapter Twenty-Eight

Present Day (2022)

Palmer had been pretending to sleep when Hartman quietly came back a few minutes after Calum left. Palmer had felt him kiss her cheek and brush the hair from her face. When he leaned over her she could smell him, he smelled like cedar and spearmint. When he stood up she heard him step toward the little side table where she had set the necklace from Calum. She heard him open the box, look at it for what felt like forever, and then snap it closed. He had walked quietly to the chair beside her and she had assumed that he had stayed there the entire night.

Palmer wanted to be annoyed at his insistence on being near her at all times but she couldn't. She was actually thankful for his hovering. It meant that she wasn't alone with her thoughts. Or the weird presence in the room.

Palmer hadn't slept at all. Anxiety caused her limbs to feel jittery, and her chest heavy. Her mind was a maze of thoughts. Images of the horrifying woman that haunted her swirled through her brain, along with the near-constant worry that she was in fact going crazy. Just when she thought that she would finally snap and have that long-awaited mental breakdown, she would remember that someone believed her. The man behind her believed her. She might not know him, but at some point, she had trusted him enough to tell him her darkest secret and he had believed her. Hartman believed her.

Hours passed until finally Palmer thought it must be morning. She could hear nurses changing shifts in the hallway. She heard Hartman stand up and stretch a couple of times but other than that he had been completely silent. Eventually, she heard her parents come into the room.

"Shhh Chuck, she's still sleeping," Palmer could hear her mother whispering. Palmer was still lying on the hospital bed with her back turned to the door. She heard her parents start to talk with Hartman in hushed voices.

"How's our girl?" asked Chuck.

"She's been out like a light all night," responded Hartman.

"Good. She needed the rest," said Emilia. "Any news from Dr. Walters?"

"No, she went home for the night but she'll be back soon. She thinks Palmer is doing well enough to come home today as long as we keep a good eye on her. The police stopped by yesterday evening after you left wanting to ask Palmer some questions but Dr. Walters sent them away for now. Palmer can't remember anything yet and Dr. Walters said Palmer is probably a little fragile right now."

"Palmer still can't remember what happened at that house?" asked Chuck.

"No, not yet. As soon as she does, the police will want to interview her. They did collect the clothes she was wearing while they were here though," answered Hartman. He didn't sound happy.

"Mmm," Chuck grunted in reply.

"That's good news though! Right? She can go home today?" Emilia said cheerfully.

"Yeah, Walters says the sooner Palmer can get back to her normal everyday life the sooner her memories will come back."

Palmer hadn't known that the police had stopped by. No one had mentioned it to her.

"Hartman, you should go get some coffee and something to eat. We'll stay here with her. Don't worry."

"I'm fine," he reposed.

Palmer could imagine the hard look her mother had likely given him in response.

"You sure?" Hartman said reluctantly. Clearly he was hesitant to leave.

"Go on. We'll call or text when she wakes up," said her mother.

Palmer heard the chair under Hartman scrape against the floor as he stood. She could have sworn some part of him, either his knee or his back, pop as he stood. She felt his warmth lean over like he was going to give her a kiss on the cheek. Instead, she felt his hot breath in her ear.

"I know you're awake Palmer. I know when you're faking being asleep," he said playfully. "I'll be right downstairs if you need me." Then he really did kiss her on the cheek and left.

Palmer smiled just a little despite herself. Hartman might know when she was fake sleeping but her parents obviously did not. A few seconds after the hospital door closed behind Hartman her parents started to whisper to each other. Palmer could hear their hushed words from behind her.

"You called the recovery center this morning?" asked her father Chuck.

"Yes, I talked to his counselor. She said he is doing really well. I told her the situation and she thinks we should tell him. She thinks he can handle it. The counselor will have him call us at noon and she'll be right there while we tell him. He's going to beat himself up for not being here. I'm scared he'll leave," Emilia said.

"We'll tell him she's doing just fine. Dr. Walter said Palmer might be able to go home today as long as Hartman keeps a close eye on her," Chuck responded.

"I don't want him to relapse, Chuck."

"I don't either."

"He's doing so well. I really think this is it."

Palmer's father only grunted in response.

Palmer turned over then and looked at both of her parents. They had fake smiles plastered to their faces.

"Good morning sunshine!" said Palmer's mother. "How did you sleep? How are you feeling?"

Palmer's mother was nervously trying to fill the moment with chatter. Palmer gave both of her parent's a meaningful look.

"Mom. Where is Shawn?"

Chuck and Emilia Lane's expressions fell.

Chapter Twenty-Nine

The Static (2013)

Palmer was feeling only a little bit sweaty, and 'a lot a bit' claustrophobic. She was in her mother's kitchen with a handful of her tias and other various female family members including her grandmother. The women were bustling about cooking, chopping, stirring, and chatting. The air was thick with the smell of different foods and women trying to talk over each other both in English and in Spanish.

It was Thanksgiving break. This year Palmer had been deemed 'adult' enough to help prepare the meal instead of being banished to the living room with the other kids. She could remember a time when she had yearned to be allowed into the kitchen during Thanksgiving. But now, amidst the overwhelming chaos of women, she wished she could just relax in the next room where the kids were watching the dog show.

Palmer, Calum, Jessica, and Jessica's new boyfriend Jayce, had all driven home together during break. It was junior year and Calum had stayed true to his word as far as classes went. He still lived off campus with some friends. His parents were no longer supporting him so he was working part-time for a local landscaping company. His hours varied depending on the time of year. Lots of mowing lawns in the spring and summer, raking leaves in the fall, and snow removal in the winter. However, in late November there wasn't much for him to do. The Colorado trees had lost all of their leaves weeks ago and the first snow hadn't come yet.

Calum was having Thanksgiving with his parents this year. It was rare for his father to be home for Thanksgiving so Calum's mother had insisted. Jessica was introducing Jayce to her parents this weekend. Surprisingly Jessica had let this new guy stick around for a while. Palmer liked him. Jayce was nice, normal, and kind of quiet, but that was probably for the best given how much Jessica liked to talk.

Palmer was a little surprised that Jessica had even given him the time of day. For one, he seemed a little boring for Jessica. He had no drama, there was nothing different or weird about him for Jessica to latch onto. On top of that, Jessica had a strict *'no boys with J names'* rule. Jessica had a superstition that all men with names that start with J were the worst. Also since her name started with a J, Jessica always thought dating a guy with a J name would just sound ridiculous. Regardless, here they were. Jessica and Jayce.

It had been almost nine months since Palmer had opened up to Calum about the woman and the strange things that kept happening to her. Nine months since he had warned her to ignore it and not talk about it anymore. Palmer had taken his advice to heart. Even so, the strange occurrences continued to happen. She hadn't seen the woman again but she still felt uneasy. Like she was never really alone. She would wake up most nights in a cold sweat after dreams of running through the woods from some invisible threat. When she sat up awake she could almost make out the sound of distant whispering only for a moment. Sometimes, for no reason at all, the hair on her arms and the back of her neck would stand up. Still, following Calum's warnings, she had ignored it.

Palmer was currently in charge of whipping the potatoes. In her family, there could absolutely be no lumps. So Palmer fought to keep control of the hand mixer as it loudly made its way through the potatoes, butter, and milk. The electric humming sound of the mixer did nothing to drown out the noise of the women crowding the kitchen. Palmer's hand was starting to go numb due to the vibrations of the mixer when she heard her grandmother get into an argument with her mother.

"Mom, we can't use this. It's expired," said Emilia.

"What do you mean it's expired? It can't expire, it's in a can," explained Abuela.

"Let me see that," said a tia. "Oh my, Maria. This expired in 2002."

Abuela put her hands on her hips and gave the woman a hard expression. "So?" The two women laughed.

"Mother. We can't serve expired cranberry sauce," replied Emilia. Abuela glared before finding another task, grumbling something in Spanish as she made herself busy. Emilia only huffed and yelled over the noise, "Does anyone want to run to the store and grab a couple cans of cranberry sauce?"

Palmer immediately turned off the mixer and raised her hand. "I'll go!" she said as she untied her ruby-colored apron. She needed to get out of this stuffy kitchen. As she moved away from the bowl of half-mashed potatoes another woman stepped in to take over. Palmer made her way out of the kitchen and down the hallway to where her car keys were dangling from a little key hook. Palmer had parked down the block, knowing that if she parked in the driveway she would get blocked in.

Palmer walked out of the house and toward her car. She strode past the cluster of her male relatives on the front lawn drinking beer and attempting to deep fry the turkey. Her father was a head taller than most of them and spotted her.

"Hey, where are you going?" Chuck yelled in her direction.

"Gotta make a run to the store. Do you need anything?" Palmer hollered back at him. Palmer's father shook his head and waved her off before turning back to the turkey and giant pot of hot oil.

Half an hour later Palmer was driving back home with two cans of cranberry sauce in the passenger seat. Palmer decided to take the long way home to kill a little more time but also to drive by Calum's parent's house just for fun. She wouldn't stop unless she saw him outside. Maybe she would get to give him a quick kiss and ask him to come by later.

Palmer slowed down a little bit as she was about to drive past and craned her neck to see better. She smiled when she saw Calum on the curb just ahead. He was leaning into the window of a parked car talking to someone. Palmer watched as Calum took something out of his pocket and handed it to the driver. She blinked. She knew that car. Just then Palmer decided to pull over. A knot formed in her belly.

Calum looked up and toward her car when he noticed someone pull up behind the car he was leaning in. He made eye contact with Palmer and his face froze in shock. He stood straight up and said something to the driver. Palmer got out of her car and started walking toward Calum, and toward her brother Shawn's car.

"What are you guys doing?" she said with false lightness.

Calum looked shifty, Shawn looked incredibly guilty and just a little bit scared.

"Palmer? What are you doing here? I thought you were helping cook," said Calum. He tried to reach for her but she stepped out of his embrace.

"I had to make a run to the store. Shawn?" Palmer said, now looking at her brother. Shawn looked like he might be sick. He opened his mouth to speak but nothing came out. Instead, Calum started talking.

"Shawn was just driving by and I flagged him down to say hey, I haven't seen his new whip. It's pretty sweet. I can't believe you're old enough to drive," Calum rumbled Shawn's hair in a brotherly sort of way. Shawn still looked scared.

Palmer leveled Calum with a look and turned back to her brother. Something caught her eye in the back seat. It was four cases of beer. Palmer let out a small breath of relief and had to reign in a smile. Alcohol. Calum had bought Shawn alcohol for a party and they were trying to hide it. That's why they were acting weird, she thought to herself.

"You guys chill out. Did you really think I cared about you buying my brother some beer?" Palmer pointed to the back seat. She looked at them incredulously. "He's sixteen, we were sixteen not that long ago. I get it. If anything I'm just a little upset you guys were trying to hide it from me."

Calum laughed. "I'm sorry, I just didn't want you to get mad at me."

Palmer smiled now and turned to her brother who still looked unsure. "Just don't be a dumb ass. No drinking and driving, yeah? Either make sure you have a designated driver or stay the night where you're at, ok?"

"Ok," Shawn said with a weak smile. "I'm sorry Palmer, you're not going to tell Mom and Dad?"

Palmer gave her brother a comforting smile. "Of course not. Just promise me you'll be smart."

Shawn smiled back. "I promise."

"Now get back home. I think dinner will be done soon. I'll meet you there. Cover this up with something or mom and dad will see," she added.

"Ok! See you in a few, thanks Cal!" Shawn said as he pulled out.

Palmer watched her brother's car drive off and turn the corner before she turned to Calum.

"What?" Cal said defensively with his hands out. "You just said you understood and it was no big deal?"

"You were going to lie to me?" She felt hurt and irritated.

Calum ran his hands through his dark, messy hair. "Look Palmer, I didn't want it to become a whole thing. I didn't feel like getting into it with you today."

Palmer shook her head in disbelief and started walking back to her car. She only made it a few steps before she was jerked back by the shoulder. Calum had stopped her.

"Don't be like that Palmer."

Palmer shook off his touch and turned to him.

"What did you hand him?" she asked.

"What?"

"What did you hand him? When I was pulling up I watched you hand him something from your pocket. What was it?" she refused to let him side-track her.

"Oh," Calum paused. "Just his change from the money he gave me for the beer. There were a few bucks left over."

Palmer took a breath and looked at him then. Really looked at him. She searched his handsome face for any sign of deceit. She found nothing. Besides, his answer made sense.

"Ok," Palmer said. "We'll talk about this later. Happy Thanksgiving Cal," she said angrily and walked back to her car.

Later that night Palmer sat in her parent's living room. All of the guests had left. Palmer's father had gone up to bed hours ago but Palmer and her mother were still awake. They were both night owls. Especially tonight since both of them had coffee with the pumpkin pie they ate for dessert. Emilia sat in her rocking chair in the corner of the room crocheting. Palmer was sitting on the couch with her feet tucked under her reading Interview with a Vampire by Anne Rice. Palmer had just gotten to the part where Louis turned Claudia into a vampire when her mother's phone started to ring.

Emilia looked down at her ringing cell phone and frowned.

"Who is it?" Palmer looked up from her book.

"I don't know the number but it's got a local area code?" said Emilia with a question. She decided to answer it. "Hello?" Emilia paused to listen. Palmer immediately knew something was wrong. "What!" Emilia looked panicked now. Palmer stood up and moved to her. "Well, is he ok?" Another pause. "Yes, yes of course we'll be right there." Palmer's mother hung up, she was crying now.

"Mom?" said Palmer.

"Go wake up your dad! I need to find my shoes!" Emilia stood abruptly, almost knocking Palmer over.

"Mom! What is going on?" Palmer asked frantically. Something was terribly wrong.

"That was the hospital! It's Shawn!"

Everything that happened after that was a blur to Palmer. They had woken up Chuck, grabbed what they needed, and loaded it into the car. Chuck had bombarded Emilia with questions she didn't have the answer to. Apparently all the doctor had said was that he was brought in by ambulance but he was stable, he would be fine, and that they should come. Emilia had been so upset that she had agreed and hung up before she could ask any more questions.

It usually took twenty minutes to get to the hospital from the Lane residence. But somehow they arrived in twelve. They were forced to sit in a large empty waiting room for what felt like forever before a doctor came out to speak with them. They were told that Shawn had collapsed at a party, and that he was extremely dehydrated when he arrived at the hospital. The doctor suspected that he had not only been drunk but had likely taken drugs as well. They wouldn't know what kind of drugs until the results came back or he woke up and decided to tell them. The doctor asked subtly if this type of thing had ever happened to Shawn before. The answer was no. Up until tonight, Shawn had never been in trouble a day in his life.

Palmer's mother wept. Her father stared at nothing and ground his teeth. Palmer, on the other hand, was dazed. Her ears were ringing and she felt lightheaded. This was her fault, she thought to herself. This was all her fault.

After a few more minutes they had been allowed to see Shawn. He was awake in his hospital bed. As soon as they walked in he began crying and apologizing. Chuck and Emilia had told him everything would be all right. They asked him what happened. Shawn had glanced at Palmer only for a moment before he said that he had been drinking and decided to try some ecstasy. That someone at the party had brought it but he didn't know who they were. He apologized over and over again to their parents. Palmer stood in the corner. Afraid to move. She knew the truth.

While her parents continued to comfort her brother, Palmer pulled out her phone. She sent one simple text.

Shawn is in the hospital. What did you do?

It only took a minute before her phone started to ring. She didn't answer. It rang again. So Palmer turned her phone off.

A few hours later the sun was coming up. Shawn was sleeping peacefully. Palmer's father had given her the keys to his truck and told her to go home and get some rest. Her parents wanted to stay with Shawn for now but they would text her if they needed her to bring something when she came back. Palmer had only nodded and left.

Nothing felt real to Palmer. She felt like she was watching herself from far away, like in a movie. She hardly remembered driving home. She got out of the truck still dazed and walked toward the front door. She was almost through the front door and into the house when she heard someone call her name from behind her. Palmer turned to see Calum racing toward her. His car was parked across the street.

"Palmer!" Calum yelled again. "Is Shawn ok? Your phone is dead!"

Palmer put her hand up to stop him before he reached her.

"I don't want to see you right now," she said. She still felt as though she was outside her own body.

"Palmer?" Calum looked at her hurt. The hurt on his face only angered her.

"You gave my little brother drugs." It wasn't a question. Calum pushed a breath out and looked at her beseechingly. Several moments passed, and still, he said nothing.

Finally, he spoke, "Palmer, I'm sorry. I fucked up. He just wanted to have a good time. I told him to only take one and make sure to drink a lot of water. I shouldn't have even offered it. I see that now. Please. I'm so sorry Palmer."

Palmer watched as a tear slid down his cheek. He was crying. But Palmer still felt nothing. Just the overwhelming numbness she had felt for hours. This was all her fault.

"Go home Calum," she said coldly. "I can't even look at you right now."

Calum sobbed.

"Please Palmer! I'm sorry!"

Palmer snapped. The numbness was replaced by pure rage.

"YOU'RE SORRY? YOU'RE SORRY? Seriously Calum?" she could feel the anger boiling up inside her. "What is wrong with you Cal? My brother could have died tonight. Do you even realize that? He collapsed at a party in the middle of nowhere. What if the kids at the party had been too afraid to call 911? Or what if the ambulance couldn't find the place? Oh my God," Palmer was pissed now.

"I know Palmer, it was stupid. I'm sorry. I'll do better, I —" she cut him off.

"YOU ALWAYS SAY YOU'LL DO BETTER! But you never do! Did you ever even stop doing drugs or did you just get better at hiding it?" she asked. He didn't answer, only swallowed. It was enough for Palmer.

"Holy shit. I'm a fucking idiot," she laughed angrily. "I believed you. I believed IN you. Did you know that?" She was fighting back tears now. "Go home Calum," she said again.

"Palmer." That was all he said.

"LEAVE. GET OFF MY DOORSTEP CALUM," she yelled and he flinched.

"Can I come by and talk to you some more tomorrow?"

Palmer laughed coldly. "No. You can not 'talk to me tomorrow'. I don't want to see you."

"For how long?" he asked.

Palmer gave him a meaningful look. Her heart was shattering in her chest. But she realized that it had been shattering for a long time now.

"I — don't — want — to — *see* — you — anymore," she said slowly.

Understanding dawned on his face. Before it crumpled.

"No," he whispered.

Palmer turned to go inside.

"Wait Palmer, no!" he yelled but she had already closed the door and locked it behind her.

Palmer wasn't sure what to expect after that. Maybe she thought he would go to his car. Instead, he started to pound his fist into the door. Palmer jumped in surprise. She had never known Calum to be violent. She had never seen him this way. The banging was deafening and coming in quick succession. Palmer stepped back slowly, thinking for sure he would stop any second. But he didn't.

Palmer was sobbing in fear. He was going to break down the door. She could hear him yelling her name over and over. Behind her, in the living room, the television came on. It wasn't a show or a movie, just the grainy black-and-white static from no connection. The volume got louder and louder until the whole room was filled with white noise. The sound of Calum's violent assault on the door was nearly drowned out now.

Palmer had to cover her ears. She slid into a crouch and took steadying breaths. Her senses were on overload. She wasn't sure how long she stayed in that position. Finally, she realized the pounding had stopped and she stood up. The television was still blaring the sound of static from behind her. Palmer apprehensively walked to the door and looked through the peephole. Calum was gone. So was his car. She took a deep breath.

Palmer turned to the television and walked to where the remote was usually kept. She picked up the remote and pointed it toward the television, pressing the button to turn the volume down. Nothing happened. Palmer pushed the power button to try and turn the television off. Again, nothing happened. Palmer finally walked up to the big screen and reached around to the side, attempting to turn it off manually. Nothing happened.

Palmer studied the salt and pepper pixels quizzically. Exasperated, she followed the black cord from the back of the television to where it was plugged into the wall. She yanked hard. Finally, the television turned off, the deafining static noise gone. Palmer sniffed, wiping her wet cheeks and nose with her sleeve. She stared at her parent's TV with bunched brows before turning to walk up the stairs to her room. She rubbed at her puffy eyes as she walked up the steps.

Once Palmer was safely behind her closed bedroom door, the television turned back on.

Chapter Thirty

Present Day (2022)

"Rehab?" asked Palmer. "Shawn is in — rehab. Like rehab rehab?" she couldn't believe what her parents had just told her. Her happy-go-lucky baby brother was in rehab. But he wasn't a baby. Was he? Palmer had to adjust her image of her brother. He wouldn't be a teenager anymore. He was a grown man now. Palmer did the math real quick in her head. Shawn would be twenty-seven years old now. His life was a mystery to her.

Palmer's memories were slowly coming back. Like a small trickle in the back of her brain. Some memories came to her crisp and clean like biting into a cold granny smith apple. Others were hazy, the details just out of her reach. Sometimes all she had was a feeling. A small nagging feeling in her gut. Still, Palmer waited patiently for everything to come back to her so she could finally feel like she had her feet under her.

Palmer closed her eyes and pushed her brain to remember Shawn and his dark past. She could remember who had first sold drugs to Shawn but she didn't want to dwell on that right now. She had a feeling that Shawn had borrowed a lot of money from her in the past. She also had a bad feeling that he had broken her heart and her trust a few times. Her gut told her that she loved Shawn, but he had burned her many times.

"What happened?" She asked.

Emilia and Chuck looked at each other. Chuck shrugged.

"It started in high school. Just experimenting we thought. Only, it got worse and worse —" Palmer's mother's voice trailed off.

"This is his fourth rehab," mumbled Chuck. Palmer stared at him.

"This is the one though, I just know it. He's doing really well. His counselor says that he is really motivated in therapy and engaged in all of the activities. He's made some friends and he keeps a detailed journal. He chose to go this time all on his own. That's the difference," Emilia said hopefully. "Addiction is a terrible disease," she added. Emilia's eyes were watering a bit. Chuck sat silent, his back hunched, and looked at his hands.

"What is he — addicted to?" Palmer asked.

"Anything he can get his hands on," grumbled Chuck. Emilia glared at her husband.

"Opioids mostly," Emilia said under her breath. Palmer was still in disbelief.

"When was the last time you saw him?" Palmer asked.

"Well, we moved to Arizona a few years ago after he relapsed and entered the recovery center. He's at that same one again now. We had been thinking about moving somewhere warmer anyway —" Emilia said. Chuck grunted. "We haven't gotten to tell him what happened yet. He doesn't know you had an accident or are in the hospital yet. We didn't want to worry him, he would want to be here and we didn't want to give him an excuse to leave treatment," Emilia explained.

Palmer's stomach was in knots. How did this happen? How had she let this happen?

Several silent minutes passed between Palmer and her parents. Finally, her mother broke the silence.

"Hartman said that Dr. Walters should be here soon to check on you. He also said that she is thinking you might get to go home today! That's exciting!" Emilia chirped.

Palmer's stomach rolled with nausea. She was barely processing all of this new information here in the hospital. How was she going to handle it all at home? Where even WAS home anyway? Hartman had told her that they had a house together but she still had no memory of it, let alone him.

Amidst her anxiety and all of her foggy memories, there was one question that had been burning a hole inside of her the last few days. Palmer swallowed and made up her mind. She would finally ask the dreaded question. The question she was sure she already knew the answer to.

"Where's Abuela?" Palmer asked. Her voice was low and quiet but it still sliced through the silence. Palmer's parents didn't lift their heads or move at all. As if they had been waiting for this question for some time. They only looked at each other sideways under lowered lids. Chuck took a deep breath. Palmer spoke again. "She's dead, right?"

Both of Palmer's parents looked up at her then but it was Chuck who spoke.

"Yeah, baby. She died."

Chapter Thirty-One

The Last Talk (2013)

Palmer hated spring. Why anybody liked this season was beyond her. Maybe spring in other places was nicer. But spring in Colorado was a wet, muddy mess. When spring showers came there was usually still snow stuck to the ground that the rain would turn into brown sludge.

Palmer kicked some of that sludge off of her crimson rain boots and onto her grandmother's front door mat now. Palmer let herself into the house and proceeded to take off her boots and layers of wet clothing. As she did so she could hear thunder off in the distance. Palmer shivered and called out to her grandmother.

"Abuelita?"

"Hola hita, I'm in the living room!" Abuela yelled back.

Palmer padded into the living room. Her grandmother was lying on the big couch with several blankets on top of her. The bluish glow from the television was the only light in the room. Palmer took a seat next to Abuela's little socked feet. They didn't speak for a couple of minutes, waiting for a commercial to come on. Abuela didn't like interruptions during her novelas.

"How was your day?" Abuela finally asked.

"Good," Palmer responded blandly.

It was spring break. Jessica and a bunch of Palmer's college girlfriends had all gone to Mexico but Palmer had declined. Jessica had thrown a fit and pulled every trick she could think of to try and sway Palmer into going. Jessica had even gone so far as to say that Palmer was putting all of the girls at risk since Palmer was the only one who could speak Spanish. Jessica had gone on and on with what-ifs.

'What if we get lost because we can't read the signs?'

'What if we agree to do something dangerous because we can't understand what someone is asking us?'

'What if we get sick because we eat or drink something we aren't supposed to because we can't understand people's warnings?'

On and on. Jessica had finally given up and gone to Cancun after telling Palmer 'If I die it'll all be your fault'. She was joking of course. Palmer had hugged her and told her at the airport that they would be fine as long as they didn't leave the resort. Jessica had meant well. Palmer knew Jessica only wanted Palmer to go so desperately because she wanted to help Palmer.

Palmer hadn't seen or spoken to Calum since Thanksgiving break. It was like he had disappeared completely. Somehow they hadn't run into each other once even though they lived in the same city. He hadn't reached out and tried to speak to her at all. She hadn't tried to either.

Still, Palmer suffered. She was a shell of herself. Palmer's life had been bathed in gray. Food didn't taste as good, movies were uninteresting, jokes weren't funny. She cried herself to sleep almost every night. She had pulled Calum's number up on her phone more times than she could count. Her thumb hovered over the green dial button before she closed it. They had never gone this long without talking to each other.

Abuela looked at Palmer every once in a while like she saw all of this and disapproved. They continued to watch the end of Abuela's shows in silence. Palmer chewed her nails and tried to focus on the show. Abuela was currently into a show called Santa Diabla. It was Abuela's favorite show. She had been watching it for two years now. It was a story about a woman trying to get revenge for her husband's murder. Abuela had no idea that the 'good' brother was actually the 'bad' brother and vice versa. Palmer had predicted that twist last year and she was pretty sure they were going to reveal it soon.

The show finally ended and Abuela sat up to turn on the lamp on the side table. It was a vintage Tiffany lamp so it showered the room in warm colors. Abuela turned off the television and turned toward Palmer.

Abuela made a *tisking* sound with her mouth before speaking. "Don't bite your nails. You'll make your beautiful hands look like a man's."

Palmer immediately pulled her fingers out of her mouth.

"Are you staying the night?" Abuela asked. Palmer had shown up unannounced. She often did that. Palmer's grandmother only lived a couple blocks away so sometimes when Palmer or her brother were bored they would walk over to Abuela's.

"I was thinking about it. Is that ok?" Palmer asked.

"Of course, that's always ok hita," Abuela responded mid-stretch.

It was late, Palmer looked at her phone for the time since none of the clocks and Abuela's house ever worked. It was well past eleven o'clock. Palmer and her grandmother were both night owls but Palmer watched as Abuela yawned.

Palmer got up and helped Abuela to her feet. Abuela groaned and something popped in her back. Once both women were on their feet they walked to the kitchen and each filled up a glass of water before walking up to the bedrooms.

Palmer hovered behind Abuela while the old woman made her way up the stairs. It used to be that Abuela could go up and down these stairs two at a time when she was in a hurry. Now Abuela took the steps slowly and purposefully. Her arthritis and brittle bones made the steep incline treacherous. Abuela used to stand straight up, making herself seem taller than the five feet God gave her. Now her back was curved and she had a small hump. Her daily activities looked more and more painful to complete. Palmer had overheard her parents recently discussing how they would convince Abuela to move in with them. Palmer shuddered to think how that discussion would go.

Finally, Palmer and Abuela made it to the top landing of the stairs. Palmer escorted Abuela to the door of the master bedroom and kissed her grandmother goodnight before steeling herself to one of the guest rooms. Abuela always had one of the guest rooms ready for her grandchildren to stay the night. Sleepovers with Abuela were very common for Palmer, Shawn, and all of their cousins.

Palmer stared at the made-up guest bed for some time. She allowed the full weight of her sadness to wash over her. Where was Calum sleeping tonight? Palmer let memories flash by in pictures like one of those View-Master toys that were all the rage in the 90's. They were these little red binoculars that you could put round disks into. You would look through them and when you pressed down on the lever a new picture would appear. There was Calum leaning down to kiss her for the first time next to her locker. There was Calum lying on her bed watching her try and give herself bangs. There was Calum riding up to her house on a bike when his parents took his car away. There was Calum's horrified face after they saw Saw IV in theaters. There was Calum, there was Calum, there was Calum.

Finally, Palmer blinked back tears and pulled back the comforter to get into bed. She could hear rain starting up again outside. Palmer hoped distantly that the sound would help her sleep. She laid her head down and closed her eyes, trying to quiet her mind.

The rain grew louder and louder until it sounded like the roof was getting pelted by millions of small rocks. Then thunder clapped loud enough to make Palmer jump. More thunder rumbled.

Palmer eventually sat up and decided to check on Abuela. She walked down the hall and peered into Abuela's room. It was pitch black but then lightning flashed twice very rapidly. The first flash revealed a woman lying in Abuela's bed tucked in. A young woman, staring right at Palmer. Palmer jumped and her heart skipped several beats. But before she had time to panic the lightning flashed again. It was just Abuela. Her face was back to the normal soft, leathery, brown that Palmer loved. Palmer took a steadying breath. The light and her imagination must have played a trick on her. Lighting flashed a third time and revealed Abuela still staring at Palmer but now with a concerned look on her face.

"Hita? Are you ok?" Abuela said. Palmer could barely hear her over the pounding rain.

"Yeah, I'm fine Abuelita. I just can't sleep with this crazy storm."

"Come here, you can snuggle with me like when you were little. Hurry quick, before The Coco Man gets you."

Palmer walked to the other side of the bed, careful not to stub her toe on anything. She crawled into her grandmother's bed and savored the familiar smell. Palmer could hear Abuela turning toward her. Another bolt of lightning flashed through the room and Palmer could see her grandmother's sweet face. She felt Abuela's small hand touch her face.

"Abuelita, will you tell me about the Coco Man?" Palmer asked. She could hear her grandmother much better over the rain when they were this close.

"You know about the Coco Man hita," replied Abuela.

"It's been a while, refresh my memory."

"It's a spooky night to be telling stories like this. Are you sure you want to hear about it right now? Oh, I forgot which granddaughter I am talking to. You love scary stories, yes?"

Palmer smiled. "Yes," she replied.

"OK then. Let me think. El Coco had been around for a long time, hita. Longer than anyone can say for sure. But he loves to come and steal naughty little children. Children who don't listen to their parents. He comes and puts them in a sack while they sleep. Then he takes them away and eats them. My mother told me that he was tall with red eyes that glowed in the dark. She said he had bat ears that could hear anything and long sharp teeth. She said he moved in the shadows." Abuela paused then before speaking more. "At least that is what my mother told me and my abuela told me something similar. But I have heard that he looks different in different places. A nun from Brazil stayed with my family once when I was very little. She said he looked more like a dragon or an alligator. She said he had fire in his eyes. He would wait under the beds of little kids and wait for them to get out of bed when they weren't supposed to. That's when he would eat them." Palmer shivered. She had never heard The Coco Man described like that before.

"Why is he called El Coco? Coco means coconut," Palmer had always wondered. She thought that was rather silly but had been too scared by the stories to pose the question.

"If you turn a coconut around in your hands there is a face, no? A spooky little face. You can see the eyes and the mouth. At night, from the shadows that's what he looks like. All you can see from the shadows is his hairy, brown face before he takes you" responded Abuela. She was in full storytelling mode now, her voice rose and fell to dramatize the tale.

Palmer smiled. "Where does he live?" Palmer had decided tonight was the night she would ask all of her silly little questions that had been nagging her since she was a child. Growing up it had always felt like if you questioned The Coco Man or said his name enough times he would appear. Like Beetlejuice.

"El Coco roams around all over. Anywhere we speak Spanish. Maybe he liked the way we taste best!" Abuela raised her voice at the end for extra flare. Palmer was smiling even bigger now despite herself. It was fun listening to her grandmother's embellishments.

"You're a good storyteller Abuelita," Palmer said. Abuela said nothing. Palmer's smile faded. Moments passed before Palmer's grandmother spoke again.

"I don't think The Coco Man is a story mi hita," Abuela said in a low voice.

"What do you mean? Of course, he is just a story. A way to scare young people."

Abuela paused again before speaking. As if she wanted to plan out precisely what she would say.

"Once, a very long time ago, I think I may have maybe seen El Coco." Abuela's voice had dropped to a very light whisper. Almost as if she was afraid that someone else would hear her. Palmer's chest tightened and she leaned in to hear better.

"I was a young woman. In my twenties. I hadn't yet married so I still lived in my parent's house. My father was very strict. He had many rules. One of his rules was that I always had to be home by ten o'clock. No matter what. No exception. But one night my friends all wanted to go dancing and I also wanted to go. So I snuck out of my window that night and went with my friends. I danced and I had a great time. Afterward, they dropped me off a couple of blocks from our house so the sound would not wake up my parents. I thought I was very clever. Until my friends drove away and I was walking alone in the dark to my house. Every step I became more and more frightened. I was only one block away when I started to feel — not alone. Like a bunny when it knows a cat is close by. Natural inside me. Instinto —" Abuela stopped to think of the English word. "Instinct. Something in me just knew. So I ran very fast. I climbed through my window and locked it behind me. I've never felt fear before like that night. When I looked out the window I saw only darkness at first. Then I saw him. He was across the street. At first, I thought it was a man. He was tall and wore a hood. I couldn't see his face but I knew he was no man by the way he stood. I saw his eyes shine red in the street light, only for a moment." Abuela trailed off, lost in her terrifying memory. "I never snuck out again after that night. And I never walked alone at night. I never told anyone about that night. I never spoke of who or what I saw. I was afraid they would say I was silly. But I know what I saw. But I tell you now. So you remember. So you think."

Palmer could taste her fear on her tongue. Ice had crept down her spine during Abuela's tale. "So it's not just a story?" Palmer asked her grandmother.

"My beautiful Palmer. The eldest daughter of my eldest daughter. My first granddaughter. I have lived for a great many years. I have known great gladness and great loss. I have seen many things and known many people," Abuela's voice had become serious. Palmer knit her brows together in concern. Abuela continued.

"In all of this time that God has given me I have learned many lessons. There is one thing in particular that I have come to understand very well. That is, there is no such thing as 'just a story'."

Palmer didn't respond. She willed her grandmother to continue.

"These stories we tell our children and their children are like protective heirlooms. We tell you so that you do not get hurt but also so you tell your children so they do not get hurt. Do you understand?" Abuela reached for Palmer's hand and squeezed. Palmer squeezed back.

"I understand," Palmer said.

"Is El Coco prowling about on rooftops looking for children to eat? I don't know hita. But there are plenty of things in this world that are just as scary and waiting to get you."

Palmer shivered. The room was suddenly very cold and the rain was dying down so the room seemed much quieter.

"Thank you for telling me your stories Abuela," Palmer said.

"Your welcome hita, just promise me you will tell them to your children as well," Abuela said with a yawn.

"I love you," said Palmer.

"I love you too. Now say your prayers and go to sleep."

Palmer closed her eyes and said The Guardian Angel Prayer quickly before falling asleep.

Angel of God, my guardian dear,
To whom God's love commits me here,
Ever this day, be at my side,
To light and guard,
Rule and guide.
Amen

Palmer woke up the next morning alone in Abuela's bed. Palmer had slept better than she had in months. She had even slept in until almost nine in the morning. She wasn't surprised to find that Abuela was already up. She usually woke up with the sun.

Palmer stretched and made her way downstairs expecting to smell coffee and maybe even eggs and bacon frying. But the kitchen was empty. Palmer thought that was odd so she made her way into the living room. Abuela was asleep sitting up in her favorite chair next to the window. Palmer also thought that was odd. She had never seen Abuela asleep sitting up like that before.

Palmer started to walk toward the chair. With every step an icy feeling began to creep up her spine, but still she walked forward. When Palmer had gotten closer she could see that Abuela's chest was not rising and falling. Palmer hardened her heart and pushed back her rising panic. She reached for her grandmother's hand. It was cold.

Chapter Thirty-Two

Present Day (2022)

Palmer was being wheeled through the hospital again. Only this time Hartman was driving and she was wearing pants. A little red foil balloon shaped like a heart that said 'Get Well Soon' was attached to the wheelchair. It bounced along in the air above her.

Dr. Walters had come by this morning to tell Palmer that she was cleared to leave. Dr. Walters had said she was confident Palmer's memories would continue to return to her over the next couple of weeks, maybe less, maybe more. Dr. Walters had sent her home with pain medicine for her headache and instructed her to take it easy. She had also made Palmer an appointment to follow up with her on Monday. Palmer nodded and agreed to everything.

Palmer was nervous about going home with Hartman but she knew that's what she needed to do. She found out that her parents were staying at Abuela's old house. When Abuela had died she left it to Palmer's mother. Emilia had never gotten rid of it and instead rented it out sometimes as an Airbnb. Palmer had been half tempted to ask her parents to stay with her and Hartman for a few nights but she had decided against it. Dr. Walters mentioned several times that it was best to get her life back to normal in order to get her memories back faster.

Palmer could hear Hartman and Dr. Walters talking behind her as Hartman pushed her through the maze of hallways.

"Rest and hydration. She doesn't need to take the prescription unless the headaches get bad. Tylenol should be fine but I want you to have those other ones just in case. I'm just a phone call or text away if something changes or she needs anything," Dr. Walters said.

Palmer was so full of nerves that she hardly cared that they were talking about her like she wasn't even there. Dr. Walters continued to give Hartman instructions.

"You still have the card for that detective?"

"Yes," Hartman replied.

"Good, I think he'll give you a couple more days of peace but I'm sure he'll come and hunt you down soon. If she remembers anything about the accident —"

"I'll call them ASAP," Hartman interrupted.

Dr. Walters smiled at him and squeezed his shoulder before turning to Palmer.

"Rest my dear. And try not to worry. It'll come back to you when you're good and ready," she said.

"Thank you for everything," Palmer said with a weak smile. "Really."

Dr. Walters genuinely smiled back. "You're so welcome dear. Call me if you need anything."

Palmer wondered absently what she would call her with. Palmer didn't have a phone. Palmer looked up at Hartman to ask.

"Do I have a cell phone?"

Hartman frowned. "Yeah, but the cops took it. I'm sure they will give it back eventually or we'll get you a new one."

Palmer just nodded her head and watched as Dr. Walters and Hartman hugged before Hartman wheeled Palmer out of the front doors and toward the parking lot.

"You guys are friends?" Palmer asked.

"Yeah, we've worked together for a long time."

"You seem close?" Palmer wasn't sure why she was asking. It wasn't like she was jealous. How could she be jealous over a man she didn't even know? Still, she wondered.

Hartman raised his eyebrows in surprise, then spoke.

"When I met her she was going through a hard time. A really hard time. Her kid had passed away a few years before. That's actually why she became a doctor."

The idea of the kind and caring Dr. Walters losing a child made Palmer unbelievably sad.

"Oh my God. That's terrible," Palmer said under her breath. "What happened?"

"SIDS," Hartman replied. He must have understood Palmer's silence as confusion because he continued. "Sudden Infant Death Syndrome. Sometimes little babies just go to sleep and they don't wake up. It's sad but it happens. There's no reason, no one's fault."

Palmer breathed deeply. That was the saddest thing she had ever heard.

"She and her husband couldn't get through it. They divorced and she went to medical school. She's a Neurologist now. She saves lives every day."

They were pulling up to an enormous black pickup now. "Oh, this is us," he said after realizing she wouldn't be able to recognize their car.

"Jeez. Compensating for something?" Palmer said laughing. She hoped he would take the joke well. She was right. Hartman laughed heartily.

"This is YOUR truck, Palmer," he said mid chuckle.

Palmer gaped at him.

"This giant monstrosity is mine?"

"In your defense. I sent you to the car dealership with explicit instructions to not get something small and therefore unsafe. I think this was your way of messing with me. You think I can be —" he paused, "a little overprotective?"

"So this was my way of making a joke?" Palmer said, gesturing to the ridiculously large pick-up truck.

"Yeah. I think you were trying to prove a point."

Palmer paused and then shrugged. "That actually sounds about right."

Before Palmer could protest Hartman was lifting her out of the chair and setting her into the passenger side seat. Palmer went rigid and tried to lean away from him but he hardly noticed. He leaned over her and belted her in before closing the door and walking the wheelchair back to the entrance.

Palmer sat in silence for a moment. Her nerves were coming back. Her stomach felt a little queasy. She was about to go 'home' with her 'husband'. But she didn't know where or what this 'home' looked like. And she barely knew her 'husband'.

Hartman eventually came back, opened the driver-side door, and hopped in. Turning the ignition he said, "Alrighty, here we go." The truck roared to life, making an obnoxiously loud noise. Palmer laughed. Hartman turned to her with a smile before he spoke again. "I think the real joke is on you. It's actually a really, really safe vehicle so

—," he trailed off. Their laughter died down and Palmer had a sudden idea.

"Hey, on the way home can we make a pit stop?"

"Yeah, sure?" Hartman responded. "Where too?"

"Actually, I just realized it might not be on the way. I have no idea where home is." Palmer said, looking at her feet.

"Then we'll take a detour. Where are we going?"

Palmer rubbed her lips together considering if she really wanted to do this.

"The cemetery?"

Chapter Thirty-Three

The Casket (2013)

Palmer stood in front of her childhood bedroom mirror and looked down at herself. She hated wearing black. Somehow it always seemed to bring out her paleness. She did a full body sweep and frowned.

"Yup. I look like a character from Sweeney Todd," Palmer grumbled to herself. She reached behind her and tried to zip up the back of her dress. It was difficult. She had managed to get the zipper halfway up but then her arms wouldn't bend anymore. She tried a different angle, going from the top. His fingers could barely touch the zipper handle. She readjusted and tried to grasp it again from yet another angle. All the while she held her breath. The back of her hair was getting in the way of her fingers and the front of her hair was getting in her eyes. The dress was tight and itchy. And she couldn't get the stupid thing zipped no matter what she did.

"UGH!" Palmer let out a loud frustrated sound and straightened. She clenched her fists to try and calm them. The urge to rip the dress off of her body was very strong. She looked down at her fists through tear-heavy eyes and realized they were shaking. Then the tears started to flow down her cheeks.

Today was Abuela's funeral. It had been five days since Palmer found her seemingly asleep in her chair. After realizing that Abuela was gone Palmer had tucked the blanket in around Abuela's lap and took Abuela's cup of tea to the sink. She washed out the cup and placed it in the drying rack. She went back upstairs to get her phone and she called her mother. Her mother had instructed Palmer to sit on the front porch and she would be there in just a moment. So Palmer had calmly put on her muddy boots and sat on the front steps. It could have only taken her mother a couple of minutes to run from her parent's house to Abuela's but it felt like an eternity. Palmer absently had wondered why she was so calm. Her favorite person in the whole world was dead, her corpse was in the house right behind her. This must be what shock is like, Palmer thought to herself.

Everything after that had been a bit of a blur. Palmer's mother had come sprinting up to the house. Then Palmer's father's truck pulled up. Then some police and an ambulance. Then a van from the funeral home. Palmer had sat on the front porch the entire time, her ears were ringing. At some point, her brother Shawn had come and sat next to her. Neither of them spoke. Palmer watched as a gurney moved past her, down the steps, and into the van with her grandmother's covered body on top. The people from the funeral home slammed the doors to the back of the van and Palmer flinched.

Everything since that day had been depressing and tense. Palmer's house was full of relatives, all of them telling stories of Abuela and pulling out pictures of her. Spring break was over but Palmer had stayed. She was needed here for now. She would go back after the funeral when she knew her mother was ok. She was ahead on all of her class assignments anyway.

Palmer still stood shaking in front of the mirror, tears running down her cheeks in black steaks. She wiped at her cheeks angrily and moved to her old vanity. She pulled out some waterproof mascara but it had dried with age. All of her good makeup was at home in the house she rented with friends near the university. She had packed lightly, thinking she would only be here for spring break. Frustrated she threw the tube of mascara back into the drawer with more force than was necessary.

Palmer walked down the hall and to her parent's bedroom. She could hear how crowded the house was on the first floor already. She opened her mother's vanity and searched for waterproof mascara. Finally, she found it and applied it using her mother's mirror. Then she pulled out her phone and checked it. There were no notifications.

The night after Abuela had died, after the shock had started to wear off, Palmer had messaged Jessica on Facebook asking her to call her from the resort as soon as she could. Jessica called less than ten minutes later. Jessica had found an early flight home and came over immediately. Jessica had gone back to school once break was over but only because Palmer had sworn up and down that she would be fine. Jessica had promised she would be back for the funeral today.

Palmer had stared at her phone for days trying to figure out if she should call Calum. Finally, the day after Jessica had left she gave in. She tried calling him twice but he didn't pick up. Then she texted him.

Abuela died. Can you call me? I need you.

He didn't respond. So the next day she called again. Still no answer, so she texted him again.

Calum. Please pick up. Can we talk?

Again, nothing. She texted him again yesterday.
The funeral is tomorrow. Please come.
Then last night, feeling desperate she typed.
I miss you.

Palmer looked at her phone now, but still no response. She had wondered if maybe he lost his phone or he got a new one. But he had an iPhone just like her and she could see that all of the messages had been delivered. Palmer sighed and slipped her phone back into her dress pocket. She blinked back more tears. Today was going to suck.

A few hours later Palmer sat in a cushioned chair at the back of the funeral home viewing room. Apparently the immediate family would all meet here first so that they could be together and look at Abuela's remains. Then they would all load up in limos and be driven to the church where the service would be held. Palmer felt like she might be sick. She stared absently at the coffin sitting just twenty feet in front of her. It was propped open but she couldn't see inside from this far.

Palmer had watched as several mourning family members had made their way up to the casket and peered inside. Many of them had walked up clutching tissues and holding onto one another. Some had merely looked, nodded, and walked on. Palmer had overheard several tias discuss how good she looked and how Emilia had picked the best outfit for her. No one paid Palmer any mind.

Palmer knew she would need to muster up her courage and go up soon. She wasn't sure why she was glued to her seat. She didn't know why the idea of looking at her grandmother in this state was causing her so much anxiety. Maybe it was the finality of it. Once she looked they would move on to the funeral portion of the day, then the burial, then the dinner, then she would go to bed and when she woke up Abuela would still be dead. Life would go on, but Abuela would not.

Palmer's mind was reeling, but finally, she had a thought that gave her courage. What was in that box at the end of the aisle wasn't Abuela at all. Abuela had moved on to the next place. Holding onto that knowledge Palmer took a deep breath and stood. Slowly she walked up to the casket. Everyone had their turn to look and now they were milling about crying and talking in low voices far away from the coffin.

As Palmer walked she made a mental note to request she be cremated. She did not want her closest family looking at her embalmed body like some kind of spectacle. No, she thought. She would much rather they look upon a pretty little vase that held her ashes instead.

Palmer approached the casket finally. There were two large vases of assorted flowers on either side of the box. Their sweet smell permeated the air and made Palmer even more nauseous. Palmer could see the white satin that lined the inside of the coffin first. Then she saw her grandmother's tiny feet.

Palmer's mother had chosen some sensible black heels for her grandmother's corpse to wear today. Palmer noted that someone had put pantyhose on Abuela. Then Palmer's eyes trailed up and saw that Abuela wore a purple floral skirt suit. She had never seen her grandmother wear that outfit before, Palmer wondered if it was new. Abuela wore a cream shirt under the suit and on her neck was a silver necklace with a cross. Under the harsh neon lights of the funeral home, the little diamond in the middle of the cross glittered. Palmer's eyes continued to trail up Abuela's little frame until she finally reached her face.

It wasn't Abuela's face at all. Palmer's heart leaped up into her throat. Instead of Abuela's familiar comforting face, there was a young woman. The woman's eyes were closed and her dark lashes were long, nearly touching her cheeks. She had dark, almost black hair that hung thickly on either side of her thin shoulders. She had rosy cheeks and full glossy lips. She was lovely, but then she started to change. The women's skin started to become paler and started to sag. It almost looked like she was melting at first. The skin around her eyes darkened and her lips pulled back into a sneer. The woman's hair started to thin and fall apart, becoming dry and brittle. The longer Palmer stared the more terrifying she appeared. One second the face was soft and lovely, the next it was the face of a rotting corpse.

Palmer wanted to scream but she was frozen to the spot. Just then the eyes of the monstrous face opened and looked right at her. Palmer blinked and the face changed again. No longer was it the strange woman with the rotting face. It was Palmer. Her own green eyes stared back at her from inside the coffin. Palmer made eye contact with herself. The eyes of her doppelganger lying in the coffin widened in what appeared to be fear. Palmer's hands were shaking and she squeezed her eyes shut.

Palmer swallowed and eventually opened her eyes again. This time it was only Abuela. She looked exactly how Palmer had expected her to look. Palmer swiveled her head from side to side and quickly looked at the groups of people in the room. She prayed nobody had witnessed her momentary lapse in sanity. They all faced away from her, deep in conversation, apparently oblivious to what had just happened.

Palmer turned to her grandmother's body again. Yup. Still her grandmother. Abuela looked like herself but also she didn't. It was her grandmother's wrinkly, worn face but someone had put too many layers of makeup on it. Her skin wasn't quite the right shade, neither were her lips. Palmer had gone to Las Vegas once with her mother and they had visited Madame Tussauds Wax Museum. Palmer thought Abuela looked a little bit like the wax statues. Almost too perfect in some places but not quite right in others.

Palmer felt a hand on her shoulder and she flinched hard. A little gasp escaped her mouth.

"Honey, you ok?" Palmer's mother asked.

"Yes, I'm sorry," Palmer replied.

Emilia Lane put her arm around her daughter's waist and they both looked at Abuela's body.

"It's going to be ok kiddo," Emilia said between tears.

"I'm so sorry Mom," Palmer said and hugged her mother.

The two women stayed like that for some time until finally Chuck came up and told them it was time to load up into the limos. Emilia and Palmer squeezed each other and started to walk back down the aisle between the chairs. Palmer turned back once to look at Abuela. Yes. It was still Abuela. Palmer took a reassuring breath and continued to put one foot in front of the other.

It had been the longest day Palmer had ever experienced. Everyone kept commenting that the funeral was 'lovely', but to Palmer, it had felt terrible. The sound of annoying sniffling was only drowned out by the deafening sound of the church pipe organ in the back. After the service, the immediate family loaded into the limos while the rest of the church loaded into their cars. Everyone followed the hearse to the cemetery where they placed flowers on Abuela's casket and watched as she was lowered into the ground. Palmer had stood staring into the six-foot-deep hole until nearly everyone had cleared out and her parents had come and ushered her to the limo.

Now Palmer sat alone in the porch swing on her parent's front deck. The windows to the house were open and she could hear the bustle of the funeral reception her parents were hosting. The voices of the funeral goers trailed out to her and she listened to stories of her grandmother.

Jessica had left a little while ago. She had come to the funeral with her parents, Palmer had seen them sitting in the back of the church. They had even come to the reception. Palmer had told Jessica she was fine and wanted to be alone. Jessica had hugged her tightly and told her to text her later. Palmer had meant what she said. She needed some time to process.

Palmer rocked the porch swing lightly with both of her feet. It was tucked back far enough to the right of the house that most people didn't notice her as they left. Every once in a while someone would notice her and she would casually wave them off. A few close family members had stopped to kiss her on her cheek as they left, they would sometimes give her shoulder a little squeeze. No one had lingered too long or tried to make conversation about her grandmother with her. Maybe there was something in her face or posture that elicited her need to be alone right now.

The majority of people had finally left. The house was much quieter now. Palmer would need to go inside soon to start helping her mother and do what was left of the dishes. No doubt Palmer's tias had helped do most of them but she was sure there was some sort of final tidying up that her mother would need help with. Palmer closed her eyes and took a deep breath of the cold spring air. Her arms were crossed and she tried to rub the goosebumps off of her arms.

Just as Palmer was about to stand up to go inside she had the familiar sense that she wasn't alone. Palmer opened her eyes and saw Calum standing with his hands in his pockets at the bottom of the porch steps. He was looking right at her but he hadn't come closer. He stood on the sidewalk like there was some kind of invisible forcefield around the house he couldn't cross.

For a few awkward moments, Palmer and Calum stayed like that. Palmer sitting on the porch swing, and Calum standing on the sidewalk. Both of them were staring at each other from twenty feet away. Palmer wasn't sure what she should be feeling right now. In fact, she wasn't sure what she was supposed to be feeling all day. Was she sad, depressed, angry, irritated or upset? She had mostly just felt numb. Calum showed no emotion on his face, but he never broke eye contact.

Palmer stood slowly and walked across the porch. She made her way down the steps until there was only one left, putting her face to face with Calum. Neither of them spoke. Palmer wasn't sure what she would even say. There was so much hanging between them. It was Palmer who spoke first.

"What are you doing here?" her voice was raspy. The words sounded more harsh than she had meant them to. Calum flinched.

"You texted me," Calum whispered.

"That was days ago," Palmer responded.

Calum sighed and ran his hands through his hair. "I know, I'm sorry."

"You're always sorry Calum."

Calum clenched his jaw and looked like he wanted to say something but decided better of it.

Palmer repeated her earlier question, "What are you doing here?"

"You said you needed me," he said.

"I've called you a dozen times. I left you voicemails. I texted you," Palmer threw her hands up in exasperation.

Calum closed his eyes and nodded. "I know, I'm —"

"Sorry?" Palmer said loudly, interrupting him.

Calum clenched his jaw again.

"Oh my fucking God Calum. Say something better. WHERE WERE YOU?" Tears were threatening to fall from Palmer's cheeks.

Calum said nothing.

"Make it make sense Cal. Make an excuse that makes sense. Did you lose your phone? Were you out of the country? You're in witness protection? You got possessed by a demon? You fell down a well? Something Calum. Anything. Give me something here." The tears had started to spill onto her cheeks. Her voice sounded panicky and shrill.

Calum said nothing. He looked at her pleadingly, but no excuses came. Finally, he spoke.

"I'm here now."

Palmer laughed angrily. "Holy shit Cal," she said between angry sobs. Palmer wiped at the tears under her eyes with both of her thumbs. "The funeral is over. You're too late."

"Palmer," Calum started to speak but Palmer interrupted him.

"Didn't you hear me?" she said, shaking her head. "It's too late." Palmer emphasized each word. As the words left her mouth she realized just how much she meant it. No amount of Grade-A Calum bullshit would get him out of this. No amount of flattery or schmoozing. He wouldn't be able to spin this into something they could laugh about later. He had fucked up over, and over, and over. Palmer no longer had the energy to accept the bare minimum he would offer.

Palmer watched as the realization hit him. She saw him realize that he wasn't just too late for the funeral, but too late to fix what he had broken. Palmer turned and took a step up the stairs only to be jerked back by her arm. Calum was gripping it tight, too tight. She could feel his fingertips on her bones. His nails were digging into her pale flesh, making little red half-moon indents.

"Don't turn away from me," Calum growled. His eyes were blazing with anger and his jaw was clenched so hard she could see the veins pulse in his neck. He looked crazy. Palmer tried to yank her arm away but she was unsuccessful.

"Cal, you're hurting me," Palmer tried to speak calmly. When they were younger Palmer's brother Shawn had stumbled too close to a nest of rattlesnakes on a hike. Shawn had frozen in fear. Palmer remembered having to give Shawn instructions in a low calm voice so that he wouldn't panic but also so the rattlesnakes wouldn't strike. She was using that voice now. "Let go please," Palmer said.

Calum's grip loosened but not enough for Palmer to pull free. Palmer's heart rate was escalating. She nervously glanced back at her parent's house but Calum jerked her arm.

"Look at me." Calum commanded her. Palmer had never seen him look like this in all the years she had known him. The crazed and pissed-off look from before was gone. It had been replaced by a glazed-over indifferent look. Palmer made eye contact with Cal then. His gray eyes had always seemed dreamy and mysterious to her before. But now they seemed empty and cold. Palmer calmed her mind and willed herself to speak firmly.

"Calum. Please let go of my arm," Palmer said evenly. She started to gently pull her arm out of his grip. Calum glanced down at where Palmer removed her arm with vacant eyes. He didn't try to stop her.

Palmer eventually freed her arm and rubbed it with her other hand. Small red smears moved where her hand rubbed. He had broken the skin just barely. Calum stared at the blood with zero emotion. Then Palmer watched as the realization of what he had done hit him. Shock overtook his face. His eyes widened and his mouth popped open. He looked down at his hands and froze, staring at them like they weren't attached to him.

Palmer kept her breathing even and started to walk backward up the steps. He didn't move an inch. When she made it to the porch she turned and faced the door. She walked at a normal pace to the door and once she was inside she closed the door. Palmer locked the door and moved to look out the parlor window that looked out onto the porch. She pushed the curtain back just a bit.

Calum was still standing exactly where she had left him. His fists were now clenched tightly at his sides and he stared at the spot where she had stood earlier. His hands were shaking slightly. Palmer backed away from the window and stumbled into an umbrella stand. The stand along with all of its umbrellas clattered to the ground and Palmer scrambled to pick them up as fast as possible. Once everything was set to right Palmer took a deep breath and put her hand on her chest to calm her heart. She pushed her hair out of her face and slowly walked back to the window. She pushed the curtain back again to see what Calum was doing now. He was gone.

Palmer pushed the curtain back further and looked out all over the porch and yard. Nothing. She even went to the peephole and looked out. Still nothing. He had disappeared. Palmer pulled her phone out of her pocket. No notifications. Palmer backed away from the door and spoke out loud to herself.

"What. The Fuck."

Chapter Thirty-Four

Present Day (2022)

Palmer sat silently in the passenger side of her giant truck while Hartman drove. Hartman apparently wasn't the type of man who felt the need to fill silence with idle chatter. He seemed perfectly content sitting in the quiet with her. At first, the silence made Palmer feel a little awkward. She knew it wasn't fair to compare Hartman and Calum but she couldn't help it. Calum was never very good at embracing silence. Sure he knew when to shut up if he needed to but he usually found something to talk about constantly. He never would have been able to stand the silence for this long. Especially if the moment felt awkward in any way. Not Hartman though. In fact, he didn't seem like he felt like this ride was awkward at all. Palmer thought that maybe it was just her. After a while, she started to feel comfortable in the silence too.

Palmer watched out the window as her hometown flew by. So many things have changed, she thought to herself. There was a second grocery store north of town. That was good, maybe the main one wouldn't be so crowded now. The parking meters had been painted a dark green and she thought it looked really nice. There were a few new restaurants downtown that looked really interesting. Hartman pointed out a little shop nestled between a sporting goods store and a coffee place.

"That right there is your store," he said. Hartman slowed down a bit to let her peer at the storefront.

It had big windows that displayed a bunch of funky antiques. The right window had a cute wooden table and chairs painted mint green set up with a tea set. On the chairs were a couple of handmade Raggedy Anns. There was a fresh bouquet of flowers in the middle of the table and doilies set under the tea cups. There was a pink and purple Persian rug underneath the display and twinkling lights everywhere. In the window to the left of the large oak door was a display of bookshelves absolutely filled with old books, records, picture frames, and 'nic-nacs'. More twinkling lights glittered from between the shelves. On the front of the door, a sign was flipped to say 'closed'. Above the door, there was a large sign in big loopy letters that spelled out 'Tiffany's Epiphanies'.

Palmer thought the shop was lovely and she craned her neck to look a little more as they passed it.

"Do you want me to stop? I can turn around and we can go check it out?" Hartman offered.

"Not today, it's lovely though. Maybe tomorrow," Palmer sighed. "Who's Tiffany?" she asked. Hartman smiled from ear to ear.

"Tiffany Valentine," he said, still smiling like he was in on some inside joke. Palmer scrunched her nose and thought for a moment. She was trying to figure out where she knew that name from. When it finally hit her she smiled as well.

"The Bride of Chucky?" Palmer asked. It was one of her favorite movies.

"When we opened the shop you were too self-conscious to include your name in the name of the store. When we first met you used a lot of aliases, and you always used the names of female horror movie characters. You came up with 'Tiffany's Epiphanies' as kind of a joke but it stuck. Besides, I think you like that most people don't even know it's your shop. You like the anonymity. You find all of the inventory and sometimes you come in to organize the displays but Susan mostly runs it."

Palmer let everything he told her sink in. "Why was I using a lot of aliases when I first met you?" she asked.

"You were sneaking around, doing research. Mostly though I think you did it to be funny," he said smiling again.

"What was I researching?" Palmer asked.

Hartman took a wide turn and the gates of the town cemetery came into view. "You were looking into a cold case of a missing relative back then."

Palmer's eyes widened slightly. Was he talking about her grandmother's lost sister? Palmer was trying to decide what to ask next when the cemetery gates opened before the truck. They must have a motion sensor. Once the gate was open all the way they drove through and Hartman navigated his way through the maze of pavement. He must have known exactly where Abuela was buried because he didn't have to check with Palmer. After a couple more minutes he pulled to the side of the road and parked.

Hartman stepped out of the truck and walked around to Palmer's side. She had started to open her own door to let herself out but Hartman shook his head at her sternly through her window.

"Jeez, old-fashioned much?" Palmer said as Hartman opened her door for her and helped her step out. He only shook his head in amusement. The height from the truck steps to the concrete was a lot bigger than Palmer had originally thought and she nearly stumbled but Hatman caught her. Hartman's touch still made Palmer feel uncomfortable even though their conversations were getting less and less awkward every minute.

"Easy does it," Hartman said.

"This truck is stupid," Palmer replied with a huff. Once she was on the ground she glared up at it and Hartman chuckled. Setting herself to rights Palmer looked around her. The sky was still overcast. The air was frigid and there were patches of snow on the grass. Some of the headstones in shadier areas, like under trees, had a bit of snow built up on their tops. She knew already that walking through the grass would get her feet wet but she didn't care.

Palmer turned to Hartman. "Can you, you — stay here maybe? I think I want to do this alone."

Hartman looked hesitant. He didn't look like he wanted to leave Palmer alone but still wanted to respect her wishes. Finally, he nodded. Palmer gave him a reassuring smile and headed off in the direction she knew Abuela was. Palmer turned back once to see Hartman leaning against the truck and staring at her. She gave him a little wave hoping it would help his anxiety.

Palmer crunched through dead grass, passing headstone after headstone. The plaques that were shaded by trees had a few inches of snow frozen to the stop. The cemetery was large even though their town was fairly small. This was mostly due to the town's age. Some of the headstones in the very back of the cemetery dated back to the early nineteen hundreds. The names and dates of death of the people beneath them were barely visible anymore.

Palmer was nearly fifty feet away from Hartman and the truck now, the trees were getting thicker and the grass had a small dusting of still-frozen snow. This part of the cemetery was made up of mostly her older deceased family members from her mother's side. The name Rivera was on pretty much every headstone. Finally, she stopped in front of her grandmother's grave.

Abuela had been laid to rest next to her husband. They even shared a headstone. Abuela's husband had died of a heart attack before Palmer was even born. Palmer had no memories of her grandfather, Abuelo. But he was spoken about often and lovingly. Emilia had taken Palmer to this very spot on numerous occasions to visit. When Abuelo died and they needed to buy a headstone, Abuela had decided to get a double headstone and put her name on it too. Even though she was still very much alive at the time.

Palmer could still remember coming to visit her grandfather's grave as a child but being deeply disturbed by the fact that next to his name was Abuela's name and her birthday. The only thing not engraved was the day of her death. Palmer had always felt that this was a little bit off-putting. Like it was a reminder, a promise, that one day Abuela would be here too. She hadn't liked it at all.

Now Palmer looked down at the double headstone. It was lovely. It was dark gray and glossy. There was a picture of a cross with flowers draped over it engraved into the stone. But this time, the day Abuela had died was etched into the previously blank spot. The finality of that carved date hit Palmer hard. She knelt down, the knees of her sweatpants becoming instantly wet but she didn't care.

Palmer used her index finger to feel the indent of her grandmother's name. Maria Rivera. Then she bowed her head and said a silent prayer. When she was done Palmer took a deep breath, wiped at her wet eyes, and stood. As soon as she stood up a chill crept up her spine. She could feel someone watching her. She was well acquainted with the feeling.

Palmer glanced back at the pickup and could see Hartman still leaning against the truck watching her like a hawk. Palmer shook her head and spoke to herself.

"Jeez, that guy is wound up tight," she said under her breath, jokingly. Palmer smiled tightly and gave Hartman the thumbs up. Hartman, obviously taking the hint, smiled back with a self-deprecating shrug and took out his phone. He was swiping through it when Palmer turned back to the headstone. Before her eyes landed fully on the headstone she thought she caught sight of something moving just over the ridge.

Palmer placed her hand on her forehead to try and block out some of the sun in order to see better. She was scanning the ridge of trees just past the fence to the cemetery. As her eyes searched a man stepped out from behind a tree. He was barely visible from this distance, especially with the shadow of the trees but Palmer could see him clearly. He was tall and lean, his hands were in his pockets and he stared at her unabashedly. It was Calum.

Palmer stood frozen to the spot. Nervously, Palmer looked back toward the truck. Hartman was still there but he was now flipping through his phone because she had made him feel overbearing. Palmer turned back. Calum was still looming in the distance.

Calum. The boy she had loved. She still couldn't remember everything, but she remembered enough. Palmer watched as he took a step toward her. She took a step back instinctually. Calum paused and narrowed his eyes at her. Palmer had a thought. Maybe she didn't know Hartman, but maybe she didn't really know Calum either. Palmer had thought she knew Calum better than she even knew herself. But that wasn't true. Calum was just as much a stranger to her as the man behind her.

Mustering all of her resolve Palmer slowly turned her back to Calum and walked deliberately back to the truck. To Hartman.

Chapter Thirty-Five

The Teeth (2015)

It had been two years since Abuela died. Two years since Palmer and Calum ended things. She hadn't even seen him since then. He had disappeared from her life entirely. No texts, no calls, no running into each other, nothing. He had deleted all social media and completely dropped off the face of the earth.

Additionally, the woman who haunted Palmer had also disappeared. Along with all the creepy occurrences that usually came with her. The only thing that lingered was the nightmare, but even that had dissipated. She only had it every once in a while now.

After Abuela's death and Calum's abrupt exit from her life, Palmer threw herself into her school. She studied hard and relentlessly. Even Jessica's nagging couldn't get her to lighten up that last year of college. After graduation, Palmer got a job as a bookkeeper for the local newspaper in her hometown. Chuck and Emilia were ecstatic when she asked if she could move back home.

Palmer could probably afford to get an apartment on her new salary but she had a plan. Or rather, a start to a plan. She would save up as much money as possible and eventually, she would open up her own business. Or invest in one. She wasn't sure what type of business yet but it would be local and it would be hers.

Palmer had a job and a plan. Everything was running smoothly. The only issue had been that she had too much time on her hands. She had too much time to think about how much she missed Abuela. Too much time to think about Calum. She needed a project. Something to fill up the empty space in her brain so it didn't fill itself up with unwanted thoughts.

A few months after she started her new job Palmer was going through old newspaper clippings at work when she stumbled across an article about a missing girl from 1957. Gabriela Rivera. Abuela's missing sister, Palmer's great aunt. Palmer's side project spiraled out from there. Over the next year, Palmer made it her personal mission to solve the cold case. Maybe she did it to distract herself from her grief but part of her thought she needed to solve the case for her grandmother. Abuela had been absolutely certain that Gabriela had not just run away. Her family had been so sure that they had even given her a tombstone to mourn her. A part of Palmer felt like she owed it to Abuela. Another part of her, a part of her buried deep, wondered if Gabriela could be the woman Palmer was cursed with seeing. The reason for all the strange things that happened to her.

Palmer had found every newspaper article the local newspaper had ever printed about Gabriela's disappearance. Palmer had detailed notes about the police officers involved in the investigation, the areas where volunteers had searched, the people who had been questioned, etc. One of the only clues Abuela had left her regarding Gabriella's disappearance was that she was maybe seeing a man named 'Nick'. Abuela had said that Gabriella had written the name multiple times in a notebook but no one in the family knew a Nick. Palmer had googled men named Nick who had lived in this town around that time but it had resulted in pretty much nothing. At one point she had called the local retirement homes and enquired about all the men named Nick. Again, nothing. For an entire year, Palmer's free time had been filled with researching. There wasn't much. But she had been relentless in finding everything she could.

Now Palmer sat in front of her car outside of a dentist's office shuffling through a thick accordion binder of paperwork. She was trying to settle her nerves and get her story straight. She would need to be confident and straightforward in order to get the information she needed. Palmer was trying to track down Gabriela Rivera's dental records.

Through Palmer's research, she determined that her aunt's case was never actually treated like a real investigation since there was no evidence of a crime. The police had conducted a very minimal inspection into what could have happened to her. There was no mention of the name Nick in any of the news articles. Most of the major efforts in looking for her came from her family. Palmer had left several messages for the sheriff's department but they hadn't returned her calls. However, the police receptionist informed her that the case was still open.

Palmer hoped that by obtaining Gabriela's dental records she could bring them to the police, after she made copies of course, and they could compare them to the dental records of unidentified bodies of women who had been found around that time. Based on the nonchalant statements the sheriff made to reporters for the paper at that time, Palmer felt fairly confident that they had not gone through the trouble of obtaining Gabriela's dental records.

The town had a notoriously low crime rate, especially in the 50's, so there had of course been no Jane Does found at that time. But Palmer had looked into unidentified bodies in neighboring counties during that time period anyway. She had been able to find a few in Colorado during that time and a few more in northern New Mexico. She had compiled a list of Jane Does and as soon as she had Gabriela's dental records she would present everything to the sheriff's department. Or at least, if they ever agreed to meet with her.

Palmer adjusted the collar of her black blazer, smoothed out her scarlet sundress, and adjusted her necklace before walking up the steps of the office. Finding dental records that were nearly sixty years old was a long shot. Palmer was well aware. There were currently a handful of dentists in town and none of them were old enough to have remembered seeing her aunt. But Palmer had been prepared to call every single one of them to see if they would be willing to check old records.

Palmer, however, had gotten very lucky. After sorting through old local yellow pages Palmer had discovered that in the 1950's there had actually only been one practicing dentist in town. His office had been at this location. Palmer tried not to get her hopes up but it was difficult. This was the first time she was actually investigating and not just obsessing over news articles in the newspaper archives.

Palmer pushed the doors open to the dentist's office and was greeted with a rush of cool air. Palmer walked directly into a relaxing, chic waiting area. A large ornamental fan hung from the ceiling and sent a light breeze throughout the room. The floors were dark hardwood. In the middle of the area was a cool-tone Persian rug and comfortable gray cushioned chairs lined the wall. At the far end of the waiting room was a built-in desk with a blonde receptionist. To the left of the reception desk was a long hallway that Palmer assumed led to the patient rooms.

The waiting room was empty aside from Palmer and the receptionist smiled at Palmer welcomingly.

"Hi! How can I help you?" the woman asked brightly from behind the counter. Palmer straightened and tried to walk up to the desk with confidence.

"Yes! Hi, I'm here to try and get hold of some dental records?" Palmer said, trying to match the woman's tone.

"Of course, I'd be happy to help you with that. What is your name and date of birth?"

Palmer paused. "Oh! No, not my dental records. I'm actually trying to get hold of the dental records for a relative?"

"I see, are you the legal guardian of the relative?" the woman asked.

"No," Palmer responded. She had known this would be a bit tricky, she was trying not to lose any of her resolve. "It's kind of a long story. I need to get the dental records for my great aunt."

"I see — well unfortunately I can't legally give out medical information unless it is your own medical information or if it is the medical information to someone who you have legal guardianship over. It's called HIPPA. I'm sorry," the woman seemed a bit uncomfortable but genuinely sorry she couldn't help.

Palmer's confidence was starting to deflate. She took a deep breath before speaking again. "Look, I totally get it. It's just, that this is kind of a unique situation. It's complicated but they would be really old records. Like, maybe around fifty years old," Palmer was leaning closer to the receptionist, trying to plead with her.

The receptionist's eyebrows shot up in surprise. "Oh, well Dr. Roth hasn't been practicing that long, are you sure your aunt was seen by him?"

"Actually no, I think she may have been seen by the dentist who used to practice out of this building before him. I think the practice was maybe called something else back then," Palmer could tell by the woman's expression that she thought Palmer was nuts.

"Um..." the receptionist was clearly trying to figure out what to say next. Before she could speak a large man came out of the first room down the hall. He was massive. He wore navy scrubs and crisp white shoes. Over the scrubs, he wore a white lab coat. He walked behind the counter and cleared his throat before speaking.

"I'm sorry to interrupt, I'm Dr. Roth. You can hear just about everything in this office, especially when it's this quiet. You're trying to get hold of old records?" he asked. His voice was deep and smooth. The receptionist looked up at the dentist in surprise but moved her chair back to give him room.

"Uh, yeah," Palmer said, swiping at her hair. She was trying to get her bearings again after his interruption. "It's complicated. But I'm trying to get hold of my great aunt's dental records. I think she was seen by the doctor who used to practice here. The records would be old. Maybe from the 1950's."

Dr. Roth looked at her sternly but with interest. "Well, the dentist who practiced out of this building before me was actually my father, Dr. Klaus Roth. He was old school and did mostly paper charting."

"I'm not sure what you mean by paper charting. Like, as opposed to..."

"We use EHRs now. Electronic Health Records. Everything is computerized now. It's faster and more efficient. But before 2009 it wasn't mandatory and a lot of older doctors were still recording everything on paper and storing it all in boxes," he must have noticed the hope in Palmer's eyes because he shook his head before speaking again. "All of this doesn't really matter though because Vanessa was right," he gestured to the receptionist. "We can't give out any medical information unless it's your own medical information or medical information for someone you are the legal guardian of. And even then you have to have the paperwork that shows you are the guardian."

Palmer rubbed her lips together, thinking. "What if the person is deceased?"

Dr. Roth's handsome face lit up with shock. "Oh?" he paused. "You need the dental records for your dead aunt?"

Palmer could tell that she was not handling this encounter well at all. Every time she spoke she seemed to make things more and more confusing and complicated. She huffed. "Kind of? Like I said, it's a really long story and I'm not doing a very good job of explaining. I'm sorry." Palmer's skin was feeling hot and she wanted to get out of here but not before she got the information she needed.

Dr. Roth examined Palmer with a look. He must have seen something because he nodded his head and spoke a little more gently. "Why don't we go back to my office and you can try and explain a little bit better." He turned toward the secretary. "Vanessa, I still don't have any patients until one o'clock, right?"

Vanessa looked a little surprised. "Um, no sir."

Dr. Roth nodded again and gestured for Palmer to follow him. "Right this way," he said with that deep soothing voice. Palmer walked around the desk and down the hall. Dr. Roth stopped in front of the first door on the right, the door Palmer had seen him come out of. He waited for Palmer to walk in first.

The room was similar to the waiting room in the sense that it was covered in cool-toned decor. There was a plush rug on the hardwood floor that had a bluish hue and two pieces of abstract art hung on the opposite wall. Under the art was a dark wooden desk with a large, sleek computer. The desk was incredibly clean and organized, everything set 'just so'. On the right side of the desk was a small zen garden.

Hartman walked into the room behind Palmer and moved around her to pull out a chair for her to sit. Palmer sat awkwardly and tried not to fiddle with her hands. Dr. Roth moved to the other side of the desk and sat. Somehow he made the oversized desk look small.

"I'm sorry I don't think I caught your name earlier," Dr. Roth said smoothly.

Palmer panicked. Her earlier confidence in the car was starting to fade and she was feeling more than a little intimidated.

"Tangina," Palmer said before she could think. "Tangina Barrons." Palmer thrust out her hand to shake his a bit more forcefully than she had intended.

Dr. Roth smiled slightly and took her hand in his. His hands swallowed hers up completely. He released her hand, still smiling. "So, you're trying to get hold of old dental records for your deceased aunt? Is that about right?" he asked.

"Basically," Palmer replied.

"Can I ask why?"

Palmer chewed her lip and considered her words carefully. "She's actually not — 'confirmed' dead. She went missing over fifty years ago and they never found her. I was hoping to get her dental records so that I could ask the police to compare them to a list of Jane Does that I have. I know that sounds a little — well it sounds like a lot. I know," she finished.

Dr. Roth clasped his hands together on top of the desk and regarded Palmer carefully. "Wow. That IS a lot."

Palmer tried not to let her shoulders slump. She waited for him to speak first. Finally, he started again.

"Well —," he nodded his head to himself, considering. "Medical records are only protected until fifty years after someone has died. But that doesn't really help us here since she isn't actually considered dead. Right?"

Palmer nodded and he continued. "Anyway, that might not even be helpful at all since legally doctors are only required to keep medical records for ten years. Plus, my dad, Dr. Roth senior, passed away about five years ago."

"I'm so sorry for your loss," Palmer responded automatically. Palmer felt her heart deflate. All that research on Jane Does. For what?

"Thank you," he responded. Dr. Roth was deep in thought. "You might be in luck though, my dad was a bit of a hoarder. And I inherited all of it. It's possible he has old patient records in one of his old storage units or maybe he kept a record of where he put them." Dr. Roth pushed a sticky note and a pen toward Palmer. "Right down your phone number and I'll give you a call once I know anything."

Palmer wrote down the fake name she had given him as well as her cell phone number. Once she was done she pushed the sticky note back to Dr. Roth.

"Oh, why don't you write down your great aunt's name and date of birth too just in case," he pushed the sticky note back toward Palmer. Palmer wrote down Gabriella's information.

"Here, I'll walk you out." Dr. Roth stood and walked Palmer out and into the lobby. He opened the door for her to step outside and Palmer was greeted by the warm sun on her skin. She turned to him.

"Thank you, for hearing me out and for trying," she said thoughtfully.

"You're welcome, I'm sorry it's a little more complicated than you were hoping. I wish I had what you wanted."

Palmer smiled genuinely and put out her hand to shake his again. He took her hand and shook it gently. "I'll give you a call as soon as I can," he promised.

"Thank you, Dr. Roth," Palmer responded.

"Oh, please call me Hartman."

Palmer noticed that their hands had been clasped together for longer than appropriate. She carefully pulled her small delicate hand from his bear-sized one. "Thank you, Hartman," she amended. Then she carefully turned and walked down the steps of the office.

Hartman began to speak again. "Hey," he said, so Palmer turned around. "Don't you think since you know my full name now it's only fair that I know your's?" he asked.

Palmer froze and her mouth popped open.

"I was born in the 80's, I've seen Poltergeist a million times. Tangina Barrons? She was the medium with the funny glasses right?" he was grinning. In any other circumstance, she would have appreciated just how handsome this man was when he smiled. However, she was currently too embarrassed, having been caught in a lie.

Finally, Palmer composed herself enough to speak. "Palmer Lane," she said and smiled sheepishly. He was still giving her that huge smile from above the steps.

"Well. It's nice to meet you, Palmer Lane."

Palmer walked back to her car. She put her hand on the door handle but before she opened the door she decided to turn back around. The sun was bright so Palmer put her hand up to shield her eyes. Dr. Hartman Roth was still standing on the steps of his dentist's office watching her. Palmer smiled. Behind her, next to her own reflection in the driver-side window, was the reflection of another woman. A woman also staring at the same man.

Chapter Thirty-Six

Present Day (2022)

Palmer sat quietly as Hartman drove them toward the other side of town. Palmer gazed out of the window and watched as houses went by. Eventually, the houses stopped, replaced by snow-covered trees that got more and more crowded as they drove. Finally, they turned off onto a side road that led deeper into the forest. The road was paved and plowed so no snow stuck to it but all around Palmer was a winter wonderland. Palmer was so preoccupied with looking at the sun dancing off the snow that she almost missed the giant house that appeared before her.

It was a massive two-story log house, with a green roof covered in snow. There was a beautiful balcony held up by stone pillars that overlooked the forest. It had a big brick chimney and oversized windows with dark green trim that led to the balcony. The balcony ran all along the front and she could see that there was a firepit with a bunch of chairs surrounding it.

Hartman must have hit a button for the garage because Palmer watched one of the garage doors open. There were three double-car garage doors. One of them was insanely bigger than the other and she had no idea why they would need that one, let alone all of the others. She watched as he pulled into the spot, right next to a dark gray Range Rover.

Hartman got out of the car and this time Palmer knew to let him open her door for her so she waited. He came around the side, opened her door, and helped her out. Palmer whistled as she took in the garage. It was the biggest, and cleanest, garage she had ever been in. It smelled like new tires, concrete, and those wipes people use for the leather seats inside their cars. Parked in the garage was her massive stupid truck, the Range Rover, a silver Prius, an old cream-colored Ford Thunderbird, and a big ass boat. Palmer realized that was what the oversized garage door was for now.

"You think we have enough vehicles?" Palmer asked sarcastically.

Hartman chuckled. "I drive the Range Rover in the winter because of the four-wheel drive. The snow can get pretty crazy up here, but I try to drive the Prius when there is no snow since it's better for the environment. The Thunderbird was my dad's so she's strictly sentimental. Every once in a while though you and I take her out for date night. You usually get a pretty big kick out of that. And the boat is for fun."

Palmer whistled again. "Damn, so we're like... RICH rich."

Hartman laughed loudly. "We do ok," he finally said mid-laugh. Then he led Palmer up some steps and into the house.

The door from the garage into the house led into a small mudroom. If there had ever been any mud in this room there was absolutely no evidence of it. It was pristine. There were a couple jackets hanging from the coat rack and a couple of boots placed neatly on a shoe rack just underneath.

The mud room led directly into an enormous kitchen. Hartman flipped on the lights. The ceiling was at least twenty feet and from it dangled a beautiful ornate light fixture. It was a very modern style and made of dark metal with grayish glass orbs scattered all over it. Inside the orbs were Edison light bulbs. Palmer thought it looked like something you would see in a New York art gallery. There was a large island in the middle of the kitchen with dark gray, granite countertops that gleamed. The cabinets were dark wood and had steel handles. The sink was also steel and must have been commercial grade.

The kitchen opened up directly into the living room. There was a large stone fireplace with oversized, light gray, leather couches surrounding it. On the couches, perfectly placed and fluffed were a handful of brown throw pillows.

"Here's the kitchen," Hartman said pointing to the kitchen, "and here is the living room."

Palmer was starting to feel a little overwhelmed again. Here she was. In her home. Only, she had no memory of ever being here. She had no memory of them buying this house. Or was this already his house when they got together? Maybe they built it. Palmer's head was reeling. How was she expected to just keep rolling with all of these punches? This was all just too much.

"Hey, are you ok? Come here, sit down." Hartman pulled out a tall chair from one side of the kitchen island and she took a seat. "I know it's a lot. It's going to take time." Hartman continued talking as he pulled out a glass from the cabinet and filled it with cold water from the fridge. "Drink some water," he said as he set the glass in front of her.

Palmer chugged the water quickly. A little bit dribbled down her chin and she wiped at it with her sleeve.

"I'll make you some dinner ok? You must be hungry. I have the stuff for chicken alfredo, your favorite!" he said the last part with fake excitement and Palmer smiled. He was trying to help her feel more comfortable.

Palmer sat at the counter that was so clean Hartman probably could have performed surgery on it, and watched as he made her favorite meal.

Chapter Thirty-Seven

The Morgue Pizza (2015)

Dr. Roth, or rather, Hartman as he preferred her to call him, called Palmer a couple of days after their first meeting.

"Hello?" Palmer answered the call.

"Yes, I was calling for a Ms. Barrons?" Hartman said mockingly.

It took Palmer a couple of seconds to get in on the joke. She smiled.

"Hi Dr. Roth," she said. She held the phone between her chin and her shoulder as she closed out of Excel on her laptop. Palmer had been working at her actual job and not just on her side project.

"It's Hartman," he corrected her. She rolled her eyes.

"Any news? Did you find anything?" Palmer asked. She could feel the hope in her chest.

"Yes. I have good news and bad news,"

"Bad news first please," Palmer responded.

"I looked through all of my dad's old storage units I hadn't had the chance to sort out yet and I didn't find any old patient records."

Palmer waited for him to continue but he didn't. "But...?" she pushed.

"But... I found out that sometime in the 60's a bunch of the smaller local medical practices started storing their overflow of records in the basement of the hospital. I think it's possible that my dad did that too. I don't remember him holding onto old records in the office. The basement would have been the obvious choice but it was full of old equipment when I was a kid."

"So you're saying there's a chance that my great aunt's dental records are somewhere in the hospital basement?"

"Exactly. But again, it's just a guess."

"How do I even get access to that?" Palmer asked.

"You don't," Hartman responded. "But I can."

The next afternoon Palmer met Hartman in front of the local hospital. She had shown up a few minutes early, she was excited. Hartman was already standing in front of the automatic doors.

"Wow, how very punctual of you," Palmer remarked.

"I like being on time. And if you're not early, you're late," he said back with a smile.

Palmer rolled her eyes under her red sunglasses before admiring how truly handsome he was. Hartman must have come here directly from work because he was still wearing his navy scrubs, but he had taken off the white lab coat. Palmer could now see just how crazy jacked he was. His arms were roped with muscle and his neck was thick with it as well. The short sleeves of his scrub top hugged his abundant biceps. Palmer raised her eyebrows. His biceps were almost as big as her thighs and she wasn't exactly considered 'petite'. Hartman must have noticed her staring because he cleared his throat and shifted uncomfortably.

"You ready?" he said.

"I guess so? What's the plan exactly?" Palmer asked. Palmer removed her sunglasses and tucked them into her purse. It was starting to get too late for them anyway.

"Just follow my lead, I do surgeries here all the time. I've never been in the basement before but I've got a buddy who works here. She gave me the layout and the name of the guy who works down there. She let him know we were coming."

"Ok," Palmer replied. She wasn't really sure she was allowed to be down in the basement with the records but Hartman seemed confident.

Hartman walked through the sliding doors and into the lobby. He steered her toward the first elevator they came across and pushed the button to go down. Palmer tapped her foot nervously as they waited for the elevator to reach the floor they were on.

"You ok?" Hartman asked.

"Yeah, just nervous. And I'm a little excited I guess."

"Do you mind if I ask you kind of a personal question?"

Palmer shrugged and let him continue.

"Why are you working so hard on this? I get that it's your great aunt and no one knows what happened to her but it feels like maybe there is more to it. You've taken on the case personally. You're going above and beyond to figure out what happened to someone you haven't even met right? So, why?"

Palmer stopped tapping her foot and glanced up at Hartman. He looked down at her with concern and interest.

"My grandma passed away two years ago. Gabriella was her sister. My grandmother lived her whole life not knowing what happened to her baby sister. I can't even imagine how hard that must have been for her. I guess I just feel like, maybe if I can get some closure on this whole thing then maybe I can also get some closure with my grandma no longer being here." Palmer swallowed down a lump in her throat and commanded herself not to cry.

The door to the elevators opened and they both stepped in. Hartman was so big he seemed to take up most of the space. He pulled on an ID tag that was attached by a retractable cord on his front pocket. He scanned the ID card on a card reader attached to the elevator just above the buttons. It must have accepted his clearance because the little light on the reader turned from red to green. Hartman pushed the button with a big B on it and the elevator lurched downward.

"You must have had a very special relationship with your grandmother," Hartman said finally.

"I did," Palmer responded with a sad smile.

Hartman looked at Palmer then. "You're a good person Palmer."

Palmer looked up at him a little confused. She wasn't sure what to say.

"Thank you. Honestly, though, don't go thinking that I'm some kind of saint. It's not a totally unselfish project," Palmer said, shaking her head.

"What do you mean?"

"I mean, I needed a distraction and this was a pretty good one."

"Oh," Hartman said understanding.

The mechanical sound of the elevator filled the air until finally, the doors opened to a long, wide hallway. It was brightly lit by fluorescent lights. Hartman gestured for Palmer to step out first so she did. Hartman started walking confidently down the hall.

Finally, at the end of the hall, there was a pair of swinging doors. Above the doors was the word 'MORGUE', underneath which were the words 'Authorized Personnel Only'. Palmer froze. At first, Hartman didn't notice that she was no longer following him. It wasn't until he reached the doors, pushed one of them open, and turned to her, holding it open for her to go through, that he realized she had stopped following him. She was still nearly halfway down the hall looking up at the ominous words.

Hartman let the door go and it swung back. He walked back and peered down at her with concern.

"You ok?" Hartman asked Palmer. He put his hand under her elbow to try and comfort her.

"We're going into the morgue?" she asked blankly.

"Well yeah," he admitted. He looked a little ashamed that he had forgotten to warn her. "Most of the rooms down here are storage. Some have equipment, some have cleaning supplies. A lot of them have boxes of old records. But the really old ones, the ones we are looking for, were stuffed back here I think."

"In the morgue," Palmer repeated herself.

"I think so. I called down and talked to the coroner. He said there are a couple of large closet-sized rooms back here that have a bunch of dusty old records," he continued to explain when he saw the confusion and doubt still on Palmer's face. "This hospital wasn't always this big. It was much smaller actually. It was originally built sometime in the early 1900s. They added onto it in the '80s and then again in the early 2000s. It seems like every few years they add on a new wing or an annex. But THIS part of the hospital, the morgue, is part of the original hospital," Hartman squeezed Palmer's elbow gently. "The most likely place for records from the '50s to be packed away and forgotten about is through those doors."

Palmer swallowed and straightened her spine before letting Hartman lead her again towards the morgue doors.

Hartman spoke again but this time his tone was lighter. "I thought you were into scary movies. I didn't expect a morgue to affect you so much," he was smiling jokingly.

Palmer huffed a laugh. "I like scary movies, I don't want to be in one."

Hartman pushed the door open and Palmer walked in. It was a large room with brick walls and old green tiled floors. There were two steel autopsy tables placed in the middle of the room between a large drain on the floor. Against the side walls were built inside tables with microscopes, books, and other ominous-looking equipment. The back wall was made up entirely of small steel doors with latches stacked on top of each other. Palmer had seen enough scary movies to know that was where the bodies were kept. She repressed a shiver. There was a hallway just to the right of the back wall. It wasn't nearly as awful as Palmer had expected. A little cold, but not unbearable.

"Hey there!" said a chipper male voice. The owner of the voice came into the room from the back hallway. It was a small man with rimless round glasses and sandy blonde hair. He was older than Palmer but not by much she decided. He had a clean-shaven face and a smile that was too chipper for someone who worked in a basement full of dead bodies.

"I'm Carl, the morgue tech. You must be Dr. Roth," Carl and Hartman shook hands. Then Carl turned toward Palmer. "And you are?" Palmer hadn't thought about this part. She obviously wasn't authorized to be down here but Hartman hadn't said anything about a plan to get around that. Before she could say anything Hartman spoke.

"This is my dental assistant, Regan MacNeil. She's here to help me dig through those old records. I figured two hands are always better than one."

Palmer fought hard not to stare at Hartman. Instead, she tried to pretend that everything he just said was true.

"Alrighty. Well, I talked with the coroner and he said you guys would be stopping by tonight. Follow me and I'll show you where he thinks those boxes are."

Carl walked back down the hall and Palmer and Hartman followed. Palmer nudged Hartman's arm with her shoulder.

"Regan MacNeil? The little girl from The Exorcist?" she whispered.

Hartman only smiled knowingly and lifted his pointer finger to his lips for her to be quiet. Palmer couldn't believe it. He had used HER *'fake name from a horror movie trick'*. Despite herself, Palmer felt a small familiar flutter in her stomach.

Carl led them down the long hallway. Along the left-hand side of the wall were several cluttered offices with old shag rugs and outdated furniture. Hartman was right, this part of the hospital was old. After the offices were storage rooms. Carl led them to the ones in the very back and opened the doors with a key.

"Stay as long as you like, I'm here all night. It's slow so I might be sleeping on the sofa in the first office. If that's the case just leave when you're done and I'll lock up later." With that Carl gave them a salute and turned back down the hall.

Palmer and Hartman looked at each other and shrugged before getting to work. The two closets were stacked high with old brown banker's boxes. The boxes were dusty and smelled like moth balls. Some of them had water damage from leaks that were likely decades old. Palmer pulled out box after box. She heard Hartman doing the same but with noticeably less grunting on his part. Every once in a while Palmer would get a little tickle at the base of her neck when she remembered she was alone in a closet inside of a morgue. But she did her best to push that aside and asked herself WWLSD; What Would Laurie Strode Do? She would straighten her spine and get shit done. That's what she would do. So Palmer continued to sort through dusty boxes in the creepy morgue.

After about an hour of sifting through boxes and moving things aside, she heard Hartman speak.

"Found something!" he said.

Palmer dropped the box she was currently bringing down and rushed to his closet. He was holding two boxes with the name 'Roth Family Dentistry' on them.

"These are my dads!" He sounded as excited as she felt and her stomach did the little flutter again.

Palmer hadn't let anyone close in years. She had built up sturdy walls and chosen to be alone. It was easier that way. And yet, here was this guy. She was sure Hartman had better things to do on a Friday night than dig through old boxes in the hospital basement.

"What?" Hartman asked.

Palmer corrected her face. She realized she must have been looking at him funny. "Nothing!" she said.

Hartman walked out into the hallway and set down the boxes against the wall. "There's gotta be some more of my father's boxes back here," his voice was muffled as he stuck his head between some shelves. Palmer squeezed herself into the already tight space and tried to look with him. They were both too preoccupied to hear Carl sneak up behind them.

"Hey guys!" he said loudly in his overly cheery voice.

"Aaaahhh!" yelled Palmer.

"Fuck!" Hartman gasped as he hit his head on the shelf.

Carl jumped at their surprise and fumbled the box of pizza he was holding, nearly dropping it.

"I'm sorry! Jeez, you guys gave me a fright! I was just letting you know that I ordered some pizza. I didn't know if you maybe wanted a slice?" said Carl.

Palmer's hand was on her chest trying to steady her heartbeat. Hartman was rubbing the top of his head.

"Yeah sure man, thanks," Hartman replied.

Carl handed them the box and explained that he already had two slices and was full so they could have the rest. Hartman thanked him again and Carl went back to the office to do God knows what.

Palmer and Hartman sat on stools next to the open closets and set the box of pizza on top of a banker's box. Palmer was starving, she realized. In her excitement, she had forgotten to eat something before she came here after work so she was the first to grab a slice of the pepperoni pizza. Hartman gladly took a slice and ate in four bites before reaching for another.

Palmer raised her eyebrows. "Hungry?" she asked sarcastically. Hartman only nodded and continued to devour the next slice.

"Hey, in case I forgot to say it before, thank you for helping with this," Palmer said genuinely.

Hartman shrugged and smiled. "It's no big deal. Really. I probably needed to track down these old records and dispose of them anyway since they were my dad's," he stopped to take another bite. Palmer was impressed. Even stuffing his face he managed to stay clean. "Besides, I could tell it was important to you when you came into my office the other day, and I wanted to help. It feels important," he finished.

"Still. Thank you for spending your Friday night down here. In the morgue. With me and probably dead people." Palmer mused.

"There is no death. There is only a transition to a different sphere of consciousness." Hartman said in between mouthfuls of pizza.

Palmer gaped at him.

"Did — did you just quote Poltergeist?" she asked. She was shocked.

He smiled broadly at her. "Yes 'Tangina Barrons' I did."

Chapter Thirty-Eight

Present Day (2022)

Palmer ate nearly the entire bowl of chicken alfredo Hartman had made her. It was delicious. Perfect. Probably the best chicken alfredo she had ever had, and she had had A LOT of chicken alfredo in her life. Hartman had whipped it up quickly and she had watched from the kitchen counter. He was the type of person that cleaned as he cooked so when the meal was over all you had to do was put your plate and utensils in the dishwasher and presto, everything was done.

"Do you need anything? Water? Your medicine? How's your head?" Hartman asked her.

"I'm fine, Hartman really. A little tired maybe," Palmer responded.

"Right," he said. Palmer could see the concern on his face.

"Hartman," Palmer started to say. She intentionally reached over and put her hand on top of his across the counter and squeezed. "It's going to be ok. I'm ok."

Hartman's shoulders sagged and he released a breath. Palmer started to speak again.

"It's just going to take some time. Everything is a little overwhelming right now but it'll get better right? We just need to take it one step at a time."

Hartman nodded. "What do you need right now?" he asked gently.

"Maybe a shower. And then some sleep," Palmer gave him a reassuring smile which he returned.

"Alright," Hartman said before leading her upstairs.

The stairs were made of log like the rest of the house and Palmer ran her hands along the smoothness of the rails as she made her way up. Hartman was switching on lights as they moved through the house since the sun had gone down while Palmer had eaten dinner. The large windows of the house had previously opened up to beautiful mountain views but now they only revealed a black void that seemed to leech its way into the house.

Upstairs was a large loft that had a second living room. This one looked out over the downstairs living room and the kitchen. However, this one had a large flat-screen television on the wall. Opposite the television was another couch. This one was gray suede and had gray-toned throw pillows placed just so on its cushions. There was a small bar just to the right of the couch. Palmer had paused to look into the room but Hartman had continued on down a hallway so she followed.

Along the hallway were a couple of pieces of framed artwork. They were modern and abstract. The art was the same grayish and brown town as the rest of the house. It must have been chosen with care. Finally, Hartman turned right and led Palmer into the master bedroom, flipping the light switch as they entered. The master bedroom was gorgeous.

There was a large A-frame window against the farthest wall that she assumed would look out over the forest in the daylight. In the middle of the room was what Palmer could only assume was a California King size bed. That made sense she thought, since Hartman was so large. The bed was piled high with a crisp white down comforter and gray fur pillows. It was placed on a large, Native American style rug that had lovely green accents. Above the bed was another piece of abstract artwork, this one larger than the others she had seen. The nightstands were simple and sleek. On top of each nightstand were matching modern-style lamps with silver bases.

Palmer's gaze swept across the room. The head of the bed was pressed against the right wall but on the left wall was a large doorway that led into what she guessed was the master bathroom. Instead of a traditional door to the bathroom, there was a large barn-style door. In order to close the opening to the bathroom you had to pull the door sideways. Only this one was made of industrial metal instead of wood.

"So, uh, here we are. This is our room. It feels really weird to say that, since it is our room. You've been in here countless times," Hartman laughed nervously. "Oh my God. I'm sorry, I'm just now realizing I probably should have given you a tour of the whole house! I didn't even think of that," Hartman said. He looked like he was going to turn around and insist on giving her a tour.

"Hartman," Palmer said firmly. Hartman turned to her and composed himself. He took a deep breath.

"Tomorrow?" He suggested. He was talking about giving her a tour.

"I would love a tour tomorrow. Maybe then you can explain how there isn't a single dust bunny in this entire place. I'm assuming you require the maids to go off their OCD meds before hiring them?"

Hartman laughed and the earlier stress that had lined his face disappeared. Palmer smiled genuinely. She was starting to love how she could relax him with a simple snarky remark.

"Shower?" Palmer asked.

"This way," he said and he led her toward the master bath. It was much bigger than she had expected, and based on the rest of the house she had expected it to be fairly large. There was a big two-sink vanity with sparkling gray marble and an oversized mirror hanging above it. Opposite that there was a deep jacuzzi tub. Next to the tub was a two-person shower with shower heads on both sides of the wall. Palmer could tell which side must be hers because the shower head was hung lower. She could see all of this through the clear shower walls. Palmer tried not to blush thinking about her and Hartman showering together here.

"There's uh, towels in that cupboard over there. And that one is your closet," Hartman said, nodding his head to the door to the right of the sink. There was a matching door to the left of the sink that she assumed would be his closet. Hartman looked unsure of what to do with himself.

"Thank you, I can take it from here," she said and saluted him. Hartman smiled and rubbed the back of his neck before exiting the bathroom and sliding the door closed for her.

Palmer moved to the cupboard where Hartman had indicated the towels were located and pulled out a fluffy gray one. Then she leaned into the shower and turned on her shower head. While the water warmed up she hesitantly stepped out of her clothes and kicked them into the corner. She was painfully aware that there was no lock on the door. The shower heated quickly and soon the room was full of steam.

Palmer stepped into the scalding hot water and sighed. She let the water cleanse her and she relished in its feel. She grabbed the nearest loofa and selected a body wash from the rack of unknown shower products. She squirted the soap onto the loofa and started to lather it. Immediately she realized the soap must be what Hartman usually washes with because she was enveloped in his cedar and spearmint smell. It smelled incredible. She felt oddly erotic here in the shower, naked and rubbing something that was his all over her. The hot water made her skin flush and the feel of the rough loofa on her nipples made her core feel warm.

Despite herself, Palmer started to imagine what it would be like for Hartman to be in here with her. What his hands would feel like on her slick body. What he would look like flushed and wet from the hot shower. Palmer imagined Hartman leaning down and pressing his lips to hers. She continued to lather her body with his body wash, making slow deliberate circles.

Palmer shook herself and continued to wash and condition her hair. She could have cried from relief when she found a lady's razor for her to shave her legs. It had been days since she shaved and her legs were beyond prickly. Finally, Palmer stepped out of the shower and onto the fuzzy bath mat. She grabbed the towel from the sink counter and noticed that Hartman had laid out some pajamas for her to change into. Palmer dried herself off, all the while blushing thinking about Hartman in the bathroom while she was showering. She also noticed that he had picked up the dirty clothes she had kicked into the corner. Her blush deepened. She hadn't heard or noticed him while she was washing herself. She had been showering and thinking of him. Palmer chastised herself. She needed to grow up, she told herself, he was her husband after all.

Once she was dry she pulled on the soft pajamas and applied some moisturizer to her face. She had determined which bathroom drawer must be hers based on the process of elimination. One drawer had been neatly organized with men's products. The other had been messy and full of women's products. When Palmer opened her drawer all of the tubes and containers rolled around noisily. She smiled to herself thanks to the small familiarity.

Palmer assessed herself in the mirror. Satisfied she turned to open the bathroom door and froze. Hartman would be out there. In their bed. And she would sleep with him, obviously. It would be weird if they didn't. Palmer willed herself to look braver than she felt and slid the door open.

There he was, sitting up in bed with the lamp turned on. He was reading a book and he had a pair of reading glasses on. When he saw her he set his book on the nightstand and placed his glasses on top of the book. She was still just standing there awkwardly.

"Is — is this ok?" he asked, gesturing to himself. Obviously he was referring to sleeping together.

"Yeah, of course," Palmer said breathlessly. She walked over to her side of the bed and crawled under the sheets. They were slick and cold.

Hartman leaned over and turned off his light. The room was bathed in darkness. The only light was from the nearly full moon outside the window. Palmer listened as Hartman adjusted himself into the bed, getting comfortable. She could hear him breathing.

Palmer flipped over onto her side so that she was facing him. He must have been facing her too, probably in a similar position she thought. She could feel his hot breath on her face, it was minty.

Palmer heard the sheets rustle and she felt Hartman's hands stroke her wet hair. She didn't flinch.

"Hartman," Palmer said. It wasn't a question. She just wanted to say his name. Somehow it made her feel safe.

"Palmer," he replied. Only when he said her name, it almost sounded like a prayer.

Later that night, as Palmer slept next to Hartman, a man stood out in the forest. He was nearly invisible thanks to the cover of the tall, thick trees. The only indication that he was there at all was the small orange light coming from the end of his cigarette. The man gazed up at the large house, sucking in the smoke. Behind him, even deeper in the mountain trees was someone else. But instead of standing still, looking at the house in a silent vigil, she walked slowly between the trees. No animals stirred around her, and her bare feet left no footprints in the snow.

Chapter Thirty-Nine

The Cemetery (2015)

After several hours of reading through paperwork, Hartman and Palmer finally found Gabriella's dental records. Palmer was filled with hope. She had made copies, keeping the original for herself. Then she had placed the copy of Gabriella's dental records, a list of Jane Does that had been found around that time, and a detailed letter for the detective now in charge of the case in a big manilla envelope. The letter politely requested, or rather pleaded, for the detectives to please compare Gabriella's dental records with the records of the Jane Does in hopes of finding a match.

Palmer had taken the big manilla envelope to the police station and handed it to the receptionist. The receptionist had said that she would make sure it would get to the detectives in charge but she looked at Palmer with pity. Palmer tried not to get discouraged. It was a long shot but at least it felt like she was getting closer. As she was leaving the police station her phone rang. She pulled it out and smiled despite herself when she saw who it was.

"Dr. Roth," she said in a mocking tone.

"Carrie White," Hartman responded. That was their thing now. Every time she called him Dr. Roth instead of Hartman like he had asked her countless times, he always called her some iconic female horror movie character's name. This time it was Carrie White, from Stephen King's movie and book Carrie. Palmer's smile widened.

"Did you drop it off?" he asked.

Palmer had assumed that Hartman's interest and involvement in her project would have ended after he helped her find Gabriella's dental records. But even after that joyous moment, even after they had shared a particularly awkward hug that had ended in a high five, he had kept in touch. He had asked to see the list of Jane Does and had even sent her a few articles about cold cases that had been solved thanks to persistent family members as encouragement.

Palmer was grateful for the unexpected friendship. And it was nice having someone to talk to about her side project who didn't think she was crazy. Her parents hadn't said anything about her being overly obsessed with the case or being worried about her, but Palmer had noticed the little looks they shared with each other every time she chose to stay in and do research instead of going out.

Jessica, on the other hand, had been extremely vocal about what she thought about Palmer's new 'reclusive' lifestyle. Jessica had moved to California after they graduated college but she still called and texted often enough. Jessica had gone on and on about how Palmer needed to get out of the house, how she needed to find someone new to 'play with', how worried she was about her social life, how Palmer was a hermit now, about how boring she was, etc.

Jessica made frequent jokes about how long it had been since Palmer had sex. She made off-handed comments about how Palmer had cobwebs *down there* or bats. She even made a joke that it had been so long since Palmer had sex that she had probably 'grown a new hymen'. Palmer always laughed, it was all in good spirits. She knew Jessica was just worried and this was her way of expressing it. But Palmer DID look up the hymen thing just in case and was relieved when Google said it wasn't true.

Palmer focused her attention back onto the conversation she was having with Hartman.

"Yeah, I literally JUST dropped it off," Palmer said as she adjusted the phone on her ear. She walked down the steps to her car. "The receptionist still thinks I'm annoying and a little sad I think, but she seemed genuine when she said she would give it to the detectives."

"You're not annoying or sad. Even a little. I think what you're doing is noble." Hartman said. Palmer rolled her eyes. "So," Hartman continued. "What's next?"

Palmer had just gotten into her hot car and was about to turn the ignition but she paused. "What do you mean?" she asked.

"With the case? What do we do next? I mean while we wait for the detectives to get back to us about the dental records."

Palmer's chest was full of emotion. 'WE'. He had said we, not YOU, WE. That one simple word had threatened to completely undo her. Palmer swallowed a lump in her throat before speaking again.

"Palmer?" Hartman said. She had paused for too long and he was checking to see if she was still there.

"Sorry, I'm here. Just getting in my car," Palmer turned the ignition and was rewarded with a blast of air from the vents. Palmer buckled herself up and continued to speak. "Well, I was thinking about maybe going to visit Gabriella's grave when I get off work. I know that sounds — creepy..."

"Creepier than eating pizza in the morgue?" Hartman said mockingly and Palmer laughed.

"It's just that my grandma said she and her siblings bought a gravesite and a tombstone for Gabriella a few years after she disappeared so that it would maybe give their parents some closure. I've been to the cemetery hundreds of times, my family is — large, and we're always buried in the same sort of area. But I've never noticed hers. I think when we would go visit when I was a kid my grandmother would purposely avoid Gabriella's spot." Palmer took a deep breath. Talking about Abuela in the past tense was still hard. "I think I'd like to see the spot where she could possibly be laid to rest. If I'm successful, I think it would — motivate me or something. I know how stupid that sounds."

"It doesn't sound stupid. Mind if I tag along?" Hartman said.

Palmer closed her eyes and marveled at how lucky she had gotten to find a friend like Hartman.

Palmer and Hartman made plans to meet up after they both got off work. Hartman would meet Palmer at the newspaper at 6:30 pm and they would drive together to the cemetery in Palmer's car. Palmer had insisted that she drive. It felt a little too weird to let him drive since it was her personal mission. Her great aunt's empty grave. Palmer tried not to watch the clock as she worked.

At 6:20 pm sharp Palmer heard a knock on the opening to her office and looked up in time to see Hartman step into the cramped space. Palmer's 'office', if you could even call it that, was located in the very back of the newspaper building. It was more of a makeshift mini cubicle more than anything.

"Hey," Hartman said.

"Hey," Palmer said back. She smiled at his punctualness. "I forgot about your whole 'if you're not early you're late' thing." She said the last part in a deep baritone to imitate his voice. "I just need to finish this up real quick before we take off, is that ok?" She said the last part as she gestured toward the spreadsheets on her computer screen.

Palmer's desk was a mess like always. She liked to think of it as organized chaos. Paperwork was piled high in a jumbled heap, illegible sticky notes were pasted all over and Palmer had pictures of her family and friends tacked up wherever she could find some spare space. Hartman stared at the mess with wide eyes for only a moment before shaking himself and speaking.

"Yeah! Of course. Is it ok if I sit here?" He pointed to the little stool she kept in the corner of the cubicle. Her workspace was so small she could never have fit a real chair in it. No one had ever actually sat on the stool. In fact no one ever really came into her cubicle at all. People usually just dropped off their receipts and other financial information into her drop box.

Palmer shrugged. "Um — yeah sure," she said with false confidence. She turned her gaze back to her screen but from the corner of her eye, she watched as Hartman tried to fold his overly large body onto the tiny stool. Palmer tried not to wince when she heard the wood of the stool groan under his weight. Miraculously it held firm. She had found it at the flea market last summer. Someone had hand-painted bright multicolor flowers all over it. Palmer loved that it brought a little pop of summer into her workspace even in the dead of winter.

Palmer continued to enter a few more numbers into her spreadsheet, her red-painted fingernails clacked away. But it was hard to focus. Hartman took up nearly all of the extra space in the little area and his scent was filling her nose. She could hear every breath he took behind her, in fact, she could almost feel it on her neck. It gave her the shivers, an involuntary tremble traveled from her shoulders down to the base of her spine.

"Are you cold?" Hartman asked. He immediately shifted to take off his light jacket to give to her. The small adjustment caused the stool to groan even louder and Hartman's balance shifted dangerously. Palmer shot her hand out to steady him and stop him from moving further. Her hand landed flat on his hard pec muscle. At the same time, his own hand instinctively went to her hand to also stabilize himself. Once they both realized the stool was not going to break they started laughing.

"Holy shit, your face was priceless just now," Palmer said chuckling. Hartman was smiling like a fiend. They both looked down at their hands and their smiles faded to something a bit more serious.

Palmer's hand was still placed on Hartman's chest, and his hand was covering hers still. Palmer stared at where they touched, unable to move. She watched as Hartman's thumb stroked the top of her hand. The urge to pull her hand away was almost as strong as her urge to stay like this for as long as possible. Hartman must have noticed the war she was battling inside herself because he spoke gently.

"Do you want to talk about it?" he asked.

Palmer looked at Hartman dumbly. "Talk about what?" she asked.

"The hurt I can see in your eyes." His thumb was still stroking slowly. His hand was a little cold but she watched the muscles and tendons work as he stroked her. Palmer didn't say anything, so he continued to speak. "Someone hurt you right? Pretty badly if I'm correct."

Palmer shook her head but then she shrugged. Closing herself off, keeping all of these walls up was exhausting. Maybe, just maybe, it was time she started to let them down. In response, Hartman squeezed her hand.

"Well, I'm here if you want to talk about it," he concluded. He removed his hand from the top of hers. Palmer's hand remained on his chest. She could almost still feel his hand on top of hers still, like a phantom touch. After another moment she moved her hand back to her lap.

Palmer cleared her throat before speaking. "I'm pretty much done here, you ready?" she asked.

"Yep," he said as he stood up. If he was just a little taller his head would bump into the ceiling tiles.

Palmer stood up as well and brushed the wrinkles from her sundress as she stood. When she looked up she noticed Hartman staring. Blushing, she grabbed her bag and pulled out her keys. Her rabbit's foot keychain swung at her side. Together they walked to the front of the building. The newspaper was pretty much empty aside from the cleaning people who came in to vacuum and take out the trash. Palmer walked to her car with Hartman following closely behind her.

Palmer unlocked the car from several feet away but when she neared the driver's side door she noticed that Hartman hadn't moved to the passenger side. He was still beside her. She watched quizzically as he reached for the handle and opened the car door for her, gesturing for her to get in. Palmer stared up at him for a moment but decided to let it go. It wouldn't be nice to make fun of someone for doing something nice for her. Besides, it kind of made her feel special. Like she was Princess Diana or something.

Palmer was pretty certain that any notion Hartman had of her being like a princess or ladylike would dissipate pretty quickly. Especially after he saw the pile of take-out trash and random shit in the back of her car. Luckily she had cleaned out anything gross that had previously been in the passenger seat since she knew he would be riding with her tonight. To Hartman's credit, he barely glanced at the garbage truck she called her car. Palmer did have to help him adjust the seat so that his legs would fit but eventually, they got him comfortably inside her vehicle.

Palmer drove them through town and toward the cemetery. The sun was starting to dip behind the mountains so the light filtering through the car was a lovely pink. The song Love Me Like You Do by Ellie Goulding was playing lightly on the radio. When they neared the cemetery, Palmer realized they had hardly spoken since leaving the newspaper. And yet, somehow she was more relaxed than she had felt in ages.

Palmer pulled up to the black, wrought iron cemetery gates and they opened automatically. Palmer waited until they were open all the way before she drove through. She wound her way through the pavement that organized the tombstones and headed toward the Rivera plots. When she was as close as she could get she pulled to the side and put the car in park. Hartman immediately got out of the car and rushed to the driver's side. Palmer watched in awe as he opened her door for her again and helped her get out.

"Thank you," she said nervously. Hartman didn't respond, he just continued to gaze out over the cemetery.

"Which way?" he finally asked.

Palmer pointed with her finger. "My mother's family is usually buried in this direction. Any Rivera who has lived in this town and died here is buried right over there." Hartman only grunted in response. Palmer thought he seemed a little tense.

They started to walk in the direction Palmer had indicated. The cemetery was lovely this time of year. Or at least as lovely as a cemetery gets. The trees were green and full, the flowers were in full bloom and the grass was lush. It was warm enough that Palmer didn't feel the need to put on a sweater. Hartman had taken off his light scrub jacket before he got into her hot car but he was carrying it now. She was pretty sure he wasn't planning on using it. Actually, Palmer had a feeling that he was carrying it in case she got chilly later.

Finally, after a small trek, the tombstones started to bear the name Rivera. Palmer gestured around her and spoke.

"Well, here lies pretty much all the Riveras. Except for Gabriella of course, but her headstone should be around her somewhere." Palmer's voice trailed off as she started to search. She and Hartman split up but stayed close as they read name after name aloud.

Palmer paused as she came upon Abuela's grave. She put her index and middle finger to her lips. Then she placed those same fingers on the cold stone and smiled weakly before moving on.

"I found it!" Hartman yelled a few moments later. Palmer walked quickly over to where he stood.

Under the shade of a willow tree stood a small light gray tombstone. It may have stood two feet tall and was likely made of zinc. It was dirty and weather-worn from decades of Colorado sun and snow. There was only a small inscription.

In Memory of

Gabriella Guadalupe Rivera

Just above the inscription was a small engraving of The Virgin Mary. The image was of Mary's entire body standing with her arms at her side, palms facing up.

Palmer's hand instinctively went to the necklace around her neck. The image on the headstone was the same as the one on the necklace. Palmer tried to shake off the odd feeling. They were Catholic after all. That image of The Blessed Mother was all over the place.

Palmer glanced up to see if Hartman had caught onto any of her weirdness, but he was too busy staring at another part of the cemetery. His jaw was set and he looked like his thoughts were far away.

"You ok?" Palmer asked. She watched as Hartman's throat bobbed.

"My dad is buried just over there," he finally said.

Palmer's lips parted in surprise. He had mentioned that his father had died not too long ago. Maybe five years ago she thought she had remembered him saying. Palmer wanted to kick herself for not thinking about that before dragging him here.

"Do you — should we go visit?" Palmer suggested.

Hartman shook his head. He was still staring off at a set of gravestones a few yards away.

"Can I tell you a secret?" Hartman said in a hushed voice.

A light breeze moved through the willow causing the long hanging branches and leaves to move eerily.

"Of course," Palmer replied. He seemed very sad and distant.

"My father was an awful person. Nobody knew though. They still don't. To the world, he was Dr. Klaus Roth, the friendly neighborhood dentist. He donated to local charities, volunteered once a month at the food bank, he was even an usher at church. But I knew. It was just a show. A mask."

Palmer wasn't breathing. Her heart was breaking for Hartman but at the same time, she was touched by his vulnerability with her, and his willingness to share something so painful with her.

"He was a different person when he came home. When no one was watching except for me. If there really is a heaven and a hell, I know he didn't go to heaven." Hartman dropped his voice to a whisper as if to hide his next words from a father who could no longer hear him. "I think I may have hated him."

Palmer slipped her hand into his. The body contact seemed to pull him from whatever spell he was under because he looked at their joined hands quickly and then down into her eyes. Palmer looked up into his eyes as well and willed herself to be brave and vulnerable like him. His eyes were impossibly blue, like the sky on a perfect day.

"Do you want to talk about it?" she asked. Hartman shook his head gently. Palmer blazed forward. "Can I tell you a secret too?" Palmer said, dropping her voice.

Hartman looked at her quizzically but nodded. "Yes," he said hoarsely.

Palmer swallowed and let her giant internal wall down. She felt anxious but somehow free. "I think I am being haunted by the ghost of Gabriella Rivera. I see her sometimes. Or at least, I'm pretty sure it's her. For a long time, I wasn't sure who it was. All I knew was that I was different. Strange things would happen to me. But now, I know. Either that or I'm maybe schizophrenic. Honestly, I'm not sure which one would be better at this point." Palmer finished her verbal diarrhea and waited for Hartman to withdraw his hand. She waited for him to confirm that it was indeed most likely some sort of mental psychosis. He would stop talking to her after this and she would be alone again.

Hartman did none of that. He only squeezed her hand and turned to face her fully. His other hand came up and stroked her arm. He seemed to lean down a bit so that their faces were closer.

"I believe you," Hartman said.

He believed her. Palmer had to repeat it inside her mind. He believed her. Nothing in his face made her feel like that was a lie to make her feel better. He was being genuine. He believed her. He said nothing else. Nothing about her needing to keep it to herself. Nothing about how she needed to stop watching so many scary movies. Just the words 'I believe you'.

Without thinking Palmer went up onto her tippy toes and wrapped her hand around Hartman's neck pulling him down to her level. She crushed her lips to his. He reacted immediately, molding his lips to hers. He tasted like winter and the promise of spring. He lifted one hand to the back of her head and the other to stroke her long dark hair. Her heart stuttered in her chest and she felt weightless.

Hartman kissed her like she was precious. Like she was made of porcelain and could easily break under his hands. He lightly caressed her cheek and her jaw before pulling away from her lips and gently pulling her into his chest. He wrapped his big arms around her and squeezed just enough. Palmer breathed in his scent and smiled. Palmer felt safe.

Chapter Forty

Present Day (2022)

Palmer woke up to the sun glaring through the A-frame window of the master bedroom. It was way too bright for her liking. She squinted toward the other side of the bed and sat up when she found it was empty. Hartman wasn't there.

She had woken up sometime in the middle of the night to Hartman spooning her from behind. Her head had been resting on his bicep like a pillow, his large frame had molded to her smaller one. Their feet had been entwined and his arm had been wrapped around her middle, his hand resting flat on her stomach. Palmer had been confused at first, thinking it was Calum. She and Calum had slept like that a long time ago when she was in college. Her dorm bed was tiny and in order for them both to fit they had to sleep in that position. Calum had always joked that he didn't mind since it gave him perfect access to her ass.

But it wasn't Calum spooning her last night. It was Hartman. Her husband. Somehow that was starting to bother her less and less. Last night instead of moving away from him she had settled in deeper into the cuddle. She had shifted her hips just a little causing Hartman to readjust in his sleep as well. When he did he pulled her hips closer to his own and Palmer's heart nearly toppled out of her chest when she felt the outline of his dick on her backside. It had taken a long time for her to fall back asleep after that.

Now Palmer reached over to his pillow and picked up a note he had left.

Palmer,

I went to the corner market

to get some groceries.

You were so beautiful

sleeping, I didn't

want to wake you.

Be back soon.

Hart

Palmer smiled to herself. She was starting to remember him finally. Not everything. Not yet. But enough for her to start feeling like she really knew him and trusted him. He was no longer a stranger.

Palmer stretched and got out of bed. She was about to walk into the bathroom when she looked back at the bed. Hartman's side was already perfectly made and put together. Like he physically couldn't leave without making it. Feeling guilty Palmer walked back and tried to make her side look as good as his. After several minutes she gave up and decided it would have to do.

Palmer padded into the bathroom to relieve herself. She laughed out loud when she saw the toilet. She must not have noticed last night in her exhausted state but now in the light of day, she could see the ridiculous commode in front of her. It was the fanciest toilet she had ever seen. It must be one of those bidets people in Europe have. She hesitantly sat down on it and did her business. She was too intimidated to use any of the buttons on the side. Palmer was hit with another fit of giggles when she realized the toilet had its own remote.

Palmer exited the little inner room where the toilet was inside the giant bathroom and washed her hands in the sink. She then proceeded to brush her teeth with what she assumed was her toothbrush based on the crushed bristles. Palmer had a tendency to brush a little too hard. Then she washed and dried her face before applying some moisturizer.

Palmer decided to take a peek in her closet and see if she could find something comfortable to wear for the day. Palmer opened the closet and gasped. It was a walk-in closet nearly the size of her childhood bedroom. Vintage dresses and colorful tops hung from hangers. There were drawers filled to the brim with pants and patterned skirts. There was almost an entire wall dedicated to an impressive shoe selection. In the center of the room was a retro-style, red velvet sofa. Palmer was immediately in love with the piece. She walked over to it and stroked its soft upholstery. On the farthest back wall hung a large mirror outlined in gold swirls and flowers.

In the corner of the vast closet, Palmer spotted something that threatened to completely undo her. There, tucked between the mirror and some faux fur coats, was a large standing jewelry case made of gleaming cherry wood. The top of it was opened to reveal a mirror and a bunch of glittering rings. Many of which were recognizable to Palmer. It was Abuela's armoire.

Palmer swiped at her now wet eyes and moved to touch the small bit of her grandmother that was here with her. She ran her hands along the smooth wood and gently touched some of the rings. Absently Palmer's hand went to her neck where her necklace usually laid. The first time she had ever seen her necklace was in this jewelry case. She remembered that day vividly. Abuela had caught her sneaking around her room. Instead of being angry, she had given the necklace to Palmer.

She had worn it every day since. Or at least, up until recently. Up until her accident.

Palmer felt a bit odd. Like she was standing on the edge of a cliff and she didn't know whether to jump off or to take a step back. Like she had an itch she needed to scratch only she didn't know where the spot was. Like when someone makes a movie reference and you don't remember the movie right away but you know you've seen it.

Palmer shook her head. She was frustrated with herself for being so nostalgic and silly. She gave the armoire a small smile before stepping away and continuing with her mission to find something to wear for the day. She wanted something lazy, and comfortable. Palmer pushed apart a couple of dresses on hangers and smirked. Some of these outfits were ridiculous. Palmer looked closely at a red, puffy dress made of gauze before throwing her head back to laugh. It was a replica of the iconic dress Winona Rider wears in the movie Beetlejuice. Yes, she thought to herself, this was definitely HER closet.

Deciding today was definitely not the day to wear Lydia Deetz's wedding dress, Palmer continued to search for something suitable to put on. She started to pull open drawers. After a few moments, she pulled out a white cotton tee shirt and some leggings. She slipped on the outfit and looked in the mirror. The bottom half of the tee shirt was missing. Apparently crop tops were back in style. Palmer laughed at herself. She had forgotten her entire life, of course, she had forgotten what the current style trends were.

Palmer pulled open a few more drawers looking for socks. She finally found a messy drawer stuffed with crazy socks in every color imaginable and pulled out a pair of bright orange ones. They were soft and looked handmade. She immediately loved them. She pulled them onto her feet and relished in the warmth. The house was a little chilly, especially the floors.

Palmer walked out of the closet, through the bathroom, and back out into the bedroom. She decided to take a look outside the A-frame window at the view and let out an impressed whistle. It was exactly how she had pictured the night before. The house sat up on a hill, maybe even pressed against a mountain, so she could see out for miles. A huge expanse of snow-covered trees splayed out before her. She could see where their long driveway eventually met with a road and wound into town. The town was visible a long way away but only as a conglomerate of specks. Palmer peered into the trees, looking left and right. There were other houses up here but they were definitely a long way away. At least a half a mile or so she thought.

Palmer turned away from the view and ventured out of the bedroom. Her socks were slick on the hardwood. She wandered from room to room trying to get reacquainted with her house. She found two more bedrooms up on the second level along with another bathroom. They were neat and tidy, definitely spare bedrooms that were likely not used very often. There were no signs that anyone stayed in them frequently.

Also on the second floor, Palmer found what she assumed was Hartman's office. It was decorated in the same cool tones with brown accents, just like the rest of the house. There were books lined along one wall, most of them were boring medical books but some were classics like The Count of Monte Cristo and Crime and Punishment. On the back wall was a large desk made of dark wood complete with a comfortable-looking chair behind it. Beside the desk was a trolly filled with expensive liquor and glittering glasses. In front of the desk and in the middle of the room were two high-backed chairs made of gray leather. Underneath which was another ornate, Native American rug. Palmer noted that Hartman's office had the same view as their bedroom. Finally, Palmer noticed that there was a large gun safe next to the desk. She knew what it was immediately. Chuck had always been a hunter when she was growing up and they had a similar case in their home. However, the one Chuck had was a fraction of the size of this one.

Palmer turned back down the hall and continued her exploration. She made her way back down the stairs and to the first floor. She had already seen the kitchen and the main living room so she didn't pause to take them in. Instead, she kept on moving. On the first floor, she found another bathroom and a guest bedroom. The first-floor guest room was a little warmer than the rest. On the nightstand next to the bed was a framed photo of her, her parents, and Shawn. She hardly recognized Shawn at first. He had a beard and his face was much leaner than she remembered. His cheeks were a little sunken and his eyes weren't as bright as they had always been. Palmer couldn't remember taking this photo so she assumed it must have been taken during the time she still couldn't remember. Palmer tried not to get frustrated with that fact so she forged ahead.

Palmer discovered that they had a basement. It was even colder than the rest of the house. She made a mental note to ask Hartman to start a fire in the giant fireplace when he got back. The basement was carpeted with a lush light gray carpet. Against the back wall and along part of another was a bar big enough to quench the thirst of the entire town. The wall behind the bar was mirrored and lined with shelves filled with every kind of alcohol Palmer could think of. At least ten stools were pushed into the bar on the side Palmer was on. In the corner behind the bar was a television mounted and facing the stools.

In the middle of the room was a pool table, an air hockey table, and a foosball table. Along one of the walls were a couple old school arcade games. There was another bathroom down in the basement along with a big room for storage. Palmer walked back into the middle of the basement and peered around again. Just then she heard the front door to the house slam shut and she jumped.

"Palmer?" Hartman yelled.

Palmer breathed a sigh of relief. It was just Hartman.

"I'm in the basement!" she yelled back.

She heard Hartman's footsteps walk just above her. She thought she could maybe hear the footsteps of someone else as well. Maybe a couple of different footsteps. Palmer bunched her eyebrows pondering who could be here. A few moments later Hartman popped his head through the door to the basement.

"Hey you," he said tenderly.

Palmer smiled. "Hey."

"There are a couple of police officers here to talk to you? I ran into them in town and they were pretty persistent about having a chat with you. Are you up for it? If not I can just tell them you're not feeling well and we can try again tomorrow?"

Palmer's stomach soured and she rubbed her lips together. Part of her wanted to send the officers away so she could deal with all this later, hopefully when her memory of that night came back. But another part of her wanted to get it over with. Besides, maybe they could give her phone back to her now. Maybe they had even found her necklace. With that idea, she made up her mind.

"No, I'm good. I'll be right up," she said to Hartman.

Hartman looked at her with uncertainty but nodded his head before closing the door again. Palmer took a deep breath and rubbed her eyes with the palms of her hands. Then she straightened her spine and walked up the stairs. With every step she imagined herself getting one more step closer to the truth.

Chapter Forty-One

The Reunion (2016)

P almer sat at a small outdoor table in front of her favorite coffee shop. The early spring wind blew her long dark hair lightly so she pushed one side behind her ear. It was a relatively warm day for this time of year but she still wore her light jacket. She was waiting for Hartman to meet up with her. They had made plans to get lunch during their breaks. Palmer was twenty minutes early. She had wanted to surprise Hartman by being the first one there. He was always the first person to arrive at everything thanks to his silly rule about always being ten minutes early. Palmer smiled to herself thinking about how confused he would look when he saw her sitting there patiently waiting for him.

It had been eleven months since she first met Hartman. Almost a year. They had taken things slow. Very slow. They still hadn't even had sex. But Hartman, apparently the most patient man in the world, never pushed her on it. It was one wall Palmer was not quite ready to let down. She wasn't sure when she would be. She wasn't even sure what the hold-up was. Deep down she thought maybe it was just too hard to let herself be that vulnerable again. She had always imagined she would be the type of girl who would only ever be with one man, the man who would be her husband. That was how confident she had been that she would end up with Calum. But she had been so, so wrong.

Palmer promised herself that next time she would be right. It would be right. She wouldn't get hurt that way again. She hadn't explained all of this to Hartman yet. But she would. Soon. She swore to herself that they would have that conversation soon. He deserved to hear it. Hartman was one of the kindest, most even-tempered people she had ever met. He had zero qualms with the slow and steady pace that Palmer had needed so far.

After their first kiss in the cemetery, Hartman had asked her on a date. It had felt a little awkward at first but then they had their second date and it felt less weird. Then another date, and another, and another. Before Palmer knew it she heard Hartman introduce her to someone as his girlfriend and it didn't scare her. He met her parents and they loved him. Palmer thought that she was maybe starting to love him too.

After a few months and a lot of phone calls to the police station, a detective finally called her back about the dental records and list of Jane Does she had dropped off. The detective told her that they had passed along the dental records to the counties that had open cases with Jane Does that matched but there was no news. They had assured Palmer that they would contact her as soon as they had anything concrete to go on.

Palmer tried not to let the disappointment of not getting an immediate match discourage her. She continued to research her side project. But these days she found she had less and less time to obsess over it.

Instead, she spent most of her free time with Hartman in his studio apartment above his dental practice. He would help with her research when he could, often giving her new ideas and avenues to go down.

Lately, Hartman had been encouraging her to get a small business loan to open up her own store. Palmer had briefly mentioned to him how she would love to have an antique store one day and ever since then, he had been dropping hints about how she should take the next steps.

Palmer warmed her hands on the outside of her to-go coffee cup and let the sun shine on her face. Hartman would be here any minute.

"Palmer?" said a voice from the sidewalk directly in front of her.

Palmer's heart stopped. Her throat tightened with dread. She slowly moved her gaze to where the voice came from. It was Calum. The world seemed to stop turning.

"Cal," she said in a near whisper.

Calum shoved his hands into his pockets and smiled awkwardly. Palmer was frozen. She had absolutely no idea what her face was doing. Her brain was empty.

Calum cleared his throat before speaking. "How have you been?"

Palmer didn't respond, she was still frozen in shock.

It had been three years since she had last seen him. Three years of nothing. He had completely disappeared from her life. He had never believed in having social media so there was no way to see what he had been doing since then. He had never called or texted her. A few months after Abuela's funeral she had called him in a desperate moment, just needing to hear his voice. The number was no longer in use. Realizing he had changed his number without telling her had led to a particularly dark spiral that had lasted longer than Palmer was proud of.

Then a few months after that, she drove by his parent's house and there was a for sale sign staked in the front yard. She had gotten out of the car to investigate. When she looked through the front window the house was completely empty. Emilia, her mother, had overheard someone at the grocery store say that Mr. and Mrs. Murphy had moved to the east coast somewhere. Palmer realized then that Cal was really, truly gone. She had expected another dark spiral but this time she had only felt numb. That numbness had lasted far, far longer than she ever dared say out loud.

But here he was. Cal. In the flesh.

Calum shifted on his feet. Palmer still had not responded to anything he had said. She just stared at him like an idiot. Palmer could feel the tension in the air like electricity. She tried to think of what to say. She willed her mouth to say words. But nothing came out. She just gaped at him.

He had vanished, backed away so quickly and efficiently from her life that a small part of her had been convinced that he was never actually real. He had been just a figment of her imagination, a way to cope with high school. But when she had moments like that she would dig out the box she kept high up in her closet. It was full of movie ticket stubs of all the movies they had ever seen together. It had her dried-up corsage from prom and the park pass from the class camping trip where they lost their virginities. It was also full of pictures of them. They were difficult to look at. If she looked too hard at the photos she could hear his laugh, feel his warm hand in hers, smell him. It was always too much. The photos made her feel like she was drowning. So she kept them in the box tucked away, only to be pulled down to prove to herself he was real.

"Palmer?" Calum said her name again. Concern etched his face.

Palmer swallowed and straightened her spine. "Calum." This time she said his voice with more confidence. He looked good. He wore dark gray jeans and a crisp white shirt. His black boots were scuffed but everything else about him looked clean and put together. His hair looked slightly wet like he had just showered not too long ago. Calum had been on the skinnier side in high school but he had filled out now. His skin was tan and his arms were toned like he maybe worked outside for a living.

"It's been a long time," he said. He moved closer to her.

Palmer fought off a shiver. "Three years," she said.

Calum nodded. "How are you?"

Palmer bunched her eyebrows together. The awe of seeing Calum in the flesh was starting to fade, replaced by anger. "How am I?" she asked.

Cal took a deep breath. "Yeah?"

Palmer huffed out a laugh. "Seriously?" she asked.

"I uh —, " he rubbed at the back of his neck.

"Cal. You disappear for three years without a trace and the first thing you decide to ask me is 'How are you'?" There was no sarcasm in her voice, just confusion. Palmer thought absently that maybe she was dreaming.

"I —," his words trailed off and he ran his hands through his hair. It was longer than it had been. "Jesus Palmer, I don't — I don't know how to do this," he said, gesturing between them.

"Clearly," she said as she stood up quickly. She needed to leave. Her head was too full of emotions.

"You look beautiful," Cal blurted out.

Palmer gawked at him. "Are you fucking kidding me right now Cal?" Palmer noted that her voice was shakier than she would have liked.

"I miss you," he blurted out again.

Palmer's eyes widened. "Wha — what is this?" she said in a low voice.

Calum continued with his verbal vomit. "I miss you so much that it hurts Palmer. I'm so sorry. For everything. I know that's not enough. It will never be enough, but I would do ANYTHING to make it right. If I could I would go back in time and pull a Marty McFly and fix everything. I would be a better guy. I thought— " he swallowed and looked at Palmer with pleading eyes. "I thought I was doing the right thing by you when I left. I was a piece of shit and you were the best thing that had ever happened to me. I loved you so much, I wanted the very best for you but I knew that wasn't me. You deserved so much better than me. And like an idiot and a coward, I left. I know now that I should have done everything in my power to be better for you then. To be the kind of man you deserve THEN. I was going through some shit. I was struggling with myself. My sense of self-worth, my absent parents, my life. And instead of asking for help from you, my best friend, I chose to struggle with it alone. You were the only person who ever really loved me and I pushed you away like a dumb ass. I'm still not good enough for you now, I probably will never be but I swear I will try every single day for the rest of my life to be a better guy if you let me." Calum paused and sniffed. "I thought about you every day. Everywhere I went, everyone I've met — you were there. Your memory *haunts* me, Palmer. Images of you, of us, play in my head on a loop like movie clips. Punishing me for losing you. Now I know what a curse it was for you to always know the ending of every movie because thinking that I know the ending of our story, knowing that our ending is this awful has destroyed me. You are the air that I breathe and I tried so hard to learn to breathe something else, anything else because I wasn't worthy. But I can't. I still love you, Palmer. I came back to find you and beg you, on my knees if I have to, to take me back. I can't let our movie end this way. I can't live the rest of my life knowing that I didn't try to change the ending. Change the ending with me Palmer, please." The words had exploded out of him. He had spoken so fast that he had barely taken a breath.

Palmer stared at Calum. Her coffee cup slipped from her hand and spilled onto the pavement but neither of them noticed. Calum looked like he wanted to move toward Palmer desperately but was holding himself back. Palmer only gaped at him with wide eyes. He had never, in all the time she knew him, spoken to her so openly and honestly about his feelings. He had never laid himself so bare. Now on top of the shock from seeing him again Palmer was faced with the shock of everything he just said. Her mind was whirling so fast she felt a little dizzy. Calum continued to stare at her earnestly, willing her to say something. Looking more vulnerable than she had ever seen him before.

"Uh, Palmer? Everything alright?" Hartman said from behind Calum.

Palmer's veins filled with ice. Hartman was standing directly behind Calum. He was wearing his navy scrubs, a slightly irritated look on his face. The look was directed to the back of Calum's head. Cal turned slowly and then looked at Hartman with confusion. They were both exceptionally tall but Calum seemed to have at least an inch on Hartman. Although Hartman likely had at least fifty pounds on Calum.

"Who's this guy?" Cal asked Palmer. Calum's voice had changed from the sincere one he was using with Palmer to his usual snarky one.

Palmer couldn't have spoken to save her life. Her brain was short-circuiting.

Hartman rolled his shoulders back and spoke. "I'm Hartman. Her boyfriend," he said confidently.

Cal whipped his head back to Palmer, then to Hartman, and finally back to Palmer almost comically. "THIS GUY?" he asked incredulously, his finger pointed at Hartman. Palmer still had no words. Cal turned back to Hartman. "What even are you? The world's largest male nurse?"

Palmer had never heard anyone talk to Hartman that way. Clearly, by the look on Hartman's face, he had also never heard anyone talk to him that way.

"What?" Hartman asked.

"Do you work at a retirement home for elderly WWE wrestlers or something?" Cal said sarcastically. He had switched from giving Palmer the most honest and sincere speech he had ever given her to classic Cal sarcasm so quickly Palmer felt like she was going to get whiplash.

Hartman looked at Cal coldly. "I'm a doctor," he said in a dry tone.

Calum nodded his head and pierced his lips slightly. Then he turned to Palmer. To anyone else, he would have seemed fine. But not to Palmer. She knew he often put up a mask to cover her feelings and she knew he was doing it now.

"A doctor. Wow. Way to go, Palmer," Cal said to her. Palmer parted her lips. She had no idea what to say or what to do but she desperately wanted to help him.

"Cal," she said in nearly a whisper.

Cal only smiled nonchalantly. Like he wasn't breaking and shook his head.

"Don't worry about it Beautiful," he said casually. But Palmer knew. She knew and it was killing her.

Hartman moved around Cal, bumping him ever so slightly on the shoulder. Cal gave him a lethal smile. Hartman had moved to Palmer's side and put his hand on Palmer's lower back. Calum tracked the movement with his eyes, sneering the entire time. A muscle ticked in his jaw.

"We didn't get to properly introduce ourselves, I'm Hartman," Hartman said, sticking out his hand. Calum didn't take it.

"Calum," he said back. He had a wicked twinkle in his eyes.

Hartman slowly put his hand back down to his side. "Ah, the infamous Calum," Hartman said in his business voice. "Well, we were just about to have some lunch, 'Cal'," Hartman said 'Cal' in a tone that spoke volumes as to how much he knew about Calum. The tone in Hartman's voice when he said Cal's name only caused Cal's devilish smirk to deepen.

"Nah, I'll have to pass this time," Cal said mockingly as if Hartman had invited him to join them. Then he turned to Palmer and his face changed to his real one. The one he seemed to only save for her. "I'll see you around," he said gently. Cal looked at Palmer's necklace then. It was peeking out from her jacket. He smiled. "You still wear that?" he asked her.

Palmer was still reeling from this entire interaction but she responded. "I never take it off," she said. Calum smiled genuinely. "Some things never change," he was speaking to her like Hartman wasn't even there.

To Palmer's shock, Cal started to reach toward her necklace slowly. His eyes were fixed on the pendant. Palmer could feel Hartman stiffen behind her but she didn't so much as flinch. Calum seemed transfixed. His index finger paused millimeters from the image on the pendant, the engraving of The Virgin Mary. Calum's eyebrows were knit together in deep concentration. His lips parted slightly. It felt like time had stopped. Then without warning he quickly pulled his hand away and looked up and behind Palmer, directly at Hartman. Palmer couldn't discern the look on Calum's face. It was like that look zoo-goers have on their face when they are looking for the tiger in the tiger enclosure but they can't seem to find it in all the greenery.

Calum shook his head, looked back to Palmer, and laughed nervously. "Anyway, like I said. I'll see you around." He said to Palmer. Cal gave her a sad smile and winked. He looked above her to Hartman and his face changed in an instant. A fierce, suspicious look spread over his features. His eyes narrowed and a muscle ticked in his jaw. Then he turned and walked away.

Palmer stared at Cal's back until he turned the corner at the end of the block. Then she stared at the space where he had been. Hartman was talking to her but she couldn't hear him. She was thinking too hard. What the fuck just happened?

Chapter Forty-Two

Present Day (2022)

Palmer sat awkwardly on the living room couch across from two police officers while Hartman made coffee in the kitchen behind her. She stared at her ridiculous orange socks and watched as she wiggled her toes. One of the police officers cleared her throat.

"Mrs. Roth, I understand you've been through a lot the past few days. Thank you for taking the time to sit down and chat with us," the female officer said.

Palmer shook her head. "Of course. I'm not sure how much I can help with. I still don't remember anything about what happened."

"I understand. Your doctor explained that you are experiencing some amnesia. We were anxious to speak with you right after the incident but your doctor was pretty adamant that we give you a few days. It's our understanding that you are starting to get back some of your memories. Is that correct?" the female officer asked.

Palmer nodded. "Yeah, I'm constantly remembering stuff but nothing... current yet. If that makes any sense."

The female officer nodded. The male officer grunted his understanding. Palmer could hear Hartman from somewhere behind her pull down some coffee mugs.

"What exactly is the last thing you remember?" the female officer asked. She was taking notes in a little yellow notebook.

Palmer looked down at her socks again and scrunched her nose, thinking. "When I woke up in the hospital the last thing I could remember was being a freshman in college. That was twelve years ago. But now —, things have been coming back. Now I remember when Hartman and I first started dating. Thank God." The last part she said under her breath. She heard Hartman fumble something in the kitchen.

Both officers nodded.

"But you don't remember anything from the night you were found? No idea why you were at the cabin? Anything you can give us would be helpful." the woman said.

Palmer shook her head. "I'm sorry." Palmer touched her head where steri-strips still held a small gash closed.

The male officer sighed but the female officer smiled encouragingly.

"Let's try this. I want to show you some pictures of where you were found and see if it sparks anything. Is that alright with you?" The female officer was still doing most of the talking. Obviously they had decided that she should take the lead.

Just then Hartman walked up and set down two mugs of black coffee in front of the two officers. He peered back at Palmer with a questioning look. Palmer gave him a nod, letting him know she was fine. He nodded back and took a seat next to her. His leg was warm against hers and she felt his arm come around her and rest on the back of the couch. The simple gesture made her feel less nervous.

The male officer put a folder on the coffee table between them and opened it up to reveal some large photos. The female officer pointed at a photo of a run-down-looking cabin covered in snow. The windows were dark and foggy.

"Do you remember if you've ever seen or been to this house before?" The female officer spread a few more pictures out on the table. Some of the pictures were of the inside of the cabin. It was almost as creepy and run down as the outside. It was covered in dust and cobwebs. The majority of it was made of rotting wood. It was small but had a main level and a second story. There was a treacherous-looking staircase with a big hole in one of the steps. In the photo, there was a yellow marker next to some dried blood at the bottom.

Palmer took a shaky breath and shook her head. "I'm sorry, I don't — I don't think so? It doesn't look familiar. Is that my blood?" she asked.

"Yes, you were found at the bottom of the steps. The blood is presumably from that gash on your head." The female officer responded.

The male officer began speaking then. "The paramedics thought that you may have slipped and fell on the stairs but it didn't add up. The bruising on your arms for one. But also, the force with which you landed was more consistent with someone pushing you or throwing you than just a simple fall. Once we got there and took a closer look we noticed some other evidence that made us think someone else had been there. Someone other than your husband that is."

Palmer whipped her head to Hartman then. He turned to her slowly and gave her a weak smile.

"You were there?" she asked.

"Yes. I found you," he said in his steady voice. "We got lucky. You have a location-sharing app on your phone. I made you download it when you started the antique shop years ago. You were all over the place going to garage sales and estate sales in other towns. You were meeting up with strangers on the Facebook marketplace to buy items for the shop. It gave me some peace of mind."

"And thank God you did otherwise this could have ended very differently," the male cop added. The female police officer nodded her agreement.

Palmer still looked confused. So Hartman continued. "I had a surgery that day that ran late. When I came out of the operating room I decided to check the app to see if you had gone home or if you were at the shop still working late. But you weren't at either. According to the app you were way out in the middle of nowhere. I tried calling you but you didn't answer so I panicked. I got in my car and followed the directions on my phone. When I saw you lying there —," Hartman's voice cracked.

Palmer reached her hand over to his and squeezed gently. He squeezed back.

The female officer started to speak again. "Your husband called 911 but we have no idea what happened up to that point. Like I said, once we started looking around it was obvious someone else had been there. There were footprints. Not large enough to be your husband's." She slid out another photo and pointed. There were footprints in the dust on the second floor. Not shoe prints. Literal footprints. Like someone had been standing there in their bare feet. A chill ran down Palmer's spine.

In a different photo, Palmer saw another yellow marker next to a phone. The screen was cracked.

"Is that my phone?" she asked.

"Yeah," the female officer said and pulled out something from her bag. It was an evidence bag with the phone from the picture inside. "We're done with it on our end. You're free to have it back now."

The officer took the phone out of the bag and set it on the coffee table between them. "We went through it but weren't able to get any answers. We're still not sure why you drove up there or who was there with you. Other than your car and your husband's car there was no evidence of any other vehicle."

"Did you find my necklace?" Palmer asked a little too quickly.

The officers looked at each other and frowned.

Finally, the female officer spoke. "I'm sorry, what necklace?"

"It's gold. It has a religious pendant on it. An image of The Blessed Mother?" said Palmer.

Hartman chimed in. "She wears it all the time. Never takes it off. I called your office and left a message about it a couple of days ago."

"We must have missed the message. When did you notice it was missing?" the female officer asked.

"A few hours after I woke up at the hospital. The hospital staff said they didn't have it. I was hoping you guys would find it at the scene," Palmer said hopefully.

"No. I'm sorry. We didn't find anything like that and we turned that place upside down," the female officer responded.

Palmer's heart sank.

Hartman spoke up then. "Do you guys have a working theory?" he asked.

The officers looked at each other then before the male one spoke. "We have a few. Maybe someone got into your vehicle with you and forced you to drive up to that shack. We searched your truck though and didn't find anything to support that theory. The other theory, the one we're leaning toward is that you drove out there by yourself for some reason. Maybe you were meeting up with someone to purchase something for the store? When you got there maybe things got heated and you were pushed." The officer shrugged before his partner continued where he stopped.

"There's a few issues with that theory though as well. First of all, we combed through your messages on your phone and didn't find any conversations that would support that idea. Maybe you had a conversation though in person. Who knows. Second, whoever was there with you disappeared without a trace. There were no tire tracks from any mystery vehicle. They would have had to leave on foot. That being said they wouldn't have gotten far in the woods this time of year. We looked for any tracks and found none."

"To be honest Mrs. Roth, we are at a bit of a loss. We don't have any answers for you. That being said, it would help us out a bunch if you could let us know as soon as you remember ANYTHING from that night," the male officer finished.

Palmer nodded her head but it was Hartman who spoke up. "We have your number and we will contact you the second she remembers anything significant."

The officers and Hartman stood up so Palmer gingerly stood up as well. She was feeling a little shaky.

Hartman started to escort the police toward the door.

"Thank you Mrs. Roth for agreeing to see us. I do apologize if we caused you any additional distress. We hope you get to feeling much better soon. And Dr. Roth thank you for the coffee and the hospitality. We'll be in touch."

The female officer hesitated by the door and turned then, walking back to where Palmer stood. She reached into her pocket and pulled out a card with her name and phone number on it. She handed it to Palmer.

"Your husband has our info but I wanted to make sure you had it as well. Don't hesitate to call," she added.

Then both officers left, leaving Palmer and Hartman alone in the house. Palmer turned and walked toward the window. She watched as the police car turned and slowly made its descent down the driveway.

Chapter Forty-Three

The Map (2018)

Palmer sat on a short stool in the very back of her store. She was sifting through some boxes of random crap she had picked up at an estate sale a few weeks earlier. She had tucked them back here to sort through when she had the time. Right now she was trying to make the time.

Palmer's antique store, "Tiffany's Epiphanies", had been open for about a year and a half. It was Palmer's baby. She poured herself into it. She worked tirelessly to give it just the right vibe. Finding the most unique and unusual items to stock it with. Business had been slow at first but had been picking up here the last few months. Palmer's projections that she frequently checked and updated on her computer weren't stellar but weren't necessarily bleak either. She couldn't have been more thrilled.

Palmer's side project had taken a back seat in her new life. Sure she still occasionally thought of a new part of the case to explore, a new explanation for what could have happened. She sent emails to podcasts that covered cold cases at least twice a year. She checked in with the police station every so often just to make sure there weren't any new leads. But it was less and less often these days. Palmer was busy with the store and with Hartman.

Additionally, the weird shit that usually happened to her had almost completely stopped. No more dead birds or other ominous shit. No more creepy lady sightings. No more shadows. Sure she still had the creepy feeling she was never actually alone but these days she just chalked it up to anxiety.

The back of the store was closed off from the front by a couple of mismatched vintage folding room dividers. The front of the store was neat and organized. Everything in its place. But behind the dividers was a disaster. It looked like a bomb had gone off in a time machine. Books, dishes, furniture, jewelry, and appliances from every decade were scattered and tossed all over in unorderly heaps. It never bothered Palmer one bit. If anything it made her feel exhilarated. Like she was standing in a real-life I Spy book. Anything was possible back here.

Palmer was hunched over shifting through a large box of paperwork. She had found this particular box at an estate sale of an older gentleman who had passed away. The man had been a real local, born and raised in this town. He had also been a real historian based on his belongings. While Palmer had of course been saddened by the news of his passing she had also been admittedly excited to get her hands on some of this local junk. That kind of stuff sold like hotcakes in her store.

In the box were aged photographs of some of the town's oldest families. Foggy black and white photos of unsmiling people stared back at Palmer as she rifled. There were other photos mixed in as well. There were photos of some of the oldest houses in town and Palmer set them aside to show to the historical society. There were old newspaper clippings from the town's founding and she set those aside as well. Palmer still had some contacts at the newspaper and she made a mental note to contact them tomorrow. Whatever the newspaper or the historical society wasn't interested in she would frame and sell in the store. There were old maps and land surveys also tucked in the box and she pulled them out, setting them on her lap.

Palmer flipped through the sketches and maps of the county. She was familiar with most of the surrounding area around her hometown. You don't grow up in a small isolated mountain town without being familiar with the majority of the trails that exist around it. Palmer's father Chuck had been a hunter when she was growing up and had always made sure Palmer knew where all the public lands and reservations were.

Palmer pulled out one particularly detailed map of the woods just north of town and studied it. Her eyes trailed the small road that led up a mountain to a beautiful cliff with an amazing view that only some locals even knew about. She found the spot on the map where Calum had pulled the car over to show her that particular view for the first time. The spot where he told Palmer that he loved her for the first time. Palmer's chest ached ever so slightly and she nearly folded the map back up when her eyes caught on something else in the map.

There was a smaller road indicated on the map that she had never seen before. It connected to the main road just a little ways past where Palmer remembered her and Calum stopping. She followed the road with her finger, trying to determine where it led. It wound through the woods eventually stopping in the middle of nowhere. Palmer bunched her eyebrows together. Then she gripped the paper a little tighter. She remembered seeing something, maybe some kind of building off in the distance all those years ago when she had looked out at that view. It had been only a small brown speck back then but Palmer remembered the irrational dread it had given her. A fraction of that fear passed over her now even though she knew it was ridiculous.

A hand gripped her shoulder from behind and Palmer screamed, nearly toppling off of the stool.

"Palmer! It's just me!" Hartman said forcefully. He had grabbed her by both arms trying to keep her upright.

"Oh my God! Hartman, you scared me half to death," Palmer gripped her chest. She tried to steady her breathing.

"I can tell. Good Lord," Hartman said. He looked nearly as shaken up as she did.

Palmer laughed a little. "I'm sorry, I thought I was in here alone. I didn't hear you come in. I was just sorting through some of this inventory," she explained.

"I just got off work and changed clothes. We were supposed to grab dinner tonight, remember? The closed sign is up but the door isn't locked. I've told you a hundred times how unsafe that is," he said sternly.

"I'm sorry, I must have forgotten." Palmer pushed her hair back and out of her face. Hartman nodded but still looked stern. "I can sort through the rest of this tomorrow. It's not going anywhere," Palmer added before she stood up. She straightened her clothes and turned to leave but noticed Hartman's attention on the map she had dropped.

"That's a cool map," Hartman knelt down to pick it up.

Palmer looked down at the map as well. "Yeah, I got it at that estate sale a few weeks ago. It was mixed in with a bunch of cool old photos of the town and some of the founders. There's a bunch of cool maps in here." Palmer pulled out a few of the other maps. Some of them looked as though they were hand-drawn.

"My dad was a big map guy," Hartman said lightly. He looked at the map for another second before getting up and dusting himself off.

Palmer took a moment to drink him in. He wore dark gray pants, dress shoes, and a button-up shirt. Hartman always looked like he was one flex away from ripping any shirt that wasn't made of stretch material. Palmer smirked at the thought. She just knew that he would be ogled by every woman at the restaurant. He was hard to miss.

Palmer had worn a dress to work today knowing that they had dinner plans. She had picked out one of Hartman's favorites. It was white and flowy with little red flowers all over it. It was one of the only dresses she owned that hadn't been secondhand. Palmer typically bought vintage or preowned clothing.

"You ready to go?" Hartman asked.

"Yep," Palmer responded.

Palmer walked to the front of the store and grabbed her purse from behind the counter where the cash register sat. Hartman held the door to the store open for her and she stepped out. Once it was shut she took out her keys and locked up.

They walked in silence, hand in hand to their favorite Italian restaurant only a couple blocks away. Palmer's heart sank when she noticed the closed sign on the door. She turned to Hartman. "Oh no, I'm sorry Hart. They're closed. Should we try somewhere else?"

Hartman only smiled at her sheepishly and knocked on the door. Palmer watched in confusion. A waiter came to the door and let them in without saying a word, only giving Hartman a knowing look.

The moment Palmer walked in she knew something was happening. The restaurant was completely transformed. It was empty of any customers except for them, and instead of multiple tables like there usually were, there was only one small table set with pristine white roses in a vase. There were twinkling lights hanging from the ceiling and romantic music was playing from somewhere.

Palmer had made it halfway to the table before turning to Hartman. She began to say his name. "Hartma —" her voice trailed off.

The waiter had disappeared and Hartman was behind her. He was down on one knee. Palmer froze in shock. He was holding a small red velvet box that was open to reveal a ring nestled inside. It was a thick-banded platinum ring with a large round diamond in a bezel setting.

"Palmer. You walked into my life three years ago and changed everything. I had no idea that day that I would be meeting the woman I would want to spend the rest of my life with. You were a surprise. The best surprise. I love you. Would you do me the greatest honor imaginable and be my wife? Marry me Palmer," Hartman said.

Palmer looked into one of his blue eyes and then the other. She chastised herself for not seeing this coming. Nearly three years they had been together. Of course, he had been thinking about marriage. Jessica had gotten married two years ago to Jayce and they had their first baby less than a year later. She was twenty-six years old. That was about the right age she assumed. And Hartman was older, well into his thirties. She didn't technically live with him but she stayed at his apartment at least four to five nights a week.

Palmer realized Hartman was still looking at her earnestly. Waiting for an answer.

This was Hartman. The man who had somehow slowly but surely pulled her out of the dark hole she had dug herself into the years following Abuela's death. He had gently knocked down all of her walls until there was nothing left. Well, except for one. They still hadn't had sex. He never pushed her, but he had asked her about it once. In his gentle way. She had explained her past and explained her desire to wait this time. He had respected her and didn't bring it up again. He was the most dependable and kind man she had ever met. He was her rock. He was hers.

She understood then that he was asking her for more than just her hand in marriage. He was asking her to let down that one last wall she had put up. He was asking her to trust him.

"Yes," she answered firmly.

Hartman's eyes lit up and a huge smile overtook his face. A panicky laugh bubbled out of Palmer before Hartman stood and picked her up, swinging her in the air. Eventually, he set her down and smothered her with kisses before slipping the ring on her finger.

Chapter Forty-Four

Present Day (2022)

Palmer stood at the big window in the living room that looked out over the driveway and the forest. The winter sky was overcast with the promise of a storm. It had been that way for days. The two officers had left just moments before after asking her questions she didn't have the answers to. At least not yet.

Palmer felt Hartman's presence behind her. He was remarkably quiet for a man of his size.

"You remember me?" he asked her in a low deep voice.

The police had asked her during their interview about her most recent memories. She had responded that she could remember dating Hartman but not much after that point. Hartman was only feet away when she had said it. He must have been surprised. She hadn't told him that she remembered him yet.

Palmer looked down at her ring finger. In the hospital, she had noticed she wasn't wearing a wedding ring. Looking now she could see that there was a band of skin around her finger that was lighter in color than the rest of her hand. Indicating that she usually wore a ring there.

"Where is my wedding ring?" she whispered.

Palmer heard Hartman shift behind her so she turned. He was digging through his pocket. Finally, he pulled out a ring. It was the same one he proposed to her with only now there was an additional band that had been soldered to it. Hartman twirled the ring in his big fingers.

"They had to take it off of you for x-rays when they first brought you in. Dr. Walters gave it to me to hold onto. I would have given back to you right away but —," he shrugged slightly. His face looked so sad. "But when you woke up and I realized you didn't remember... I guess I just didn't know how to give it back to you. Or if you would even want it. So I held onto it."

Palmer reached up and put her right hand on Hartman's cheek. He leaned into it. Then she put her left hand out, silently asking him to put the ring on. He looked her in the eye. His eyes were watery and he gave her a hopeful smile as he slipped the ring on.

Palmer looked down at the ring and watched how it glittered in the light. It was heavier than she had expected.

Hartman spoke again. "You never answered my question," he said.

"Hmm?"

"You remember me?" he asked.

"I remember you, Hartman," Palmer said with a smile. "Or at least, I remember you up until you gave me this ring. You said I was a surprise, the best surprise," her smile widened as she spoke and Hartman chuckled. "But everything after that is still blurry. I'm still waiting for the rest."

"It'll come to you," he said and he leaned down so their foreheads were touching.

Palmer could feel his breath on her lips. The urge to tilt her head up and kiss him was so strong she was nearly shaking.

"Maybe tonight we could have dinner?" Hartman said before she could act on her impulse.

"We've established that we're married right? I know my brain still isn't working right but I'm assuming that we eat dinner together pretty much every night, right?" Palmer responded.

Hartman chuckled and took both of her hands. "We do, but I want to do something special."

"Ok, what did you have in mind?" she asked.

Chapter Forty-Five

The Best Day (2019)

Palmer stood in front of a large ornate mirror and examined the details of her wedding dress. It was a cream ball gown with a drop waist and delicate sleeves that hung from Palmer's shoulders. Palmer gently traced the lace and beadwork on the sweetheart neckline. There was even more lace and beadwork toward the bottom of the gown. She had found it at a vintage bridal shop in Denver and had fallen in love with it immediately. She hadn't told anyone but she had chosen it because it looked almost identical to the one that Christine Daae wore in Phantom of the Opera.

Palmer's hair was curled and held half up with glittering, delicate hairpins. She wore no veil but had long dangling earrings made of multiple pearls. They had been Abuela's. Palmer met her own eyes in the mirror and took a deep breath. She leaned in a bit closer to the mirror. There was a fly on her cheek and she swiped at it and it flew off before returning and landing on her cheek again. It walked along her cheek and toward the bridge of her nose. Palmer went to swat at it again with her hand but paused. She realized she could see the fly in the mirror but she couldn't feel it on her face. She couldn't hear it buzzing either. That was odd.

Palmer leaned even closer to the mirror. She watched as the bug walked down her nose toward her nostrils. Then she sucked in a breath as she watched it stroll right up her nose. But she still felt nothing. No tickle in her nose. Then, in horror, Palmer watched as the bug crawled out of the tear duct of her right eye. Palmer stepped back but it was too late.

The Palmer in the mirror had started to change. She watched, glued to the spot, as her reflected face started to decay. Her full rosy cheeks became pale and sunken then the skin started to rot rapidly. Her previously green irises faded to silver. The curls in her hair became lank and stringy. Her skin was decomposing and pulling back to reveal patches of her cheekbone and her skull.

An awful smell hit Palmer then. The smell of rotten meat and fruit shoved itself up her nose. It was strong enough that she almost gagged. Then Palmer saw her. There, in the corner of the mirror, standing at the far end of the room, was the woman. It had been years since Palmer had seen her. Palmer's knees threatened to buckle. She ignored her disgusting reflection in the mirror, focusing only on the woman.

"Gabriella?" Palmer whispered.

The woman said nothing but her arm slowly started to come up, as if she was reaching for Palmer from very far away.

Just then Palmer heard a knock on the door. Palmer jumped slightly and in one blink the woman was gone. Palmer looked back at her reflection. Her mirror self was back to normal. Palmer gently placed her hand on the mirror.

The knock on the door came again and Palmer's mother stuck her head in.

"Are you ready?" asked Emilia.

Palmer turned toward her mother, trying to get a hold of herself.

"Oh honey, are you nervous? You're going to do fine. Everyone gets a little nervous on their wedding day. Take a deep breath. They are just about ready for you."

Palmer turned back to the mirror. Still normal. She ran her hands down her dress again and took a deep steadying breath before turning back to her mother.

"I'm ready," she said firmly.

Emilia smiled at her daughter and gave her a big hug, a kiss on the cheek, and took her hand.

"Let's go get you married huh?" said Palmer's mother.

Emilia led Palmer out of the dressing room and down the hall toward the entrance to the main part of the church. Palmer's bridesmaids and Hartman's groomsmen were already paired off and lined up, ready to enter the church at any moment. At the back of the line was Jessica, Palmer's matron of honor.

Jessica's hands were full, she was carrying her own small bouquet as well as Palmer's giant one. Not to mention her swollen belly, she was seven months along with her and Jayce's second baby. Even with a toddler and another one on the way she had refused to pass off her maid of honor duties to one of Palmer's cousins. God bless her. Jessica had been paired off with Hartman's best man, a buddy of his from dental school.

Jessica turned and found Palmer. She gave Palmer a wide smile and handed her the larger bouquet. It was jam-packed with velvety white roses, Hartman's favorite. Then she reached her hand out for Palmer's.

"You just say the word and I'll get you the hell out of here. We can pull a Julia Roberts in Runaway Bride," Jessica said with a wink.

Hartman's best man looked at them in shock, clearly not hearing the sarcasm in Jessica's voice.

Palmer laughed nervously. Of course, Jessica was joking but a part of Palmer paused at her words. Was she really doing this?

Before Palmer could panic her father stepped in beside her.

"You doin' ok kid? You look a little pale," Chuck looked her up and down before adding, "Well, pale-ER."

"Thanks, Dad," Palmer chuckled. She slipped her arm around his and watched as the wedding party slowly started to trickle into the church. Palmer focused on her breathing. This was happening.

It was almost Palmer's turn. She watched as Jessica waddled her way through the door arm in arm with Hartman's best man. Moments later the music changed, signaling that Palmer was coming next. She heard nearly two hundred people stand all at once and stopped breathing.

"Just hold on tight baby, I got you," Chuck said under his breath and he started to walk. Palmer's feet followed suit even though her brain had shut off. They walked through the door and too many faces stared back at her. Her eyes bounced from face to face rapidly taking it all in. Colorful, warm light filtered in through the stained glass windows illuminating the church. The wood of the pews glowed and white rose petals littered the floor beneath her.

Palmer heard Chuck sniff next to her as they made their way to the altar. The altar. Palmer looked up then and toward the front of the church where the wedding party stood. There, next to the priest, stood Hartman.

His eyes were locked on her, tracking every step she took as she came closer and closer. Before she knew it she was standing in front of him. The priest was saying something to Chuck and Chuck responded but she didn't hear them. She only saw Hartman. Finally, Hartman reached his hand out for her. Palmer looked at his open, big strong hand. She raised her hand to place it inside of his but paused inches from touching his palm.

Palmer looked up at Hartman. He gave her a warm smile and nodded his head. Palmer looked back down at her hand for another moment. Then she placed it gently in his.

Forty-five minutes later Palmer walked out of the church hand in hand with Hartman. Palmer had never seen a bigger smile on Hartman's face. The new Dr. and Mrs. Roth were led around the side of the church along with the wedding party and immediate family to take pictures. Palmer was hugged and kissed over and over again by family and friends.

The photographer started with Palmer and Hartman first, directing them to stand in certain places and pose in different ways. From where they were currently standing Palmer could see the wedding guests make their way out of the church and mingle in front before getting in their cars to go to the reception. Palmer's eyes drifted from guest to guest trying to identify them from this distance. Palmer paused.

Among the sea of people moving out of the church stood a still, tall figure all in black. He was facing the side of the church where they were getting their photos taken. His hands were in his pockets, his tie hung loose around his neck, and his hair was disheveled. He was looking right at her. She could barely make out his face but she knew it was him.

"Palmer?" The photographer said her name in a way that made Palmer think it wasn't the first time she had tried to get her attention. Hartman's hand squeezed hers.

"I'm sorry what?" Palmer responded.

"Can you look directly at the camera?" the photographer asked.

"Oh I'm so sorry," Palmer apologized. She gave a fake smile but her eyes drifted back to where she had thought she saw Calum.

He was gone.

Chapter Forty-Six

Present Day (2022)

Palmer sat in front of the vanity inside her colossal closet and applied bright red lipstick to her full lips. She had straightened her long dark hair and applied a generous amount of mascara to her long eyelashes to accentuate her green eyes. She hadn't yet picked out what she would wear tonight for her date with Hartman so she still wore a robe from her shower.

Hartman had been very secretive about what he had planned for their date but he seemed so excited about it that Palmer hadn't pushed him for details. The majority of Palmer's day had been spent with Hartman giving her a tour of their home. She didn't tell him that she had already given herself a little tour. Instead, she let him lead her around and tell her about various design choices, artwork, and furniture. It was helpful, she still didn't remember the house at all. She had assumed they bought it after they got married but according to Hartman, they had built it just a few years ago.

Apparently he had designed the house before they had even met. He bought the land when they were still engaged and surprised her with the property and the blueprints after they were married. Hartman explained that it took just over a year to build so they had only actually been living in the house for about two years now. Hartman had walked her around the property showing her the lay of the land and giving her details about what he still had planned. A shed here, maybe a barn there, a garden here, etc. Palmer's head was swimming by the end.

Pain had started to press into Palmer's temples so she had excused herself to take a nap. On the way to the bedroom, she grabbed the phone the officers had left. It was dead. She took it upstairs and plugged it into the charger.

She wasn't sure what Hartman had been up to while she slept but it sounded like he was doing something in the basement. When she woke from her nap she found another note from him. This time it was on her nightstand.

Palmer,

Had to run to town again.

I'll be back by 6 pm for our date.

Dress up for me.

Love you,

Hart

Palmer looked at the clock now. It was nearly 5:45 pm. Palmer looked back into the vanity and rubbed her lipstick together between her lips before standing. She still hadn't decided on what she would wear. The sheer size of her closet still overwhelmed her. She started to separate the clothing that hung from hangers trying to find something suitable to wear. She had no idea what Hartman's plans were. No idea where they were going or what the dress code was so she decided to go formal. She found a sleek black dress that hugged her curves and stopped mid-thigh. It was a little slutty but she was *feeling* a little slutty. Embarrassingly enough Palmer still didn't remember her and Hartman's first time together. She had only started remembering their wedding day this afternoon. Butterflies flooded her stomach at the thought.

Palmer slipped her feet into some black heels and stepped in front of her mirror to get the full effect. She felt only a little ridiculous. After all, she was excited to go on a date with her husband she was just starting to remember. It was a bit incredible.

Palmer sprayed some perfume on her neck and wrists before grabbing a peacoat off of its hook. It would be cold tonight and she was sure she would need it. She slung the coat on her arm and started to make her way downstairs. She was certain Hartman would be here any minute. Palmer's heels clicked on the wood of the stairs and she heard the door to the garage close.

"Hart?" Palmer called out. Just then she saw his broad frame walk through the door. He was wearing a suit, but he was also holding two pizza boxes. Palmer's eyebrows knit together in confusion and she cocked her head.

"Hey!" he said brightly.

"I thought we were going out?" she said, gesturing to her outfit. Palmer had finally made it to the first floor and started to walk toward him. Hartman let out an impressed whistle.

"Wow," he said in awe. Palmer paused her walk and allowed him to take in every inch of her. Hartman took his time. Eventually, he spoke.

"I uh, I'm sorry. You look incredible," he said, chastising himself for not being able to find the right words to say.

"Thank you." Palmer smiled. His attention warmed her core.

Hartman shook his head and looked down at the pizza boxes still in his hands. "I um, I thought we could stay in. I had an idea," he walked toward Palmer and kissed her on the cheek. Palmer savored his woody, minty smell. She hadn't flinched and Hartman looked pleased when he moved back.

"Right this way, Mrs. Roth," he said and guided her toward the basement stairs.

Hartman opened the door and started to walk down first. Once he was a couple steps down he took his free hand and offered it to Palmer to help her take the steps in her heels. Once she was halfway she could see everything he had done to the basement that afternoon.

The room was dark except for the twinkling lights that Hartman must have hung from the ceiling. He moved the furniture so that a small table could be set in the middle of the room. On the table was a vase with crisp white roses and a bottle of wine. On one wall he had pulled down a large white projector screen.

"What is this?" Palmer asked. Hartman walked to the small table and set down the pizza. He picked up a remote and pointed it at the screen. Alfred Hitchcock's Psycho started to play on the screen. Palmer followed Hartman to the table with a confused look on her face.

Hartman smiled at Palmer. "Pizza in a basement," he said, shrugging a little.

Palmer smiled nervously and shook her head. Then understanding dawned on her face.

"Pizza in a basement," she whispered. Then a laugh bubbled out of her throat.

"Like our first date," Hartman said. Palmer laughed even harder. She had to wipe her eyes with her fingers to keep her mascara from running.

"You think THAT was our first date? The pizza in the morgue?" she asked.

Hartman looked genuinely taken aback. "Well yeah, of course. Don't you?" Palmer laughed even harder.

Hartman guided Palmer to her seat. There was a small handmade place card on the plate and she read it silently before bursting with laughter again.

"Marion Crane?" Palmer asked.

Hartman smiled broadly and took his seat. He reached into the first pizza box and served them each a slice. Palmer's heart was full to bursting. He had done all of this for her. They ate and talked, all the while Psycho played in the background. Palmer loved every second of it.

Two hours later Hartman walked Palmer up to their room, one hand on her back and the other hand holding her shoes. Palmer's skin felt warm from the wine and she giggled at how responsible Hartman was as he switched all the lights off as they moved up to the master bedroom. Palmer paused in the door frame, staring absently into the dark room. She could feel Hartman move behind her, his breath on her neck. Palmer shivered slightly.

Hartman's hand moved under Palmer's hair and she felt the back of his finger caress the top of her spine. Palmer turned then and looked up into his bright blue eyes. His large chest rose and fell rhythmically and Palmer laid her hand on it. She felt his heartbeat beneath her palm. She reached up on the tips of her toes and put her lips on his gently. His free hand pulled her to him by her waist and the kiss deepened. Palmer pulled back, turned, and walked to the bed. She pulled her dress over her head, revealing her red lingerie. She climbed into the bed and looked at Hartman. Her heart was beating wildly in her chest.

Hartman watched her from the doorway with predatory focus. The top few buttons of his suit were unbuttoned, his hands were at his sides. In one hand he still held her shoes, the other was clenched into a hard fist.

"Hart?" Palmer said quietly. Hartman seemed to come out of his trance and he looked her in the eye as he walked into the room. He set her shoes down neatly on the floor next to the door. Then he removed his jacket and laid it on the chair that sat in the corner. He slipped off his own shoes and placed them next to hers. Hartman's eyes never left Palmer's.

Finally, he walked to the bed where Palmer sat waiting for him. Instead of climbing in with her, he knelt down before her. He was so tall that his face was level with hers. Hartman gently rubbed his hands up and down Palmer's thighs. Little bolts of electricity shot to her core at his touch and she trembled. His palms slowly moved to her waist, his eyes never leaving hers.

Palmer leaned forward and kissed him then. His taste was safe and familiar to her. Hartman started to stand and he lifted her further onto the bed. He stood over her and stared for a moment. Drinking her in. Finally, he took off his shirt revealing his toned upper body. It was so perfect. Palmer thought briefly that he looked like a statue of some god in a museum. Slowly he started to take off his pants and Palmer sucked in a breath once he fully revealed himself to her. So with shaky hands, Palmer removed her bra and sipped out of her panties. With predacious focus, Hartman tracked every move she made.

He watched her for a moment longer before getting onto the bed and moving on top of her. Palmer was vibrating with energy. His painfully slow pace had only caused her nerves to skyrocket. Hartman kissed her while his hands explored her naked body. The calluses on his palms caused goosebumps to form along her milky skin.

Palmer was desperate for more, to see him unleashed. So she reached down and found him. Hartman made a deep feral sound in his throat, it vibrated on her lips where they kissed. She started to stroke him and she felt the muscles in his biceps shudder, the muscles holding him up like they might give out.

Hartman flipped them then so that he was laying on his back and she was straddling him. His large hands gripped her waist. Palmer looked him in the eyes as she licked her middle finger and slowly touched between her legs, readying her entrance. Hartman clenched his jaw so tightly Palmer was worried he would break his teeth. Then she slowly lowered herself onto him. Palmer tilted her head back and panted as she took in his full length. She felt Hartman's grip tighten on her love handles but not enough to hurt her. Once she was fully seated she looked at him again. He looked like his self-restraint was being held together by a string.

Palmer started to move her hips, finding her pleasure. She closed her eyes and felt one of Palmer's hands move from her side and she nearly came apart when she felt his thumb on her most sensitive spot.

"Look at me," he said in a commanding tone. Palmer had never heard him use that tone before and her eyes flashed open. The circles his thumb was making became faster and Palmer felt the beginning of her release. She went to throw her head back in ecstasy but the hand Hartman had on her side moved with lightning speed to the back of her neck. He pulled her face down to crush his mouth to hers right as she climaxed. He kissed her hard, sucking on her tongue. Palmer's body shuddered around him and he growled into her mouth as he came as well. His teeth bit into Palmer's lower lip and she thought she tasted metal.

Hartman stroked Palmer's back and lifted her up, laying her on the bed next to him and covering her up. He kissed her forehead and stroked her cheek.

"I love you," he whispered to her.

"I love you too," she whispered back.

Hartman touched his forehead to hers for a moment before getting out of bed and walking to the bathroom. He switched on the light. Palmer lay there in the massive bed and tried to stop smiling like a weirdo but she couldn't. She grabbed a pillow next to her and covered her face, trying to smother the giddiness. The light from the bathroom illuminated the bedroom. Palmer removed the pillow from her face and looked at it quizzically.

There was a small, bright red stain on the white pillowcase. Palmer wiped at her mouth and looked at the back of her hand. She was bleeding slightly. Hartman had bitten her lip earlier and she had thought she tasted something metallic. It was her blood. Hartman had bitten her and drawn blood.

Chapter Forty-Seven

The Feeling (2021)

Palmer folded a couple of embroidered cloth napkins and stuffed them into a picnic basket. She stood back and took a short mental inventory to make sure she had grabbed everything. She had wanted to surprise Hartman with lunch today. Palmer had called his office earlier and made sure his schedule was light and he would be free for lunch.

Palmer grabbed a couple of forks and stuck them into the basket as well before picking it up and placing it on her arm. She had put the lunch together in the back of her shop and had used a basket from her inventory. She smiled thinking about how surprised her husband would be with this little lunch.

She made her way to the front. Palmer caught Susan's eye and gave her a little wave. Susan was talking to a customer and Palmer didn't want to interrupt. She had hired Susan a couple of years ago to help run the store part-time. But last year Palmer had offered her a full-time position and Susan had gladly accepted. It had been Hartman's idea.

Palmer loved the shop but running the front, selling the items to customers, was not her favorite. No, her true passion was the hunt. Finding the treasures that stocked the store. The shop was doing well enough now that Palmer could take that step back and it felt good.

Palmer opened the big wooden door to her shop and stepped out into the cool autumn air. The bell on the door dinged as she exited. Palmer pulled her cardigan together and started to walk the couple blocks to Hartman's office. It was sunny but just chilly enough that Palmer was glad she had decided to put on the long red cardigan.

It was a Tuesday afternoon in a small town so the streets were fairly bare of cars. The sidewalk was mostly free of people. Palmer crossed the street to the next block. Palmer could hear the sound of her shoes on the pavement, and the wind moving through the trees. Every once in a while a car would drive past.

Out of nowhere, Palmer felt cold dread wash over her. A light sheen of sweat formed on her upper lip. Palmer stopped walking and turned around. There was no one there. Her fight-or-flight response had turned on so quickly that she could have sworn there had to be someone or something behind her. Palmer shook her head and berated herself silently for being so silly. She walked on.

The fear remained coiled tight in her belly. Palmer looked over her shoulder again. Still nothing. She looked to her right, to the street. Nothing. There was no one on the other side of the street. She looked to her left. Just familiar storefronts.

Palmer continued to walk. She heard something from behind her. Like a scuff. She whipped her head around. Again nothing. Now Palmer's heart was racing. Panic flooding up to her throat. She started to walk faster. Only another block to go and she would be at Hartman's office.

Then she saw it. The shadow in the corner of her eye. It was so familiar to her. Palmer closed her eyes gently. It had been years since anything weird had happened to her. Palmer took a deep breath and slowly turned her head to the left where she had barely caught a glimpse of the shadow.

Palmer saw her reflection in a storefront window. The light was shining off the window brightly, causing the window to look dark but Palmer's reflection to be more vivid. Palmer looked at herself then her gaze moved to the reflection that stood directly behind her. The shadow. It was in the shape of a person, someone a little shorter than her. There were no details. Just a basic outline. Palmer's eyes darted to the spot behind her where the reflection indicated someone should be standing. Only there was no one there.

Palmer's eyes darted to the unmoving shadow figure reflected behind her. Her mind tried to make sense of it. Maybe it was just a trick of the light, or maybe Palmer was getting a migraine and she had a dark spot in her vision. But deep down, Palmer's intuition knew none of that was true.

Palmer took a step forward and watched in horror as the figure moved a step as well. Palmer moved another step, and the figure's reflection remained close behind her. Maybe only a foot or two away. Palmer's hands started to shake and she started to walk quickly. She tried not to look at the storefront windows as she walked but she couldn't help it. Halfway down the block, she looked and there it was again only this time its arms were starting to come up as if it would try and grab her.

Palmer took off in a sprint running down the sidewalk like a mad woman. She refused to look at her reflection again but she could have sworn she saw the shadow in the corner of her eye as she ran.

Finally, she reached Hartman's office and yanked the door open only to run face-first into something hard. She nearly dropped the basket. Palmer thought for a moment how absurd it was that she was still holding onto the basket at all.

"Whoa! Palmer? Are you ok?" she heard Hartman say. She had run right into his chest.

"Hartman!" she cried.

"What is it? What's wrong?" he asked sternly. He started to check her all over, assessing her for injury or distress.

Palmer quickly explained what had happened. Hartman only listened intently until she was done.

"Show me," he nodded his head toward the door. Indicating that he wanted her to show him the shadow.

Palmer cautiously walked back out of the door, Hartman close behind her. She walked to the side of his office where the biggest window was and stood in front of it. She saw her reflection but no shadow reflected behind her.

"Walk down the street a little bit and let's check in the other windows," Hartman suggested. Palmer did as he asked. Still, she only saw her reflection and nothing else. Palmer shook her head.

"I'm sorry Hartman," she started to say but he grabbed her basket out of her hands and set it on the ground. Then he folded her into a bear hug. Her cheeks were pressed against his pecks. She took a deep shuddering breath and let it out.

"I believe you," he said. Palmer squeezed him in thanks. "Maybe it was a trick of the light or something with the physics of the window. Maybe it was something else altogether. Who knows. But it's gone now. Ok?" he said.

Palmer nodded and Hartman kissed the top of her head.

Chapter Forty-Eight

Present Day (2022)

Palmer gasped and sat up in bed. Her hand clutched at her chest, her heart was racing underneath. She was covered in sweat. Her hair stuck to her neck and forehead. It took Palmer a few moments to realize where she was. White duvet and sheets, shiny wood floors, modern style light fixture above her head, and the first light of dawn streaming through a large a-frame window. She was in her and Hartman's home. She tried to calm herself but jumped when she felt a large warm hand on her bare back.

"Hey, shh shh shhh..." Hartman tried to soothe her. "You just had a nightmare," he added. His eyes were still halfway shut and sleepy. Obviously Palmer had woken him up with her night terror.

"I'm sorry," she said and stroked his cheek. "Go back to sleep," she tried to order him.

"No I'm up, come here." He pulled her back down and close to him. Palmer nuzzled her face into his chest, the hairs on his pecs tickled her face. She relished the way his strong arms felt around her, how his smell mixed with hers.

"I love you," she whispered to him. After last night she felt like she finally remembered that she really and truly did love him. Finally, she thought. The fear of the unknown no longer felt like something she couldn't handle because at least she had Hartman. At least she remembered him. If none of her other memories ever came back she would be just fine with that because at least she remembered Hartman.

Hartman squeezed her. "I love you too," he said. He moved his head lower to kiss her and she tilted her own head up to meet his lips. The kiss started slow and gentle but quickly started to deepen. Palmer felt his hardness against her stomach and her core tightened at the thought.

"Palmer —" Hartman growled in between kisses. Palmer reached down to touch him and Hartman moved on top of her. Palmer smiled on his lips and knew that she was about to have an excellent start to her morning.

A couple hours later, and another romp in the sheets, Palmer and Hartman were in the car on their way to see Palmer's shop. Hartman had insisted that she needed to get out and suggested she take a look at the shop. He said he had been communicating with Susan and she had said that everything was running smoothly. Susan had told Hartman that she could handle whatever needed to be handled until Palmer was feeling better and he relayed that message to Palmer now.

Palmer sipped on her to-go mug of coffee and nodded her head. She had a lot of faith in Susan and her ability to run the shop for an extended period of time if need be, but Palmer would feel a lot better if she could at least stop by and take a peek. She was still missing at least a year of time and she had no clue what her inventory looked like right now.

"Is it ok if we stop at my office? I need to check on a couple of things real quick. In and out I swear," Hartman asked.

Palmer nodded her head. "Of course," she said automatically. It was convenient having Hartman's practice so close to the shop. "Is it ok if I stay in the car? My head is aching a little."

Hartman continued to drive but looked over at her with concern. "Do you need your medicine?"

"No I'm fine, I swear." Palmer lifted her coffee. "Nothing a little caffeine can't fix," she said and smiled. Hartman still looked worried. Palmer wondered if he ever relaxed about her general well-being but then reminded herself of everything that had happened the past few days and didn't blame him one bit.

They had taken Palmer's truck since the weather forecast had said a snowstorm was coming in later. The weatherman had predicted several feet of snow. Palmer was certain he was right. The sky was an angry gray color and the air smelled like snow. The world felt a little bit quieter like it always does before a storm.

Hartman pulled the truck into the parking space at the front of his practice and put the car in park.

"I'll just be a couple of minutes. You're sure you're ok to stay here?" he asked.

"Hartman," Palmer said with a laughing huff. "I'm fine. I promise."

Hartman nodded his head and got out of the truck smoothly. Palmer watched as he walked up to the office and went inside.

Palmer sipped her coffee and realized she hadn't brought her phone and regretted it. It was still charging where she had plugged it in the day before. She hadn't even thought to grab it so she could look through it.

Instead, Palmer decided to look around her truck. It was as clean as a whistle. No doubt Hartman paid someone to detail it on a regular basis. Palmer was a naturally untidy person. Palmer opened the glove box and looked at the papers inside. Nothing interesting. There were a couple of packets of diablo sauce from Taco Bell and Palmer smiled. At least she knew now that her taste in fast food hadn't changed.

Palmer moved to the middle compartment and looked inside. She found some chapstick, a rosary, and some sunglasses. Palmer closed the lid and looked in the backseat. Hartman's sweatshirt was folded neatly in the back. Palmer shook her head, silently making fun of him, and then paused. There was a significant lump in the gray sweatshirt.

Palmer unbuckled her seatbelt and reached back to grab it. She pulled the sweatshirt to the front and opened it up to find the source of the lump. Hartman's familiar smell filled her nose. Palmer reached into the pocket and pulled out a small, dark green box.

It was the one Calum had given her in the hospital. Palmer opened it gently to reveal the new saint necklace. It was silver and shiny but the image of the Virgin Mary was the same. Palmer touched the image with her finger. She had almost forgotten about it with everything else going on. Palmer hadn't even wondered what happened to it after she left the hospital. She hadn't asked.

Palmer realized Hartman must have grabbed it at some point and put it into his pocket. She wondered if he knew who it was from. Then she wondered why he hadn't given it back to her.

Chapter Forty-Nine

The Link (2022)

Winter was a bitter bitch this year. Palmer's cheeks stung from the cold as she walked up the front steps to Abuela's old house. Palmer's parents were in town and were having a family dinner there. Most of the houses on the block still had their Christmas lights up even though they were weeks into the new year now. Chuck and Emilia weren't here for Christmas this year so no lights hung from Abuela's house. Palmer's parents had stayed at their home in Phoenix so Palmer's brother Shawn wouldn't be alone for the holidays. Palmer didn't blame them. Shawn was checked into a rehab there just after Thanksgiving. He needed them more than she did.

Palmer and Hartman had spent Christmas alone together. He had offered to fly them somewhere warm and tropical but Palmer had declined. Palmer preferred her Christmas to actually look like Christmas. Colorado was perfect for just that reason. Colorado Christmas almost always looked like the inside of a snow globe. Unless it was a particularly warm year, which it was not this year. Besides, Christmas was the shop's busiest time of year.

Palmer could hear the noise of her extended family emanating from the house before she even reached the door. Palmer didn't knock, instead, she let herself in and shrugged off her cherry red pea coat. She hung the coat on the hook and stepped inside. Palmer smiled as the familiar sounds and smells of home hit her. Family members bustled about the entryway in front of the stairs, moving from the living room to the kitchen and vice versa. Everyone spoke in a raised voice trying to be heard over the chatter. The smell of posole wafted through the house.

Aunts, uncles, and cousins all greeted her warmly as she walked in. She was also embraced by her more distant family members. Great uncles and great aunts, second cousins, etc. Anyone significantly older than Palmer was just called Tia or Tio. People stopped to tell her how beautiful she looked and asked where Hartman was. Hartman had been called in for an emergency surgery and she explained as much. Some of the nosier tias had of course asked Palmer when she was planning on having any babies. Palmer was an expert at brushing off those kinds of questions. She had been navigating awkward questions like that for four years now. Ever since she and Hartman were married.

It wasn't that Palmer didn't think about having babies. She had always imagined herself as a mother. It just never really seemed like the right time for Hartman and her. There was always something going on. Between Hartman's crazy work schedule, running the shop, and building a house it just hadn't seemed right. Not to mention everything happening with her brother lately. Her parents tried to put on optimistic faces but she could see their devastation. Palmer had flown out to Arizona twice already to try and help where she could.

Shawn's counselor was very optimistic and Palmer had never seen Shawn so determined before. Maybe this really would be the end of his addiction. And if that was the case maybe things would slow down this year. Maybe Hartman would finally take on a partner at his practice to help with the workload. Tiffany's Epiphanies was getting busier all the time and Susan had casually mentioned that she would be interested in helping with finding the inventory if Palmer hired another person to help with the front. Palmer would have to crunch some numbers but she was fairly certain that could work out. It would definitely give Palmer some more free time. On top of everything, the house was built and furnished now. Hartman still had some plans for adding on some other details but in general, it was finished and way too big for just the two of them. Maybe this would be the year she would talk with him about it. About babies.

Hartman had never brought up children. Palmer wasn't sure why. Maybe it had something to do with his family. He had no siblings and his mother had died when he was really little. Hartman had said it was a car accident and didn't talk about it. His father had died a few years before they met and other than that time at the cemetery he didn't talk about him intimately. People frequently brought up Hartman's father. He had been one of the only dentists in town for a long time and he had been very involved in the community. Additionally, Hartman now practiced out of the office his father had so his name was brought up fairly often. Hartman always brushed it off in a professional, practiced manner. Whenever Palmer tried to bring him up Hartman would simply say that he wasn't worth talking about.

Hartman had some distant relatives back in Germany that he sometimes spoke about but other than that he had no family. Over the past several years her family had become his family. Hartman had charmed everyone just as thoroughly as he had charmed Palmer. Even when Palmer was certain that her family must be overwhelming him he acted just as calm and collected as always.

Palmer walked into the kitchen and moved through the crowd of women to get to her mother. Emilia was in the middle of speaking feverishly to someone else, so Palmer silently kissed her cheek and moved toward the living room. On her way, she heard a loud boisterous cheer come from the garage where she was sure most of the men were drinking. Palmer walked into the living room where some of the older members of her family sat and looked through old photo albums.

When Abuela passed away she had left the house to Palmer's parents and they had turned it into an Airbnb for most of the year. The town was a hot spot for tourism thanks to the skiing and other outdoor activities it offered so her parents did pretty well. They had sold the house Palmer grew up in and moved to Arizona a few years ago to be closer to Shawn. Now when they came home they stayed here.

They had kept the house almost the same after Abuela died. All the furniture and most of the decor was the same. They had decluttered a lot of it and taken down all the family photographs to make it more Airbnb friendly. All of the photos had been put into albums that now stayed locked up in a giant chest. The chest was open now and family members were looking through them and reminiscing.

Palmer took a seat next to a couple of tias and after giving them each a kiss she focused on what they were all looking at. Her Tio had an extremely old, tattered-looking album out and was flipping through it slowly. He pointed to a picture of Palmer's great-grandparents when they were fairly young. Everyone smiled warmly and made remarks on how lovely Great Grandma Rivera was.

The Tio turned the page and everyone leaned in closer to look at an old family portrait. It was black and white. In the middle and toward the back stood Great Grandma and Grandpa Rivera. Next to them stood two older boys, Palmer's great uncles. In the front were six little girls all dressed in matching outfits, Palmer's great aunts. They all looked similar, but Palmer knew that the tallest and oldest would be Abuela. Palmer heard the room around her go silent as everyone looked at that picture. They were all looking at the smallest little girl. She was likely only about two years old. It was Gabriella, the lost sister.

No one said a word. After a few moments, Palmer's Tio turned the page and there was another picture. This one must have been taken around Christmas time several years after the previous photo. It was a staged photo of just the little girls. Again, at the end of the line stood the smallest sister. Palmer's Tio continued to flip through the pages slowly. Picture after picture. Some of the whole family, some of the boys, and many of just the girls. The ages of everyone continued to increase slowly as the pages were turned.

Finally, he flipped to a black-and-white high school photo of Gabriella. Palmer watched two of her Tias reach out to hold each other's wrinkled hands as they looked at their sister.

"Gabriella," one of the tias said sadly.

"She was so young there," the other tia said softly and touched the picture.

Palmer stared blankly at the page, unmoving. She had seen only one picture of Gabriella, this picture. It was the one the newspaper had printed when she went missing. Abuela hadn't kept any pictures of Gabriella hung on her walls, the memory had been too painful. Palmer's Tio turned the page again.

The next picture was of all the tias when they were young, including Gabriella. They were sitting around a table eating and laughing. Gabriella's head was thrown back, her dark hair flowed behind her and she was laughing with abandon. The image looked so much like Palmer that Palmer's heart skipped a beat. The rest of the room must have thought the same thing because every head turned toward her. Palmer froze under their gaze.

One of Palmer's cousins who was around her age spoke first. "That looks exactly like Palmer," he said a little too loudly.

The tias that had started to hold hands, Gabriella's sisters, smiled at Palmer. One of them put her hand on Palmer's cheek. Silently saying everything Palmer needed to hear. The tio flipped the page again. It was a photo of Gabriella and Abuela when she was much younger. They were standing in front of their church wearing their finest mass outfits. They both had on little hats with small veils. Abuela and Gabriella were holding each other by the waist and smiling broadly at the camera. Palmer marveled at how beautiful Abuela had been but also how much Gabriella looked like herself. Palmer felt the eyes of some of the people in the room on her as they made the same conclusions. Then Palmer saw something that made her entire body feel like someone had thrown a bucket of ice water over her.

Around Gabriella's neck was a gold necklace with a little oval pendant. The picture was too old and granny to make out what exactly was on the pendant but Palmer knew. The tio went to turn the page again but Palmer leaped forward and stopped him.

"Wait," Palmer said. "What is that?" she pointed to the necklace on Gabriella's neck.

The tias leaned in closer. Then one of them, the older one, spoke.

"That was her necklace. She started wearing it one day out of the blue. It had a little picture of Santa Maria on it. I don't know where she got it. One day she didn't have it and the next she did. I remember being a little jealous. It was real gold and we didn't have much money those days. Someone must have given it to her. She wore it all and refused to talk about it no matter how much we teased."

The other tia started to talk. "She took it off though a couple of days before she — before she was lost." The tia said sadly. "Remember?"

she said to her sister. She turned to Palmer. "Maria, your grandmother always thought that was strange. I think she kept it."

Palmer reached into her sweater and pulled out the chain, the pendant following after. The tias eyes widened slightly when they saw it.

"I have it. Abuela gave it to me when I turned fourteen." Palmer said frantically. "I didn't know. I didn't know it was hers!" Palmer frantically attempted to take off the necklace. "One of you should have it. Take it!" She was close to crying, but she wasn't sure why. Her cheeks were hot with the eyes of everyone in the room on her.

"No mi hita," one of the tias said gently. "Maria gave it to you. The necklace came to you. It is yours," she said in a soothing tone. The other tia leaned over and clamped her hand over Palmer's, stopping her from undoing the clasp. Palmer wasn't sure what she should do. The old woman adjusted Palmer's necklace again so the clasp was in the back and then she gently tucked it back into her sweater before gently patting where it now lay hidden.

Chapter Fifty

Present Day (2022)

Palmer sat silently in the passenger side of her truck while Hartman drove them home. The visit to the shop had been successful. Susan was doing a great job of keeping everything going. She had even moved some of the pieces that Palmer had bought before the accident to the front of the store. She had placed them and priced them exactly how Palmer would have. Palmer felt a little bit of the weight that had been resting on her shoulders lift after they left.

Before heading back up the mountain and toward home they had stopped at Abuela's house to visit her mom and dad. They had fussed over her, bringing her tea and asking about her memories. Palmer explained that she still didn't remember what happened that day and they tried not to look worried. Hartman never left her side. After allowing her mother to force-feed her half a sandwich and some fruit, Palmer and Hartman left. Palmer's mother had chastised her multiple times for not having her phone. Palmer explained that it was plugged in and charging at home and swore she would try and keep it on her. Hartman and Palmer promised they would be back.

Now Palmer watched as Hartman pulled into the driveway of their secluded home. She watched the dark trees tower over the car and become denser and denser as they neared the house. Hartman parked in the garage, got out, and came around to let Palmer out. He helped her to the floor and held onto her hand for a moment. He looked at her with concern.

"Are you ok?" he asked.

Palmer shrugged. "Yeah. Just a headache," she admitted.

"I know you don't want to take the pain meds Dr. Walters prescribed but you should really try and at least take some Tylenol. I really think it would help."

"Ok, I will." Palmer gave her husband a small smile. "I'll take some and then maybe take a nap."

Just then Hartman's phone started to ring. He gave her a smile before picking it up.

Palmer could only hear his side of the conversation. "Hello?" he said. There was a long pause as he listened. Hartman looked like he was concentrating hard. "Ok. Yeah. I'll be there in a few. No, it's fine, she's doing much better. Mild headache at most." He paused again to listen. "No, she still doesn't remember." Another pause. "I'll tell her. Yeah. See you soon." He clicked the button on the phone to hang up and looked at Palmer. "That was Dr. Walters. She has a case she needs my help with. She was also wondering how you're doing. I'm sorry honey, I need to head to the hospital. You ok if I go?"

Palmer nodded her head. "There's no point in you staying. I'm just gonna lie down for a bit."

Hartman nodded and kissed her on the forehead before exchanging her keys for the ones to the Range Rover.

"I'll be back home before the storm hits," he said. Palmer felt a little bubble of worry in her stomach but she pushed it down. Palmer watched as he backed his car out of the garage and waved to her from the front window and then he closed the garage.

Palmer walked inside and hung her coat up. Then she walked up to the bedroom and into the master bathroom where the medicine cabinet was. She located the Tylenol, popped two of them in her mouth, filled a cup with water, and drank. Then she walked to her closet to pull out some comfy clothes, maybe even some pajamas.

Palmer walked to the dresser where she knew her pajamas were and went to open the top drawer. She stubbed her toe on something and yelped, grabbing her toe and hopping on one foot. There was something under the dresser. She remembered then that she had stashed her 'Calum Box' there a long time ago. Her heart did a little flip. She had felt guilty for keeping it so she had stashed it in this room, her closet. The one place Hartman never came in.

Palmer got on her hands and knees and looked. Her 'Calum Box' was just a plain brown box and she saw it stuffed in the corner but she also spotted another familiar-looking box. This one was red and it was filled with all the research she did on Gabriella Rivera's disappearance. She sat down on the floor and pulled out both boxes.

She opened 'Gabriella's box' first and looked through the stacks of documents she knew like the back of her hand. She sighed. Knowing that no matter how hard she stared at the contents, there was no answer there.

Then she pulled out the 'Calum box'. Her fingers hovered at the edges, unsure if she should open it. She knew the contents of this box even better than the contents of 'Gabriella's box'. Palmer wasn't sure why, but she opened it anyway.

It was exactly as she remembered it. Movie stubs, a dried-up green corsage, a hollowed-out pen for shooting spit wads, sand from the Pacific Ocean, and pictures. So many pictures. Palmer thumbed through them and smiled. One was a Polaroid picture of just Palmer and Jessica when they were only fifteen. Babies. It was in the 'Calum box' because Calum had taken it. Palmer stood up to get her phone so she could take a picture of the picture and send it to Jessica.

Palmer walked to the nightstand and picked up her cracked but fully charged phone. She took the picture of the old photo and opened up her text messages with Jessica. She sent the photo and looked at their last conversation. It wasn't a conversation at all, just a couple of pictures of Palmer with Jessica's kids at the Denver Zoo. Palmer was pushing two of them in a double stroller. It was from the last time Jessica came to visit.

Palmer paused and looked at the picture closer. Then she nearly dropped her phone. Her hands started to shake. There was a tingling sensation in the back of her head like a memory was starting to trickle in. Palmer opened up the photo gallery on her phone and started to look through picture after picture.

A photo of Palmer and Hartman at the ski lodge. A photo of Palmer, Shawn, and her parents at the carnival. A selfie of Palmer and her mother at lunch. Hartman giving Palmer a piggyback ride at the Fourth of July parade. Palmer flipped through more and more photos.

Something between a gasp and a sob escaped her mouth and she covered it with the back of her quivering hand.

In an alarming number of her photos, there was a figure of a man in the distance. Not just any man. Calum. Dozens of photos of Palmer living her life. And in each one, she could just make out Calum in the back.

Palmer dropped her phone and grabbed her temples with both hands. A jolt of pain like she had never felt before wrapped around her head and she nearly screamed. She squeezed her eyes shut as one last memory flooded back to her.

Chapter Fifty-One

The Last Memory (2022)

Palmer sat in the back of her shop absolutely giddy over her recent finds. She had gone to a storage unit auction in a neighboring town that afternoon. Palmer had put a large sum of money, more than she usually offered up, on unit number nine. She had a good feeling about it that had only been validated by the fact that nine was her lucky number. Something about it had called to her and when they had given her the key and she had opened it up she was NOT disappointed.

The storage unit had been chock-full of priceless antiques and local artifacts. She spent hours looking through it, only getting more and more excited as she sorted. Palmer didn't realize how much time had passed until her phone buzzed and she saw an incoming text from Hartman along with the time above the notification. It was already nine o'clock at night and extremely dark and cold outside.

"Shit," Palmer said under her breath.

Palmer opened up the text from Hartman.

Need to stay late for an
emergency surgery. Won't be
home until late late.
Maybe the morning.
Don't wait up.
Love you.

Palmer texted back quickly. Maybe he would read it before he scrubbed in.

Still at the storage unit.
HUGE finds. I'll head
back in a couple minutes.
Might stop at the store.
See you when you
get home.
Love you too.

Palmer pressed send and looked at all her new inventory. She sighed with happiness. It would take her weeks to sort through everything. Palmer grabbed a few boxes that were filled with tchotchkes, framed photos, art, and papers she wanted to look through as soon as possible. She locked the storage unit and walked through the freezing cold parking lot to her truck. She tucked the boxes into the back seat before climbing into the driver's side. She turned the key and blasted the hot air. Then she turned on the radio and started the hour-long drive to get back to her own town. Palmer sang every song as loud as she possibly could no matter how off-key she was the entire ride.

It was nearly half-past ten when she parked in front of Tiffany's Epiphanies. The street was empty and dark, she could have just driven home but she was wired from the excitement of the auction and all her treasures. She wanted to sit at her little desk in the back and go through the boxes she grabbed.

Palmer locked the truck as she walked to the front doors of the shop. The confirmation honk from the truck was harrowing in the silence of the main street. Palmer struggled to open the front door with her key while balancing both boxes but eventually, she got it. She set down the boxes and locked the door behind her. She walked through the dark shop toward the back, vintage dolls, photographs, and paintings stared back at her.

Palmer turned on the Tiffany lamp on the cluttered desk in the back and set her boxes down. She pulled out her phone and checked it. No reply from Hartman. Palmer shrugged and sat down to wade through her precious finds.

Several more hours passed and Palmer rubbed her eyes. It was well past midnight now. Palmer had started to sort the items and figure out what pieces she needed more research on. There were only a few pieces of paper at the bottom of the last box. Most likely trash but Palmer pulled them out anyway. There was a faded receipt for six cans of beans and a half gallon of milk from 1962. Palmer shuddered thinking about anyone eating that weird combo. There was also a water-stained flier for a hunting cabin for rent. Palmer almost tossed it in the trash with the receipt, but she paused.

There was a crudely drawn map to the cabin's location. Palmer tried not to panic. She took the flier and walked to the front of the store, turning on a couple of lights as she went. She went to the area where she kept the majority of her local interest pieces and held up the flier to the framed map she had on the wall. It was the map she had found years ago, the map that showed the road that led to the brown spec that had elicited so much fear in her. The cabin. The flier and the map on the wall matched. Palmer was looking at an old flier to the house that haunted her dreams.

Palmer swallowed. Before she could change her mind she grabbed the framed map off of the wall and took it to the back. She set it on the desk and slowly removed it from its frame. She stared at it. What did it mean?

Just then Palmer's phone buzzed alerting her to an incoming text. She expected it to be Hartman but it was Jessica. It wasn't unusual for Jessica to text her so late, they lived in different time zones these days. Palmer opened the text. It was a couple of pictures of Palmer with Jessica's kids.. Palmer smiled and zoomed in to get a better view of the little happy faces.

Palmer froze. What the fuck? She zoomed in more. There in the back of the picture, yards away from them, was Calum. Palmer couldn't believe it. What was he doing there? Her brain tried to make sense of it. Maybe it was just a coincidence. Palmer sat back in her chair and tried to think.

She wasn't sure why she did it. Perhaps it was intuition or perhaps it was years and years of feeling like she was being watched. Palmer pulled out her phone and started to look through her photo gallery.

"No, no, no, no, no, no..." Palmer said under her breath. There he was in the background of another picture. And another. And another. Palmer's heart was hammering in her chest. Was Calum following her? This was stalking, right? Why hadn't he just reached out? Tried talking to her. Palmer's brain was working too fast.

Palmer looked down at the map and the flier then. Calum had been the one to show her the cabin for the first time. He had taken her to that lookout spot years ago. Why? And why did she have such a visceral reaction to it?

Palmer stood up quickly, the wood chair making a loud sound on the floor. She grabbed the map and the flier and started walking fast through the store and to her truck. It was almost one in the morning.

Palmer pulled out her phone and called Hartman, maybe he would be out of surgery soon. No answer. She tried one more time even though she knew it would be pointless. Hartman would know what to do. He always knew what to do. No answer. She climbed into her truck and threw her phone, the map, and the flier onto the passenger seat in frustration. She turned the ignition in the truck and roared to life. The hot air blasted her in the face and she turned it down so she could think.

Palmer toyed with her necklace. What would Hartman do? Palmer closely stared at the steering wheel and contemplated. She could picture exactly what he would do. Hartman would tell her to meet him at the hospital. He would take care of everything. He would drive them home, turn on all the security alarms and lock all the doors. He would probably even take out one of his guns from the gun safe when Palmer wasn't looking. He would load it and put it under his side of the bed just in case. Then in the morning he would call the police station and report Calum. The police would have Palmer come down and give a statement and show them the pictures. Hartman would have her file a restraining order against Calum. Then Hartman would go way over the top to make sure Palmer was always with someone if not with him. He would insist she not stay at work after dark and then there would be security cameras at the house and before Palmer knew it her whole life would change.

And for what? It was Calum. Palmer knew Calum. He wasn't a stalker. There was an explanation. There had to be. She had no idea what it was but she knew deep down, where it counted, that Calum would have a good explanation. Obviously he needed help. Maybe he was drinking or doing drugs again. Maybe he was following Palmer around because he wanted to ask her for help but was too afraid.

Palmer didn't know. But it didn't matter because it was Calum. She knew Calum, and she knew she could reach Calum.

Palmer glanced down at the map. Her intuition told her it was important. Maybe Calum was staying there. It was on the same mountain her house was on. It was probably only a twenty to thirty minute drive past her house. What would Laurie Strode do? She would be brave as fuck that's for damn sure. She would face her fears. Palmer made up her mind and started to drive.

Palmer leaned forward in her truck as she drove trying to find the little road that would lead to the cabin. She flicked her brights on. It would be small and most likely not paved. If she wasn't careful she would miss it. Palmer tapped her brakes. There it was.

Palmer turned carefully and her tires dipped onto the bumpy road. The dirt road was thin and full of potholes. The forest looked ominous with her high beams on. The bright lights only reached so far before the blackness between the trees swallowed them up. Palmer started to regret her decision but there was no turning back now, the road was too slim and the trees too thick. She would just have to keep moving forward. Adrenaline started to pump through Palmer's veins making her feel light and weightless.

Palmer continued down the deserted dark road in the middle of the mountain forest. Frozen tufts of snow clung to branches on the trees but for the most part, the road remained clear. She tried not to think of movies like The Blair Witch Project or The Village. She didn't need to think about fake horror movie forests when a genuinely horrific forest was laid out before her.

Finally, the road veered right and Palmer's headlights lit up an ancient-looking cabin. Palmer's blood went cold. Here it was. Palmer looked through the front truck window and tried to determine if anyone was home. If Calum was there. She didn't see any signs of life. No car out front, no lights. Palmer looked at the time on her dashboard, it was 1:45 am. Palmer sighed. She had been wrong. Calum wasn't here. The house wasn't calling to her. She moved to put the car in drive so she could flip around in the open space in front of the house but she paused.

There was a light in the upstairs window. Palmer blinked. He really was here. Palmer squeezed the wheel of her truck and mustered all of her bravery. She grabbed her phone and turned on the flashlight app. Then she turned the truck off and climbed out. She started to walk toward the house, her eyes never leaving the warm light emanating from the upstairs bedroom.

The forest around her was eerily quiet. The only sound was the crunch of her boots. It was cold, likely below freezing and Palmer realized she had left her jacket at the shop. She had left in such a hurry that she had completely forgotten it. She shivered slightly in her red sweater.

Finally, Palmer made it to the door and she raised her hand to knock. She paused. Knocking somehow felt stupid. Instead, she tried the handle. It opened right away and the door made a painful squeak as it opened. Palmer peered inside. Besides the light from her flashlight, it was dark. Palmer stepped into the house. It was musty and dank. The floors were covered in dust and grime. Palmer started to doubt herself again.

"Cal?" she called out. Her own voice echoed in her ears. There was no reply. Palmer was about to turn around and go back to the truck to lecture herself about how stupid she was when she heard a creak from upstairs.

Palmer rented every horror film that the Blockbuster had in stock before it closed down nearly ten years ago. She had seen every scary movie that her local movie theater had come out within the last two decades. She had watched every thriller that was offered on every streaming service she could get her hands on. Palmer was a horror movie expert. So she knew that it was at this point in the movie that the audience usually yelled at the main character to get out. Palmer knew that this was where the heroin made a grave error by not going back to the car.

Palmer knew all of this. She had spent her entire life unknowingly studying for this exact moment. But even knowing everything she did, Palmer had zero fear. It was the strangest feeling. She should be afraid. Any normal person would be afraid. But she did a quick mental scan and there was nothing. Just a strong urge to search the house. There was something here that needed finding. Palmer knew that simple fact with impossible clarity.

Palmer's feet started to move on their own accord. She reached the staircase and put her hand on the railing. It was dusty but she slowly walked up the stairs. They creaked in a worrisome way under her, and there was a large hole she had to side step but Palmer continued on. Palmer reached the second-story landing and walked into the only room that was up there. It was empty. Palmer walked into the middle of the room and let her flashlight illuminate every corner. This had to have been where the light came from. Palmer was so confused.

Just then a loud blaring noise erupted in Palmer's ears. Palmer dropped to the floor and covered her ears, her phone skidded off into the dark. It was the loudest, highest-pitch sound she had ever heard. Like some kind of siren. It was almost like a woman's scream but amplified by ten. Palmer's mouth was open in a scream but there was no way to hear it over the sound. Palmer's nose began to bleed and she knew she had to get out of the house. She scrambled to her feet and tried to make her way back to the stairs. She ran through the bedroom doorway in the dark and turned toward the top of the stairs.

Instead, she ran face-first into something hard, like a wall. But it wasn't a wall. It was a person. Their hands grabbed Palmer by the upper arms impossibly hard and jerked her sideways. Palmer felt her brain rattle in her skull. The alarm was still going off and Palmer couldn't see. The person shoved her hard and Palmer could no longer feel her feet on the floor. She felt the person grab at her necklace at the last second and the chain snapped. Just before Palmer plummeted down the stairs she swore she saw a pair of red eyes. *The Coco Man*, Palmer thought. She heard a deafening crack. Everything went black and the light turned green.

Chapter Fifty-Two

Present Day (2022)

Palmer remembered. She stood in the master bedroom of her and Hartman's home. Her hands were still gripping the side of her head trying to ease the pressure from moments ago. She was in utter and complete shock. Her memory was back.

Palmer scrambled to find her phone. She had dropped it right before her head had nearly exploded from pain and the memory had come back. Finally, she found her phone and with trembling fingers, she pulled up Hartman's contact info.

"C'mon, c'mon..." Palmer said under her breath. She prayed he wasn't in surgery. It was taking too long for him to answer, the call would go to voicemail soon. Palmer counted the rings she could hear on her end to calm her nerves. She almost made it to nine rings when Hartman picked up.

"Hey, you ok?" Hartman asked.

"I remember Hart. I remember what happened," she said frantically.

"WHAT?" he said loudly on the other end.

"I remember going to the cabin! It was Calum! Calum has been following me around for a long time I think. I found all of these pictures. And Hart..." she paused. "He's in them. It sounds crazy but I think he's been staying at the cabin or something and then sometimes he — I don't know. He watches me or something. I don't know why but I think it was him at the cabin with me. It was dark so I can't be sure but I think I surprised him and he pushed me down the stairs. Maybe he didn't know it was me or maybe he did. I have no idea. The important thing is that I REMEMBER!" Palmer had spoken so quickly that she needed to take a deep breath when she finished.

Hartman didn't say anything. For a moment Palmer thought she had lost him, the cell service wasn't always great this far up the mountain.

"Hartman?" Palmer said.

"I'm here," he responded. "Make sure all the doors are locked. I'll be home in five minutes."

"Hart, it's a twenty-minute drive from the hospital."

"I said I'll be there in five, I'll be there in five." Hartman's voice was cold and harsh.

"Ok," she whispered. Hartman hung up.

Palmer held onto her phone but quickly walked downstairs and checked all the locks. They were secure. Feeling a little sick to her stomach she moved to the giant window between the living room and kitchen. She stood to the side and peered out. The sky was an angry dark gray, the sun was nowhere to be seen. Palmer could feel the hairs on the back of her neck rise, a chill traveled down her arms. She embraced the all too familiar feeling that she was not alone. Her eyes darted through the trees trying to find any evidence that someone was out there but she saw nothing. She gripped her phone so hard in her hand that her fingers started to turn red. While Palmer continued her vigil, it started to snow.

Dr. Walters stood quietly behind Hartman in the hospital hallway.

They had been leaning over a computer looking at a patient's medical results with another physician when Hartman had gotten a call. Dr. Walters had seen Palmer's name pop up on the caller ID just before Hartman excused himself and walked out into the hall. Dr. Walter wasn't sure why she had followed him. She told herself that it was because his wife was her patient and she was concerned. Maybe it was just curiosity. She had known Hartman for years and she valued him as a colleague and even a friend. But there had always been something about him that she found a little off. Dr. Walters had never been able to quite put her finger on it.

She had listened to his short conversation and become more and more worried. Hopefully, Palmer was ok. She was just about to walk toward him to ask and also to offer her help but she paused. In one hand he held his phone but the other was clenched into a fist. Dr. Walters could see the veins in his hands bulge and his fist started to shake violently. His broad back rose and fell and she heard him take a deep breath before unclinching his hand. He cracked his neck and then he reached into his pants pocket. She watched as he pulled something out, looked at it for a moment, and then shoved it back into his pocket.

Dr. Walters walked toward him then and he must have heard her footsteps because he turned toward her. There was an odd look on his face but it was quickly covered with deep concern.

"Is Palmer ok?" Dr. Walters asked.

"Yeah. I mean, I don't know. I need to go. She uh — she said she remembered what happened. An ex-boyfriend she thinks. I'm sorry but I really need to leave. Can you handle this without me?"

Dr. Walters nodded. "Oh my God. Yes, yes of course. Go," she assured him.

Then without another word Hartman turned and left.

Chapter Fifty-Three

Present Day (2022)

Palmer watched as Hartman drove up the driveway like a bat out of hell. He had gotten to the house in five minutes, exactly like he had said. He must have flown up the mountain at NASCAR speeds to get here that fast. Luckily the roads weren't slick yet. He didn't bother parking in the garage for once. Instead, he parked his charcoal Range Rover haphazardly on the pavement in front of the house. The car looked like it was barely in park when he got out, he left the driver-side door wide open. Palmer watched as he tucked something down the front of his pants before he started to walk around the house. His gaze swept from side to side, assessing.

Palmer waited and watched from the window. Eventually, he must have been satisfied with his sweep because he unlocked the door and opened it with a loud thud. His hair was disheveled and his shirt was untucked. With a stern face, he walked quickly to Palmer and pulled her into a fierce hug.

Palmer immediately started to explain in better detail what she had found and what she believed happened. She told him about the shack. About when she first saw it, the map and flier. She told him about seeing Calum at the wedding and she showed him the pictures. She described what happened at the cabin in detail. Hartman listened intently all the way to the end.

"I'll call the police," he said into her hair. Palmer nodded into his chest.

A few minutes later Hartman hung up the phone. He had called the detectives directly and told them everything Palmer had told him. The detectives said they probably wouldn't be able to come out to interview Palmer today because of the storm but they would try tomorrow. In the meantime, they said they would look into Calum Murphy. Hartman had thanked them cordially before hanging up.

Palmer and Hartman sat across from each other on the couch. Hartman leaned forward and took her hands in his. Palmer took a deep breath.

"I want to go back to the cabin," Palmer said evenly.

Hartman didn't react in any way. Instead, he only said, "No."

"Yes," she said back firmly.

"You're not going back there, Palmer," he said in the same indifferent tone.

"Calum isn't a bad guy. I know you don't like him. But I know him. This is just a big misunderstanding. He might be in trouble," Palmer felt like she was trying to put together a puzzle that was missing a couple of crucial pieces.

"You think you know him, Palmer, but you clearly don't," Hartman was still speaking in his annoyingly even tone.

"Maybe," Palmer admitted. "But he's not the only reason I need to go back to the house. I think — I think there is something calling me there. Something I don't quite understand. All I know is that I NEED to go back."

"No," he said again.

"Hart, you've always believed me when I've told you about the strange shit that happens to me. You've never once doubted me or made me feel crazy. I need you to believe me now. I need you to trust me."

Hartman said nothing. He just sat there silently. No emotion on his face.

"WWLSD," she whispered. "What would Laurie St —"

"I DON'T GIVE A FUCK ABOUT WHAT LAURIE STRODE WOULD DO!" he yelled so loud that the light fixture above them shook.

Palmer jumped back in her seat, letting go of his hands. She looked at her husband in shock. Hartman seemed to compose himself. He rubbed his face with his hands before eventually looking at Palmer again.

"I'm sorry," he took a deep breath. "I hear what you're saying. And I believe you. I really, really do. If you want to go back to the cabin so badly I will take you. We'll go together." His words were calm and purposeful again.

Palmer was still reeling from his outburst but she nodded her head.

"I *need* to go back, Hartman."

Hartman nodded solemnly. "Ok."

Chapter Fifty-Four

Present Day (2022)

Palmer leaned forward in the passenger side seat to try and get a better view of the road. The snow was really starting to come down now. It wasn't quite a whiteout but it was getting there. Hartman didn't seem to notice. They drove in eerie silence.

Palmer held her breath as he turned her truck onto the little road that was barely visible. She had nearly missed it. The little dirt road was even more snow-packed than the paved one they had just left.

"Good thing we got those new snow tires on Black Friday," Palmer said, trying to lighten the mood. Hartman didn't laugh. He was not at all happy about her insistence to go back to the cabin. They continued on in silence. Night time was approaching and the sky was dark but the white of the snow cast the world in a purplish hue. Finally, they veered right and the sinister, ramshackle house came into view. There were no cars except for their own. No tire tracks in the snow except for the truck's.

Hartman put the truck in park and Palmer immediately went to open her door but Hartman reached over her and shut it.

"Hold on," he said. "Are you sure?" he asked.

"Yes," Palmer said with confidence. Hartman nodded and got out of the truck. Palmer watched as he walked around the front of the truck and came to her side. He opened the door for her and helped her out. The snow was only a couple of inches deep but soon it would be even deeper. Fat, chunky snowflakes fell and stuck to the red beanie Palmer had put on right before they left the house.

They walked up to the house together, Hartman just slightly ahead of Palmer. Their shoes made satisfying crunching sounds on the snow. Palmer looked up at the house as they walked toward it. It was just an abandoned shack. Someone must have built it a long time ago and it had been forgotten. Left to rot and fester by itself. Palmer looked into the window where she had seen the light the night of the accident. There was no light now. The window was dirty with age and neglect. The room behind it was dark.

When they reached the front of the house Hartman stepped up to the door and opened it with a creek. He looked inside and then stepped back to let Palmer in. It was almost exactly the same, only this time there were many muddy footprints on the ground and dried blood on the floor by the bottom of the simple staircase. Palmer reached her hand up and touched the tender spot on her forehead, just shy of her hairline, where she had hit the ground.

Palmer walked further into the room and her eyes scanned her surroundings. She was overcome with the same feeling she had the night she fell. There was something here she needed to find. There was a simple kitchen to the left and a tiny sitting room to the right. Palmer already knew from last time that there was a bedroom upstairs. That was the entirety of the cabin. Palmer decided she would check the kitchen first. She walked into the room and felt Hartman close behind her. There were empty cans of food and beer on the floor covered in dust. A small table sat in the center of the room with a single chair pulled up to it. There was another one on its side in the corner.

Palmer started to open the cupboards and look around. There was nothing but old garbage and cobwebs so she moved to the lower cupboard under the sink.

"What are you doing?" Hartman asked from behind her.

"I'm looking," she said. She wiped some dust on her jeans.

"I see that. What are we looking for?" he asked.

"I don't know," she responded. "I'll know it when I find it," she said in a frustrated tone.

Just then a pair of headlights flooded the kitchen through the small broken window. Palmer's heart started to hammer in her chest. Hartman moved quickly.

"STAY HERE," he commanded. He moved to the entryway of the tiny space and opened the door just as the car that had driven up turned its engine off. Palmer stood rooted to the spot, stuck in the kitchen. She heard the car door open and Hartman speak through the open door.

"Stop right there," he said in a deep commanding tone.

"Where's Palmer?" a familiar voice answered back. It was Calum.

Palmer's feet began to move and she barreled her way to where Hartman stood.

"Cal?" she cried out.

Calum stood just to the side of his car, his hands were in the air in a mock show of submission. He seemed to relax a little when he saw Palmer.

"Hey Beautiful," Calum said to her. Hartman stiffened. Calum put his hands down and took a step toward them.

"Don't come any closer," Hartman growled. He pulled Palmer behind him. "Why have you been stalking my wife," he asked. He emphasized the words 'my wife'. Palmer stepped to the side so she could see Calum better.

Calum gave Hartman a wicked smile. "I wouldn't say I've been stalking her per se. I just like to check in on her from time to time. Gotta make sure you're taking good care of our girl." Calum took another sneaky step toward them.

Hartman made a sound of disgust. "I take excellent care of my wife, thank you very much. Why are you here?"

"I followed you," Calum admitted.

"Why," Hartman growled.

Calum made a tisking sound. Like a mother scolding a child. "I know what kind of man you are, Dr. Roth. I knew it the day I met you. There was something just a little bit off about you. But you know that. You do everything you can to make sure no one else sees it."

"Is that right?" Hartman challenged him.

"You know, I looked into you. No family. No close friends. You were always top of the class. Your IQ score is through the roof, kudos by the way. Your record is spotless, you've never been in trouble a day in your life. On the surface, you seem like the perfect guy." At some point while he was talking Calum had taken another step forward.

"Is your little speech just about over?" Hartman's fists were shaking at his sides.

"I couldn't find ANYTHING on you. It drove me nuts. You just didn't sit right with me. No one is *that* perfect. But then you finally fucked up didn't you." Another step.

"Shut the fuck up and leave," Hartman said between clenched teeth.

Palmer decided she needed to intervene and she stepped forward.

"I get it. You convinced yourself that Hartman wasn't good enough for me, so you checked up on me from time to time. Ok. But why throw me down the stairs? Why this cabin?" she asked.

Calum's eyebrows rose up. "Palmer, I didn't push you down the stairs. I've never been here before. I'm only here now because I followed you guys here," he sounded genuine. He turned his gaze back to Hartman and his expression changed to disgust and anger. "I've never been here before. But Hartman has, isn't that right Dr. Roth."

"I was the one who found Palmer, luckily. So yeah, I've been here before." Hartman's voice sounded strange to Palmer. She looked up at him, he didn't look right either. When she turned back to Calum he was a few steps closer.

"Cut the shit Doc. I found the map and the little flier about the cabin in your duffle bag at the hospital. I found it very interesting that you never gave them to the police."

Palmer took a step back from Hartman. She had almost completely forgotten about the map and the flier. They had led her here and she had left them in her truck right before the accident. The detectives had said they went through her truck and found nothing. They had been stumped as to how she had made her way to a remote cabin out in the middle of the woods.

"Hart?" Palmer said under her breath. Hartman turned and looked at her with anguished eyes, but he didn't speak. He stepped toward her but she took two steps back. What Calum had said was starting to sink in. Palmer's eyes widened in fear.

"I would bet big money that he has your necklace hidden away somewhere. Something tells me he's a bit of a narcissist. So I'd wager he carries it on him. Go ahead, big guy, where is it?" Calum had taken advantage of Hartman's back being turned and snuck up behind him.

Hartman must have felt Calum's nearness because he turned quickly and took a step to the side. They were all in the house now.

Hartman's hand absently went to his pocket. Palmer and Calum both tracked the movement. Hartman's eyes flicked back to Palmer and realized where she was looking.

"Palmer —," he seemed like he might try to explain, but he stopped. Instead, he slipped his fingers into his pocket and pulled out Palmer's necklace. The chain was broken.

Chapter Fifty-Five

Present Day (2022)

Energy crackled through the room. It had to be below freezing in the shack as well as outside, but Palmer felt a trickle of sweat bead its way down her back. Calum looked like he was ready to move toward Palmer at a moment's notice. Hartman looked like he had been hit by a truck. They stood in the shape of the world's weirdest triangle in the middle of the entryway.

"Make it make sense, Hartman," Palmer begged him.

Hartman swallowed and looked like he would say something, but Calum interrupted.

"Hartman Gunther Roth. Born January 3rd, 1984 to a pair of German immigrants. You were raised by your father though, weren't you? The late, great Dr. Niklaus Roth. Mom died under 'suspicious circumstances' when you were pretty young, isn't that right Hartman? What did dear old Papa Nik do to her I wonder. And what pray tell, did he do to you to make you into the perfect little neurotic psychopath you are huh?" Calum was starting to slowly inch his way in front of Palmer.

"SHUT THE FUCK UP!" Hartman yelled. His eyes looked crazed.

Palmer was thinking too hard to flinch at Hartman's outburst. She finally felt like one of those missing puzzles was sliding into place.

"Nick," she whispered.

Both men looked at her then. Calum with confusion and Hartman with panicked alarm. She looked up at Hartman.

"Your dad. His name was Klaus. That's short for Niklaus. Isn't it." It wasn't a question. She continued. "Nik is another nickname for Niklaus." Palmer's voice trailed off as horrible ideas started to take root in her mind. Nick. The name Gabriella had written in her notebook over and over again. Like a young girl in love. Nick. Nik. Niklaus. Klaus. Dr. Klaus Roth.

Palmer thought that she might vomit.

"My dad used to rent out this cabin for hunting when he immigrated here. My dad always said that Colorado looked the most like Germany out of all the other states," Hartman's voice was haunted. Palmer had never seen him look as rough as he did now. He was always perfectly put together, but now he looked like something that fell off a train. Palmer stared at him in horror. Calum inched closer.

Hartman continued to speak in that spooky far-off voice. "My father was a monster. I could never prove that what happened to my mom was his fault. But I knew. My childhood was —," he paused. He lifted the broken necklace in his hands and looked at it absently. "My mother wore a necklace just like this. I mean EXACTLY like this. She wore it every day. She was even buried in it. It was a gift from my father. It was so unique and I had never seen another one like it. Until the day you walked into my office." He looked up at Palmer then. Calum froze. He had been in the middle of taking another step in front of her.

Hartman went on. "You were so beautiful that day. I wanted you instantly. I had to have you. But I lied. I had all my father's old things. I went home that day and tore through everything trying to find the dental records you wanted. I wanted to make you happy, you were so sad. But instead, I found a dark secret that my dad had kept for over half a decade. I found a box full of letters from him and your great-aunt. It had pictures of them and even a lock of what I assumed was her hair. It was romantic at first. But then I found all the newspaper clippings from her disappearance. I found a map to his hunting cabin and when I read through the letters I put it together. He did something to her. Here." Hartman was crying. Fat, wet tears streamed down his face in ugly little rivers. Palmer felt weightless. Like she was in a dream.

"I know that you're thinking that I should have told you, but I did the right thing. I know I did. If I had told you then you would never have let *us* happen. We never would have gotten together. But we're MEANT to be together, Palmer. I know that. You know that. I had to do whatever it takes to keep you," he released a loud sob.

"Why did you throw me down the stairs, Hartman?" Palmer asked the question but it didn't sound like her voice.

Hartman wiped at his face. Calum was almost directly in front of her now.

"I panicked. I got out of surgery and I checked my phone. You had called me twice so I called you back. It went straight to voicemail. I got worried so I checked the location sharing app and it said your last known location was just up the road. The service is really spotty up here. I realized where you were heading and I assumed you had figured it out. I thought you had come up here to find evidence. I thought you knew I had lied. I thought you were going to leave me."

Palmer was appalled. "You thought I was going to leave you, so you tried to kill me?"

"You don't understand. I love you so much. I couldn't bear the idea of you leaving —"

Palmer interrupted him. "SO YOU TRIED TO KILL ME?" she yelled. Hartman's face changed from anguish to fury so fast Palmer felt a jolt in her stomach. For a brief moment, she could have sworn she saw his eyes flash red. Then he tried to move toward her.

Hartman only made it a step before Calum tackled him.

Chapter Fifty-Six

Present Day (2022)

The two men went crashing into the closest wall. Palmer wasn't sure what to do. Her body said run but she knew Hartman was bigger and she was worried about Calum. Besides, Hartman had the keys to the truck in his pocket and she had no clue where Calum's car keys were.

Calum miraculously had Hartman pinned against the wall and he was punching him in the face repeatedly. Hartman put his hands up defensively, then tackled Calum in the opposite direction, right toward where Palmer was standing. Right before the two giant men crashed into her, Palmer felt a cold hand grab her and pull her out of the way. Palmer landed on her side with a thud. The men barreled into the wall and she couldn't tell who was hitting who.

Palmer looked around to see who had grabbed her. There was no one else in the room. Palmer's eyes caught on something in the open doorway. A woman in a white nightgown stood just on the edge of the forest. Her nearly black hair was blowing in the wind, her bare feet stood in the snow and her mouth hung open at an awkward angle. Palmer couldn't make out the fine details from this distance but she knew without a doubt that if she got closer she would see that the woman's flesh was rotting. Her eyes would be bulging out and there would be a reek of death.

"Gabriella," Palmer whispered. Her voice was drowned out by the sound of the fight next to her. Palmer made a split-second decision and scrambled to her feet. She clumsily ran toward the door and out into the snow-covered forest.

Palmer was ten feet away from Gabriella's ghost when it turned and started to move quickly through the forest. It left no footprints and Palmer noticed that the snowflakes coming down from the sky didn't stick to her. Palmer continued to follow Gabriella through the forest. She was panting and her breath came out in little puffs of smoke in the frigid air. She was close to finding whatever it was. She could feel it.

Gabriella moved slightly to the right and a tree blocked her from view. Palmer hurried her steps and scanned ahead but Gabriela was nowhere to be seen. Palmer made it to the tree where she had lost Gabriella. She wasn't there. But just beyond the tree was a small clearing. In the middle was a pit. It was filled with debris, trash, logs, and little sticks of wood. Palmer knew what it was. It was a burn pit.

Without thinking Palmer slid in. It was only a couple of feet deep. She started to pull things out, throwing them to the side.

'C'mon Gabriella, I know you're here," she grunted as she tossed a particularly heavy log out of the pit. She needed to hurry. Palmer wished she had worn gloves. Her hands were red and raw from the cold. Still, she dug through the debris. She finally made it to the bottom but it was just dirt.

"No!" Palmer cried out in frustration. Tears were streaming down her cheeks and she sank to her knees in the frozen dirt. "This isn't how the story is supposed to end," she whispered to herself. Palmer stared at the dirt. Then she started to dig with her hands.

The earth was hard but she used her nails to dig. She didn't have to dig far before she felt something smooth and hard. Palmer let out a sob and started to dig more frantically trying to uncover what was underneath.

"I'm here! I'm here! I found you! I have you!" she cried out as she dug. Palmer had scratched the dirt away to reveal part of a skull. The eye socket and part of the forehead were the only things visible.

A loud gunshot went off in the direction of the shack. Palmer jumped and looked back in the direction of the house.

"No, no, no, no, no... " Palmer looked back at the skull. She kissed her dirty fingertips and placed them gently on the brow. "I'll be back. I promise."

Palmer stood on shaky legs and climbed out of the pit. She took off in a sprint toward the shack. Toward Calum. When she neared the edge of the forest, just before the little clearing in front of the house, Palmer slowed. The door to the cabin was open and she could see someone on the floor trying to stand up. It was Calum. He was gripping his arm.

Palmer looked all over the clearing but couldn't find Hartman so she booked it across the clearing and toward the house. Calum saw her and his eyes bulged out in surprise.

"What are you still doing here? You gotta leave, Palmer, he's fucking nuts!"

She ignored him. "What happened?" she asked. She grabbed his arm and he winced. His left arm was covered in blood.

"He had a gun. He just grazed me. I'm fine. He took off into the woods. I think he's looking for you. Palmer, Palmer!" She was still assessing him and he was trying to get her attention. Palmer looked up at him. He continued. "Where are your truck keys?" he asked.

"Hartman has them," she said absently. She was thinking. "But he's been sloppy lately —," She paused again to think harder. "He didn't lock the car!"

"So?" Calum had positioned them behind the door, using it like a shield.

"WWLSD," she whispered mostly to herself.

"You're still using that fucking mantra?" Calum looked dumbstruck.

"Of course I am. And you know what Laurie Strode would do?" she asked. She was smiling slightly and Calum looked at her like she had lost all her marbles.

"What?" he said nervously.

"She would make sure to learn the fucking combination of her husband's gun safe." She took off at a sprint for her truck.

Palmer made it to the driver-side passenger door and wrenched it open. The dome lights came on. She reached under the back seat. Just then she heard Hartman call her name.

"Palmer!" it sounded like he was almost singing it. "Palmer!" he sang again. This time it was closer. His voice was coming from the other side of the forest.

Palmer pulled out a shiny twenty-gauge shotgun. She had been surprised to find it among Hartman's huge collection of much larger guns in his safe. Most men didn't bother with a smaller caliber shotgun. But there it was, tucked in the very back. The least likely gun for him to notice if it went missing. Palmer had grown up hunting with Chuck, she knew guns.

Palmer opened the driver's side door and rested the gun in the space between the door and the truck. She adjusted her bright red beanie so it wouldn't be in her eyes. She lined up her sight, aiming the bead exactly where she knew he would come out. Palmer knew exactly where he would walk out. She pumped the shotgun, loading a shell into the chamber. It made a foreboding sound in the darkness.

Hartman walked out of the forest and into the clearing. His handgun was raised and he was sweeping the area, looking for Palmer. He made it another two steps into the clearing before he found her. A pair of red eyes looked right into her, all the way down to the soul. Palmer pulled the trigger and shot him square in the chest. He dropped to the ground almost silently, the snow absorbing much of the impact.

Palmer lowered the gun just a fraction to make sure he was really down. Calum shot out of the house and ran toward where Hartman was lying unconscious and possibly dying. He grabbed Hartman's gun with his good arm and then started to run back to Palmer.

A siren wailed in the distance. Then another one. Palmer set the shotgun down on the passenger seat just before Calum grabbed her in a fierce hug. They said nothing. No words. They didn't need them. Palmer and Calum were still hugging when the red and blue lights of the police cars lit up the snow around them.

Chapter Fifty-Seven

Present Day (2022)

The police came, thanks to Dr. Walter's intuition. She called the police and requested a welfare check after she saw Hartman with Palmer's missing necklace and had described it. The police had driven out to Palmer and Hartman's house and hadn't needed a warrant to come inside. Hartman had left his car parked oddly in the driveway with the door open. The garage door was open and the house door was left ajar. On top of all that, the cops had sent out an all-points bulletin on Calum. A good samaritan with a police radio called it in when he saw Calum's car heading out this way. Gotta love small towns.

Hartman was still alive when the paramedics got there. He was a big guy and it was a small gauge shotgun at a long range. He still looked like shit though. The paramedics had cuffed him to the gurney, loaded him up, and taken him away extremely fast. Palmer was sure he wouldn't die, just like Michael Myers.

Palmer and Calum explained everything to the police. Everything except the paranormal weirdness. Palmer told them all about Gabriella and all the research she had done. She told them about the necklace and Hartman's confession in the cabin. Palmer had happily walked them back to where Gabriella's remains were. Relief flooded her as she watched the cops go into the burn pit and come back up with confirmation that it was human remains. They said they wouldn't be able to confirm it was Gabriella Rivera until after they ran some tests. But that was fine. Palmer knew.

It felt like the police spoke to them for hours. Calum's arm injury was superficial, thank God. The paramedics bandaged it and recommended that he ride into the hospital to get it checked out but he declined. Other than that, he only had a few bruises and scrapes from his fight with Hartman.

Finally, Palmer and Calum were told they could leave but that they would be questioned again sometime tomorrow. Palmer was offered a ride home by one of the officers since her truck would need to be looked at further. She had shot her husband off of it after all.

While her truck still needed to be checked out, Calum's was cleared to leave. Palmer had looked between the officer who had offered her a ride and Calum.

"I got you, Beautiful," Cal said and he led her to his car.

It wasn't until Palmer got closer that she realized his car was the exact same shitty Toyota Corolla he drove in high school. She let herself into the familiar passenger side and slipped into the seat.

"Woah, you still have this thing? She asked as he got into his side.

"Yep," he responded and started to back out.

"That's crazy. I can't believe she still runs. Why don't you just get a new one?" Palmer asked.

"It's a perfectly good car. She's got a lot of character. Plus I don't mind fixing her up whenever she has issues. I worked on cars for a bit." He straightened the car out and started to drive back up the sketchy dirt road. The snow was at least pushed down from all the cop cars and the ambulances. "Let's just pray she can make it up this road," he admitted. He paused for a brief moment. "Ya no, the first time I ever made it to third base was in the back of this thing." He pointed to the back seat with his thumb.

Palmer stared at him dumbly. "Yeah, I know Cal. That was me," she said dryly.

Calum gave her a devilish side smile. "You don't say."

Palmer rolled her eyes but couldn't help but smile.

"I'm guessing I'm not taking you back to The Bates Motel tonight right?" He was talking about Palmer's home she shared with Hartman. Palmer sighed.

"My husband's father murdered my aunt over fifty years ago. My husband knew but kept it from me. My husband tried to kill me. Then he tried to kill you, then he tried to kill me again. Is that about right?"

"You forgot the part where you shot your husband in the chest," he said comically. "Oh! And you solved a cold case with the help of a ghost!"

Palmer frowned. "I thought you didn't believe in all that,"

"Of course I believe in all of that. But when you first told me I was young and stupid and scared. I believed you, I was just afraid no one else was going to and I gave you shit advice," he admitted.

Palmer looked ahead. They were almost back to the main road.

"I'm definitely not going back to The Amityville Horror House," she said. Calum smirked at her reference to her and Hartman's house. "Can you take me to Abuela's old house? My parents are there."

Palmer rested her head on the back of the seat. She let out a long breath. "I have no idea how I'm going to explain all of this to them," her headache was coming back just thinking about it.

"I'll come in and help if you want?" Calum offered.

Palmer whipped her head toward him. "You would do that? But they hate you," she admitted.

Calum shrugged. "I feel like I could win Emilia back," he said with a grin. "And I really want to see the look on Chuck's face when he finds out Hartman tried to kill you twice so you shot him in the chest with a shotgun," he laughed. "Chuck's face is gonna be all like —," Calum screwed his face up into a perfect imitation of Palmer's father when he's shocked. Palmer laughed too despite the traumatic night. Palmer marveled at Calum's gift for doing that.

"Where have you been staying anyway?" she asked. "Obviously I was wrong about you and the cabin."

"I have a pretty sweet little RV, it's parked at the motor home lot just outside of town. It's kind of a necessity for my job. I lied at the hospital. I don't do odd jobs anymore. I haven't done that for a while. I've been a bounty hunter now for almost seven years."

Palmer thought about all the research he did into Hartman's background. Then she thought about how he had been able to follow her around without her even noticing. She shrugged.

"Yeah, ok. That checks out," she said. "Although, doesn't being a 'bounty hunter' put a bit of a damper on your lifestyle?"

"I don't think I get your meaning?" He looked genuinely confused.

"You know," she said. He only looked at her even more confused so she went on. "The party life. The drinking and the drugs. I can't imagine that mixes well with your occupation."

Calum's expression turned serious for once. "I've been sober for almost nine years now." He paused. Then a little bit of his sparkle came back. "I've got the chip and everything," he said comically. But Palmer knew from his tone that he wasn't joking.

They drove back into town for a few minutes in silence but Palmer could tell it was killing Calum. Calum would have to fill the noiselessness soon or he would explode.

"Look, I know you're probably thinking through a lot of things right now. But I just want you to know that it's all going to be ok. I know pricks like that tend to get away with certain shit, but I won't let that happen. And I know you might be worrying about money because your surgeon husband is now in the slammer but that part will be ok too. We'll get it all squared away. I'll hook you up with my financial guy."

Palmer stared at him. "You have a financial guy?" she said in disbelief.

"Yeah, of course. Why?" he asked.

It was Palmer's turn to smirk. "You live in a trailer park, you drive a thirty-year-old car, and you work as a bounty hunter."

Calum looked at her with mock indignation. "Madam. I drive this car because I like it. I live in an RV because I'm a bachelor and I'm actually the best bounty hunter in the state. I make a shit ton of money. I also feel like you have forgotten my parents are loaded. I actually have a trust fund," he admitted that last part a little quietly.

If Palmer had been drinking anything she would have done a perfect spit take. "A trust fund?"

Calum imitated her voice but made it infinitely more annoying. "*Yes, I have a trust fund.* Shut up."

Palmer laughed and Calum continued to drive in a broody state.

"Why don't you buy a nicer car or live in a house? Or for that matter why do you work?"

Calum shrugged and spoke honestly. "I like my job. It's the one thing that I've found I'm actually good at. As for the other stuff, I don't really know. I just like to live simply I guess."

Palmer leaned back again and smiled at that. They were pulling onto Abuela's street. The clock in the car indicated it was nearly two in the morning.

"Hey, Cal?"

"Yeah?" he responded.

"Thanks for watching out for me all this time. And thank you for coming for me, to the cabin," she added.

Calum pulled up in front of Abuela's old house. He put the car in park and turned to Palmer. "Of course, I'll always be here for you Palmer."

Palmer looked at him for a long moment. They had both changed so much over the years. All the differences were even more obvious and fresh in her mind due to her recent bout of amnesia. Calum's eyes were still the same though. She looked into those dark gray eyes now, searching for something she thought was long lost but now she wasn't so sure. She contemplated what he had just said.

"Always?" she asked.

Calum's smirk fell. He blinked back the wetness in his eyes that threatened to spill over. Then he swallowed before he spoke.

"Forever," he answered back.

Chapter Fifty-Eight

Epilogue

Palmer walked slowly between the tombstones of the cemetery. The trees above her were starting to come back to life after their winter slumber. The grass was starting to turn green again and spring flowers were beginning to bloom. Tulips, daffodils, and azaleas poked through the earth.

Palmer made her way to Abuela's tombstone and she knelt down. She said a quick prayer and dropped a bouquet of fluffy red roses into the little attached vase. Palmer stood and moved through the plots. Stones with the Rivera family name engraved on them stared back at her as she walked.

Finally, she arrived in front of Gabriella Rivera's headstone. Instead of green grass in front, there was a brown mound of fresh dirt. She had finally been laid to rest. There hadn't been much of Gabriella left after half of a century of her body being exposed to the elements. The police had only been able to find her skull, her femur, and a handful of some other random bone fragments. But what was left of her was now here, where it was meant to be.

Palmer reached into her pocket and pulled out Gabriella's necklace. Palmer had taken it to a jeweler and had the chain fixed. She knelt down and set it gently on the stone just underneath the image of the Blessed Mother engraved into the surface. The image on the rock mirrored the image on the pendant.

Palmer stepped back and stood there for some time. Gabriella was at peace, and for the first time in seventeen years, Palmer felt like she was finally alone. It felt odd yet calming. Palmer thought that maybe now she could find her own peace.

Palmer pulled her green cardigan closer around her as a light breeze blew through the cemetery. Palmer took a deep breath to steady herself before she walked back to her truck.

A few minutes later Palmer pulled up to Tiffany's Epiphanies and parked in her usual spot. Calum was unloading two wooden chairs from the back of a trailer and was about to move them inside. Palmer jogged to catch up and held the door open for him.

"Hey Beautiful," he said as she rushed past. He winked at her as he passed through the door. "Where do you want these? I've still gotta grab the matching table and it looks like there's still six or seven more chairs just like these."

Palmer let out an impressed whistle. "That's a big dining table. I'm gonna have to find a big family to buy it." She was already trying to figure out how she would price the table and chairs in her head.

Calum followed her with the chairs to the back.

"Nothing wrong with a big family," he said as he set them down. The corner of Palmer's mouth lifted slightly. "You sure you don't want to keep it? It could probably fit in your new place?" he asked.

Palmer had sold the giant house on the mountain without a second thought. Someone had bought it, furniture and all. The only things she took with her were the contents of her closet. She sold the boat and all the cars too. Selling the cream Ford Thunderbird had been the most satisfying. She kept the giant black monster truck though after the police gave it back. It was growing on her.

Palmer bought Abuela's old house from her parents. They had offered to give it to her but Palmer had insisted that she buy it. Chuck and Emilia confessed that they had planned on giving it to her and Hartman as a wedding present but Hartman had declined and told them about his plans to surprise Palmer with the big house

"I'll think about it," Palmer answered Calum. She adjusted her silver necklace. It was the one Calum had given to her in the hospital.

Calum started walking back to the front of the store to grab the rest of the chairs and the table. Palmer followed close behind. Susan was behind the register and he gave her a devilish smile. Susan's cheeks turned bright red and she dropped the vase she had been holding.

Palmer shook her head and spoke so that only Calum could hear her. "Please stop doing that to poor Susan. That's the fifth thing you've made her break this week. I'm going to start charging you," she huffed.

Calum only looked back at her mischievously. His grin was wide and his tongue touched one of his canines. Palmer tried not to swoon like Susan. They continued to walk back to the trailer.

"I spoke to your brother this morning, he said hi," Calum said. He started to pull another couple of chairs out.

"Oh yeah?" Palmer asked. Calum and Shawn had reconnected since the incident.

"Yeah, he said he wanted to come visit once the program is done," he said as he stepped down from the trailer.

"That would be great," she said smiling.

Palmer turned and walked to the mailbox at the front of the store. Behind her Calum carried the two chairs with one arm and used his free hand to check his pocket. He patted the little lump, reassuring himself that it was still there. Inside his pocket was a little green box he had been carrying around for almost seven years. The box held a ring. It had a thin gold band with a large emerald cut Colombian emerald surrounded by tiny glittering diamonds. He had found it in a vintage shop and knew exactly whose finger it was meant to be on. Not today, but one day.

Palmer grabbed the mail and started to sort through it. She pulled out bills and put the magazines and advertisements in the back. Then a letter caught her eye. It said the shop's address but it was addressed to a recipient named "Pamela Voorhees'. Palmer's heart stopped. That was Jason Voorhees's mother in Friday The 13th. She checked the return address. It said 'La Vista Correctional Facility' with a Pueblo Colorado address.

Palmer stopped in her tracks, ripped the envelope open, and stared at the piece of paper inside. There were no words, just a charcoal drawing. It was a drawing of a perfect white rose, the thorns uncut and sharp.

Acknowledgements

This book would not have been possible without the overwhelming support of my family and friends. Out of the blue one day, I told my husband Andreas that I thought I had a good idea for a book. His response was, "Write it". So I did. His unwavering belief in me kept me writing even when I wanted to give up.

Additionally, my grandmother RaeAnn read and edited this story with me from the very beginning just like she did with my grandfather when he wrote a book. She and my husband were the cheerleaders who helped me take this book all the way to publication.

I would also be remiss if I did not acknowledge the help of my dear cousin Kennedy Fockler, who designed the beautiful cover art for this book.

I'd also like to thank all of the people in my life who read my book before it was published and gave me their feedback. I don't know what I would have done without each and every one of you.

Finally, I would like to thank the catalyst for this entire story. My grandmother Dolores. Who truly was the inspiration not just for the character Abuela, but for this book. Without the stories she told me when I was young, I probably wouldn't have been so obsessed with all things macabre and I definitely wouldn't have written this novel.

About The Author

Laken Hyson Schmalz is a Hispanic-American author raised in the small mountain town of Durango Colorado. Her debut novel COCO MAN, a thriller romance, explores the line between oral legends and reality. Laken has a Master's Degree in Healthcare Administration and over a decade of experience working in the healthcare industry. She now lives in Derby Kansas with her Dentist husband, their daughter, and their two small dogs. When Laken isn't writing romantic thrillers she can be found crocheting, gardening, watching horror movies, and laughing with her family.

Printed in the USA
CPSIA information can be obtained
at www.ICGtesting.com
LVHW051633050924
789970LV00001B/64